Nightingale
Way

ALSO BY EMILY MARCH

Mistletoe Mine
Angel's Rest
Hummingbird Lake
Heartache Falls
Lover's Leap

Nightingale Way

An
Eternity Springs
Novel

EMILY MARCH

BALLANTINE BOOKS • NEW YORK

A Ballantine Books Mass Market Original

Copyright © 2012 by Geralyn Dawson Williams
Excerpt from *Reflection Point* by Emily March copyright © 2012 by Geralyn Dawson Williams

Published in the United States by Ballantine Books, an imprint of The Random House Publishing Group, a division of Random House, Inc., New York.

BALLANTINE and colophon are registered trademarks of Random House, Inc.

This book contains an excerpt from the forthcoming book *Reflection Point* by Emily March. This excerpt has been set for this edition only and may not reflect the content of the forthcoming edition.

ISBN: 978-1-62090-330-8

Cover design: Lynn Andreozzi
Cover illustration: Robert Steele

Printed in the United States of America

For Steve

Nightingale Way

ONE

༜

February
Alexandria, Virginia

Catherine Ann Blackburn heard the grandfather clock on the landing chime twice and knew she'd delayed the moment long enough. She had a special visit to pay this afternoon. She'd better get moving. She saved her work, blew out the cinnamon-scented candle burning on her desk, and rose to leave her home office. The phone rang, but she allowed the answering machine to pick up. She crossed the hall to her bedroom, where she stripped out of her jeans and George Washington University hoodie. Inside her walk-in closet, she stared at the racks of clothing, and debated which of her cemetery dresses to wear. She had four from which to choose. Cat spent way too much time in cemeteries.

A year and a half ago she'd joined Arlington Ladies, an organization of volunteers who attended military services at Arlington National Cemetery in order to make sure that no soldier was buried alone. When she paid her respects to the fallen, Cat represented the thanks of a nation for the soldier's service and sacrifice, and she was proud to do so. No one should be laid to rest without someone there to note the passing of a life. Not a soldier, not an old man or woman.

Not a baby.

Grief washed over Cat and she shut her eyes, accepting it. Today was a day for remembering, the one day of the year when she allowed herself to wallow in her heartache. Today she wasn't going to Arlington, but to Rose Hill Cemetery in Hagerstown, Maryland.

She scanned her closet's contents again, but nothing felt right until she spied the red cashmere sweater. Forget the black dresses. Today, she'd wear red—the color of love.

She donned the sweater and a pair of gray wool slacks. She had just slipped into her shoes when she heard her doorbell ring. Immediately she tensed. Surely this wasn't her dad, not after the lecture she'd given him last year. You'd think that after five years, George Blackburn would get the fact that she needed to do this by herself.

Her bedroom window overlooked the front yard, so she glanced outside. The only car in her driveway was her white Mercedes convertible, a recent gift to herself for having won the Goldsmith Prize for Investigative Reporting for her series on fraudulent charities. Nor did she see her father's eight-year-old Volvo station wagon at the curb. When the doorbell rang again, followed by three raps against the wood, a pause, then two additional raps, she relaxed. That was her next-door neighbor's usual knock.

Marsha Wells, the bubbly stay-at-home mother of a second-grader and a toddler, stood on the stoop. She began speaking the moment Cat answered the door. "You won't believe this. It's the most horrible thing."

Concerned, Cat waved her inside. "What happened? Are your kids okay?"

"They're fine. This isn't about us. I spoke to Janie from Paw Pals a few minutes ago. Boy, was she furious."

Janie Pemberton was the director of Paw Pals, the canine rescue organization that was another of Cat's volunteer causes. "Something to do with Paw Pals?"

"Indirectly. She says she's stumbled upon a dogfighting ring operating here in town. Some prominent people might be involved."

"With dogfighting?" Cat shook her head. Prominent people in this part of the world meant politicians. Politicians and prostitution she'd believe. Drugs wouldn't surprise her. But dogfighting? Other than child porn or murder, she couldn't think of anything that would derail a politician's career faster than being involved in dogfighting. "I don't believe it."

"She's convinced. And Janie is no fool. You know that."

Cat nodded. Janie was a dynamo of energy with a quick, intelligent mind.

Marsha continued. "I think you should call and talk to her about it, Cat. This could be right up your alley."

The old, familiar buzz that she experienced whenever a new story came her way shot through Cat, but she immediately dismissed it. Such things could wait. This was not the time. "Thanks for the tip. I'll call her this evening."

"Excellent." Her eyes gleaming with satisfaction, Marsha shifted the topic of conversation by giving Cat's outfit a once-over. "You're all dressed up. Looking gorgeous as always, I might add. How is it that you can wear red so well when you're a redhead? If I didn't like you so much I'd hate you."

"Thank you. I think."

"I thought you had an Arlington Ladies commitment today."

Cat frowned. She wouldn't have booked anything for today. "Why did you think that?"

"When I handed you my grocery shopping list last

night, I'd have sworn I saw 'cemetery flowers' written on yours."

Oh. Cat didn't know how to respond to that. She didn't like to lie, but Marsha didn't know anything about her past. Hardly anyone did. Luckily, she didn't need to respond because Marsha continued to talk.

"Thanks again for coming to my rescue. We were down to our last diaper, and I would never have heard the end of it if Aiden didn't have a banana for his breakfast this morning, but the thought of loading him into the car seat one more time . . ." Marsha shuddered dramatically.

"I was glad to help." And she was thrilled to avoid talk about cemetery flowers. "Speaking of rescue, how are things going at your house with your new foster? Is he settling in okay?"

"So far so good. He has an appointment at the vet tomorrow for heartworm treatment. How about you? Are you ready for your next baby?"

Inwardly, Cat winced. Today of all days, she didn't want to think of the dogs she fostered as babies. "Actually, I'm taking a break from fostering for a little while. I told Janie I'd help with the website and shelter visits and even do some sitting when our volunteers need help, but I'm trying to schedule some major remodeling so it's probably best I don't have dogs here full time."

"I know that Janie is thrilled to have you do anything you want to help out," Marsha said. "Don't take this the wrong way, Cat, but I'm so glad the newspaper laid you off."

"I'm not complaining. I like the freelance life more than I ever imagined. And the dogs who come to your house are lucky, too."

"I don't know about that." Exasperation wrinkled Marsha's brow. "Aiden keeps stealing their food. Fosters at your house don't have to compete for their supper with an eleven-month-old kibble thief."

Cat worked to keep her smile on her face as she finished up the conversation. Once she'd shut the door safely behind Marsha, her smile faded. Tears stung her eyes and she blinked them away. "It's okay," she lectured herself aloud. "It's natural that the mention of Aiden breaks your heart today. Perfectly normal. Don't sweat it."

She pulled her coat from the closet, locked the front door, then went to the refrigerator where she removed a bouquet of yellow roses wrapped in green tissue. Five minutes later, she was on her way.

A cold, blustery wind buffeted the car and patches of snow clung to the shady spots beside the road. Cat cranked up the heater in her car. She listened to a classic rock station on the radio during the first half of her trip, but as she drew nearer to her destination, she switched off the noise and allowed silence to settle over her.

Had someone asked Cat what she thought about as she drove, she couldn't have said. She spent the trip clearing her mind and preparing her heart, and by the time she turned in to the entrance to the cemetery, she was as ready as she ever would be. Though she hadn't been to Rose Hill since this same day last year, she knew exactly where to go—the Angel Land section. She walked the rows of flat markers, knelt beside the grave she'd come to visit, then opened her mind to dreams she ordinarily kept locked away.

She imagined a toddler with dark curls playing with a fluffy white puppy. She pictured a preschooler with finger paint on her hands standing in front of a child-size easel. Next, it was a second-grader sitting in her lap and learning to read, then a fourth-grader coming up to bat at softball practice.

Today would have been Lauren Ann Davenport's fifth birthday.

Cat remained beside the grave for almost an hour. She reflected on her memories, said a few prayers, and allowed the tears to fall as she mourned those things that she had cherished and lost. When the moment felt right, she laid the bouquet of yellow roses below the marker, pressed a kiss to her fingertips, then touched the raised letters of the name recorded there. "Happy birthday, baby. I love you."

Cat Blackburn turned and walked away from the grave of her only child.

She never noticed the figure of the man who stood behind the shelter of a nearby evergreen, silently watching.

Five months later

"She calls that security?" Jack Davenport muttered with disgust, watching as the idiot wearing a shoulder holster flashed Cat Blackburn a smarmy grin.

Moments before, Cat's little Mercedes sports car had pulled in to the driveway of her home in a quiet suburban neighborhood. From inside her house, Jack noticed that the pretty-boy bodyguard hadn't paid any attention to the pool service truck parked next door in the Wellses' driveway. While it was true that the truck sported the same logo as the service used by the vacationing Wells family, any security guard worth his permit would check out the vehicle before allowing his charge to exit her car.

What surprised him was that Cat remained so oblivious. After all, she's the one whose house had been firebombed earlier this week. She should be more careful! It was almost as if she were daring the culprit to have another go at her.

It made Jack want to wring her neck. Right after he made the bodyguard pay for his inattention.

Jack had followed Cat and her escort from her home, to the dry cleaners, then a pet store, and finally to an animal shelter where she picked up a dog. The security loser never looked at Jack's ride twice. He was too busy checking out Cat's chest and ogling her ass.

Jack wanted to shoot him on principle. He'd seriously considered breaking bones—a leg would be good—in order to demonstrate to the incompetent jackass that a career move was in order. Doing so would be a public service. Instead, once the bug he'd planted in her car picked up the order she'd made for takeout at her favorite neighborhood Italian restaurant, an indication that she was finally headed home, he'd postponed his contemplated punishment and made his way to her house ahead of her.

Now, the sound of Cat's laughter drifted through the window he'd cracked open, and he set his teeth. She wore a flirty yellow sundress, strappy heeled sandals, and oversized sunglasses. She pulled a designer dog tote filled with a puffball of four-legged fur from the backseat of the Mercedes. Her wavy auburn hair was pulled up in a ponytail, and as she approached the house, she looked more like a coed than a woman in her mid-thirties who paid no more attention to her surroundings than did her sorry excuse for security.

No wonder Melinda had assigned this job to him. Cat Blackburn couldn't bat her pretty eyes and turn him into a worthless blob of testosterone. No, he was immune to the woman's admittedly significant appeal. He'd been vaccinated.

Beautiful, stubborn fool, he thought as he watched her pause halfway to the kitchen door, hand the dog to the bodyguard, and dig in her purse for her phone. Blithely, she stood right there out in the open and double-thumbed out a text message. He had thought the woman had more sense than to leave herself exposed that way, but maybe not. After all, she'd managed to stir up a hornet's nest with her blog exposé about the dog-fighters.

The piece had gone live on the Internet three weeks ago. The day before yesterday, someone had firebombed her house. True, it hadn't been a big explosion, but fire was fire. Fire was serious business, and Jack knew that better than most. Luckily, she'd been sitting on the living room sofa when the Molotov cocktail sailed through the picture window and exploded in her dining room.

Imagining the moment, his stomach took a sick turn.

And what had been Cat's response? To hire protection who was more bodybuilder than bodyguard. What the hell was she thinking?

As much as he wanted to teach Mr. Ass-gazer a lesson, Jack knew he had to restrain the urge. This operation needed to be slick and quick. Better he stick to his original plan.

Though when the security guy reached up and play-fully tugged Cat's ponytail, Jack reconsidered. Maybe one well-placed kick wouldn't hurt anything.

She dropped her phone back into her purse and resumed her stroll toward her kitchen door. Silent as a ghost, Jack moved past the brand-new dining room window and into the kitchen, taking up position. Waiting for her to slip her key into the lock, Jack realized with a touch of chagrin that his pulse pounded in a way that it rarely had on missions. Honesty made him admit that he worried more about dealing with Cat than he ever did about dying on the job.

Bodyguard Ken entered the kitchen ahead of her. "Idiot," Jack muttered as he took the man down and knocked him out with a pair of smooth, practiced, lightning-quick kicks.

He'd be lying if he denied the pleasure it gave him, or the satisfaction he felt when he plunged the hypodermic needle into Cat Blackburn's shoulder and she collapsed, unconscious, into his arms.

He used duct tape to secure the idiot guard, then lifted Cat over his shoulder and carried her to the garage, where he transferred her into the scroungy old SUV she used for hauling dogs as part of her work for the rescue group. As a precaution, he used the tape to bind her ankles and wrists and muffle her mouth. He'd gone heavy on the drug. The last thing he needed was to have her come to on the highway and cause a wreck.

He climbed into the driver's seat, then hesitated. What about the dog? He hadn't planned for that particular complication, but he liked dogs. For all he knew, Bodyguard Bozo would wake up angry and take it out on the purse pet.

He went back and got the dog.

They exited the garage and the neighborhood without incident. Once they'd gained the beltway, he phoned Melinda. She answered on the first ring. "Yes?"

"I have her. We'll be wheels up within the hour."

"Excellent. The guard?"

"Is a tool. I put him on the sofa in the den."

"I'll take care of him." After a brief hesitation, she asked, "How is she, Jack?"

"Not a scratch on her. She'll have a slight headache when she wakes up, but we knew to expect that."

The relieved sigh was almost inaudible. "Yes. All right, then. Safe travels. You'll be in touch?"

"Absolutely." He hung up and made the rest of the trip to the airfield in silence. Though he concentrated on driving, he remained intensely aware of the woman slumped in the seat beside him and stole glances whenever traffic allowed.

She no longer looked like Coed Barbie. This was the

soft, slumbering Kitten he'd known and loved once upon a time.

Afternoon sunshine beamed through slatted wood blinds and woke Jack to the sound of the surf, the musty scent of sex, and soft snuffle of the naked woman lying next to him. He filled his lungs with air and a lazy grin stretched across his face. He couldn't ever recall feeling so . . . pleasured.

Rolling up on his elbow, he watched her sleep. Cat was an apt name for her, he decided. Two hours ago, he'd watched her stride along the beach, sleek and strong, confident and utterly feminine in her next-to-nothing bikini. He'd been in their room on a phone call— an important work call—and he'd completely lost his train of thought. She stopped outside on the room's lanai and finished off her ice cream cone. She gazed into the room and licked her fingers, slowly, one by one.

Damned if he remembered hanging up the phone.

She was a tigress in bed—bold and adventurous and enthusiastic. When they mated, when he made her purr, she made him feel like the king of the jungle.

Now, though, relaxed and sated and drowsing, Cat was a soft, cuddly kitten.

Her eyes opened. Gorgeous soft green pools that he could drown in. She blinked once, twice, and when her gaze shifted and met his, she smiled. His heart swelled. My Kitten. My Cat.

Not anymore.

Driving the SUV, Jack took a corner a bit too sharply and her weight shifted. Her shoulder fell against him and he felt the heat of her like a brand. The truck cab was too small, his memories too big. He pushed her back where she belonged—far away from him—and returned his focus to the road.

Ten minutes later, she came to.

She tried to hide it, but he was too experienced to miss

the subtle signs of awakening. He wished he'd given her a stronger dose of the drug and kept her out until they'd left the city. Stupid of him to let his own dislike of the aftereffects of the drug guide him in this case. Even bound and gagged, she could cause him trouble. Hell, she'd caused him trouble when they occupied opposite hemispheres of the globe. Soothingly, he said, "Don't be afraid. I'm doing this to help you."

At the sound of his voice, her eyes flew open wide. Shock filled those familiar green eyes and color drained from her face.

Guilt slithered through him and sparked his temper. *What, she'd rather be abducted by a stranger?*

Knowing Cat, yeah, probably.

He gunned the engine and zipped around a slower-moving car. "Believe it or not, I'm still one of the good guys, Catherine."

This time, anyway.

In reaction, she shut her eyes and slumped back into her seat.

She didn't move or speak, and he said nothing more until he'd pulled the truck up next to the hangar and switched off the engine. "I'll be back in a moment. Behave."

He took the dog with him as he entered the hangar's side door. His longtime pilot saw him and turned away from the Citation jet, clipboard in hand. "Everything's ready on this end, Jack."

"Good." Jack handed over the dog and gave the man some last-minute instructions before returning to the truck and a fuming Catherine Ann Blackburn.

Had this been a real abduction he'd have carried her to the plane, but now that the time had come to hold her close, he found he didn't want to do it. The drug had worn off, and he wasn't ready for the intimacy. Disgusted with himself, he yanked out his pocketknife and slashed the duct tape binding her ankles.

He took hold of her upper arm and when she went stiff, tugged her from the truck. The moment her feet hit the ground, the woman twisted in his grip, as slippery as an eel. Her eyes flashed. She made a growling noise in her throat.

Then she kneed him in the junk. Hard.

Pain radiated through him and only the force of will kept him from dropping to his knees. As his grip on her arm loosened, she yanked herself free of him. But instead of fleeing, she stepped calmly toward the Citation, her three-inch heels clicking confidently against the concrete floor. Once he could breathe again, Jack cursed. Once he could move again, he hobbled off after her.

Jack eyed her long, lovely legs and scowled. The shoes had worked against her, and she obviously knew it. Had she not been wearing those ridiculous shoes, she could have dashed toward the more public buildings at this private airport and perhaps found help before he pulled himself up off the ground. Those shoes were something else Security Guard Ken should have cautioned her against.

With that, his temper reached the boiling point. He was as filled with fury as he'd been since . . . well . . . since Melinda told him someone had firebombed Cat's house. Gritting his teeth, he caught up with her. He scooped her up, threw her over his shoulder, and hauled her up the jet's staircase in a fireman's carry. Inside the fuselage, he tossed her into a seat with a curt "Stay!"

Her mouth said not a word, but the furious glare in her eyes spoke loud and clear.

Again, he drew his knife and sliced the tape that bound her hands. She could remove the tape from her mouth herself. "I sit up front during takeoff. After that, we'll talk. There's water there"—he pointed toward a cabinet—"and the head is in back if you'd like to use it before takeoff. Be in your seat, buckled in, in five."

He was halfway to the cockpit door when her voice stopped him cold. "Why am I not surprised to discover that you are still Melinda's lapdog?"

Jack's spine snapped straight and he stiffened. Melinda's lapdog?

The barb struck that place deep within Jack's heart where the doubts had always dwelt. Is that what she had thought of him, even when she professed to love him? Her mother's lapdog?

Coldly furious, he glanced back over his shoulder and forced a smile. "You know, Cat, I don't recall you being such a bitch when we were married."

He slammed the cockpit door behind him with a bang.

Jack Davenport was back.

Cat sat buckled into her seat, a bottle of water clenched tightly in her fist, as the plane climbed. She couldn't believe this was happening. And to think that she'd thought the day before yesterday had been crazy. Having a Molotov cocktail come smashing through her dining room window should have been the insane moment of the month, but oh no. That was just the beginning.

Now Jack Davenport was back.

She didn't want to believe it. She'd never thought she'd see him again. She'd never *wanted* to see him again.

A little voice whispered in her head, *Liar.*

The nervous panic that had simmered inside her ever since she'd regained consciousness rolled to a boil. Maybe this man wasn't Jack Davenport, she told herself, reaching desperately. Maybe she hadn't recognized his voice, recognized the scent of him. Maybe this was all part of a nefarious plot against her and this guy was an impostor, an employee of the powerful senator she'd ruined with her story or a crazed fan of the major league pitcher whose team had cut him loose after she'd proved he owned fighting dogs.

Yes. That's it! Jack isn't back. This isn't Jack!

After all, this man was bigger than Jack. He outweighed Jack by ten or fifteen pounds. Ten or fifteen pounds of muscle. Jack's shoulders weren't that broad. He'd never been fat, but he hadn't had a six-pack like this guy did, something she couldn't help but notice when his shirt rode up as he dumped her into the airplane's seat.

She chugged back a gulp of water as if it were whiskey. The real Jack had walked out on her four years ago and she hadn't heard a word from him since. For all she knew, the real Jack Davenport could be dead. He could be living in Timbuktu. She'd never tried to find him after the divorce was final. She might be an investigator by profession, but Jack Davenport was one individual she left alone. Been there, done that, got the broken heart.

This man wasn't Jack. He was an impostor. This man was Jack Davenport's doppelgänger.

And you are certifiable. Get a grip, Blackburn. Now is no time to be writing fiction.

She recognized his walk. She recognized his *scent*. She recognized his voice and his thick black hair and his strong jaw and the tiny little crook in his blade of a nose where he got hit with an elbow during a basketball game at her parents' house. She recognized his striking blue eyes.

Jack Davenport is back.

"No," she said, and it came out in a little moan. As the cockpit door opened, she softly added, "Oh, heaven help me."

"Sure, Celeste, put me down for as much as you need," her ex-husband said into a cell phone as he stepped into the main cabin. "It's a good cause."

No matter how much she'd like to pretend otherwise, he *was* Jack Davenport. No one else on earth had eyes like his, the crisp blue like a gas flame that, once upon a time, had burned with passion for her. Now when they settled on her, they were cold as ice.

"Sure," he said into the phone. "I will. Absolutely. All right. Good-bye, Celeste."

By the time he ended the call, Cat had decided that going on offense was her best defense. "What is this all about, Jack? I don't hear a word from you in over four years, and then you show up out of the blue one day, drug me, and abduct me? Why in the world would you do this?"

He looked hard. He looked formidable. He looked dangerous. She wasn't afraid of him physically, but emotionally, he scared her to death.

He smiled mirthlessly. "Your mom and dad asked me to."

Had she not been sitting down already, she would have fallen down. "Dad! You've talked to my dad?"

He nodded once.

Of course he had talked to her mother. But her dad? "When?"

Now he shrugged. "We talk from time to time."

What? "Since when?"

"You were with a guy named Alan the first time."

Cat sucked in a sharp breath. She'd dated Alan two years ago. Jack had been talking to Dad for two years? And he'd never bothered to mention that little detail to Cat? "You took my cell phone out of Peanut's carrier. I need it back, please."

"Why?"

"I need to call my father."

"Why?"

"He never said a word to me about your calls!"

"I asked him not to."

"So? He's *my* father. He should have told me!"

"I'm not giving you your phone."

"Why not?"

For the first time in forever, she saw a genuine smile flash across his face. "You've been kidnapped. Kidnap victims don't get to call their daddies."

Oh, how I've missed that smile. Dismissing that disturbing thought, Cat lifted her chin. "Sure they do. I watch TV. It's proof of life for the ransom."

"But I'm not asking for ransom. Besides, your father already has proof of life—me. I'm your proof of life, Catherine. I'm going to keep you alive—in spite of yourself."

She winced with chagrin. "I didn't—"

"Sure you did," he interrupted. "You ruined the career of two politicians, three sports stars, and a freaking *America Sings* winner with your little exposé."

It wasn't little, she wanted to point out. It had been a twenty-thousand-word series.

"As if that wasn't enough," Jack continued, "two of the names you tied to the dogs are also connected to the mob. I'm surprised these guys started with arson. You're lucky you weren't taken out in a drive-by shooting the day the story came out."

He put her on the defensive and she didn't like it. "I took precautions."

"Sure you did. I took out your 'precaution' with a couple of kicks. Where did you get that sorry excuse for a bodyguard anyway? Who recommended him?"

Cat figured he didn't need to know that her hairdresser had recommended the agency, and that she had already decided she needed someone less . . . flirtatious.

She folded her arms and crossed her legs. "Look, I can understand why my parents might have been concerned, but why didn't they just talk to me about it? Why bring you into it?"

Jack waited, obviously debating with himself. Half a

minute ticked by before he responded. "Because there is a slight chance this wasn't about you. It's remotely possible that this was a warning."

A warning? About what? To whom? But as soon as the question formed, she knew the answer. *Melinda.* "A warning to my mother."

"We have a situation. Your mother has been tugging on some threads in-house. People are feeling threatened."

"What sort of threads?" she asked, though she knew he wouldn't answer. Officially, her mother was what she called "a run-of-the-mill bureaucrat" at the CIA. She'd never hidden the fact of where she worked, but she'd always been quick to say that every organization needed an HR department and that somebody had to process benefit plan paperwork. Cat had always known there was more to Melinda Blackburn's job than that. HR department personnel didn't attend meetings at the White House or make extended trips overseas. Or, for that matter, recruit subordinates the likes of Jack Davenport. "Is my mother in danger?"

"She's taking precautions. She's seeing that your father is protected, too."

"Good." Cat was concerned about her father. He was a brilliant man who too often got lost in his thoughts and forgot his surroundings. If someone was targeting Melinda Blackburn's family, Dad would have a bull's-eye on his back, for sure. He needed protection. Skilled protection. "Why aren't you watching over Dad?"

Again, Jack hesitated. "Actually, I volunteered for that job."

Okay. Well. That certainly put her in her place, didn't it? "But Dad asked you to look after me instead."

"Yes."

"And Melinda agreed to it?"

"She insisted on it."

This boggled Cat's mind. Her mother had never liked Cat's relationship with Jack. She'd just about blown a gasket when they eloped, and she'd been the one with a divorce lawyer's name at the ready the moment paperwork arrived from Jack.

"Since she knows your medical records, she even gave me the knockout drug to use on you," he added. "She knew which one would be safest."

"There is nothing like a mother's love, is there?"

His gaze cut sharply to hers and for a long, awkward moment, a ghost hung between them. Cat quickly changed the subject. "I thought you had transferred to a different department and were stationed overseas."

A brow arched above ice-blue eyes. "You checked up on me?"

"Absolutely not. Melinda mentioned you a time or two."

His smirk suggested he didn't believe her, but Cat was telling the truth. On two separate occasions, Melinda had made it known that Jack was no longer based in D.C. She'd said that she feared that Cat had still carried a torch for Jack, and she'd wanted to make sure her daughter knew that no reconciliation was in the cards.

The only thing Cat carried where her ex was concerned was a grudge. Melinda could have saved her breath. "Of course, I know better than to believe anything she says if it concerns her work. I figure it's a fifty-fifty chance that you're still her golden boy."

"As opposed to her lapdog?" he asked, a winter's chill in his voice.

She opened her mouth to apologize—it had been an uncharacteristically snotty remark—but she stopped herself. The man had drugged and abducted her, after all. Neither he nor her parents had bothered to present their case and request her cooperation before setting such high-handed plans in motion.

That's because they all know you better than that. They know you wouldn't have agreed to go to the grocery store with Jack Davenport, much less . . . "Where are you taking me?"

"A place I own. It's called Eagle's Way."

Eagle's Way? Eagle was his code name. She wasn't supposed to know it, but she'd overheard a phone call of her mother's one time and the context made it clear that she'd been talking about Jack. "How long?"

"That's impossible to know right now."

"I need to be home on Sunday." She nodded toward the dog who slept peacefully in her carrier belted into a seat opposite the aisle. "I am only sitting Peanut until her owner comes home after the Fourth of July holiday."

"That's not your dog? You got her from the pound."

"You followed me to the shelter?"

"I followed you the entire morning. Bodyguard Ken was worthless."

Bodyguard Ken? "The dog belongs to a sick little girl named Megan who is going to a cancer camp in the Adirondacks. I promised her I'd watch Peanut like a hawk and that she'd be waiting for Megan when she gets home."

Jack shut his eyes and mouthed a curse. "What day does the kid get home?"

"Sunday night."

"All right. I'll make sure the dog is waiting for her."

"The dog and me?"

"The dog. I'll make the decision about when you go back at the appropriate time."

He'll make that decision? Cat had the urge to go six-year-old on him and stick out her tongue and say, *You're not the boss of me.*

"We're going off the map for a little while, Catherine," he continued. "You might as well sit back and enjoy it."

Enjoy it? With you around? Yeah, right. "Off the map? Where exactly are you taking me, Jack? Mars?"

Again, he showed her a real smile. "Not Mars, but it is a little bit out of this world, I'll admit. We're going to the mountains, Cat. Near a little town in Colorado called Eternity Springs."

TWO

☙

After an equipment malfunction kept them grounded
overnight in Colorado Springs, Jack finally set his helicopter down at Eagle's Way the following day. *Hallelujah,* he thought as he cut the engine. Thank God this trip
was over. The last time he'd felt this much tension while
piloting a bird, he'd been flying through the mountains
of Pakistan with bullets chasing his ass.

He needed a dose of Eagle's Way in the worst way. He
owned houses all over the world in some gorgeous lo-
cales, but none of them soothed his soul quite like this
Rocky Mountain hideaway. Today, his soul needed
soothing more than ever. Dealing with Cat Blackburn
was proving to be every bit as difficult as he had anticipated, and more.

He'd expected her to be a challenge. He'd been prepared for hot temper and frosty anger. He'd expected a
slap in the face or a punch in the gut, and even the kick
in the balls hadn't completely caught him by surprise.

What he hadn't anticipated was his response to her.
He had thought that any sexual desire he'd felt for her
was long gone, dead and buried like their marriage. In
fact, he had counted on it. Instead, he'd flown halfway
across the country with an extra stick in the cockpit.

He removed his headset. "Welcome to Eagle's Way."

"Who are those women?" Cat asked, referring to the two females standing near his pool as they flew over.

"Sarah Reese owns a bakery in town. Her daughter, Lori, is with her."

Lori was also the college-aged daughter of Cameron Murphy, a distant cousin and relatively recent friend of Jack's. He hadn't met Lori yet, but Sarah had shown him pictures of the young woman. Looking forward to the opportunity to meet Cam's daughter while putting some space between himself and his ex, Jack exited the helicopter with a smile on his face. His long legs ate up the ground between the helipad and the pool area where pretty little Sarah Reese waited.

She was no bigger than a minute with gorgeous violet eyes and dark hair cut short and sassy. Jack had taken her to dinner a few times and her good night kiss had packed a punch, but he'd figured out quickly that she was meant for Cam. Cam had recently returned to Eternity Springs, himself, and Jack was glad to see that Sarah and his cousin might be finding their way back to each other. His smiled widened even more at that thought.

"Hello, beautiful." He gave Sarah a quick, friendly kiss. "I didn't anticipate arriving home to such lovely scenery."

Sarah accepted his compliment with a bit of a blush. "Please don't arrest us for trespassing. Cam brought us up."

"More scuba lessons?" he asked, even as he turned his attention to Lori. What a beautiful young woman. "You're Lori. Lovely Lori. You have your father's eyes and your mother's smile. Welcome to Eagle's Way, cousin."

When he gave Lori a kiss, too, her complexion flushed to match her mother's.

He saw Sarah's curious gaze shift to a spot over his shoulder. Jack braced for a cutting remark or attack from Cat, but he guessed wrong. She marched right by them, carrying her purse and the pet, without saying a word.

That loose-hipped, rolling walk of hers attracted Jack's gaze like a magnet. He'd always liked watching her walk, especially when she wore a formfitting skirt and heels as she did now. Sex on stilts. He recalled the time—

Stop. Don't go there.

Cat halted beside Sarah's car and glanced inside. *Oh, crap.* Frowning, Jack asked, "You didn't leave your keys in the ignition, did you?"

"No."

"Good."

Cat continued on, but instead of turning toward the house, she walked in the opposite direction, toward the gate. Sarah asked, "Where is your friend going?"

Jack smiled with honest amusement. "Not as far as she thinks. She doesn't realize how isolated we are up here. The exercise will do me good."

"Do *you* good?" Lori repeated.

"We've been cooped up together traveling for a while. She's not very happy with me. I'll let her walk off some of her steam, then I'll go pick her up." Glancing toward the house, he added, "So where's Cam?"

Sarah relayed a story about some trouble that Cam's son, Devin, had landed in. They discussed that situation for a few minutes before Sarah looped her arm through Lori's and said, "We're going to head back to town now. How long will you be in Colorado this time? Will we see you in Eternity Springs?"

Jack considered Sarah's question. When he'd first built the house, Jack's trips to Eagle's Way had involved his work and thus demanded secrecy. He'd rarely paid a visit to town, and Cat had never visited when they were married. In fact, she hadn't known this place existed.

More recently, he'd begun using the estate as a personal retreat rather than a safe house, so he'd started going in to Eternity Springs more often, and he'd made friends—as much as a man like him ever made friends.

Jack's gaze trailed back to Cat, who had stopped and released the dog from its carrier. Once Peanut did her business, Cat scooped her up into her arms, abandoned the pet purse in the field, and continued her march away from him.

Sarah continued to wait for his response. Until Melinda or the local authorities or the private talent he'd hired to investigate the incident determined who had tossed that flaming bottle into Cat's dining room, they needed to keep a low profile, even in a place as small and out of the way as Eternity Springs. Eagle's Way had top-of-the-line security. She was safe here at the estate. She probably would be safe in Eternity Springs, too.

But he couldn't be certain.

"I'm not quite sure, but I'll ask a favor of you. It's fine if you mention that you were here when I arrived, but please don't tell anyone that I have a guest."

"Why not?" Lori blurted out, then blushed in chagrin at her temerity.

Jack rolled his tongue around his mouth as he watched Cat's little Yorkie-mix dog scare a rabbit from its hole. He could duck the question or lie to Lori, but he hated to do that. She was family, after all. "It's a long explanation, but technically, I kidnapped her."

Lori's eyes bugged in surprise and Sarah exclaimed, "You what!"

"Don't worry. She's my ex-wife." And if everyone in town knew her as Catherine Davenport—a name she'd never used, a fact that still stuck in his craw—who would connect her with Cat Blackburn, the blogger? A satisfied smile spread across his face as he added, "Besides, her mother asked me to do it."

* * *

Cat turned her back on the huge log house nestled against the base of a mountain and started across an alpine meadow blanketed with wildflowers in a rainbow of hues. She wasn't walking *to* anywhere. She was headed away. Away from Jack. Away from her interfering parents. Away from incompetent bodyguards and firebombers.

She had reached her limit at six twenty-three this morning. That's when she'd awakened in her room of the two-bedroom cottage at the Broadmoor resort in Colorado Springs and upon hearing the murmur of her ex-husband's voice coming from the patio, had eavesdropped on the telephone conversation between him and her mother.

Listening to them talk about her had been humiliating. They spoke as if she were a child in need of babysitting. All the old resentments and insecurities that had plagued her through the years about Jack's work with her mother revived as if they were brand-new. It was bad enough having a mother whose job always seemed to be more important than her daughter, but entering into a relationship with Melinda Blackburn's right-hand man had been failure waiting to happen.

But oh, how she'd fallen for Jack Davenport—against her better judgment, against her own self-interest, against her mother's wishes—she'd tumbled head over teacup for the man the first day she met him.

And today, twelve years later, she could walk away from the man, but she couldn't outrun her memories.

She had found the perfect gift for her mom in a Georgetown antiques store earlier that afternoon, and she'd decided she simply couldn't wait the five days to her mother's birthday to give it to her. She knew the chances of actually finding Mom at home were slim, but since she was close to their Wesley Heights house, she thought she'd give it a shot.

It was a beautiful afternoon in the fall of her junior year at GWU, and she walked from the bus stop with a spring in her step. Her journalism professor had returned papers today. She had two bright and shiny A's in the folder in her backpack. That was another reason she'd decided to pay this unscheduled visit to her parents. She didn't think she'd ever outgrow the need to preen about grades to her computer-science-professor dad.

As she turned a corner and her parents' home came into view, she saw something that told her that her father, at least, was home. The Geek Fleet was back, embroiled in a driveway basketball game.

Cat had been in middle school when she bestowed the Geek Fleet moniker on the group of students her dad tended to collect and bring home like lost puppies each year. Cat usually liked the students that George Blackburn befriended. Computer nerds, they were always brilliant, often awkward, and usually nice as could be. Cat had enjoyed those times when "Prof B" invited his students home to work on a project or watch a ballgame on TV or play a game of cards. It had been nice to have people in the house. With her mother at work almost all the time and just Cat and her dad roaming around the house, she'd been happy to have company—even if they were science geeks.

She drew closer and got a better look at the fleet, divided into shirts and skins for the game. Cat did a double-take. This year's Geek Fleet had a new member. Wow oh wow, what a member! Wasn't it lucky for her that he happened to be on the skins!

He was tall, well over six feet, she guessed. Whipcord lean with broad shoulders and tanned skin glistening with sweat, he moved with fluid grace as he drove to the basket, feigning left, moving right, jumping. Gym shorts rode low on his hips and framed his butt, and Cat's mouth went dry at the sight as his hook shot found nothing but net.

Then he turned around and she got her first good look at his face. Mercy! Maybe she should start hanging around the computer labs at school. The guy was drop-dead gorgeous with a thin blade of a nose and ice-blue eyes. He must be a grad student rather than an under-grad, because he was older than the other players, older than she by at least a couple of years, she'd guess. He'd had a haircut recently, too, because he had whitewalls around his ears and the back of his neck. For some rea-son, Cat found that cute. Maybe because it was all that kept him from perfection.

She didn't miss the quick once-over he gave her when she approached. She told herself to play it cool, to treat him no differently than she did the other guys. In an ef-fort to act as she would if he weren't there, she called out hello to one of the guys who she already knew and asked, "Can I play?"

"You can be on our team," Studly Nerd quipped, flashing her a flirtatious grin as he held the basketball. "I'll be glad to help you with the uniform."

"Very funny." She swayed her hips a little as she walked up to him and smiled sweetly. "I choose shirts."

Then she stole the basketball right out of his hands and headed for the goal, scoring two points before any-one touched her.

He laughed. She shot him a smug look and felt a secret thrill at the admiration she spied in his eyes.

The basketball game continued and so did their flirta-tion. His name was Jack, he told her as he intercepted the pass she meant for a teammate. He teased her. She taunted him. Cat was a good athlete and she'd played basketball in high school. Her parents had installed the goal for her when she was ten, so this was her home court, after all. She knew every crack and dip in the driveway and she took full advantage of it.

Cat hadn't had this much fun playing ball since her team won the midwinter tournament her junior year.

The game ended abruptly when her father walked out of the house carrying a metal tub filled with ice and soft drinks and accompanied by two more students toting platters filled with sandwiches and bowls of chips. Upon seeing her, George Blackburn beamed with delight. "Sweetheart, I didn't know you were stopping by today."

"Hi, Daddy," she replied. "It was a spur-of-the-moment thing."

"Daddy?" Jack murmured, the grin fading from his face. "You're Cathy Blackburn?"

"Cat. I go by Cat." Cathy was what her mother called her. Her easy smile dimmed when he took a physical step away from her. What was that all about?

Her father continued, "This is a wonderful surprise. Come have a sandwich with us. Have you met everyone?"

"Not everyone."

"Let me introduce you, then. Guys, this is my daughter, Catherine. Cat, meet my students. You know Brandon, Will, and Reid from last year, of course."

Cat waved to the guys she already knew, then shook hands with four newcomers when he presented them. He introduced Jack last. "And this is Jack Davenport. He's not officially one of my students, but he soaks up information like a sponge. Jack works with your mother."

He works with Mom, hence the "Cathy." Well, great.

Jack had taken a small physical step away when he'd learned her name. Upon discovering his occupation, Cat took an enormous mental step backward.

The last thing she needed, the very last thing she wanted, was to get tangled up in any way, shape, or form with an associate of her mother.

Cat Blackburn drew the line at dating spies.

"If only I'd listened to myself," she muttered to Peanut, whose ears perked at the sound. Cat stooped to pluck a goldenrod from the field of flowers and blinked away tears.

She hadn't listened. She'd told herself that he wasn't really a spy but a bureaucrat. Washington was full of bureaucrats, and most of them went home to their families every night. Just because her mother worked all the time didn't mean that Jack would, too. She told herself that he could be as attentive as any other boyfriend, and then husband, and for a time, that's how their relationship had been.

Then they decided to have a baby and couldn't get pregnant and he was working more and more, had more and more out-of-town trips. She'd wanted him to quit. He'd gained access to his trust fund on his twenty-eighth birthday and the man was filthy rich. He didn't *have* to work. He *wanted* to work. Just like her mother wanted to work.

Somewhere during that time, he had gone from bureaucrat to agent.

She'd known better, but she hadn't listened to herself. She'd been the moth and Jack Davenport the flame, and eventually he'd burned her.

Cat sucked in a deep breath. She would not cry over the man. She'd sworn off doing that four years ago when she signed his divorce papers. She refused to backslide now.

At the sound of an engine starting, she glanced over her shoulder to see the woman and her daughter driving away. Jack was climbing the steps to the front door of his house.

Good. He was giving her some time to herself. Cat needed that more than anything. Ever since she broke the dogfighting ring story, her life had been a storm.

She heard the bubbling rush of water over rocks from off to her right and turned toward the sound. She had noticed the creek snaking through the valley as they'd flown over. The thought of sitting beside a flowing stream with only the dog for company sounded wonderful.

Determined to clear her mind of worry and concern, she followed the sound of water to the bank of a clear mountain stream. It was a beautiful spot. She spied a boulder with a nice flat surface a short distance upstream on the opposite bank. She slipped off her shoes and gingerly tested the crystal-clear water with her bare toes.

"Brrr . . ." Cold, but bearable. Holding her shoes by the heels in one hand and the dog in the other, she picked her way carefully around slippery stones, through icy water that at its deepest hit her just below the knees. Upon reaching the opposite bank, she climbed out of the water and up onto the flat-topped rock. It was big enough to lie down on, so she did exactly that.

With her hands beneath her head and Peanut snuggled up against her side, Cat stared up at the bright blue sky dotted with fluffy white clouds. Sunshine toasted her skin, chasing away the chill that lingered as much from her memories as from crossing the mountain stream. Slowly, the tension gripping her began to seep away.

Maybe having been kidnapped wasn't such a bad thing after all, she decided. Since being laid off from the newspaper, she'd adopted the attitude that every problem had an upside if one looked for it. This situation was no different. The weather was gorgeous. The accommodations were certain to be first class— this was Jack's home, after all. As long as he had Internet access, she could work from here as well as from home.

Maybe she'd stumble across something new and exciting to investigate while she was here in Colorado. Something that had nothing to do with abused animals or sleazy politicians or false American idols. Maybe she'd find a good illegal drug supplier to look into or some misdirected public funds to explore. Or maybe not.

For the first time in memory, she hadn't enjoyed the hunt while investigating the dogfighting ring, and she didn't know precisely why. She'd done a good job on the investigation. Some of the men she'd connected to the ring had held positions of public trust—cops and congressmen. The story had been an important piece of investigative journalism. The public had the right to know what kind of man they'd entrusted with their tax dollars. So why didn't she feel the sense of satisfaction that her job ordinarily brought her? For the past eight years or so, she'd lived for this sort of thing.

Maybe that was the answer. Maybe her ennui resulted from having done it for eight years. Maybe she was tired of fighting the good fight. Perhaps her efforts to balance the ugliness that her professional life invariably brought into her life by filling her personal life with positive influences simply wasn't working anymore. Maybe she needed a break.

Money wasn't a problem for her. Jack had been ridiculously generous in the divorce. She'd worked because she enjoyed it and because except for her volunteer activities, work was all she'd had.

That hadn't changed.

"Well, maybe that needs to change," she murmured, idly scratching Peanut behind the ears. Maybe this was her chance. She could sunbathe beside that awesome pool she'd noticed and never go near a computer.

Her mother liked to theorize that Cat had never put

her marriage behind her completely. Cat had denied the charge, and she'd tried to believe it. Hadn't she dated other men since the split? Hadn't she had two serious relationships? Deep down inside, though, she'd suspected that her mother might be right.

Not that she'd ever admit that to anyone.

But if she entertained the notion that her mother's claim did have a basis in fact, then this . . . abduction . . . might be just what she needed to finally cut the cord where Jack was concerned. The man's high-handedness might turn out to be a blessing in disguise.

Feeling better about her world than she had in weeks, Cat relaxed. She dozed for a bit, then awoke slowly, soaking in the sun and drinking in the sound of water crashing over stones, and the comfort of the small dog resting beside her. This was a little piece of paradise, wasn't it?

When a yellow butterfly danced across the air above her, she watched it until something higher in the sky caught her notice.

The bird was huge, with a wingspan of at least six feet as it soared and circled above the valley. Cat sat up and shielded her eyes with her hand, watching the bird's majestic presence. Was that an eagle? She wasn't sure. She'd never seen an eagle in the wild, but since Jack had told her that his estate was named Eagle's Way, she wouldn't be surprised.

As she watched, the bird suddenly turned and dived toward the ground. As he came closer, she saw the familiar bald head and decided that yes, he had to be an eagle. How cool was this?

He swooped down upon the meadow and she heard a cry, then he rose with his prey—a rabbit—wiggling in his talons. Cat gave a little shudder, and murmured to Peanut, "I'd better keep a close eye on you whenever we're outside."

She turned her attention back to the water, and that's when she saw him. Jack stood downstream some fifty yards or so with a fly rod in his hands. She watched him work the line with a fluid, artistic grace, and an old, familiar yearning washed through her.

Those hands. Those talented hands. They'd made her body sing like none before and none since.

Suddenly he yanked back on the rod. Color flashed on the surface of the stream as he reeled the rainbow trout in. Once he had the wriggling fish gripped securely in his hand, he looked her way. The predatory triumph in his eyes brought the eagle to mind.

A frisson of apprehension skittered up Cat's spine. This might be her opportunity, but she was in his territory. She'd best keep watch on more than the sky while she was here at Eagle's Way.

THREE

Jack didn't make mistakes very often, but when he entered the kitchen to make coffee on the morning of their third day at Eagle's Way, he feared he'd made a huge one when he decided to bring Cat to Colorado. Being around her stirred up not only his libido, but also regrets. He could deal with the former, but the latter was giving him trouble.

Regrets were a waste of energy. He couldn't go back and change what had happened, but being around Cat made him entertain thoughts he had denied himself for years. Being around her made him want things he hadn't wanted since the day he moved out of their house. Knowing that once again she slept beneath his roof had Jack tossing and turning in his bed all night.

He wanted her. He despised her. Dammit, a part of him still loved her. How sad was that?

Still half asleep, he poured coffee beans into the grinder. As the motor whirred, he tried to shake off his grouchy mood.

When Cat stumbled into the kitchen a few moments later looking half asleep herself, they fell into the breakfast-making routine they'd established long ago, then revived on their first morning at Eagle's Way. Cat set out fruit and yogurt, and while the coffee brewed, Jack made toast. Neither spoke until after they'd tasted their first sip of coffee—the need for caffeine being something they still shared.

Cat spoke first. "Good morning."

"G'morning."

"Any news from Washington?"

He thought of the middle-of-the-night alert he'd received and the subsequent conference call.

In recent years, as kidnapping had become a regular method of commerce in some parts of the world, Jack's job description had evolved and narrowed. He and his team had become extraction specialists. They mounted rescue missions into places where no one in their right mind wanted to be. They worked under the auspices of the CIA, but Jack didn't know how much longer that would be the case. Life in the clandestine services wasn't much fun anymore. Politicians seemed to think they knew more about just about everything than did the people working in the trenches. Every time Jack turned around, they had set up another hoop he had to jump through.

He was about ready to tell the pols just where they could jump.

But this wasn't the sort of Washington news Cat had asked about. "No," he told her. "Nothing about your situation yet."

Not definitively, anyway. Melinda's concerns about the attack on Cat being a warning to her had just about been eliminated, and the private investigators he'd hired had turned up a couple of promising leads. Nothing was settled, however, so he'd keep those details to himself.

"Peanut needs to be home tonight," she said as she stabbed a strawberry with her fork.

"She will be." He slathered orange marmalade onto a piece of toast. "Someone will arrive here by ten to escort her back to her owner."

"Someone you trust?"

"Yes." The little girl had nothing to worry about.

They finished breakfast and cleaned up without exchanging another word. Cat took the dog outside to play with a tennis ball. Jack donned sneakers and went for a run. A long run. Physical exhaustion was the best way he'd found to manage the constant tension that resulted from daily interaction with his ex-wife.

Sharing breakfast this morning had been an unhappy reminder of those meals they'd shared—and the ones they had not shared—in the last few months before their split. Those memories rode his shoulders as he ran.

The alarm buzzed and Jack flung an arm out to shut it off. Rolling over, he reached instinctively for his wife . . . and found nothing but cold sheets.

Reality returned. He opened his eyes to an empty bed, a lonely marriage, and a hurting heart.

He sat up and listened to the patter of rain against the roof as he debated whether to reach out to her again or just go about his day. He was almost too weary to try, but this particular morning, loneliness drove him more.

He knew where he'd find her, so after he pulled on his jeans, he took the short walk from the master bedroom to the room that was a half-completed nursery.

He stopped just beyond the threshold. Cat sat in the bentwood rocker he'd given her for her birthday. Staring out the window into the gloom of a rainy day, she stroked a receiving blanket decorated with yellow ducks as if it were a pet. Her eyes were hollow and haunted, and he doubted she'd strung together eight hours of sleep in the last week.

"Hey, honey."

She didn't respond, but continued to stare out into the wet, gray morning.

Frustration rose inside him. He knew she was grieving. He recognized that she was depressed. The doctors had assured him that such a reaction was normal and to be expected. They'd advised him to give her time and he'd done that. But this . . . malaise . . . had gone on for months now and it was beginning to feel like forever.

Jack was lonely. He was sad. He was more than a little bit angry. He'd lost his child, too. Who had been there for him? Who had comforted him? Certainly not his wife.

He never claimed to have been as attached to his unborn child as Cat had been, but he didn't think he was any different from most men in that respect. The fertility treatments had been brutal on them both, and when she finally conceived, he'd been more relieved than excited. But as the weeks and months passed, that had changed. He'd looked forward to having the baby. Losing her had hurt him, too, but he'd never been able to share his pain with Cat because he'd had to be strong for her. Unfortunately, his strength or lack thereof hadn't seemed to make any difference.

He closed his eyes, drew in a breath, then tried again. "Cat, I'm going to make omelets for breakfast. Do you want vegetables in yours or just cheese?"

Finally, she turned to look at him. "How can you eat today of all days?"

Today of all days?

"You don't even know what today is, do you?" she accused, life finally sparking in her eyes as she rose from the rocker and took a step toward him.

Today? He quickly took stock. Not her birthday. Not their anniversary. Today wasn't even the date the baby had been due. That date didn't roll around until next week and he'd been trying to decide how to handle it. At a loss, he said, "I'm sorry, Cat. I don't know what today is."

"Today was supposed to be my last day of work at the newspaper. They were going to give me a baby shower today."

Jack's lips flattened into a grim line. What was he supposed to say to that? He didn't have a clue. "Why don't you come to the kitchen with me. We'll have a nice breakfast and then maybe we can go to the gym. I'll bet a yoga class would make you feel better."

You'd have thought he'd drop-kicked a puppy from the look she gave him. "Go away, Jack. Just . . . go away."

Angry now, he did just that. When his work line rang as he finished up his omelet, he didn't hesitate to volunteer for the trip. Rather than tell her good-bye, he left a note. When he returned seventeen days later, he saw no sign that she'd read it. Or, frankly, even noticed that he'd been gone.

Running beside the creek that split the heart of the valley that sheltered Eagle's Way, Jack put on a burst of speed, hoping to outrun the memories. He ran all out, harder and farther than normal, draining away his energy and the tension that hummed through his blood as a result of sharing space with Cat, until he stopped, exhausted and spent. For a moment he leaned over, resting his hands on his knees until his breathing slowed, then he turned and went back to the house at a slow, easy jog.

The run had done him good. He felt more relaxed now than at any time since he'd heard the news about the fire at Cat's house.

He arrived back at the house just in time to see his exwife exit the pool house in a one-piece bathing suit.

Jack's tension came roaring back.

After her swim and her shower, Cat settled down to work in the sunroom at Eagle's Way. A box of her belongings had arrived yesterday, gathered and shipped to her by her father. As she booted up her laptop, she also tried to stir up some enthusiasm to begin research on a new investigation to follow up the dogfight ring story.

The day after the Molotov cocktail exploded in her dining room, she'd written a post explaining what had happened and announcing a temporary hiatus from her blog. She spent almost an hour answering email—carefully, so as not to give away any details about her location—then turned her attention to her next project—whatever that would be.

She always kept a running file of ideas and possibilities so she had somewhere to start. She pulled up the file and scrolled through it. Nothing called to her, so she moved on to surfing an Internet shoe store when Jack knocked on the sunroom's open door. "Sorry to interrupt, but I want to let you know that we're having guests for lunch. Some friends of mine are bringing their twin daughters for a swim."

"Oh." She looked up from her computer. "Thanks for the warning. I'll grab a sandwich and stay in my room."

"Actually, I was hoping you'd join us. I think you'll like the Callahans." He paused, and when she didn't immediately reply, added, "Please join us, Cat. If nothing else, spending time with them will give the two of us something to talk about once they're gone. Maybe it will help us avoid so many awkward silences."

The man had a point. "All right. Do you need help with lunch?"

"No, thanks. Nic is bringing it with her." Jack hesitated, then watched her closely as he added, "I know Gabe through work. He stayed here at Eagle's Way a few years ago when he was going through some tough personal times. His first wife was killed in an auto accident, and their son died of his injuries months later. Gabe stayed up here at Eagle's Way for a while afterward."

Cat sat back in her chair. So, was he telling her that as a warning or as a test of some sort? It was the closest he'd come to mentioning Lauren since he'd snatched Cat off the street.

She supposed that she should reassure him that she didn't break out in hives or erupt into tears or sink into despair every time she spied a child. Not anymore, anyway. However, being around Jack had brought all those emotions closer to the surface—along with the old, deep resentments—so she managed only a noncommital "That's very sad."

When she didn't elaborate, he said, "They'll be in here twenty minutes or so."

"Okay. I'll finish up what I'm doing and join you then."

Taking that as the dismissal it was, he nodded curtly and left. Cat blew out a breath, her thoughts racing.

So, this Gabe Callahan guy was someone Jack knew from work. "Work" could mean a whole lot of things. He could have been a bureaucrat or he could have been a spy. He could know Cat's mother. *Oh, golly gee. Wouldn't that be nice?*

Cat shut off her computer, then made a quick trip upstairs to brush her hair and check her makeup. She knew she hadn't made a good first impression on the Reeses, the first—and only—Eternity Springs residents she'd met. Pride made her want to redeem herself.

Fifteen minutes after Jack knocked on the sunroom door, Cat joined him outside. He carried a box of toys from the pool house closet and set them on a lounge chair as an SUV came up the road toward the house. The driver pulled the vehicle to a halt in the spot where Sarah Reese had parked on the day they'd arrived in Colorado. A handsome man wearing swim trunks and a Texas Rangers baseball jersey exited the driver's side door, then retrieved a curly-headed blond toddler from a car seat in the back. At the same time, a pretty, ponytail-sporting blonde removed an identical child from a second car seat on the passenger side.

Jack approached the couple, shook the man's hand and kissed the wife, then gladly accepted the handoff of a child from her mother. Upon seeing Jack holding the toddler, emotion knifed through Cat and she caught her breath. Whoa. She hadn't expected that.

She realized that in all the years they'd been together, she'd never seen Jack hold a child.

Stupid of her, though, not to consider the possibility. Had she thought ahead, she would have braced for the blow, and she wouldn't be walking toward the group with a fake smile pasted on her face, trying to look anywhere else but at Jack, but unable to tear her gaze away.

Jack said, "Gabe and Nic Callahan, meet Cat Blackburn. Cat, the Callahans and their daughters, Meg and Cari."

Gabe's greeting was friendly enough. Nic's was both friendly and unabashedly curious. "I have to confess that after Jack told us you were up here, I went online and read about your investigation and the bomb going off and how you've . . . um . . ." She cut a glance toward Jack. ". . . gone into hiding until your safety can be assured."

Cat's fake smile transformed to a genuine smirk. "As a career newspaper reporter, let me advise you not to believe everything you read in the papers."

"Yes, well, our friend Sarah did mention that Jack said something about a kidnapping."

"I knew she wouldn't keep her lips zipped," Jack said.

Nic's grin was unabashed. "She swore me to secrecy."

Wryly, Jack asked, "Who did you tell?"

"Just Sage Rafferty."

"Just do me a favor? If anyone asks, her name is Catherine Davenport." Cat frowned at Jack, who shrugged. "Just an added, and probably unnecessary, precaution."

Gabe nodded reassuringly. "No need to worry about your safety in Eternity Springs. We take care of our own."

One of the girls—Meg—began kicking her legs, saying, "Down, Daddy. Down."

For the next little while the girls busied themselves throwing all of the toys one by one into the pool while the adults made small talk. The Callahans spoke of the Fourth of July picnic and fireworks show at Hummingbird Lake, then Gabe asked, "Did y'all come down to watch the fireworks?"

"No," Jack replied. "We were still settling in here."

What he didn't say was that neither one of them had wanted any reminder of the romantic Fourths of July they'd spent together watching fireworks on the National Mall. In fact, the word "fireworks" had taken on a special meaning to them after they made love for the first time after returning to Jack's town house following a Fourth of July show.

"Have you seen your cousin?" Nic asked, a frown line showing between her brows.

"I haven't seen Cam, but he called earlier to tell me he and Devin are returning to Australia."

Cat was more than a little surprised as she listened to the conversation about Cam Murphy and Sarah Reese's star-crossed romance. So, Jack had a cousin named Cam who grew up in Eternity Springs? She'd never heard of any cousin before. He'd always told her he didn't have any family.

Once the toys were all in the swimming pool, the Callahan twins showed signs of wanting to go in after them, and Cat wanted a distraction from thinking about Jack. She asked Nic, "Can your girls swim?"

"We've been taking water babies classes at a pool in town this summer," the other woman replied. "They can't swim yet, but they have learned to go underwater and hold their breath."

Jack got into the water with the Callahans, and after changing into a swimsuit in the pool house, Cat did, too. The toddlers laughed and splashed and squealed when their daddy blew bubbles on their tummy and Jack tossed them up in the air. While the children played, the adults talked a little politics, some major league baseball and college football, and then general news about Eternity Springs. When the girls started showing signs of fatigue, Nic and Gabe took them out of the pool, dried, dressed, and fed them, then put them down to nap in the portable beds the Callahans had brought with them. While Gabe and Nic were busy with the girls, Jack and Cat set the table for lunch.

"This looks good," Jack said as he peeked into a container. "Chicken salad?"

"Yes, it's Ali Timberlake's," Nic replied, adjusting the sunshade over Meg. "You need to give her restaurant a try while you're in Colorado, Jack. Her menu is beginning to attract foodies from all over the state."

"I'll be sure to do that."

Once the children were asleep, conversation turned to some landscaping changes that Jack had in mind for Eagle's Way. An award-winning landscape architect, Gabe Callahan had strong opinions about Jack's ideas, and once they'd finished their lunch, the men took their discussion into the house where they'd have access to the Internet so that Gabe could illustrate his points. Nic turned the conversation toward the dogfighting ring, explaining that she was a veterinarian. "Is it true that one of the men kept twenty-three dogs penned in his basement?"

Cat nodded. "Craig Gauthier."

"Okay, I must confess my ignorance of pop culture. He's the singer on TV or the race car driver?"

"The singer."

"That's just so wrong. They were pits?"

"Pits and pit mixes," Cat replied. "You wouldn't have believed what pathetic shape those dogs were in."

"I've seen a lot over the years in my veterinary practice. I don't think anything some humans do to animals could surprise me. This subject depresses me. Let's change it." Nic gave Cat a sidelong glance and observed, "Gabe has known Jack a long time. He said Jack was tight-lipped about his personal life. He didn't know about the divorce."

Cat snorted.

"The man never has been one to share much about himself."

"How long were you married?"

"Five and a half years. We've been divorced for four."

Cat wondered how much Nic Callahan would indulge her own curiosity, and she was trying to decide how much to reveal when Nic surprised her by saying, "I was married and divorced before I met Gabe. There is no way on earth that I would sit down to lunch with my ex. I might be tempted to pick up my knife and do harm."

"And you think I wasn't?" Cat drawled.

Nic grinned. "I think I like you, Cat Davenport."

"Blackburn. Cat Blackburn. I think I like you, too, Nic Callahan."

Nic must have taken that as tacit permission to be nosy, because she then said, "So, my first husband cheated on me. Why did you and Jack split?"

"He didn't cheat." At least, not that Cat knew. Those first weeks after the miscarriage he could have brought a woman home and done her on the living room floor and she wouldn't have noticed. She gave Nic her usual response whenever anyone asked. "He traveled a lot. We grew apart."

At Nic's speculative look, she asked, "What?"

"*You* cheated?"

"No!" Cat scowled at her. "You Eternity Springs people are nosy, aren't you?"

Nic grinned unapologetically. "I think you should probably know that I have a soft spot in my heart for your ex. More than a soft spot, actually. Jack is my hero. I wouldn't have my life if not for him." Nic refilled her glass of iced tea, then silently offered more to Cat.

Cat nodded and asked, "Jack saved your life?"

"He saved Gabe's life."

Nic Callahan went on to tell her the story of how Jack accomplished Gabe's rescue from a Balkan prison. Cat realized that it had happened during one of those unexplained absences during their marriage, and her gaze shifted to the twins napping peacefully in their beds.

She'd always known that Jack did important work. That had never been in doubt. But she'd grown up with an absentee mother, and because of that, she'd never wanted an absentee spouse. Unfortunately, Jack Davenport had been a force her heart had been unable to resist.

The failure of her marriage couldn't be summarized as easily as that of Nic's first one. Even if she'd wanted to spill her guts to this woman whom she'd only just met, too many factors had contributed to the breakup to be neatly enumerated. Cat wasn't sure that she could identify all of them herself, even if she tried.

"I've always known that Jack was someone special," she said, honestly touched by Nic Callahan's tale. "I imagine there are dozens of stories similar to yours that only a handful of people have ever heard. Unfortunately, it's hard to be married to a hero. We simply weren't able to make it work."

"That's too bad," Nic said softly, as one of her daughters stirred in her bed and let out a little snuffle of a snore.

Cat had nothing more to say.

The room in Eagle's Way that Jack used as an office was on the ground floor off the great room. Designed with the need for secure communications in mind, the office was the one room in the house that didn't boast floor-to-ceiling windows. The furnishings were sleek, functional, and comfortable, though the room was not designed or utilized for relaxation.

Now Jack stood behind Gabe, who was seated at a drafting table. He studied the sketch his guest had penciled on the blank sheet of paper and nodded. "You are good, Callahan."

"I know."

"I never would have thought of adding that sundial."

"That's why you pay me the big bucks to design your landscape." Gabe reached up and switched off the light illuminating the drafting board.

In a droll tone, Jack replied, "Last time I checked, I hadn't paid you anything. I wish you'd cash my checks, Callahan."

"Not gonna happen, Davenport." Gabe's expression and tone turned serious. "I could work at Eagle's Way for the next forty years and not come close to paying you back for what you did for me."

"Just doing my job—for which I received a paycheck from the good old U.S. of A., I'll remind you."

"I owe you my—"

"Enough," Jack interrupted, waving the topic away. "This is cruising too close to mush for me. When can you start on the build?"

Gabe nodded his acceptance of Jack's change of subject. "I'll want to put more thought into it, draw up a detailed design. How long do you plan to be in Colorado this time?"

"That depends. Cat needs to stay hidden until we can smoke out whoever firebombed her house."

Gabe slipped off his chair and tore the drawing from the pad. He folded it, stuck it into his pocket, and idly asked, "So, Davenport, I gotta ask. Why the secret wife?"

Jack had expected this question, and he'd thought about his answer prior to the Callahans' arrival. Gabe knew more than most, considering their history, so Jack had decided to be more open than he'd be with someone else. "Our marriage wasn't exactly secret, but I kept it separate from work. Cat wanted it that way. She had some firsthand experience with the way things worked at Langley, and she wanted to keep our life together as far away from it as possible."

"Firsthand experience?"

"Her mother is Melinda Blackburn."

A widening of his eyes telegraphed Gabe's surprise. "I wondered when I heard her name. Blackburn isn't that common. But c'mon, Jack. You married the boss's daughter?"

A defensive note in his voice, Jack replied, "I married her in spite of the fact that she was the boss's daughter. Cat's relationship with her mother was rocky as a result of Melinda's work. She didn't want to sign up for more of it."

"Then why did she?"

Jack started to deflect the question with a reply containing the usual guy-talk boast about great sex, but then he hesitated. He'd invited Gabe into the middle of this mess, and Gabe deserved better than that from him. "We fell in love."

"Marriage couldn't withstand the strain of the job?"

The job. Infertility. The death of their baby. The job.
It wasn't an easy question. "Something like that."

"How long ago was the split?"

That, too, wasn't a simple answer. Just when had they
split? When the papers were served? When he stopped
sleeping in their bed? Or when he'd come home from
what was supposed to be a three-day trip to Iraq and
discovered that Cat had lost their child?

*The front porch light of his house in Arlington, Vir-
ginia, glowed a welcome beacon through the veil of twi-
light and snowflakes as Jack pulled his Porsche into his
driveway. He was beat.*

*He'd been gone seventeen days. Seventeen dirty, mis-
erable, bloody days with a double-digit body count, a
couple of personal near misses, and a slaughterhouse
scene that was likely to haunt his nightmares for years.
Even worse, they'd failed in their mission. The infor-
mant they'd been sent to extract had been killed before
Jack and his partner had ever set boots on the ground.
They'd suspected it by their third day in country. It took
them another ten days, thousands of dollars in bribes,
and three gun battles to confirm it. Jack never left without confirmation. It was a principle upon which he
never wavered, but man, was he glad to finally be home.*

*He switched off the engine and opened the car door.
Bitter cold air swirled around him as he removed his
duffel from the car. His footsteps crunched on two
inches of fresh snow as he walked toward his front door,
frowning when his shoe hit a slick spot and slipped. The
ice on the sidewalk had been there awhile. Had the teenager he'd hired failed to show up to do the shoveling?
He needed to remember to ask Cat about that.*

*He slipped his key into the lock and opened the door.
Stepping inside, he called, "Cat? Honey, I'm home."*

No answer.

He set down his bag and hung his coat on a rack, then

walked into the kitchen, grabbed a beer from the fridge,
and headed upstairs to take a long, hot shower.

He flipped on the lights in the master bedroom and
stopped abruptly. Cat was curled beneath an afghan in
the easy chair that sat beside the window overlooking
their backyard. "Hey, darlin'. Guess you didn't hear me
come home. Were you sleeping?"

She stared at him without speaking and Jack finally re-
alized that something was wrong. Her eyes were sunken
and she was as pale as the snowfall. "Cat? What's
wrong?"

When she still didn't reply, he set down his beer on the
dresser and crossed the room to her. "Cat?"

His body tensed as wordlessly she handed him a slip
of paper. Glancing down, he frowned. "Angel Land,
row 28, place 14? What's this?"

"The location where Lauren is buried."

Lauren? Who is Lauren? The answer came like a
punch to the gut. Lauren was the name they'd been con-
sidering if the baby turned out to be a girl. "You miscar-
ried?"

The flash of temper in her eyes was the first sign of
emotion he'd seen. "I gave birth to my baby."

He sank down onto the bed.

"I buried my baby."

"Oh, Cat."

"Alone. I did it all alone."

Alone. Years later, Jack could pinpoint that moment
as the one when he began to believe that his marriage
wouldn't make it. In response to Gabe's question, he
said, "Our divorce was final four years ago."

Jack could see Gabe thinking, tracking time backward, until he gave his head a slight shake. "I never
would have guessed you were going through a rough
patch of your own during that time, Jack."

"I compartmentalize." And that compartmentalization had been part of the package that led to divorce, too.

"Yeah, I understand. You just about have to do that in your position. I guess it must not have been too bad a breakup, though, since you're helping her out now?"

"Oh, I wouldn't go so far as to say that. We haven't spoken since the divorce. I'm helping because Melinda asked me to do it."

Gabe folded his arms and studied Jack. "And Melinda is the only reason you brought your ex-wife to Eternity Springs? Sorry, Davenport, I'm not buying that."

"I didn't say that was the only reason. I'm genuinely concerned for her safety. That's what I do, Callahan. I rescue people."

Except, of course, the one person who had mattered the most.

He recalled the conversation the following day when his cousin, Cam Murphy, called with the news that Sarah Reese's mother, Ellen, an Alzheimer's patient, had driven off in the family car and become lost. With Cat along as a spotter, Jack joined the search team by flying a grid over an area assigned to him by Sheriff Zach Turner. He flew the grid twice and expanded the search area on his own. He saw no sign of the missing car and landed back at Eagle's Way at dark, tired of the tension that continued to simmer in the air between him and Cat, and deeply frustrated by having failed in his mission. So much for being a "rescuer." Jack didn't fail often, and when he did, he didn't wear it well.

He was tired. It wasn't easy being the go-to guy when someone was in trouble.

Except, he wasn't the go-to guy when Cat was in trouble, was he? For her parents, maybe, but not for her. She hadn't called him. Not this time, and not five years ago. She hadn't wanted him around then, and she didn't want him around now. It wore on a man. Made him weary.

That's why when his phone rang an hour later, he was standing in his great room staring out at the moonlit night, sipping a drink and sulking. He checked the screen and recognized Melinda's number.

"Hello?"

The conversation that followed removed one burden from his shoulders, and he only realized how heavy a burden it had been once it was gone. Just as he'd suspected, the threat against Cat had nothing to do with Melinda. That made the entire situation much less complicated and easier to solve. "If the arson investigator doesn't track down the bomber, my guys will," he told Melinda.

"I spoke with the local authorities today. They weren't happy you hired private help."

"That's just too damn bad."

They spoke about the local investigation a few moments, then Melinda asked, "How are you and Cathy getting along?"

"Fine."

"I hope she'll use this time to find her way past some of the bitterness so that she can move forward. The two of you—"

"No," he interrupted. "Those rules haven't changed, Melinda. I will not discuss my relationship with Cat with you. That's still off-limits."

In the moment of silence that followed, he could easily see the unhappy purse of her lips. "I just think—"

"I'm going to hang up now. Good-bye." He disconnected the call and sighed. Some things never changed. Keeping his mother-in-law out of his marriage—and out of his divorce—had been one of the most difficult tasks he'd faced. In fact, her refusal to keep her nose out of his business when his marriage was falling apart was one of the main reasons he'd transferred out of the D.C. office.

That, along with the fact that looking at Melinda Blackburn was like looking at Cat in thirty years. Being around her had hurt his heart.

He'd no sooner dropped his phone into his pocket than it rang again. Melinda again, he figured. He was tempted to ignore it. He'd hung up on his mother-in-law, not his boss. But just in case his boss was calling back, he knew he had to answer. He fished the phone back out of his pocket and paused. This wasn't Melinda. "Hello?"

"Jack Davenport? Is this Jack Davenport?"

He didn't know the woman's voice, but he did recognize the note of hysteria in it. "Yes."

"I'm Tony Martinez's wife. He gave me your number months ago. He needs your help. *We* need your help. He's using again and he's saying some crazy things. I'm scared. Please, help us?"

Jack dropped his chin to his chest. Tony Martinez was a former colleague and a friend. Three years ago they'd gone into Mexico together tasked with liberating a U.S. asset being held hostage by a Mexican cartel. Tony had come home a changed man—the change not for the better. "Have you called 911?"

"No. It's not that kind of emergency. I think he needs to talk. He said he needs you."

"Where are you?"

"At home. In Dallas."

Jack mentally formed a plan. He would call the sheriff and offer the use of his helicopter in the search effort for Ellen Reese to another pilot. Zach had mentioned today that the guy who had bought Sarah's grocery store earlier this year knew how to fly a bird. "I'll be there by noon tomorrow."

"Thank you."

Even as he ended the call and began developing his travel plan, his thoughts turned to Cat. She would be safe at Eagle's Way whether he was with her or not. She didn't need him here to protect her. In fact, she'd probably pop a bottle of champagne as soon as he left.

Decision made, he left his office in search of his ex-wife. He found her in the library, stretched out on the couch, typing on her laptop. She looked up at his knock on the door. "Yes? I'm . . . Jack? What's wrong?"

"A friend is in trouble, and I have a favor to ask."

"Of me?"

"Yes."

"What is it?"

"If I leave you here alone for a few days, will you promise to stay here?"

"At Eagle's Way?"

"Yes, though if you get bored, I think it's safe for you to go into Eternity Springs. Melinda confirmed to me a few minutes ago that her fear that the firebombing had been a warning to her has proved false, and the other suspects are all local to D.C. They would not have been able to follow us here. I'd ask that you go no farther than town and to keep a low profile while you're there, however."

"I can do that." She gave his face a searching look, then abruptly shut her laptop and smiled. "Want me to help you pack?"

FOUR

❦

One week later

The eagle was back.

Through the wall of windows of the great room, Cat spied the huge bird as he circled above the meadow. She grabbed her camera bag from a table beside the front door and hurried outside. Quickly, she switched to a long range lens while debating where to position herself to get the best shots.

She scanned the valley and then the house. She'd get snowcapped mountains in the background if she shot the photos from the balcony off the master bedroom. Without hesitation, she turned around and hurried inside and up the stairs.

Cat had explored most of Eagle's Way since Jack left her here alone last week, but she'd stayed clear of his bedroom. Now as she entered it, she took a quick look around, noting dark woods and a peaceful palette of blues and grays and . . . whoa.

She halted abruptly. A framed photograph of the two of them at their wedding sat on his dresser. Wow. Just wow. That was the last thing she would have expected to find in her ex-husband's bedroom.

She crossed to the dresser and picked up the photograph. How young they'd both been. How happy.

They'd eloped to Las Vegas. He had no family and she'd never cared about having a big wedding. Presenting their marriage as a fait accompli had made it easier for them both where her mother was concerned. They'd honeymooned in a bridal suite over a long weekend and left the room only twice the entire time.

Oh, Jack. Why couldn't we make it work?

Unsettled, she flipped the lock on the French doors leading out onto the balcony and tried to refocus her attention on the soaring eagle. He was a beautiful thing to watch, and once she brought her camera up and began framing shots, she was able to put the picture in Jack's bedroom out of her mind. Mostly.

She wanted to get a fabulous shot. She'd been inspired by the work of a wildlife photographer hanging on display at the art gallery in town, Vistas.

Yesterday Sarah had invited her to a luncheon she'd hosted to thank everyone who'd assisted in the search for her mother. Ellen Reese had been found safe and sound the day Jack had left Eagle's Way. At the gathering at Sarah's bake shop, Fresh, Cat had met Sarah and Nic's circle of friends: Celeste Blessing, the owner of Angel's Rest Healing Center and Spa; Ali Timberlake, the owner of the Yellow Kitchen restaurant; and Sage Rafferty, professionally known as "the renowned artist Sage Anderson" and the owner of Vistas. It had been a fun, lighthearted gathering and Cat had enjoyed herself—as Cat Davenport. These friends of new friends who knew the truth could be trusted, Nic and Sarah had assured her, but it was easier and safer for everyone to think of her as Davenport.

Easier for them, Cat thought. *Not me.*

When conversation turned to a painting Sage had recently completed, Cat expressed a desire to see it, and after lunch, Sage had taken her over to Vistas.

Cat had liked all of Sage's work very much, but for

some reason, the wildlife photographs had captivated her. One shot in particular had caught her fancy, a five-by-seven print of a nightingale perched on the limb of a cottonwood tree. She'd made a spur-of-the-moment decision to purchase it. Only after she'd paid for the photograph and was preparing to leave did she think to ask the name of the photographer. Sage had smirked a little as she told her, and Cat had felt her cheeks flush. Jack Davenport? Really?

"I browbeat him into letting me hang his work," Sage had told her. "I saw his photographs when my husband and I visited Eagle's Way earlier this year. I've been looking for someone in that field to represent. We had a horrible incident with my previous wildlife photographer—turned out he was also into kiddie porn—so I was just thrilled to discover someone local who was also so talented."

Back when they were together, Cat had done all the picture taking. Jack never touched a camera. She wondered if photography was a new pursuit or simply one more thing he'd hidden from her while they were married. She had tucked the photograph into her shopping bag, and once back at Eagle's Way, she'd buried it in her panty drawer under the assumption that Jack would never find it there. Now, though, as she attempted to capture a spectacular shot of the predator in the sky, her thoughts continued to stray back to the photograph in her lingerie drawer, and the one on the dresser behind her.

She was almost relieved when a new image entered her viewfinder. Spying the whirling blades of a helicopter, she caught her breath.

The Eagle was back.

Hoping she hadn't been spotted on his balcony, she hurried back through the master bedroom. Downstairs, she took a seat at the bar in the kitchen and pretended to idly flip through a magazine while drinking a glass of hastily poured iced tea.

The door opened and Jack stepped inside. Cat took one look at his expression and gasped. He looked ten years older than when he'd left. "Jack, what's wrong?"

He walked straight through the kitchen and into the great room without speaking. He headed straight toward the wet bar where he poured three fingers of scotch into a crystal tumbler. He tossed the drink back in one large gulp, then filled the glass again.

She had never seen him act this way before. "Jack. You're scaring me. What happened?"

"Not now, Cat. Just leave it be. Leave *me* be."

Another time, she might have been hurt, she might have pushed, but not now. Not when he was so terribly upset, so horribly raw. Shaken, she nodded once and returned to the kitchen where she took her seat, pretended to read the magazine, and listened for sounds coming from the other room.

Probably five minutes later, she heard a thunk and then a crash. Glass breaking. Not a window, though. His drink glass, most likely, smashing against the floor tile.

Next she heard the pounding of his shoes on the stairs followed by the slam of the master bedroom door. "Okay." She blew out a breath. "What now?"

Obviously, something really bad had happened. In her experience, Jack never brought his work home. Why now? Had the situation changed, his job changed, or had Jack changed?

Even as she asked the question, she heard him descending the stairs. He went straight out the front door. She walked to a window and looked out. He'd changed into gym shorts and sneakers. The Eagle was going for a run.

Cat was worried about him, seriously worried. She

glanced down at her own clothes—shorts, a T-shirt, and sneakers—and muttered, "What the heck."

She followed him, running hard to catch up, though she didn't question her ability to maintain pace with him. She had run cross-country in high school and college, and earlier this year she'd completed a half marathon. Why she felt compelled to accompany him on his run, what she thought she could accomplish, she couldn't quite say. All she knew was that she didn't want him to be alone.

He spared her one glance when she fell in beside him and then he picked up his pace. Stubborn fool. She kept up, and within minutes she could tell that he'd forgotten she was there. Jack appeared lost in his own thoughts, tortured and dangerous.

He ran and ran and ran, down the road, across the meadow, picking up his speed until finally he outpaced her and pulled away. Cat slowed to a cool-down jog, breathing heavily. She wondered if he intended to run all the way to town.

She had slowed to a walk when he looped around and turned back toward the house. He accelerated as if sprinting toward an unseen finish line until he lifted his face toward the sky and yelled. Screeched. *An eagle's cry of pain.*

Oh, Jack.

He bent over double, his hands on his knees. "Jack, what is it? What's wrong?"

"Go, Cat," he ordered, his voice strained. "Just leave me alone. Please, just leave me alone."

She heard the tiniest of cracks in his voice, and that's what decided her. "If I leave now, will you talk to me later?"

"Sure."

He said it too fast and she didn't believe him. "You promise that you'll tell me what this is about?"

This response took longer. "Yes."

Now, she took him at his word. "All right, then. I'll leave. If you need me, though, shout."

He didn't look up, simply nodded, so she blew out a breath and turned and walked away. Upon reaching the house, she decided to put off a shower for a time and she took up a position where she could watch Jack.

He lay on his back in a meadow of green grass and a rainbow of wildflowers. His arm was slung over his eyes. Cat's teeth tugged at her bottom lip. She'd never seen him this way. It worried her. Foolish of her, maybe, considering their situation, but she'd feel that way about any person, or animal, who exhibited so much . . . torment.

Minutes dragged by and he lay still as death. Spying movement in the periphery of her vision, she glanced away from Jack long enough to see the eagle land high in the branches of a tree. The eagle no sooner found his perch than Jack rolled to his feet. He stood watching the bird, neither of them moving, and something about the sight before her had Cat holding her breath. Then, almost simultaneously, the bird took flight and Jack turned toward the house. He walked slowly, his head down, shoulders stooped as if they carried the weight of the world.

He entered through the front door and climbed the stairs to his bedroom, again without stopping or speaking. Once she heard his bedroom door shut with a definite snick, she retreated to her own room and took a shower in the connecting bathroom.

She didn't hear so much as a peep out of the man for the rest of the afternoon. At suppertime, she made two chef salads and left one in the fridge with his name on it. She watched a movie in the theater room, then went to bed at eleven.

The soft knock sounded on her door at eleven-fifteen.

Cat sat up, switched on the bedside lamp, licked her suddenly dry lips, then said, "Come in, Jack."

He didn't know why he was standing here in Cat's bedroom.

All he knew for certain was that one minute he'd been lying in bed, desperate to go back to sleep, and the next he had pulled on shorts and headed down the hallway. One minute he needed to be alone, the next he couldn't bear the thought of being by himself another instant.

His gaze stole over her form. She had the sheet clutched against her chest. He wasn't surprised to see that she still slept in satin nightshirts. She had always liked the sensation of satin against her skin. The one she wore tonight was midnight blue, and it looked great against her creamy complexion and fire-streaked hair. He cleared his throat. "You still want to talk?"

"I do."

Jack advanced into the room. "First, let me apologize for being a jackass."

Her mouth quirked in a droll smile. "Which time?"

He relaxed just a little and managed a shaky grin back at her. She gestured toward the foot of her bed. "Have a seat, Davenport."

He glanced toward the guest bedroom's easy chair and saw that it was piled high with books, papers, and her laptop. He sat on the end of her mattress. Now that he was here, he didn't know what to say.

He couldn't jump into the events that had happened in Texas. He might not tell her at all, never mind that he'd given his word. Instead, he asked, "What did you do while I was gone?"

She gave him a measured look. "I spent quite a bit of time in town. Nic introduced me to her friends. They're nice women. It's a nice town."

"That's . . . nice. Did they find Sarah's mom?"

"Yes. She had driven to her and her husband's special spot—a place called Spirit Cave. A couple of guys had car trouble or ran out of gas or something and stole the car. She was confused, hungry, and thirsty, but she was okay."

"Good."

As silence fell, Cat settled back against her pillows and her sleep shirt slid off one shoulder. Jack made himself look away and grasped for something to say.

"Talk to me, Jack."

He closed his eyes and his thoughts drifted back to those times during their marriage when he would come home from a long, stressful day at work and climb into bed and cuddle with his wife. He would ask her how her day had gone and she would rattle on about this person and that story and another task. He'd only halfway listen to her, because he'd been filling his senses with the scent of her, the sound of her, the touch of her skin against his. Just by being there, she had soothed him. She'd been his port in the storm. His soft place to fall. And if she'd resented his lack of sharing, she'd kept it to herself. At least, until their decision to have a baby had changed the tenor of those peaceful moments.

Cat yanked his thoughts back to the present by asking, "Did you lose someone?"

Out of the blue, Jack felt tears sting his eyes. What the hell? He didn't cry. He never cried. Nevertheless, a lump the size of Murphy Mountain lodged in his throat. "Tony. We lost Tony."

She reached out and touched his hand. "Tell me about Tony."

Jack flipped his hand around and took hold of hers, lacing their fingers. He opened his mouth, but at first he couldn't speak. When she squeezed his fingers, the words poured forth. "He was a good guy. A really good guy."

"What was his last name?"

"Martinez." He filled his lungs, then blew out a heavy breath. "I recruited him. We worked together. He saved my butt on an extraction in Mexico a few years ago. I was seen going in. I was pinned down. Tony got the shooter. The man could be a ghost when he wanted."

Cat's eyes went round. "I think I'm really glad that you never talked about work when we were married."

"Home was an oasis, Cat."

She rose up on her knees and scooted closer to Jack. Her gaze locked on to his, her big green eyes filled with compassion and concern. It was a look he recognized from a long time ago, though one she hadn't given him in years. Seeing it again, he ached anew for all that they had lost.

"Tony was your friend," she stated.

"He was my partner. That's more than simply being a friend."

"Yes, I can see how that would be."

She might think she could understand, but she couldn't possibly. Nobody could, unless they lived it.

"What happened, Jack? Was Tony lost on a mission?"

"He killed himself. I might as well have put the gun in his hand myself."

Cat made a little sound of shock, and rather than look at her, Jack lay back on the mattress and stared up at the ceiling. Weariness tugged at his soul. He wanted to quit right there and say nothing more, but the poison was flowing and he sensed that letting it out might be the only thing to ease the wrenching in his gut. "He got hurt that day saving my ass, and the recovery was a bitch. He got hooked on painkillers."

"Oh, no."

"He fought it. He hid it." Jack sucked in a lungful of air. "He got married. Had a kid."

That little girl. That precious little baby. Moisture seeped from beneath his closed eyelids, and Jack hoped like hell that Cat wasn't looking closely enough to notice. "He started using illegal stuff—buying drugs from those same asses who hurt him to begin with. Whatever he got hold of this time made him crazy."

Ah, Tony. Dammit, man. Tony had been alive when Jack showed up. Alive, and high as a kite. Saying wild-ass things.

Waving his gun.

Jack couldn't bear to describe the events that had happened next. Neither could he banish them from his mind.

Tony with that baby in his arms. The bright yellow bow in her hair and the green stuffed turtle clasped tightly to her chest. The little girl's cries. Denise Martinez's scream. Tony's paranoid rambling.

Then the shot.

The blood.

The streak of crimson across the terrified toddler's face.

"He shot himself, Cat. Right in front of me. Right in front of his wife and that sweet little baby."

She clasped his hand hard and he squeezed hers back. He had a mountain on his chest and the pressure at the back of his eyes threatened real tears—something he hadn't experienced in years. "I couldn't save him. He was mine, and I couldn't save him. I was right there and I couldn't save him."

"Oh, Jack."

He heard an ocean of compassion in her voice, and mentally he reached for the comfort it offered. Her next words changed everything.

"I know the feeling," she said softly, hollowly. "I understand. I couldn't save our baby."

Jack's heart wrenched as if ripped in two and he trembled, quaked like an aspen leaf in autumn, but at least he didn't cry. Bitter memories and keen regret washed through him, and he breathed as if he'd run a marathon. At some point he heard Cat's soothing murmurs, sensed her comforting touch as she stroked his head, his face. She pressed a gentle kiss against his brow and Jack lifted his mouth, seeking hers. Searching for an escape from the pain, if only for a little while. Their lips met and he finally found the comfort he needed.

He wrapped his arms around her and pulled her against him. He kissed her as if his life depended on it. Maybe it did. Maybe it always had. Hadn't he sensed as much the moment he first laid eyes on her? Hadn't he known better than to fall for the boss's daughter? Hadn't he been unable to stay away?

She'd been right for him. She completed him. Life had been good, so good, until he'd lost her.

Nothing had seemed right since.

He needed something right in his life right now. She didn't fight him, which was good, because he honestly couldn't say if he would have stopped. He was desperate, aching and devastated. In that moment, he needed Cat as he had never needed another human being. So he took her, fast and furious and hard, until he lay spent. Empty.

Well and truly broken.

Ashamed.

He rolled off her, onto his back, his eyes closed, panting as if he'd run a thousand miles. He couldn't look at her, he didn't dare. Finally, he spoke from the bottom of his heart. "I'm sorry, Cat. I'm so damned sorry."

Without another word, he rose and left the room.

Cat lay dazed and aching both physically and emotionally. What the heck had just happened?

That was a stupid question to ask herself. Obviously, the answer was that she had just had sex. With Jack. Sex with Jack. Wham-bam-I'm-sorry-ma'am sex with Jack.

Holy crap.

The jerk.

You idiot. You didn't try to stop him. Have you lost your mind?

Maybe. His appearance and actions upon his arrival home following his mysterious trip had concerned her. Caring for wounded animals was part of her nature, so it was only natural that she'd reach out to him. Frankly, she'd been worried about him. Joining him on his run had been a show of support.

When she'd asked for his promise to talk to her, she hadn't believed that he'd actually follow through. She had thought that she had added an arrow to her quiver of arguments that she could pull out when she needed a weapon against him. When he'd knocked on her door, she'd been shocked.

When he actually started talking, she'd gone from shocked to flabbergasted to . . . sad. So sad. All she'd tried to do was to offer him a comforting hand.

Well, he certainly hadn't stopped with her hand, now, had he?

And you didn't stop him from not stopping. What's wrong with you? You don't do booty calls.

This hadn't been a booty call. This had been . . . what? Disaster? Embarrassment? Mistake? Certainly a mistake.

I'm sorry, Cat. I'm so damned sorry.

That had to be the most flattering après-sex comment she had ever received. Not.

Maybe she was the one who should be sorry. She'd poked the bear, after all. She'd wanted to know what was wrong. But she hadn't exactly expected *that*.

As she lay in her bed and absorbed the facts of what had just taken place, Cat began to stew. He'd said he was sorry. Sorry about what? The sex? The tears? The fact that he'd broken his cardinal rule and communicated with her about his job?

And what was that all about? She was sorry that he'd lost his friend. Truly, she was. However, a part of her couldn't help but notice and resent that he had grieved for a friend, but not for the child they had lost.

It was one thing she'd never understood. Oh, he'd been disappointed and sorrowful, she'd give him that, but he'd never shown any signs of the gut-wrenching, heart-ripping pain that had come close to destroying Cat. She'd held it against him then, and she held it against him now.

Restless, she rose from her bed and padded to the bathroom. Halfway there, she stopped as a new and unwelcome thought occurred. She'd had wham-bam-not-even-a-thank-you-ma'am sex with Jack Davenport without protection!

It hadn't even occurred to her at the time. The sex had caught her off guard, and besides, it was *Jack*. She and Jack hadn't used anything in years before the divorce when they'd tried so hard—and failed—to get pregnant.

They'd been married then. She had trusted him not to be sleeping around on her. That wasn't the case today.

Oh, no. Catherine Blackburn, you stupid fool!

Who knows how many women he'd been with since their divorce?

He could have just given her a disease. Wouldn't that simply be wonderful?

In the shower, she brooded and sulked. While she blow-dried her hair, she muttered to herself. As she reached into her closet for a clean sleep shirt, she paused. Instead of donning her nightclothes, she put on a bra and panties, then shorts and a T-shirt. If she didn't confront him now and get this off her chest, she wouldn't sleep at all. She'd be doing him a good turn, too, because she was about to distract him from his misery with a good old-fashioned tongue-lashing.

Okay, bad choice of words. Jack had always been exceptionally good at his personal version of tongue-lashing.

She exited her room and marched down the hall toward the master bedroom. Outside his door, she paused just a moment and braced herself for the confrontation to come. Without bothering to knock, she shoved open the door and stepped inside, demanding, "Just what are you sorry for, Jack Davenport?"

Dimmed ceiling lights cast a muted glow through the room. He sat sprawled in the brown leather easy chair that sat beside the wall of windows in his bedroom wearing shorts and nothing else. He didn't bother himself to even look in her direction. "Go away, Cat."

"No, I don't think I will. You owe me, Davenport. You owe me a conversation, not only because of what took place a few minutes ago, but also because of what happened years ago."

"This is not a good time."

"It's *never* a good time for you." She slammed his bedroom door behind her—not that it needed slamming; they were the only two people in the house—and doing it felt good. "This will have to do. So, I'll ask you again. What are you sorry about?"

Having stepped around to view him from a better angle, she could now see that he was sipping a drink. She wished she had one of them herself. "Talk to me, Davenport. Are you sorry about what happened to your friend? About having sex with me? Abducting me? Failing to grieve over the death of our child?"

He whipped his head around at that, fury on his face. "Stop right there, Catherine. You just stop right there."

"Why? Did one of my questions bother you? Perhaps the one about our baby? You remember our baby, don't you, Jack? The little girl who died in my womb before she ever had a chance to live? The one I named Lauren? Or wait. Maybe you don't remember her. After all, you weren't there with me when I gave birth to her still body or when I buried her all by myself."

He very carefully set down his glass, then rose to his feet and faced her. His expression was hard, his eyes blue ice. "Catherine, you are treading on a minefield. Believe me, you don't want to have this conversation right now. I don't have the ability to choose my words carefully."

"I never asked you to choose your words," she snapped back, bracing her hands on her hips. "I asked you to *use* your words. I want to know why you were able to share more about the death of your friend than you ever did about the death of our child!"

His eyes flashed with blue fire. "Because I *knew* him, dammit! I never knew the baby. I never got to hold her. You at least got to do that. You buried her before I ever had the chance. You handed me a slip of paper, Catherine. You did that to me. You took her away from me."

Guilt swirled inside her, and she lashed out with the truth. "You weren't there! You were never there!"

"You knew what the job was when you married me."

He had her there. Cat had no comeback to that.

Before she could think of what to say next, he continued, "You blame me for not talking. Let me tell you, sweetheart, you weren't exactly a fountain of words yourself in those days."

Her chin came up. "I was depressed, clinically depressed and grieving."

"I know. I tried to get you to go for help, but you wouldn't do it." Bitter temper fired his words. "It was all about you. Your pain. Your baby. How many times did you say it? My baby. My baby. My baby. It was *our* baby."

"Not *it!*" Cat fired back. "*She!* And she *was* my baby. You weren't there. You didn't go through it."

"Because you didn't let me. I tried. You pushed me away and locked me out."

"I wasn't ready then."

"And I'm not ready for any more of this now. It can't always be on your terms, Cat. I lived that way when we were married, but I don't have to now."

"My terms? What do you mean, my terms?"

"For God's sake, enough! This one time, can you cut me some slack? Please, get out of here before I say something I regret."

This one time? Cat folded her arms. She'd cut him slack plenty of times during the course of their marriage.

Jack exhaled a long, heavy sigh. "I'm going to bed. Shut the door on your way out, would you?"

He turned his back on her and walked to his bed where he dropped his shorts, yanked back the bedclothes, and climbed naked between the sheets before he reached over and shut off the lamp. It was the most effective insult he'd ever sent her way.

Cat set her teeth. Okay, then. Fine. *Jerk.*

She turned to leave and in the darkness had to feel for the doorknob. Once she found it and opened the door, she hesitated. She hadn't addressed the issue that originally propelled her to his room. Turning toward the bed, she spoke with accusation in her tone. "You didn't use any protection."

At first he gave no sign of having heard her, but just as she was about to give up and leave, he let out a bitter laugh. "What's the problem, Catherine. Are you afraid I might have gotten you pregnant?"

Cat's hand slipped off the doorknob as she reeled from the blow. Did he really just say that? For all his faults, Jack had never been mean to her before. Never cruel.

Fighting to keep her voice steady, she said, "You've changed, Jack, and not for the better. I was asking about disease. Have you been tested recently?"

After a moment of silence, he wearily replied. "Trust me or not, but you don't have to worry about that one. I'm clean, Catherine. Good night."

She returned to her room, crawled into her bed, and cried herself to sleep.

FIVE

Jack wasn't surprised when Cat failed to join him for breakfast. He didn't expect to see her much at all until she cooled down, and knowing his ex-wife, that wouldn't be any time soon. The woman held a grudge like nobody's business.

Not that he blamed her. He'd been an ass last night. He'd treated her like dirt and she hadn't deserved it. And yet, he didn't regret all the things he'd said. Some of them he'd wanted to say for years.

There had been no knockdown, drag-out, air-clearing fight before their divorce. Their marriage had ended quietly, more like the snuff of a candle flame at the end of a bad dinner date than an explosion of temper and pain.

Maybe if they had fought, they'd have found something to salvage. He hadn't fought for her. He didn't try. He'd allowed their marriage to just . . . die. *Like Lauren.* Maybe deep down he'd known that once the baby was gone, the marriage hadn't stood a chance.

At midmorning, as Jack sat at his desk in his office trying to work up the energy to deal with his email, he decided that he should probably hunt up Cat and apologize. The crack about getting her pregnant had been especially wrong.

Good thing he kept his guns locked up.

Maybe I should hand one of them over to her. Let her put us both out of our misery.

Jack felt like crap. What had happened to Tony was part of it. Being around Cat again and the daily reminder of all that he had lost contributed to his funk, too. His body was tired, his soul weary. Years of job-related stress and tensions were beating him down. The work had never been easy, but in the last year or so, the hoops they had to jump through to appease the politicians had made the work especially messy.

The whole thing was getting old. He was getting old. What did he have to show for his life's work? Sure, the men he'd helped liberate from one prison or another counted as a huge accomplishment, but the cost to him personally couldn't be ignored. In his private life he had a handful of big, empty houses all across the world and an ex-wife who despised him—for good reason.

"Might as well tackle that little problem next," he muttered, pushing back from his desk. He had just started to stand when the knock on the door kept him seated. Cat walked into his office wearing the flirty sundress she'd worn the day he grabbed her. She looked beautiful, and as cold as the summit of Murphy Mountain in January.

"Hi," he said. "I was just coming to look for you."

"I came to tell you that I'm leaving Eagle's Way."

He grimaced. "Look, Cat. I know you're upset with me and you have every reason to be, but it's not safe for you to return to D.C. quite yet. Give my people a few more days, and I am certain—"

"I'm not going home," she interrupted. "I'm staying in Eternity Springs. I've rented a room at Angel's Rest."

Oh. Surprised, Jack sat back in his chair. He thought it through quickly and decided that he couldn't see a reason why it wouldn't work. Based on what he'd learned during his quick phone call to Cam this morning, she'd had no trouble during her visits there while he'd been away. She'd be comfortable at Angel's Rest. She'd probably like being around Nic and Sarah and the rest of their friends. It was a good solution.

With those thoughts uppermost in his mind, he had no explanation for the words that came out of his mouth. "No. You need to stay here."

"No, I don't. You agreed that it was fine for me to go into town before you left on your trip. There's no reason I can't stay there."

The crazy words just kept on rolling. "You're not going. I forbid it."

That last little bit shocked them both. "Excuse me?" Cat tilted her head and studied him like a bug. "Did you just use the word 'forbid'? In relation to me?"

Yeah, he had. What the hell was he thinking?

"What the hell are you thinking?" she asked.

He didn't have a clue. His brain and mouth obviously were experiencing a disconnect.

She folded her arms. "I didn't let you tell me what to do when we were married. I'm certainly not going to let you do it now that we're divorced. Allow me to point out that I could have put a stop to the whole abduction thing if I'd truly wanted to—at least after the initial event. I'm here right now because I chose to be here. Now I'm choosing to leave. We are not married anymore. You don't have the right to stop me. You don't have the right to sleep with me. We're done, Davenport. Done for good this time."

Her lips lifted in a smile that didn't reach her eyes as she added, "Honestly, I'm fine with that. I think we both probably needed to say some of the things we've said. It's even possible that my mother was right that I hadn't moved on. Now I can. Thank you for caring enough to want to protect me. You're off the hook now . . . and so am I. My ride will be here in a few minutes." As she turned to go, the words *Please don't leave me, Cat* leaped to his tongue. He snapped his mouth against them just in time.

A few minutes later, he stood watching through a window as the Eagle's Way entrance gate opened for the Angel's Rest passenger van. Cat came downstairs carrying a suitcase and her computer backpack. He stood in his office doorway, his hands shoved into his pockets. He couldn't stop himself from making one last try. "I think this is a mistake."

"It *was* a mistake. It's not anymore. Good-bye, Jack."

She was leaving him. Again. Perhaps the method was different, but the result was the same. She was giving up on him again. He shouldn't be surprised. Hadn't he learned at a very young age that family didn't last?

The door opened and Catherine Blackburn Davenport Blackburn walked out of his house and out of his life.

As she went down the front steps to meet the van, Cat's thoughts and emotions were a soup of insecurity and sadness spiced with a dash of shame. She was leaving to protect her sanity, but at the same time she felt she was running out on Jack when he needed her. Which was stupid, of course. When had Jack Davenport, superspy, ever needed her?

Snippets from last night's argument echoed through her mind. *Your pain. Your baby. I never got to hold her.*

A wave of guilt rolled through her. Apparently Lauren's death had mattered more to him than she'd thought.

Celeste Blessing braked to a stop at the top of the circular drive. Cat tossed one last look over her shoulder toward the house before opening the door of the van.

"Hello, dear," Celeste said. A woman somewhere on the far side of sixty-five, Cat guessed, Celeste wore her silver hair in a short, stylish cut. Her sky-blue eyes seemed to always have a happy twinkle in them and her smile made a girl feel good just to see it. Silver earrings shaped like angel's wings dangled from her earlobes. "Isn't it a beautiful morning?"

"Yes, it is," Cat replied, and for some inexplicable reason, thoughts of her mother flashed through her mind.

Celeste continued, "I just love these mountains in summertime. Actually, I love them all the time, but summertime is especially pleasant. I adore seeing all the tourists in town and visiting with them at Angel's Rest. You are going to enjoy your stay, Catherine. Nothing against Eagle's Way—it's a fabulous house and everything about it is top drawer—but Angel's Rest is exceptional. We are comfortable and cozy and the energy on our estate is, well, special. Angel's Rest is a place where broken hearts can come to heal, and I do admit, our record is impressive."

Cat couldn't help but smile at the older woman's enthusiasm. "I should have come here a few years ago, in that case. My heart is healthy enough these days. The goal is to keep it—and the rest of me—that way."

Celeste clicked her tongue. "What wicked soul throws a firebomb through someone's dining room window?"

"Maybe the same wicked soul who likes to watch dogs fight to the death," Cat replied.

Celeste braked smoothly to wait for a herd of bighorn sheep to finish crossing the road. "People do disappoint, don't they?"

Naturally, Cat's thoughts again turned to her mother.

Once the animals disappeared into the trees, Celeste resumed their drive and continued to rattle on about Eternity Springs, local activities, and the people who lived there. Cat leaned her head back against the headrest and closed her eyes, listening with half an ear until she realized that Celeste had asked her a question. "I'm sorry. What did you ask?"

"I wondered if you know anyone in the hospitality

industry who would be interested in running Angel's Rest."

"You mean as your assistant?"

"No. In my place. And 'running' probably isn't the right word. I have a wonderful executive director who does all the pesky business things, but he is a quiet, private man who prefers to have someone else be the face of the operation. That's what I'm looking for, a face. Someone to be the face of Eternity Springs in the community."

"Do you not enjoy the job?"

"Oh, no. I love it. It's just, well, I think I may be moving along."

That statement was enough to surprise Cat into full attention. Nic Callahan had shared the story of how Celeste had moved to town, invested in property and businesses, and almost single-handedly saved Eternity Springs. She didn't recall Nic's mentioning anything about Celeste moving away. "You're leaving Eternity Springs?"

"It's likely, yes."

"I'm surprised. From what I can see, you've put down roots here."

"Yes, I have." The older woman's smile dimmed and turned wistful. "I love Eternity Springs and I've made some dear, dear friends here. However, Angel's Rest all but runs itself now. I may well have accomplished all I can here in Eternity Springs. My talents may be better utilized somewhere else."

"You mean like in an Angel's Rest number two? Are you thinking franchise, perhaps?"

Celeste shrugged. "It's been suggested. I admit to mixed feelings about the idea. I do love the friends I've made here. It's important, though, that a woman keep busy. Don't you agree?"

"I do." Cat glanced down at her hands and thought

that she needed a manicure. "Although in my case idle hands might have served me better. After I was laid off from my newspaper job, I figured out fast that I wasn't happy unless I had something keeping me busy. That's why I got involved with the animal rescue organization, which in turn led me to the story that got my house bombed."

"But that brought you to us, and personally, I think that's a good thing." Celeste braked at a stop sign, looked both ways, then turned left onto the state road that led into town. "You mentioned being a writer. Have you met Rose Anderson? Dr. Rose Anderson?"

"No, I don't believe so."

"She's Sage Rafferty's sister. She stayed in our attic suite for a few months when she first came to Eternity Springs and she wrote half of her first novel there, a medical thriller. She recently signed with a literary agent."

"That's exciting for her."

"Isn't it? We all have our fingers crossed that she'll sell her book. My first thought was to put you in that same suite, but after some reflection, I've decided one of our cottages will better suit. We have some that are set at the far end of the property, a little more isolated. They have a kitchenette, so you'll be able to cook meals if you'd like. Is that all right with you?"

"That sounds wonderful."

When Celeste led her toward the half-dozen small Victorian-style cabins built along the bank of Angel Creek, Cat decided she'd never seen such cute little cottages. Each had a white picket fence and a hummingbird feeder hanging from an iron bracket beside the front door. Her cabin, Nightingale Cottage, was painted a light blue with white gingerbread trim. Cheery pots of red geraniums lined the front porch, and when Cat stepped inside, she smiled with delight.

Nightingale Cottage offered a perfect retreat for a

writer. In the small living area, built-in bookcases lined one wall, and the antique writing desk made you want to sit down with paper and pen and an inkwell. A floor lamp placed beside an overstuffed chair and ottoman offered a cozy place to read. The pillow-back sofa that stretched in front of a picture window framing a spectacular view of the snowcapped mountains looked like a great place to nap. The kitchenette had a small refrigerator, a built-in oven/microwave combination, a storage cabinet, and a sink. "Wow. How great is this?"

"Come see the bedroom," Celeste told her.

It was just as wonderful as the front room with a queen-size bed on an iron bed frame and an antique chifforobe for storage. A second door led to a back porch and a yard that sloped down to where a pair of Adirondack chairs sat beside the bank of Angel Creek.

"I love it." Cat meant it, too. The lavender-scented cottage was charming. "Thank you, Celeste. I know I'm going to be comfortable here."

"I hope you are." Celeste patted a leather folder lying on the bar that separated the living area from the kitchenette. "You'll find all sorts of goodies in here—menus from our restaurant and from other restaurants in town, tourist activities, and the latest edition of our weekly newspaper, the *Eternity Times*. If you need anything, just call the front desk and let them know."

"I will."

When she was alone, Cat unpacked her bag and settled into the room. She hadn't minded staying in the lap of luxury at Eagle's Way, but being in Jack's territory, so to speak, even when he wasn't around, had been intimidating. Now, though, what to do? How should she spend her days?

She reflected on the conversation she'd had with Celeste about idle hands. While having nothing substantive to do didn't mean she was wandering into devil'splayground territory, she remained at a bit of a loss as to how to occupy her time. She had nothing new humming for her blog. Despite the fact that her email in-box overflowed with leads and suggestions, she simply didn't have the heart to dig into another investigation right now.

Her gaze settled on the writing desk and she gave a brief moment's thought to the doctor and her novel. No, Cat didn't have any desire to write a book. She'd always been a column-inch girl, and moving from newspaper reporter to blogger didn't change that.

Speaking of column inches. Cat shifted her gaze back to the leather folder, pulled out the copy of the local newspaper, and skimmed the front page.

The Eternity Times *is published every Wednesday and sent to readers in Eternity Springs and across the United States. Our newspaper covers local news and events through feature stories, weekly columns, and photographs. Subscribe to read about local government, tourism, environmental issues, Eternity Springs Community School, wildlife issues, historical facts, historical preservation, and much more. Online subscriptions are now available! Contact Emily Hall for more information.*

The front page had a tourist family profile, a wildlife sighting report, a gorgeous color photograph of a hot air balloon floating over Hummingbird Lake, and a reminder about an important town meeting tonight at seven. It was a nice little newspaper with an inviting layout, and she was impressed. She wondered what Emily Hall's background was.

Cat unpacked her suitcase, then decided to take a walk. The Angel's Rest property was lovely, with the rose garden and the hot springs pools both tempting her to explore them further. Now, though, she chose to cross the footbridge over Angel's Creek and wander through town, and twenty minutes later, she stood in front of the building that housed the *Eternity Times*. A brass plaque mounted beside the door dated the building to 1889. She eyed the door handle and asked herself, *Is this a stupid idea?*

She blew out a heavy breath, then opened the door. A chime sounded, and the woman near her own age seated at an ancient wood desk with a phone to her ear looked up. She lifted a finger, gesturing "One minute." Then she picked up her pencil, took a note, and said into the receiver, "That's a big bear, Jasper."

Cat glanced around the office. Framed copies of the newspaper graced the walls and a clear round jar of silver-wrapped Hershey's Kisses sat atop the counter that divided the work space from the lobby. A pink ribbon tied a Mylar balloon declaring "Happy Birthday" to the swinging gate at the center of the counter.

The woman on the phone had shoulder-length brown hair, a round, friendly face, and the clip of Maine in her voice as she said, "Got it. I sure will, Jasper. Thanks. You, too. Good-bye."

She hung up the phone, stuck her pencil behind her ear, and stood. "I appreciate your patience. Can I help you?"

Now that the moment was here, Cat didn't quite know how to respond. "Are you the editor of the *Times*?"

"I'm the editor, custodian, and everything in between." She extended her hand for a handshake. "Emily Hall."

"My name is Cat, uh, Catherine Davenport. I'm in town—"

"You're Cat Blackburn," Emily said, her eyes going bright.

"Uh . . ."

Emily waved a hand. "Don't worry about it. Your secret is safe with me."

Yeah, well, that's what she had thought with Nic and
the group. "How do you . . ."

"Jack Davenport has been the mystery man of Eternity Springs for years. He kept a totally low profile
around here. When Celeste first moved to town, she
asked me to help her track him down and I discovered
he was married. Your maiden name was in my files, so
when Lori Reese said that his ex was up at Eagle's Way,
I reviewed the file, did a little research, and put two and
two together. So, after they find the guy who firebombed
your house, will you give the *Eternity Times* an interview?"

This might be a small-town newspaper, but this was
no small-time reporter. "I can't say that I'm excited
about being the news instead of reporting it, but I'll be
happy to give you an interview when the time is right."

"Excellent. Thank you." Beaming, the reporter asked,
"So, Ms. Davenport, what can I do for you?"

The idea that she now realized had been hovering in
her subconscious came spilling from her mouth. "I have
time on my hands right now, and I'm not ready to dive
into another investigation. At home, I do a lot of volunteer work that keeps me busy during the downtime, but
here . . . well . . . I was wondering if you'd like some help
around the newspaper?"

Surprise flickered across Emily's face. "Oh, I'd love to
have help, believe me, but I simply can't afford it. Things
are better now that Celeste Blessing moved to town
and opened Angel's Rest, but we still operate on a shoe-
string."

"Well, see, that's the thing." Cat gave her a sheepish
smile. "I was hoping you would consider allowing me to
do it on a volunteer basis."

"You mean . . . for no pay? You'd write for free?"

"Yeah. I'd write for free."

"Pardon me if this sounds . . . insulting, but are you out of your mind? You won the Goldsmith Prize."

Cat couldn't help but preen a little. She was awfully proud of the Goldsmith. "Honestly, volunteering is not something I'd want to do long term, but I need something to keep busy while I'm here."

"At risk of sounding like I'm looking the proverbial gift horse in the mouth, I have to ask. Won't you be posting to your blog? Won't that keep you busy enough?"

"No. The biggest part of my workday ordinarily involves an investigation, and I don't have a new one going. Except for answering email, I don't have much to do."

Emily cocked her head, studied Cat for a long moment, then grinned. "Welcome to the *Times*, Cat . . . I mean, Catherine."

Cat's spirits lifted immediately. The *Eternity Times* might not be the *Washington Post*, but it was still an ink-on-newsprint publication. She'd been missing that in her life. "Thank you. What's my first assignment?"

"We have a town meeting tonight I'd love to take a pass on. The guy I've been dating moved away last month and he's here for a visit."

"Tell me when and where."

"The school auditorium at seven o'clock. I've been told there's to be a special presentation."

"Seven at the school. I'll be there."

Cat was so happy that she decided to stop by the Trading Post grocery store to buy a brand-new notebook. After that, she figured she might as well indulge in something sweet from Sarah Reese's bakery, Fresh. While choosing between a strawberry pinwheel cookie and an oatmeal apple raisin cookie, she overheard a discussion about some new handmade items being offered for sale in the quilt shop on Spruce Street, and she decided to take a look. There she fell in love with a double wedding ring quilt made of satin and silk—not the usual quilting fabrics. A discussion with the shop owner, LaNelle Harrison, led to an invitation to attend the next quilting bee. Walking back to Angel's Rest, Cat came across Sage and her little dog, Snowdrop. They talked dogs for a few minutes, then Sage invited Cat to come out to her house on Hummingbird Lake to see paintings Sage had done of the little white bichon frisé that had been a gift from her husband, Colt, when they were dating.

Cat rode one of the bicycles available to Angel's Rest guests out to the lake. She thoroughly enjoyed the afternoon and returned to town more relaxed and lighthearted than she'd been in weeks. That feeling ended when she braked at a stop sign and saw a scowling Gabe Callahan circle his car to help someone out of the passenger seat in front of the Eternity Springs Medical Clinic. Cat did a double-take. A woman in a white physician's coat hurried out the clinic door pushing a wheelchair as Gabe escorted the bloodied and battered figure of a man.

"Jack!"

"Dammit, Callahan!" Jack snapped, raising his voice to be heard over the roar of Colt Rafferty's motorcycle as it pulled up behind Gabe's car. "I can walk by myself."

"Sure you can," Gabe fired back, ignoring Jack's protest and putting the injured man's arm over his shoulder to help support his weight. "After all, you are Mr. Invincible, aren't you?"

"What happened?" Colt's sister-in-law and the clinic's physician, Rose Anderson, locked the wheels of the wheelchair and motioned for Gabe to help Jack sit.

"I don't need a wheelchair."

Colt ignored his protest. "He called this morning wanting company on a motorcycle ride on the Alpine Trail. We've done that ride before, but this time, the idiot rode like a drunken grizzly. Flat-out reckless. He went too fast and took a turn too wide. I thought he was going off the side of the mountain, but he managed to put the bike down instead. He kept himself on the road. His bike is at the bottom of a hundred-foot drop."

"I'm okay," Jack said. "Just scraped up a bit."

"He's banged up his knee," Gabe told Rose. "Can't put weight on it."

"Yes, I can." It was his arm that he suspected might be fractured.

"We'll X-ray it just to be sure," Rose said, her voice crisp and professional.

Jack's day grew even more splendiferous after they'd entered the clinic and he heard a door open behind them and his ex-wife exclaim, "What happened to Jack? Is he okay?"

"I'm fine."

Colt did his best to make a liar of Jack by explaining, once again, his version of what had happened, complete with his drunken grizzly nonsense. Rose asked Colt to help Jack up onto an exam table just as Jack's cousin strode into the clinic and demanded, "So what's this I hear about putting down your bike to keep from flying off a mountain when you weren't wearing a helmet? You dumb-ass."

"Wait a minute." Cat whirled on Cam. "Are you saying that he rode a motorcycle, he *wrecked* a motorcycle, and the reckless, moronic, demented dunderhead wasn't wearing a helmet?"

"Dunderhead?" A slow smile spread across Cam's face as Rose rolled her eyes. "Well, now, my brilliant powers of deduction tell me you must be the ex-missus. I'm the black sheep cousin. Welcome to the family."

Cam took Cat's hand and leaned down to kiss her cheek. Cat's shocked expression faded, and Jack figured she must have concluded that his injuries weren't too serious or else Cam wouldn't be hitting on her.

She addressed Cam. "You're Sarah's fiancé. She told me you're a charmer. Her engagement ring is the most beautiful thing I've ever seen."

Jack scowled. What about that honking hen's egg of a diamond he'd given her? "Excuse me, but I am in pain, here. Could you all take your dog-and-pony show somewhere else so that I can get medical treatment?" Glancing at Rose, he added, "Isn't having all these people hanging around against the HIPAA law or something?"

The doctor snapped her fingers and spoke in a droll tone as she pulled supplies from a drawer. "Oh, darn. I knew I was forgetting about something."

"Quit whining, Davenport," Gabe said. "I'm the one who needs a shot. You're being a pain in my ass. What's up with you today? This sort of behavior is completely out of character for you."

Jack's gaze met Cat's and he silently requested that she keep his confidence before saying, "Rose? Can we clear the room, please?"

Dr. Anderson sighed. "My dumb-as-dirt patient has made a request. Let's allow him his privacy while I see to his injuries, shall we?"

Colt snorted derisively. "I'm happy to go, but Rose, I don't know how much luck you're going to have. As the saying goes, you can't fix stupid."

Expressing agreement with Colt's observation, Jack's friends left the clinic. Cat hung behind until Rose said, "Ma'am?"

"Do you need some help? I don't see a nurse or anyone else."

When the doctor smiled, Cat noted her resemblance to Sage Rafferty. "We're shorthanded today, I'm afraid. I think we'll be okay unless . . ." She glanced at Jack. "Do you want her to stay?"

Yes. "No. I'm okay."

"And I'm leaving," Cat fired back. "You'll want to use the big needles, Doctor. His hide is awfully hard."

She breezed out of the clinic, closing the door behind her with such gentleness that it felt like a slam. Alone now with Rose, Jack attempted to relax. He'd never been inside this clinic before—despite the fact that he'd donated half the money to open it—and he liked it. The place had butter-yellow walls and white curtains and a clean scent that wasn't antiseptic-smelling.

The doctor was pretty easy on the eyes, too. Even scowling at him like she was right now. "I admit I don't know you very well, Jack, but I did believe you had more sense than this. Let's take a look at you. Do you need help getting undressed?"

"Wouldn't hurt, I guess. I think my knee is screwed up. Something is stuck between my ribs, too."

Rose shook her head then turned her head and went to work. An hour and twenty-two stitches later, his road burn cleaned and dressed, his strained (but unbroken) knee wrapped in a tension bandage, and a two-inch-long shard of metal removed from his side, Jack realized he had a problem. The orderly had cut his clothes off.

Just when he'd asked Rose if she had an extra pair of scrubs lying around, his cousin returned carrying a pair of gym shorts and a T-shirt with ES Auto & Sports Center tags still attached. "You owe me twelve dollars and sixty-seven cents."

"Thanks, cuz." Jack gave a mellow smile, a product of the painkillers that saved the day because putting on his clothes proved downright painful.

Refusing the wheelchair, he walked out on crutches

and wrestled his way into Cam's truck. Cam turned on the ignition and asked, "Where to? Eagle's Way?"

"Yeah."

"You sure you'll be able to get around by yourself?"

"I'll be fine. I have a lot of work to do to get ready to go. I can only do it from my office."

Cam gave him a sidelong glance. "Go? Go where? You can't put weight on your leg and you think you're gonna put your James Bond suit on? Where are they sending you this time?"

It must have been the combination of pain and pain-killers and the fact that Cam was family that loosened his tongue, because for the second time in two days, Jack opened up about his job. He not only opened up, he began to blab. "They're not sending me anywhere. I've had it with the suits. Damned politicians and political hacks and bureaucratasses."

"Bureaucratasses?" Cam repeated.

"I'm going off the reservation, going rogue."

Cam braked a little too hard as they approached a stop sign. "Want to explain that, cousin?"

"I have the money to do whatever I want. This time, it'll be my agenda, my rules of engagement. I'll play just as mean and dirty as th-th-they do."

"You sound drunk. Just how many of those pills did Rose give you? Did you eat anything this morning?"

"I'm fine," Jack said, rubbing his aching head. "I'm alive, aren't I? Tony isn't."

And Jack told him about Tony Martinez, spilling gritty details he'd never shared with anyone—not even during his other blabfest with Cat last night. Speaking the facts and his thoughts aloud served to dissolve his drug-induced mellow, but even as his mood blackened, his resolve strengthened. "I'm going after their asses. For Tony. For all the other lives they're ruining. If the suits won't do it, I will."

Cam waited until he'd negotiated one of the hairpin turns on the road between Eternity Springs and Eagle's Way to ask, "You're gonna run an operation off the books? You hiring mercs for this?"

"I'm gonna hire a whole damned army. What's the sense in having more money than the Queen of England if I don't put it to good use? Why shouldn't I do this? How many times have I've risked my life to rescue politicians and their wives and their mistresses and other Very Important Pricks? This time I'm gonna do it for a friend. For my partner. Why not rescue Tony's memory?"

"He took his own life, Jack. That's not on you."

Jack ignored him. "I'm gonna hire an army and we're gonna infiltrate that godforsaken land and its depraved cartels and take 'em out one by one. Hell, maybe I'll get myself a uniform to wear. Get some shoulder epaulets. Every banana republic leader needs some of those. Wonder if Armani could whip me up a set."

"I think Rose must have made a mistake with her drug dosages. You're talking crazy."

"Why is it crazy? Answer me that? I've spent my entire adult life fighting these sons o' bitches. I came to the job thinking it was good and noble work. You know what? It was. Back then, it was. I'm proud of the work we did, the things we accomplished, the people I helped. It was an important job that needed to be done. But it cost me. It cost me my family. Cost me Cat. And now the politicians have gotten in the way. Somehow the good guys have become the bad guys and vice versa. Where's the justice in that, Cam?" Jack dropped his head back against the headrest, closed his eyes, and repeated, "Where's the justice?"

Cam didn't respond, and Jack let the movement of the car and the effects of the painkillers lull him into sleep. When he awoke, he realized the car had stopped. Cam was no longer behind the wheel. Assuming they'd arrived at Eagle's Way, he opened the car door and reached around to the backseat for his crutches . . . and stopped. This wasn't Eagle's Way. "What the hell?"

Cam's truck was parked in the main lot at Angel's Rest. What had he missed?

Jack took stock of his situation. He ached all over and his mind was still fuzzy from the drugs, but he could get around by himself. He hauled himself out of the truck and started toward Cavanaugh House, the main building on the Angel's Rest property. He'd made it halfway there when Cam descended the front steps with a spring in his step. Upon seeing Jack, he grinned crookedly. "Hey. Feel better since your nap?"

"What are we doing back in town?"

"I'm saving my marriage."

Jack frowned. "You're not married yet."

"I'm glad you remember that. After all, you're my best man."

Oh. Yeah. The wedding had slipped his mind. "I thought Devin was your best man?"

"Y'all are co–best men. Now, about this foreign invasion you're planning. I hope you're not thinking of bugging out on me before the wedding, are you?" When Jack hesitated, Cam shook his head. "Forget it, Davenport. You made me a promise, and I'm going to hold you to it. You can go fight your war after you stand up with me at the altar if that's what you want, but you are not leaving Eternity Springs until I head off on my honeymoon the third weekend in August."

Jack gave the statement some thought. It could take him a month or longer to hire men and procure supplies. He could do that from here as well as from anywhere. Mexico wasn't going anywhere and neither were the cartels—until he arrived, that is.

If deep inside himself, Jack recognized his idea to be idiotic, he refused to let it surface. Emotion—and painkillers—continued to ride his blood. Sincerely, he replied, "I want to be at your wedding, Cam. I'm honored to be your co–best man."

"Good. I'm glad that's settled."

"So what marriage-saving task caused you to turn around?"

"Well, you're probably not going to like this, but that's really just too bad. We think that under the circumstances, it's better for you not to be alone at Eagle's Way. That house is full of stairs, and stairs and crutches and pain meds don't mix. All we need is for you to take a tumble and crack open your head or break both your legs. When Sarah heard about your accident, after she knew that you were okay, the first words out of her mouth were could you still put on a tux and stand at the altar."

"You're kidding."

"Not at all. I'm telling you, this wedding stuff is serious business. One thing I'm learning real quick is that you don't mess with a bride's idea of the perfect wedding photographs." Cam folded his arms and declared, "That's why I've arranged for you to stay here at Angel's Rest at least until you are off your crutches."

Jack eyed his cousin's belligerent stance. Nobody was making him do anything, but Jack wasn't stupid. Cam had a point about stairs, true, but he could navigate his house without climbing stairs. He'd just do all his living on the main floor. Even as he opened his mouth to say so, Cam made a statement that changed everything.

"Cat said she'd keep an eye on you."

Cat. Damn. He'd been trying not to think about Cat. "Oh? When did she say that?"

"Ten minutes ago. Sarah called her."

"Huh." Jack lifted his right hand from the crutch to scratch at one of the cuts on his face that had required a stitch and was now beginning to itch. "I'm surprised she'd agree to have anything to do with me."

"What did you do to send her running from Eagle's Way, anyway?"

"I, um, well . . ." He dragged his hand across his jaw.

Cam's brows arched. "You had sex with her."

"Yeah," Jack replied with a sigh.

"And, let me guess. You weren't exactly suave James Bond about it."

"Maybe she wants to smother me in my sleep."

Cam nodded sagely. "Now I understand her comment to Sarah. She said she's been taking in dogs for months now through her work with the rescue group, so the precedent has been set."

So, she was calling him a dog? That's better than some things he could think of. Better than some things he deserved to be called. "Where am I supposed to stay? Not in her room, I imagine."

"No." Cam waved a hello to Celeste as she entered the rose garden, pruning shears in hand, then gestured toward a red Victorian-style cabin along the bank of Angel Creek. "You're over here in one of the cottages."

The carved wood sign hanging beside the door read THE COUGAR'S LAIR. From eagle to cougar, hmm? Okay, he could work with that. "Where is Cat staying?"

A smirk on his face, Cam gestured toward the cottage next to his. "Nightingale Cottage."

She'd be closer to him here than she'd been at Eagle's Way.

"The cabins are mirror images of each other, so your bedroom windows face each other."

So he could look up and see her light at night. He

liked the sound of that. Through the years of their marriage, she'd always been the light in his darkness.

The exercise and the conversation had helped his head to clear somewhat, and Jack considered his earlier rambles to Cam. Did he honestly intend to go vigilante? Had the idea been a drug-induced, dark-night-of-the-soul idiocy or something he truly wanted to do? Right at the moment, he couldn't say for sure.

Well, it wouldn't hurt anything to make some preliminary preparations. He could do that from here with his laptop and a phone. Any arrangements that required a secure connection wouldn't be made until after the initial plans were in place, anyway. He had time.

And besides, right now, he could really use a bed and another nap.

"You think Devin would make a run up to the house to pick up some things for me?"

Cam visibly relaxed. "Absolutely. My boy said to tell you that if you needed anything to give him a shout."

"I'll make a list."

Twenty minutes later, Jack lay stretched out on a comfortable queen-size bed in the Cougar's Lair cottage. He wanted to sleep, but his mind continued to spin with images from recent days and his black mood returned.

He was tired. So damned tired. Sorrow and guilt had a vise grip on his soul.

Tony was dead because of him. His wife a widow because of decisions he'd made. Tony's daughter would grow up without her father because a few years ago, Jack had actually believed that their work made the world a better place.

It's nothing but whack-a-mole. Beat down one piece of scum and another one pops up somewhere else. Why even try?

Because the good people are worth saving, his conscience argued. *You have to try.*

With those and similar thoughts sounding a never-ending litany through his mind, he lay mired in a black morass of depression, aching both physically and emotionally, until the soothing sound of Celeste Blessing's voice lifted in song lulled him to sleep.

SIX

❦

Seeing Jack bloodied and hurt had unsettled Cat. He'd come home battered in times past, with new scars and stitches, but she'd never seen his injuries in such a fresh state. She tried to tell herself that her heart would nearly stop, her knees almost buckle, at the sight of any injured soul, but honesty made her admit that seeing a blood-streaked Jack in a wheelchair had turned her blood to ice. She'd been shaken and restless when she returned to Nightingale Cottage, so she'd gone for a soak in the hot tub pools. It had proved to be just what she'd needed, and she returned to her cottage relaxed.

After taking a shower, she'd sat down to watch a movie on TV and ended up falling asleep. Her ringing cell phone woke her and she'd listened in disbelief as Sarah had relayed news of Jack's infinitely idiotic plan to play mercenary army general and Cam's subsequent demand that Jack stay in Eternity Springs until after the wedding. "The problem is that if he stays holed up alone at Eagle's Way, we're afraid he might actually go through with it," Sarah said.

"I'm not moving back up there," Cat told her. She didn't want Jack doing something stupid like declaring war with Mexico, but she needed space from him.

That's when Sarah had suggested Jack join her at Angel's Rest—in a separate cabin, of course. "He needs someone to check up on him until he's off his crutches. Cam thinks that once life in Eternity Springs has its opportunity to work its magic, he'll see the idea of declaring war on drug lords as the idiocy that it is."

"I think it's a good idea for him to have people around," Cat had replied. "But I don't see why I need to be involved. Jack has friends in town who can check on him. For that matter, he can hire a full-time nurse if that's what he needs. He could have someone flown in today to wait on his every whim. Money isn't an issue for him, you know."

"I know. But Celeste suggested that we'd have better success getting him to see how ridiculous this private army idea is if you are the one watching over him here for the next few days. We've learned to pay attention to Celeste. She's uncanny about such things."

Private army. Cat recalled how devastated he'd been yesterday, and how completely out of character all of his actions had been since he returned from Texas. She sincerely doubted he'd do anything so ridiculous, but then again, he wasn't being himself.

She would worry about his being on crutches if he were alone up at Eagle's Way. She could picture him becoming entangled, taking a tumble down the stairs, and cracking his head open on the floor. It'd be one thing if she never knew he was on crutches, but now that she did know . . . yikes. She wouldn't sleep well from worrying about him.

Great. Just great. Would it be a big deal to look in on him a time or two? She'd do that for any injured animal, wouldn't she? Besides, in a weird sort of way, she owed him. He had gone to the trouble of abducting her, hadn't he? "Just for the next few days?"

"He'll be off his crutches in a week."

"All right. I'll do it."

"Good. Celeste said she'd put him in the cottage next

to you if you agreed. I'll tell Celeste, and someone will let you know once he's settled in at Angel's Rest."

They discussed Sarah's wedding plans for a few moments before ending the call, and not five minutes after she hung up, her phone rang again. Nic Callahan was calling to thank her for stepping up to help Jack. "I haven't seen Gabe this upset in a very long time. We were ready to bring him here, but I'm just afraid that toddlers and crutches don't mix."

Once they'd exhausted the subject of Jack's stupidity—though honestly, Cat could have gone on for hours about that—Nic asked her a question about Paw Pals and talk turned to the therapeutic value of pets. The veterinarian relayed the story of how a stray dog—now their Clarence—had literally saved Gabe's life, and that gave Cat the germ of an idea. "Does Eternity Springs have an animal services department?"

"We have someone who is lead on wildlife issues."

"Not wildlife. I mean a pet shelter."

"That would be my kennel. We don't have a large number of strays, and those we do have are part of a shelter round-robin agreement I have with other vets in this section of the state. We'll move animals every six weeks so they are seen by a broader community and have a better shot at adoption."

"That's a really good idea. So, do you have any adoptable dogs now?"

"Actually, I have two, a toy mix and a boxer. Why do you ask?"

"When you talked about Clarence coming out of the snow to save Gabe, it made me think of the cartoons when we were kids where the Saint Bernard with the keg of whiskey around his neck would come to the rescue. I think Jack needs a dog."

"To bring him whiskey if he trips and falls?"

"The excuse would be that he'd bark in the middle of

the night if Jack needs attention, but the real benefit would be giving him a companion. Jack is too alone. Maybe if he had a dog at home, he wouldn't be so quick to run off to war. If you have a dog who doesn't have any better prospects, maybe he could come to Jack as a loaner?"

The connection went quiet for a moment as Nic considered it. "Ordinarily I am against giving someone a pet as a gift, and I've never done a 'loaner' before, but I think you might be on to something here. I can't see Jack with a toy breed, but the boxer back there is as big as a house and friendly as can be. He also doesn't have any better prospects at the moment. His name is Fred."

"Fred?"

"That's what his tag read when Gabe found him. He had his dog, Clarence, with him up at the Timberlakes' new place at Heartache Falls. Clarence wandered into the woods and came out a little while later with Fred. I thought for sure someone would adopt him, but he's made the round of shelters and is back to me. I do everything I can to avoid euthanasia, but . . ."

"Can I see him?"

"How soon can you be here?"

"It's a short walk, isn't it?"

"I do it in seven minutes."

"I'll be there in ten."

"I'll gather up some supplies."

Half an hour later, Cat returned to Angel's Rest, a tote bag filled with a small sack of food and two chew toys in one hand, the end of a leash in the other. She decided to brave the beast right away. She knocked on the door of Cougar's Lair, and after a moment she heard a grumbled "Yeah?"

"It's Cat. May I come in?"

"I'm asleep."

She took that as a yes. Opening the door, a firm grip

on Fred's leash, she called out, "I know what your problem is, Davenport. You need a dog."

"Like I need a chick flick and a strawberry daiquiri," he called back from the bedroom. "I want a beer, a burger, and a ballgame on TV, but I'll settle for a glass of water. Since you're here, Cat, would you mind helping me out?"

Cat debated, glanced down at Fred who was sniffing his way around the kitchenette, then dropped the leash before she took a glass from the cabinet and filled it with water. As she stepped toward the back room, she heard him say, "Oh, you have got to be kidding."

Cat entered Jack's bedroom to see Fred with his front paws up on the side of Jack's bed, gazing adoringly up at the man who looked like an Independence Day holdover—red road burns and blue bruises against an unnaturally pale complexion. "You look terrible," she observed.

"Why did you let a dog in here?"

"Jack, meet Fred. Fred is the Eternity Springs version of that medical alert button that you hang around your neck."

"What?"

"You know . . . 'I've fallen and I can't get up'?"

Jack closed his eyes. "I know what this is. I'm still asleep and this is a nightmare."

"Tell me about it." Her lips twitched with a smile when she saw Jack give Fred a surreptitious scratch behind his ears. "You're supposed to be up on the mountain, not down here within shouting distance of me. I left you."

"Yeah, I know. So why are you back?"

"I'm not back. You followed me. In an extraordinarily stupid manner, I might add. You know, Davenport, I've called you a lot of names over the years. Stupid was never one of them. Before today."

He cocked open one eye. "Take your dog and go, Cat."

"Fred is your dog now. He was a stray who didn't get adopted. He needs to be rescued, Jack."

"That's not going to work."

Sure it would. "Then you take it up with Nic Callahan. Maybe she'll let you fill the needle she'll have to use to put him down."

Now he opened both eyes and snarled at her. He'd given in, just as she'd known he would. Fred took the opportunity to put his front paws up on the bed again and lick Jack's hand. "How is it all of a sudden I have to take care of a dog? I thought you were supposed to take care of me."

"You and I both know that you can take care of yourself. Fred will alert me if there's trouble. He has an exceptionally loud bark."

"Oh, joy." His hand rubbed the top of Fred's head.

"As long as you are at Angel's Rest, he's your alarm dog."

"Now *that's* stupid."

"No, wanting to play like Cortés conquering the Aztecs is stupid." As temper flared in his eyes, Cat asked a question she'd wanted to ask for some time. "Do you still work for my mother, Jack?"

At that, he pushed Fred off the bed and sat up. "Why would you ask me that? You know I can't answer."

The words rolled from Cat's mouth, welling up from old wounds within her she hadn't acknowledged in a very long time. "I hated your job, absolutely despised the fact that you worked for Melinda. You always said that you kept marriage and work as separate at Langley as you did at home, but that was difficult for me to believe. I know your job changed after Lauren died. Your out-of-town trips quadrupled."

"I didn't know you noticed."

She ignored that and went on, "I know that you've continued to do some sort of work while you've been at Eagle's Way. So here's what I want to know. What sort of job with the U.S. government will allow you to raise your own army? Honestly, that one I just can't wrap my head around. The only thing I can figure is that in order to do it, you would have to quit your job. That amazes me. After all, it's something you never would do for me."

As zingers went, she figured that must be one of her best ever. It was certainly one of her most satisfying. She could tell from the way his expression went blank that she'd scored a hit.

Maybe she shouldn't have said it, since it wasn't nice to kick a man when he was down, but really. The idea that Jack Davenport would declare war on Mexican drug cartels—personally—was ludicrous.

"As I said before, Catherine. Take the dog and go."

"Fred went potty right before I brought him over, so he shouldn't need to go out anytime soon. Nic assured me he's housebroken, and she sent enough food for tonight with me. I'll pick up some more at the Trading Post when I'm out this evening."

She set down the glass of water on the bedside table and unhooked the leash from Fred's collar. The boxer plopped down beside Jack's bed, making himself perfectly at home. She turned to leave and Jack's voice stopped her at the door.

"You never asked me to quit my job."

She didn't look at him. "No. I never wanted the rejection."

Cat was reaching for the front doorknob when his voice reached her. "Maybe I would have done it."

"Maybe Fred can fly, too."

She brooded about his comment as she returned to her

cottage and began to prepare for the evening's town hall meeting. No way would Jack have ever quit his job had she asked. She remembered how he'd been . . .

Cat stood staring at the contents of her pantry. The oatmeal and chocolate chips were calling out to her to make cookies. If Jack were home, she wouldn't have to worry about the temptation of cookies whispering her name because he could polish off an entire batch in two days. But he'd been gone for six days now, and she didn't have a clue when he might be back. She could gain five pounds on oatmeal chocolate chip cookies before he came home.

Firmly, Cat shut the pantry door just as the front door opened. "Honey, I'm home."

She squealed and dashed toward the front of the house, where she launched herself at Jack. He wrapped her in his arms and lifted her off the ground and twirled her around and around, even as he captured her mouth in a hungry kiss.

As they did more often than not when he returned from a work trip, they made love on the living room floor. Afterward, as they lay naked and spent, she knew from experience that this was the one time he might let slip a nugget about his job. She lifted her head from his chest and went up on her elbow and studied him. "That's quite a farmer's tan you developed while you were gone. You must have been in the sun a lot."

"I was."

"Was it hot where you were?"

"Mmm-hmm." He nuzzled her neck and Cat shuddered.

"It was a successful trip?"

"Any time I come home with all my parts it's a successful trip." His mouth stretched into a smug smile as he added, "But yes, we found what we went looking for."

Cat's heart twisted as once again she experienced that left-out feeling she invariably got whenever her husband and her mother were together. "You love the job, don't you?"

His shifted his gaze to meet hers and his blue eyes shone with an intensity that said as much as his words. "I do. It's important, Cat. It's what I was born to do."

She couldn't argue with him. The man had an uncanny ability with languages. She knew he spoke at least five fluently and she expected he had a grasp of many more—though the exact number was probably something else he'd never share with her.

"I suspect that whatever . . . task . . . you do has support staff, doesn't it?"

He chastened her with the arch of a brow. "Cat . . ."

"That's what you did when we were dating, right? Support staff? You worked long hours, just like Melinda, but you weren't gone nearly as much then as you are now."

He rolled her onto her back and rose above her. "I made you a promise and I intend to hold to it."

"It's just . . . well . . . I thought we'd be pregnant by now."

"Hey, maybe this time's the charm." He tenderly pushed a strand of hair away from her face and added, "Why don't we find a bed and work on our odds a little more?"

She didn't know if he noticed that her smile had dimmed a little. They'd missed her most fertile time earlier this month when he'd been gone. Again. For such an intelligent, observant man, he was surprisingly dense about conception.

Or else he intentionally ignored it. After all, he'd promised to transfer to a different job when they had a baby, and he did love his job.

It's what he was born to do.

His words echoed through her mind that evening, years and an ocean of heartache later. She sat in the auditorium of the Eternity Springs school, waiting for the program to start and trying to put Jack and his uncharacteristic behavior out of her thoughts. Even as she visited with the teacher beside her and waved to the Callahans and their friends who were seated toward the front of the auditorium, her thoughts continued to drift back to the Cougar's Lair cottage and the wounded beast within.

Jack wasn't acting right. Now that she thought about it, he hadn't behaved normally since the moment he snatched her off the street at home. It made sense that he would have changed somewhat in the years that they'd been apart, but to this extent? She'd caught him staring out the windows and brooding more than once up at Eagle's Way. That had been before his friend Tony had died, too. The Jack Davenport she'd been married to had never brooded. He hadn't used sex as an escape, and he certainly hadn't ridden a motorcycle like a death wish.

Maybe his response wasn't anything to be concerned about, but the way he'd acted reminded her of her own descent into depression after losing Lauren. She wouldn't wish clinical depression on her own worst enemy. Or on her ex-husband.

Realizing she'd become distracted from the program—not a good thing, since she had to go home and write about what happened—Cat tuned in. Celeste Blessing had taken the stage and was speaking a few words about the changes in Eternity Springs in the past few years. Then she asked the mayor to read a proclamation.

Mayor Townsend cleared his throat and read, "The mayor and city council of Eternity Springs, Colorado, hereby declare the third Friday in July to be Cam Murphy Day."

The auditorium erupted into cheers and applause, and Cat couldn't help but grin to see the stunned look on the man's face. Sarah had given her a recap of his history with the town. Cat understood what a sea change in attitude this represented.

She took lots of notes for her article—including the fact that instead of giving him a plaque to commemorate the honor, the town gave him a bowling trophy.

Next, Celeste gave the pair something Sarah called their "Angel's Rest wings" and Celeste referred to as the "healing center blazon." As the auditorium erupted once again, Cat noted that she needed to follow up on just exactly what that was all about.

Then Celeste Blessing spoke into the microphone once again, and as the assembly began to absorb her words, the room went silent. "Now, my friends, it appears that my Plan A is accomplished. Eternity Springs is thriving. A goodness of spirit once again occupies this valley. Eternity Springs is truly a place where broken hearts can come to heal, and you, my dear, dear friends, will spread wings of compassion and love around wounded souls. My work here is done. I'll use this opportunity to announce that I'll be moving on to another town, another place, where people have need of my assistance."

Cat noted shock and alarm on Cam's and Sarah's and the rest of the audience's faces, but what truly got her attention were the words that Celeste said about wounded souls. A moment later, Cat found herself on her feet, walking up the aisle toward the stage as she called out to Celeste. "Your work here is far from over. If you know the secret to healing broken hearts, then it's time you did something about Jack Davenport. The man is impossible."

Cam grinned and murmured something to Sarah. Celeste thumped her index finger thoughtfully against her pursed lips for a long moment while the gathering seemed to hold its collective breath until the physician who had treated Jack at the clinic, Dr. Rose Anderson, stood and said, "I agree with Ms. Davenport, Celeste. I want the opportunity to earn my Angel's Rest wings, too."

A man dressed in a sheriff's uniform called out, "Rose has a good point. I admit I'm envious of my friends who have earned their medal."

"It's a blazon," the older woman corrected in a way that told Cat she'd done so many times before. Finally, she shook her head and clucked her tongue. "Perhaps I can stay in Eternity Springs a little while longer."

Everyone clapped. Cam leaned over and pressed a kiss against Celeste's cheek. The meeting broke up a few moments later, and Cat decided to take the opportunity to ask follow-up questions of Cam about his reaction to the Cam Murphy Day announcement.

The man had a few follow-up questions of his own, and by the time the Eternity Springs Combined School auditorium emptied, Cat, Cam, the Callahans, and Celeste had concocted a plan. "Plan D for Davenport," Celeste declared. "This is going to be fun."

The sound of pounding on his door woke Jack before sunrise. The dog lying at the foot of his bed lifted his head. *Bang. Bang. Bang. Bang.* Fred looked at Jack as if to say *Well, do something about it* before lowering his head and going back to sleep.

"Some watchdog you are," Jack grumbled as he rolled to sit up, grimacing at the protest from his muscles, bones, and skin. The second day of an injury was always the worst.

Rather than reach for his pants or his crutches, Jack solved the problem by calling out, "Go away."

He wasn't surprised to hear his door open. Heavy footfalls clued him to the fact that Cat wasn't his visitor.

Anybody else, he didn't particularly care about, so he lay back down, muttering a curse against the pain the movement gave him.

Gabe Callahan switched on the light. "Wussy."

"Bite me, Callahan."

"No, thanks. I have something else in mind for breakfast. Drag your butt out of bed, Davenport, and let's go fishing at Hummingbird Lake. My mouth is watering for some fresh-caught trout."

"Mine's not." Jack put his arm over his eyes, shutting out the light. "Go away, Callahan."

"C'mon, Jack. It's gonna be a gorgeous morning, full of peace and quiet. We're going out on Rafferty's rowboat. He volunteered to do all the rowing because he needs the physical exertion. His wife is due to deliver their first child in a few weeks and his nerves are strung tight."

"Good for him. As much fun as fishing sounds this morning, I still have to pass." Jack threw out a calculated excuse. "I need to spend time with my dog."

Gabe folded his arms and leaned against the doorjamb. Jack figured he'd found a great argument because Gabe's wife was the vet and she wouldn't appreciate his deserting his new responsibility.

"I guess that makes some sense," Gabe said. "It is your first full day with him, and Fred has been shuttled around so much that Nic said he's a little insecure. We can fish here on Angel Creek. Celeste keeps folding chairs handy beside the creek, so you can sit when you need to rest. Cam said a tourist pulled a big one out of Angel Creek yesterday just a little upstream from here."

"Gabe, I appreciate the thought, but—"

"An hour. Just give me an hour."

"Why?"

"Why not? What better thing do you have to do for the next hour?"

"Sleep."

"Too bad you're already awake. Get up and fish a bit and then we'll cook our catch and you and Fred can take a midmorning nap together."

Jack tried one more thing. "Don't you have a job to go to, Callahan? You have two children and a wife to support. Where's the design plan you promised me?"

"Check your email. You've had it for a week, and I'm not taking pay for that, remember? You don't need to worry about my professional life. I have it well in hand. Quit stalling, Jack. There's a trout out there waiting for your worm."

Jack gave in and spent a pleasant hour and a half catching, cooking, and consuming breakfast in mostly companionable silence with Gabe, interrupted occasionally by Fred's spurts of energy and enthusiasm for a game of fetch with a waterlogged sneaker Gabe pulled from Angel Creek.

Once Gabe finally left, Jack hobbled back toward the cottage and his bed, thinking about that nap. At the cabin's back door, he waited for Fred, but the dog showed no interest in coming inside. "Like the outdoors, do you, boy?"

He opened the gate to the fenced area behind his cabin constructed for tourists who traveled with their dogs. Fred padded inside to a shady spot in a corner, turned around three times, then plopped down onto the thick green grass. Jack no sooner latched the gate and pivoted on his crutches toward the cottage than he heard Cam call his name. He grumbled, "Now what?"

"Hey, cuz," Cam said. "Sarah and I are headed to the hot springs for a soak. Come with us. You're bound to be sore. It'll make you feel better."

His automatic response was to turn Cam down, but he had a weakness for hot springs and a soak did sound good. It felt good, too, and as he sat submerged up to his shoulders, he relaxed and mellowed enough to tease Cam about the upcoming Cam Murphy Day.

"I can see it now. Rafferty will trailer his rowboat for Devin to pull behind his truck up Spruce Street while you sit in the boat doing a princess wave to all of your subjects."

Sarah laughed while Cam stretched out, his fingers laced behind his head, a smug smile on his face. "Maybe I should order some beads to throw like at Mardi Gras. Get the ladies to show me their—*ow!*" Cam winced. "Sarah. That hurt."

"You deserve to hurt after that remark."

"What did I say? Jack, help me out here."

"You're on your own, buddy."

Cam grabbed for Sarah's hand and brought it up to his mouth, kissing the back of it. "Not anymore, I'm not. I found me a beautiful mermaid."

"Sucking up won't work, Murphy," Sarah said.

"Sure it will. I have magic lips." He made fish lips with his mouth.

Sarah snorted and Jack observed, "That's not what she told me when I kissed her. I distinctly remember . . ."

"Ja-ack," she protested.

Cam scowled blackly at him. "And I thought the sharks off Australia were bad."

Jack felt better than he had in days. He rested his head against the side of the pool, closed his eyes, and steeped in the soothing heat of the mineral springs, contributing occasionally as the conversation drifted to topics related to Eternity Springs.

Then he looked up and saw Cat walking from her cottage to Cavanaugh House, her hips rolling with her long-legged stride, and he was glad to be wearing sunglasses. He could stare and no one was the wiser.

Or so he hoped.

So intent was he upon Cat, he didn't notice Celeste's

arrival until she spoke. "Sarah, Lori called up to Cavanaugh House looking for you. She said there's nothing wrong, but she's been trying to call you all morning and you're not answering the phone so she's worried."

"Oh, for crying out loud. My phone has been ringing nonstop with wedding vendors and I left it home to get a little peace and quiet." Sarah lifted her gaze to the heavens. "Exactly when did I switch roles with my daughter?"

"It's separation anxiety," Cam said.

"She's an adult!"

"Only when she wants to be. I know she's happy that we're getting married, but a part of her is still a little girl who is accustomed to having her mommy's undivided attention."

Celeste greeted a family of four, guests of Angel's Rest from Kansas, who arrived for a soak in the hot springs. Jack had met the two boys earlier while he was fishing with Gabe, and they'd asked if they could take Fred for a walk. They called his name and a hello. He waved back.

"I guess I should go call Lori," Sarah said, standing.

Cam started to rise, too, and she said, "Why don't you stay here and help Jack back to his cottage? I'll meet you at home later."

"I don't need a babysitter."

"No, but you need help getting out of the pool."

"My knee is sore, not broken," Jack grumbled. "I can do it myself."

Cam snorted with disgust. "Why are you so hardheaded? It doesn't hurt anything to let someone help you for a change."

The arrival of a group of chatty teenagers wearing matching T-shirts advertising a Denver church group caused Jack to decide that he'd had enough of mineral springs, and of company. "All right, all right. You can help me out now. This was a good idea and I'm glad you suggested it, but I feel a nap coming on."

After exiting the pool, they rinsed off beneath the outdoor showers. Cam and Sarah headed toward their car while Celeste asked if Jack minded if she walked back with him to Cougar's Lair Cottage. "I haven't met your Fred yet, and I need to leave something next door for Catherine."

Jack wondered if the elderly woman thought he needed her help navigating crutches. Maybe his bruises looked worse than he'd thought.

Celeste didn't betray any sign of helpfulness as they walked the path back to the cottages, though, and for that he was grateful. Instead, she asked if he was comfortable in the cottage and if he needed any supplies. She was talking about Gabe and Nic's boxer, Clarence, when the path took a turn and his cabin came into view. She broke off in midsentence, saying, "Looks like you have visitors, Jack."

He frowned as he watched Mac and Ali Timberlake step up onto his front porch. Mac knocked on his door. "Now what?" Jack muttered, casting a suspicious glance toward Celeste. "What's going on here?"

Her expression was the picture of angelic innocence. "Pardon me? Whatever do you mean?"

"How is it almost everyone I know in Eternity Springs just happens to show up on my doorstep today?"

She touched him gently on the arm and offered him a smile so warm and sweet that he felt it clear to his soul. "Jack Davenport, you have friends here. When darkness threatens your world, friends can be beams of sunshine if only you'll let them."

The Timberlakes carted him off to lunch at Ali's restaurant, after which she conned him into showing her how he prepared his one specialty dish—chili. When he finally tore free of Mac and Ali, Colt Rafferty waylaid him, looking for somewhere to watch the Rockies game since the quilt group was throwing his wife a surprise baby shower out at their house on Hummingbird Lake. Jack never did get his nap. When he finally crawled into bed that night, sore and weary from a day filled with friendship, Celeste's words echoed through his mind: *Friends can be beams of sunshine if only you'll let them.*

Maybe that was true, but they could also be pains in the ass. Nevertheless, when he finally fell asleep, he did so with a smile on his face, and Fred on the foot of his bed.

Even in the middle of summer, the nighttime air in the mountains could be downright chilly. Cat loved it. She kept her bedroom window cracked open and added another blanket to her bed. She'd always been a light sleeper, and since Jack slept with his window open wide, she didn't worry that she wouldn't hear if he called her or if Fred barked out a warning.

She'd been a busy little mountain beaver today and loved every minute of it. She'd written her article for the newspaper about the town hall meeting, then did research for an article she wanted to write about the Silver Miracle strike and Eternity Springs's three founders, Daniel Murphy, Harry Cavanaugh, and Lucien Davenport.

Lucien Davenport. Jack had told her he had an ancestor named Lucien before they got married. If Lauren had been a boy, she'd wanted to name him Lucien.

After spending two hours in the town library and one in the library at Angel's Rest, Cat was more intrigued than ever about her ex-husband's ancestor. Lucien Davenport had been a British remittance man when he went into the Rocky Mountains with friends he'd made in a Denver saloon and hit the vein of silver that had provided the basis of Jack's fortune today. Whereas Daniel

Murphy and Harry Cavanaugh had settled in Eternity Springs, Lucien Davenport had returned to England when he'd unexpectedly inherited a title upon the accidental deaths of his brothers. The Davenport fortune grew even bigger.

It had been fascinating reading. Jack had seldom spoken about his family. She knew his parents had died, but he'd never said how, and he'd never shared the fact that an ancestor was an English earl. Over the years Cat had been tempted to investigate the death of his parents, but early in their relationship when she'd quizzed him on the subject, he'd asked her not to do it. She'd given her word and she'd kept it.

She didn't figure that exploring Lucien Davenport's life counted against that promise.

She drifted off to sleep imagining Jack dressed in Victorian evening clothes leading her onto the dance floor in a glittering ballroom to the music of a string quartet.

Cat awoke to the sound of Fred's bark, Jack's hushed "Quiet," and the squeaky hinges of Cougar's Lair's front door.

He must be letting Fred out to do his business, she thought, and glanced at the red numerals of the clock beside her bed. Two forty-five a.m. She lay in bed waiting to hear the sound of man and dog returning inside, but didn't.

Groaning aloud, Cat reached for the white terry cloth robe she'd left draped over the foot of her bed. She rose and shoved her feet into her favorite slippers—the dog's head slippers she'd won as a prize at the rescue group's casino night earlier this year. They were soft and silly with dangling floppy ears, and she loved them. Quietly, Cat opened the door of Nightingale Cottage and stepped into the night.

A sickle moon and a million stars lit the night sky, but left the grounds of Angel's Rest in shadows. She couldn't see Jack and his boxer, but she could hear the scrunch of his crutches against the gravel path and Fred's soft whine from inside Cougar's Lair. Jack was moving away from the row of cottages, away from Cavanaugh House, and he'd left Fred shut inside. Where was he hobbling off to?

She'd better follow him. These were the hours of the night where the monsters lived. No telling what foolish idea he had running through his head now.

She stepped on a sharp rock and scowled. Had she known she'd be hiking, she'd have chosen shoes instead of doggie slippers. The night was dark and he'd gone off the lighted pathways. Cat followed, almost calling out to him twice, but instinct stopped her both times. He wouldn't like knowing she'd followed him. As long as his midnight mission wasn't leading to harm, she'd allow him his privacy. He would never have to know she was there.

Cat was cold. They'd walked almost the length of the estate, and her puppy slippers were soaked with dew. He hobbled to the northernmost section of Angel's Rest where the natural hot springs had been diverted into pools designed by the town's resident landscape architect, Gabe Callahan. Once she realized his intent, she scowled. He was going for a late night soak in the hot springs, while on crutches and at risk of a fall. Great.

She couldn't return to her cottage and her nice warm bed. Not until he returned to his.

"You might as well join me, Catherine," Jack called out over his shoulder. "You'll be cold otherwise."

Cat gave an exasperated sigh. "I was quiet as a mouse. How did you know I was here?"

"I learned how to listen when listening meant the difference between life and death."

Ah, yes. His job. Always the job. It was what he was born to do.

She approached the steaming pools, dimly lit by discreet lights placed for safety's sake, she thought, rather than illumination. She wrinkled her nose at the sulfur smell. "I've never seen the appeal of soaking in water that smells like rotten eggs."

He had a towel draped over one shoulder and he wore gym shorts and sandals. Propping one crutch against a rock wall, he pulled off the towel and dropped it beside a pool. When his thumbs went to the waistband on his shorts, Cat quickly said, "Wait. It might be the middle of the night, but this is still a public place."

"It's dark. Nobody's here. I'm not wearing sopping shorts back to my cabin. Did that once today already and I'm not doing it again." He stripped off his shorts and carefully lowered himself into the steaming pool, completely naked.

Cat swallowed a lump in her throat. His relieved sigh whispered across the night. "Feels good, Cat. You should join me."

"It stinks."

"You get used to it. Just takes a couple of minutes." When she continued to stand back, he added, "It's stupid to stand out there and freeze."

"Why are you doing this now, anyway?"

"My bones ache. I soaked this morning and it helped. Humans have soaked in mineral springs to ease their aches for thousands of years."

"In the daytime, surely. You couldn't wait until daylight?"

"I ache now. Go back to bed, Cat. I don't need a babysitter."

"Maybe not, but I won't be able to sleep because I'll be imaging how your crutch will slip and you'll fall and need help."

"Then get in the water. It will relax you and keep you warm."

He closed his eyes and leaned his head back against

the edge of the pool. It looked as if he'd dismissed her completely from his mind. Cat debated silently another minute, until the stir of a breeze chilled her. *Oh, what could it hurt?*

She passed Jack, thinking she'd sit in one of the pools behind him. In a low voice, he observed, "I'm not a shark. I don't bite. Or are you afraid you won't be able to keep your hands off me if you share my pool?"

"Don't be ridiculous."

He arched a brow, the look in his eyes clearly challenging. Cat couldn't resist the silent dare.

At least she wasn't naked, she thought gratefully as she loosened the belt on her robe. Beneath it she wore an oversized satin sleep shirt. With quick, efficient movements, she slipped off her robe and hung it on a nearby hook where it would remain dry. Then she stepped into the hot, smelly pool with her ex.

"I've never understood the appeal of mineral baths," she observed. Yet even as she voiced the words, a luxurious heat permeated her body.

Jack submerged his shoulders completely beneath the water and his head rested back against the side of the pool, his eyes closed. "There is a five-star resort in Costa Rica that has the most amazing natural hot springs and waterfalls. It's lush and extravagant. You'd enjoy it."

"It's your favorite?"

"No."

"What is?"

A full minute passed before he responded. "My favorite would be the hot springs I stumbled across quite by accident in . . . well, let's just say another country. The temperature had been freezing the whole week that our team had been there. Finally, we found what we went for, but circumstances changed and we had to hike out to a secondary rendezvous spot. We were crossing a valley when we saw steam rising and investigated. An old man sitting naked in a mineral pool invited us to join him. We were so cold that we couldn't resist. It was amazing. We soaked for twenty minutes, and I felt like a million dollars the rest of the day."

Cat wiggled her fingers and toes beneath the water. It felt thicker than regular water, she thought. Heavier. Definitely stinkier. Yet the gag factor was fading. Jack had been right about that much.

"So what did you do today?" he asked, just as the light nearest the pool flickered and went out, deepening the already inky shadows.

Cat regretted not grabbing a flashlight before she left the cottage. "Yesterday," she corrected. "I'm going to help out at the local newspaper while I'm here. I wrote a summary article about the town hall meeting Monday night. I guess you heard all about Cam Murphy Day?"

He chuckled and nodded, and she continued. "I also started researching an article about the discovery of the Silver Miracle Mine."

"Local color and a history piece? That's not your usual beat as a reporter."

"No, it's not. Funny thing is that I'm enjoying it. You never told me Lucien Davenport was a British earl."

"I didn't?"

"No, you didn't. You never told me much of anything about your family."

"I don't like to talk about them."

Her tone dry, she said, "Oh? I never noticed."

Now Cat settled back against the pool's smooth wall and closed her eyes, too. The crisp night air felt cool against her face, and the contrast between the heat of the water and chill of the air refreshed and relaxed her. They sat in silence for long minutes until she felt compelled to say, "I never broke my promise to you."

"Which promise is that?"

"You asked me not to investigate your parents' death. I never did."

He remained silent for a long moment. "It happened a long time ago, but I still miss them."

"I'm sure you do."

"I'm surprised you never looked into it."

"You were obviously disturbed about it even years later, so I know it must have been something horrible. If I could help you by not looking into it, then that's what I wanted to do." She waited a beat, then asked, "Will you tell me about them now?"

The question was a long shot, but he'd been more open about his job recently than in all the time she'd known him.

Enough time passed that she thought he'd say nothing more about the subject. Her thoughts drifted back to those early days of their marriage. So young and in love, and frankly, a little desperate. Looking back, she recognized that in her heart, she'd known they weren't meant to last. They'd fallen in love despite themselves. She'd wanted home and hearth and the pitter-patter of little feet on the stairs, and even then he'd been the eagle, always soaring and sailing away.

His voice emerged from the darkness, stark and raw. "There was a wiring malfunction on the hot water heater and our house caught fire. It was the middle of the night. I don't know what woke me up, but I could smell smoke. I had the attic room and I screamed for my parents, but the landing below my stairs was already ablaze. I couldn't get out that way."

Cat opened her mouth to speak but thought better of it. He was talking. She didn't want to do anything to interfere with that.

"They had fire ladders stored in all the bedrooms. I had used mine a couple days earlier when I snuck out at night to meet some friends and I'd dumped it on the floor of my closet. It was all tangled up. I thought I was going to die."

She couldn't hold back her question. "How old were you?"

"Eleven. I was eleven. Ben was eight. Andrea was a baby."

SEVEN

It was the first time he'd spoken their names in years, Jack realized. That night was something he never talked about. He'd done so once, a very long time ago to Melinda Blackburn, but not to her daughter. Never to her daughter. He didn't know why he did so now. He kept the events of that night locked away in a section of his memory that he seldom accessed, having learned at the ripe old age of eleven that survival required compartmentalization. But tonight, as his muscles ached and his heart remembered, the story churned behind his mental walls and demanded release.

He could still smell the smoke, still feel the heat against his skin. He could still hear the crackle and crash of his life going up, literally, in flames.

In the safety of the darkness, he began to speak, and in doing so, he went back.

Something was wrong. He knew it in his bones even before he opened his eyes. His heart pounded. Fear turned his limbs to jelly. He knew that he should move, but all he wanted to do was to pull the covers over his head and hide.

He smelled smoke. His eyes stung. He began to cough. Fire. The house is on fire.

Then he was moving, lunging from the bed, hollering

for his dad. He ran for the stairs, but the heat and flames below stopped him.

Okay. Not a problem. He had the fire ladder. He dashed for his closet where the aluminum-and-fabric-straps ladder lay in a tangled heap. He could hear his mother's voice in his mind: "This is for emergencies only, son. I don't want to find out you've been using this ladder to sneak out of the house at night."

"Yes, ma'am. No ma'am. I wouldn't do that, ma'am."

He'd done it every chance he'd gotten.

Safety ladder in hand, he opened the attic window that overlooked the side yard. It took him precious minutes to untangle the mess, and he knew that if he made it safely out of his bedroom tonight, he'd never disobey his mother again—and never fail to take proper care of his equipment.

Finally, he hooked the end of the ladder to the permanent fastenings his father had installed. He was coughing hard as he fed the ladder through the opening, then scrambled after it, climbing down to safety.

When his feet touched ground, he didn't pause, but dashed around toward the front of the house shouting and sobbing for his mom and dad and brother. For the baby. He saw flames engulfing the ground floor and his terror intensified. Dashing onto the porch, he tried to go inside, but he couldn't. Fire was everywhere. Heat hit him like a fist. "Mama! Mama! Dad!"

He coughed and cried. He screamed. He had to save them. He had to rescue them. He ran to the back door, then around to the front again.

He didn't hear the sirens or see the fire truck arrive. When a strong arm caught him around the waist and a deep voice said against his ear, "Come here, son," at first he thought Jesus was speaking to him.

Then he registered the black coat with neon yellow bands and knew help had arrived. Firemen. He ran toward the truck. "Help me save them. We have to save them."

"We're gonna do our best, son. We'll do our best. Now, tell me how many people are inside and where they're located."

"Everyone's on the second floor. Three bedrooms. Mom and Dad have a room and Ben has a room. The baby's room is next to my parents. They let me move into the attic when the baby was born."

The fireman spoke into his radio, relaying the information as he motioned for the paramedics to come see to Jack.

He heard a loud whoosh and he tried to run back toward the burning house, but somebody stopped him. Held him. Spoke words to him that he did not hear.

He couldn't tear his gaze off the fearsome sight before him. Firemen scurried with hoses. Jack spied the ladder resting against the siding next to Ben's window. Firemen were climbing into Ben's window. "Please, God. Please, God. Please, God."

When he saw a fireman hand Ben over to a man on the ladder, relief turned Jack's knees to water, but his gaze remained glued on the opening.

He waited.

And waited.

And waited.

He struggled against the fireman's hold. Save them. I have to save them.

Now, decades later, Jack lived those long minutes over again. His throat was tight, his voice raspy, his emotions raw, as he said, "We didn't save them. My parents and the baby died inside the house. Ben died in the ambulance. Smoke inhalation. He didn't burn. Ben didn't burn."

At the time, that had meant the world to him. He remembered that, how he'd held on hard to that one reality amid all the chaos of the aftermath. Something inside him had died right along with his family. He'd been a broken boy who, he saw now, had never completely healed.

Cat waited a respectful moment before saying, "I'm so sorry, Jack. What a horrible experience for you to go through."

He didn't respond to that. He'd never been good at accepting sympathy for the loss of his family. He always wanted to shout, "I didn't save them!"

Cat knew him well enough to pick up on his reaction, and with her next words, she took the conversation in a different direction. "What were your parents like?"

Jack lowered his gaze from the starlit night sky and peered across the hot springs toward the shadow that was his ex-wife. He could almost hear her holding her breath, waiting to see whether he would respond to her question or shut her out. Once again, his responsiveness surprised him. "My mother made the best cookies I ever had in my life. Better than Sarah's, even."

"Wow," Cat said. "That's saying something."

"I can't taste anything lemon today without thinking of her."

"That's lovely, Jack. What was her name?"

"Elise. My father was D.L. Daniel Lucien Murphy Davenport."

"Murphy, hmm? So just how is it that you and Cam are related?"

"It's one of those distant cousin things. My father's mother was a Murphy from a branch of the family that didn't stay in Eternity Springs. She was a nurse during World War II, stationed in England. Since she had an interest in genealogy and Eternity Springs, she looked up the Davenports and met my grandfather, who was a bombardier in the RAF. He died during the war. My grandmother returned to the States and eventually re-married and settled in California."

"Our marriage license lists your birthplace as Palo Alto."

"My father was a computer engineer." With that, he was done talking about himself, so in an attempt to dis-tract her, he asked, "Are you thirsty? There's bottled water by the showers."

"I'm fine. Where did you go after the fire, Jack?"

Well, hell. "I'd forgotten how nosy you can be."

"This isn't nosy. This is normal curiosity. You've just told me more about your background than you told me in all the years that we were married. Did you live with relatives after that?"

"No." He hadn't had any relatives to live with, but damned if he'd say that. Made him sound like a whiner.

Cat waited expectantly. He wanted to bare his teeth and snap at her. She asked, "Did you go into the foster system? I've always wondered how my mother dragged you into her web."

Jack figured he might as well tell her all of it and get this over with. He didn't know why he'd started blab-bing, but since he had, no sense stopping now.

"I dodged the foster system. The Davenport Trust provided for me financially, and my parents' wills named the CEO of my dad's company as my guardian." He heard Cat's quick intake of breath when he mentioned the famous man. "He was a great guy and I appreciate all he did for me, but I became another company proj-ect, the mascot in a way. They saw that I had an educa-tion with a capital E. I wanted to grow up and become a fireman, but I showed an aptitude for languages. One day my guardian called me in to his office and intro-duced me to a nice woman named Melinda."

"How old were you?"

"Seventeen." Jack thought back to that meeting. His

lips twisted in a rueful smile. "I still wanted to be a fireman."

Melinda had told him that he could fight fires the likes of which he'd never imagined if he would join her team. He'd done exactly that.

Now, though, he wondered if he might be all burned out.

Silence dragged on between them, and just as Jack began to think that she wouldn't say any more, she spoke with a faint note of bitterness in her tone. "You wanted to save the world."

"I wanted to save my family," Jack replied. He wondered why he'd never seen it quite that way before.

"Did you?" Because he knew she referred to their family, it was another shot through the heart. He closed his eyes and let his head fall back as he absorbed it. "One thing my training taught me was how to assess the odds of success. I knew that we were doomed from the first. I couldn't reach you, Cat. I did try, but in that horrible moment when you handed me the cemetery map, I knew that I had lost you. I knew I'd lost everything a second time. I didn't admit it to myself, but I knew that's where we were going. I couldn't reach you."

"I was a mess," she said, her voice barely above a whisper as it floated across the surface of the hot springs pool. "I'm sorry. I shouldn't have said that. It wasn't all your fault that we fell apart. I can see that now, and I knew it then. I can say it now."

"It was a hard time for us both."

"I was so wrapped up in my own pain that I couldn't see past it to yours. I'm sorry, Jack."

He said her name, just her name, because he didn't know what else to say.

"I've never known exactly what my mother does, and I certainly never knew what you did. I knew you served our country and that what you did was important, but I

never drew a connection between the people and the
job. Nic Callahan painted that picture for me when
she told me how you rescued Gabe. I've learned some
important things about you since we've been in Colorado. You're a rescuer, Jack. That's something to be
proud of."

In the darkness, he snarled. *Rescuer my ass.* He
couldn't save Tony Martinez. He couldn't save Mom
and Dad and Ben and Andrea. He couldn't save Lauren
or his marriage. "I'm tired, Cat. I'm so damn tired."

The shadow opposite him moved. Cat crossed the
pool to him. She leaned down and pressed a gentle
kiss to his forehead. "Then rest, Superman. Take a little
break. Give your scrapes and bruises and wounded
heart time to heal. I'm told Eternity Springs is good for
that."

Early on Friday morning—Cam Murphy Day—Cat
left Nightingale Cottage wearing shorts, a T-shirt, sneakers, and a smile. It promised to be a beautiful day
weather-wise and a fun one to witness. The town was
abuzz with excitement. From what she could gather,
the people of Eternity Springs were accustomed to having summertime, tourist-oriented festivals, but today's
event—thrown together in a few short days—was a celebration for the townspeople.

From Angel's Rest, the walk to the newspaper office
was a twenty-minute stroll, or a ten-minute power walk
if she wanted it to count toward her daily exercise.
Today, Cat was of a mind to stroll. She stopped at the
Mocha Moose for a cup of coffee to go. She brewed
a decent cup herself in the coffeemaker in her cottage,
but the barista at the Mocha Moose was a master. She
stopped to chat with LaNelle Harrison as she opened
her quilt shop and waved at Mayor Townsend, who was
taking his morning constitutional. It was a gorgeous

morning and she'd had a great night's sleep and she was downright happy. When was the last time that had happened?

Today at the *Eternity Times*, she got to be the boss.

Emily Hall had called her last night in a panic on her way out of town to deal with a family emergency. Cat had assured her that she'd be happy to fill in. While she sincerely wished Emily's family the best, she couldn't help but be delighted to have a shot at being editor-in-chief. She didn't care that the *Times* was only a little mountain newsweekly. Emily had already arranged to do a Cam Murphy Day special edition. As Cat slipped her key into the newspaper's front door, she murmured, "And now it's mine, all mine."

And she took a wicked pleasure in assigning the official *Eternity Times* photographer to document Cam Murphy Day events like the horseshoes competition and the hot dog eating contest. She had Sarah Reese to thank for that.

Ordinarily Emily took all the photographs that appeared in the newspaper. Such was the work of a one-woman newspaper. But because Sarah's daughter was in Virginia on a veterinary internship and couldn't come home for her father's big day, Sarah wanted a thorough documentation of events to share with Lori. Sage Rafferty had suggested she ask Jack to man the camera. Since he'd ditched the crutches the day after their late-night mineral spring soak, no physical limitations prevented him from helping. Still, Cat had been surprised when Sarah told her he'd agreed.

She'd been shocked when he called Emily and volunteered to take pictures for the extra edition. Cam was Jack's cousin, so it made sense that he'd go the extra mile for him, but his relationship with the town was apparently a bit more strained. Cat had learned that that was in part because of the way he'd used Eagle's Way for so long—flying in and out and visiting town so rarely that for the most part he remained anonymous. It also went back to the founding of the town somehow, though she still wasn't straight on that.

Cat sat at the desk Emily had assigned her, removed her personal laptop from the tote bag she'd carried from the cottage, and booted it up. She'd just accessed the day's calendar when the front door opened and set the bell tinkling. Celeste Blessing swept inside. "Good morning, dear."

"Good morning, Celeste."

"I intended to catch you before you left the grounds this morning, but I had an exciting phone call from a former guest. Molly and Charlie Malone got married in Eternity Springs last Christmas, and she called to tell me they are expecting their first child. Even more exciting, her mother and father are expecting, too. It's a *Father of the Bride II* moment!"

"I liked that movie," Cat said.

Celeste pulled a folded sheet of paper out of her bag and handed it to Cat. "I've revised the schedule a tad. With Sage being so far along in her pregnancy, I just didn't think it was a good idea for her to spend two hours doing face painting for the little ones."

"I can't believe an artist of such renown as Sage is going to use her talent on finger paints and children!"

Celeste laughed. "Gabe teased that he'll rent out Meg and Cari to the Denver art museum until they wash their faces."

As Cat glanced at the schedule, her thoughts returned to the history that led up to today's celebration. "Do you have a few minutes, Celeste?"

"I do."

"I've been doing research for an article about the history of Eternity Springs. I understand you are the town's guardian angel."

"Oh, I'm not a guardian angel, dear. They are much farther up the food chain than I."

"Um . . . of course."

" 'Angel' is a term used these days to describe someone who supports a project or company financially. Eternity Springs was failing economically, and after the town council tried to land a new state prison and failed, I decided to invest my nest egg in this town and its people and establish Angel's Rest."

And thus save the town, Cat thought. "Angel's Rest revitalized the town, I know. What I don't understand is why people blamed Jack for its decline."

"The Davenport family. And the Murphys, of course. It all goes back to the Cellar Bride mystery. Have you learned that particular piece of our town's history?"

"No."

Celeste related the story of a skeleton dressed in the remnants of a wedding gown that was discovered in the basement of Cavanaugh House—the centerpiece of Angel's Rest—following a fire. "This was back when Gabe was staying at Eagle's Way, before he and Nic were married. We eventually discovered that the bones were the remains of town founder Daniel Murphy's runaway bride. She'd been murdered."

"Really! Who killed her?"

"That we don't know. We may never solve that particular mystery. Anyway, way back when, Lucien Davenport had returned to England, and poor Daniel lapsed into alcoholism after his Angel—that was his nickname for her—disappeared. He was in a terrible way, flat broke. He wrote to Lucien and offered to sell him the land he'd purchased after the Silver Miracle discovery."

"Murphy Mountain," Cat surmised.

"Yes. Jack has the letters. You should ask him to let you read them. Lucien wanted Daniel—or, if not him, his heirs—to be able to recover the land he'd lost, in the same condition as it had been when sold. He had his lawyers write a sales contract and a codicil to his will that made sure the land wasn't changed."

That's when it clicked for Cat. "I get it. The Davenport heirs wouldn't allow roads to be built from this valley to the ski resorts, and isolation without any industry was killing the town."

"Yes. Of course, even if Jack had agreed, no one knew where Cam was living then—he came home not long before Jack brought you to Eagle's Way—and to break the covenant, the signatures of the heirs of both families had to be obtained."

"That's an interesting piece of town history, Celeste. Thanks for educating me."

"My pleasure. I spent some time learning the history of Eternity Springs myself, but I'm no writer. I look forward to reading your article when you get it done."

Cat wanted to get her hands on those letters. She found this history fascinating. She already had an interview scheduled with Cam; she should see if she could squeeze some information out of Jack. Who knows, maybe his talkativeness hadn't ended with the hot tub revelations.

The morning after their talk, he'd left a note on her front door saying he no longer needed the crutches and he and Fred had returned to Eagle's Way. She'd been surprised by the pang of disappointment that had fluttered through her heart, but she'd put him out of her mind—for the most part—and gone about her business.

The plan was for them to work together today. Being honest with herself, she looked forward to it. How stupid was that? So they'd passed a nice little interlude in the hot springs and he'd talked to her. Big deal. He'd talked to her once in all the years she'd known him—after they were divorced.

But he had talked, the little subversive voice whispered. That's something he'd never done before. Something had changed. Jack had changed.

So what? "What in the world does it matter to you if he's changed or not?" she muttered. "You're not his wife. You're his ex."

So when the door finally opened and Jack strolled in, she scowled rather than smiled at him.

"What's that look for?" he asked.

"You're late," she lied.

"No, I'm not." He glanced at the clock hanging on the wall. "I'm early. The parade doesn't start for another half hour."

She improvised. "I wanted to interview you before we got started covering the day."

His brow furrowed. He spoke warily. "What do you mean, interview me? I don't do interviews."

"Fine. I won't quote you. I want to ask you what you know about Lucien and the Murphy Mountain land deal."

"Oh. That. I can talk about that."

He repeated much of the same information that Celeste had given her earlier, and when she asked him what his personal feelings were about the strings his ancestor had tied, his response surprised her. "I didn't know I owned land in Colorado until your mother told me."

"My mother?"

"Part of the background check she conducted when I joined her team. Once I built here, I could see what was happening to the town. I didn't see how building a road on the Murphy property to connect to ski resorts would really hurt anything, so I went looking for Cam. In the process I found out how Eternity Springs had treated him, so I decided not to interfere."

Another instance of trying to save his family, Cat

thought. "Now that Cam is Eternity Springs's favorite son, do you anticipate the road being built?"

"Don't know. Things have changed since Celeste opened Angel's Rest. Could be that everyone is happy with the status quo. Time will tell on that question."

The wall clock chimed a quarter till the hour, and she said, "Speaking of time, we should probably be leaving. Sarah would kick us both if we missed the beginning of the parade."

"True. I suspect Cam would be happy, though."

The thought of Cam made Cat grin. "I think he's torn between being pleased and embarrassed by the fuss. So, any questions before we get started?"

"Just one."

"Okay, what's that?"

"Smile for me?" Jack lifted his camera and took her picture.

Jack didn't know what he had expected from being the official photographer for Cam Murphy Day, but he hadn't anticipated everyone's being so . . . nice. Except for the Callahans and their group of friends, his reception in town had always been distinctly chilly. Today Mayor Townsend shook his hand and Dale Parker cuffed him on the shoulder. Nobody ever cuffed him on the shoulder. Even tart old Pauline Roosevelt gave him a friendly wave. By the kickoff parade's halfway point, he realized he had a smile on his face.

What a difference a few days could make. He'd gone from self-destructive despair to grinning like a fool as he focused his camera on the wide-eyed delight of children's faces.

"Must be magic in those mineral baths," he murmured.

Cat's eyes gleamed with amusement as she looked

away from the parade of pets coming up Spruce Street. "What was that?"

She looks so beautiful, relaxed, and happy. For an instant there, he couldn't think of what he'd said. When he did, he reworded the thought a bit. "Eternity Springs is a good place."

"Yes, it is."

He followed the path of her gaze, then asked, "Cat, what do those golden retrievers have strapped to their backs?"

She actually giggled. "Those are Sarah's dogs, Daisy and Duke. They're wearing shark's fins."

He thought about it. Drew a blank. "They're wearing shark's fins why?"

"In honor of Cam, of course. He returned to Eternity Springs from the coast of Australia. Now, don't just stand there, take some pictures!"

So he did. He took photos of big dogs wearing shark's fins and a little dog dressed in what he guessed to be a princess costume. "That's Sage Rafferty's Snowdrop," Cat informed him.

"I almost feel sorry for her baby," Jack observed.

Cat cuffed him on the shoulder. *That's twice.*

The parade ended with a band of schoolchildren playing kazoos marching ahead of an antique car, a convertible, driven by Devin Murphy with the man of the hour seated beside his bride-to-be in the backseat. It was obvious to Jack that Cam had decided to jump into the spirit of things, because he sat with his long legs outstretched, his sneaker-clad feet propped up on the passenger door, his fingers laced behind his head, his elbows outstretched, and an unlit cigar clamped between rows of gleaming teeth showing in his wide smile.

Jack lowered his camera long enough to comment. "Now I get the shark reference."

"Oh, that's not his shark's smile," Cat replied. "I saw

that last night when he showed up at the quilting bee looking for Sarah and intent about changing her mind about her no-sex-before-the-wedding decree."

Jack arched a brow. "Oh, really? He hasn't shared that particular bit of news with his cousin. So, how did that work out for him?"

"She said something about a Cam Murphy Day reprieve."

"No wonder he looks so content." When the cheering stopped and the parade crowd dispersed as people began making their way to Davenport Park for the next event, Jack added, "I'd forgotten how annoying kazoos are. Eternity Springs should have a marching band for its parades. Does the school need band instruments?"

"I don't know."

"I should look into that."

"There are a lot of things around this town you could look into. I'll make a list for you, if you'd like."

He gave her a sidelong look. "Looking to spend my money, Catherine?"

She shrugged. "Someone should. You don't seem to do it very often."

For some strange reason, he felt compelled to share. "I have people whose entire job is to spend my money."

"You've remarried?"

He laughed. "I have a foundation. We award scholarships and fund research grants."

"I didn't know that. Why did you never tell me that? That's not top secret government information."

He shrugged. "I don't talk about it."

She gave him a searching look. "What's its name?"

"The Bade Foundation."

"Bade?"

"Ben, Andrea, Daniel, and Elise."

"Ah." She abruptly flipped a page on her notebook

and licked the end of her pencil. "So how long has this foundation been in existence?"

"Since I was old enough to access the Davenport trust fund." When she frowned at him, he defended, "You told me you didn't care what I did with the money."

"I didn't. We had all we needed. But admit it, you weren't exactly a wealth of information about your wealth. You told me you'd 'come into some family money.' I didn't know you were filthy rich until the divorce lawyer told me. But that's beside the point. I remember something Sarah said about a scholarship her daughter won. But it was from the Davenport Foundation."

He nodded. "That one's been around longer. My father set it up."

Someone called her name, and Jack was glad for the distraction. He lifted his camera and began shooting. Of course, the first thing of interest he found to focus on was a preschool girl and her mother. After that his attention was caught by an elderly couple who walked hand in hand along the sidewalk and next, a pair of teenagers doing the same thing.

When he finally lowered his camera and looked around, he thought Cat must have deserted him. Then he spied her leaning against the trunk of a tall cottonwood tree at the entrance to Davenport Park, her arms folded, watching him with an enigmatic look on her face. Jack wanted to shift the subject of their conversation, so when he approached her, he asked, "So, are you going to enter the hot dog eating contest? Maybe there's a ladies' bracket."

"No, there is no ladies' bracket, and I do not plan to enter the hot dog eating contest. The very idea of what goes into hot dogs makes me queasy. I'd lose my lunch right there if I tried. I'm here to report the news, not make it."

"How about the three-legged race?"

"I don't have a partner."

"I'll be your partner."

"You?" She clasped a hand to her chest in mock shock. "Jack James Bond Davenport in a three-legged race?"

"Why not? I'm not wearing a tux."

She flashed a quick grin. "Now that is something I'd like to see. If you want to run home and put one on, there's time before the race starts."

Seeing the sparkle in her eyes and hearing the laughter in her voice, damned if he wasn't tempted to do just that. "I'll think about it."

Maybe she heard a note of yearning in his voice, because she shot him a sharp look. He met her gaze with a challenging stare, and after a moment, she shook her head. "Have you been drinking the mineral water, Jack?"

He laughed and returned Nic Callahan's wave. He lifted his camera and took a few shots of the Callahan foursome—five, counting the dog—then asked Cat, "What's next on the agenda?"

"Face painting, horseshoe tournament, then it's the hot dog eating contest and barbecue for the rest of us."

"What time does the baseball game start?"

"Three o'clock. Oh, look, Jack. Cam's waving at us. Shall we go see what he wants?"

"I'd rather go give him a hard time."

He did just that. It was easy to see that Cam was both pleased and embarrassed by all the attention. Jack ribbed him a bit, then took the photographs that Sarah had requested. Jack asked how Sarah's mother was doing. "I had hoped to bring her back to spend today with us since it was Cam's rescue of Mom that won the town over completely. I woke up early to drive to Gunnison to get her, but before I left the house, Keller Oaks called. She has a respiratory infection and isn't feeling up to snuff."

"I'm sorry, Sarah," Cat said. "I hope she feels better soon."

"Thank you. I do, too. They put her on antibiotics and they've assured me she'll be fine. They also cautioned me about bringing her home too often, especially before she's had a chance to settle in. She's so easily confused these days."

"No illnesses are pleasant, but I think Alzheimer's is especially sad."

"Amen," Cat agreed. She turned her head toward Jack. "Research grants."

"I'm all over it."

Cat explained, "Did y'all know that Eternity Springs's token super-rich nabob has charitable foundations that give away his money?"

"Super-rich nabob?" Cam repeated with a grin. Cat had just handed him some ammunition to return fire in the ribbing department.

"Lori won a scholarship from the Davenport Foundation," Sarah said. "It's been a lifesaver for us. Out-of-state tuition is prohibitive."

"I'm glad. I'm not involved with the day-to-day business of the Davenport Foundation, so I rarely hear details like names. I'm happy Lori won the scholarship. If she needs more help—"

"We can manage just fine," Cam interrupted, pride showing both in his stance and in his stare. "I might not own half of Colorado, but I've done all right."

"He got an offer for Adventures in Paradise Tours," Sarah said, referring to the tour boat business that Cam had built in Cairnes, Australia. "A great offer."

"Excellent news," Jack said. "I'm happy for you."

Cam gave Jack a suspicious look. "You don't happen to have anything to do with that offer, do you?"

"Nope, I have not interfered in any way. Though I'm kicking myself for not thinking of it. That's a great business opportunity. A great investment."

"I'm a believer in the owner/operator business model for a tour boat company. Need to be a hands-on captain at the wheel. I have a great staff and they've done a fine job with me being away so long, but I'm starting to detect some slippage in effort. It'll be good to get back. I'll take a couple of days at the end of the honeymoon to whip things into shape before turning it over to the new owner."

"It won't be long now," Cat said, smiling at Sarah. Cam and Sarah were taking an extended South Sea Islands honeymoon cruise.

"I can't wait."

"Where is Devin going to stay while you two are away?"

"All our friends offered to put him up, but he's chosen to live in the Timberlakes' yurt. He'll eat his meals with Ali and Mac at their house at Heartache Falls—I don't want him being completely alone, and Devin is thrilled with that arrangement."

"Ali is a wonderful cook," Cat said. "I've heard the yurt is fabulous. I bet he's as anxious for you two to go on your honeymoon as you are."

"Not a chance," Cam said glumly, sending his fiancée a martyred look.

From that, Jack gathered that the sex moratorium remained in effect. He was amused. He didn't feel a bit of sympathy for his cousin. After all, the end of Cam's dry spell was in sight. Jack's own dry spell . . . not so much.

Sarah said, "Jack, Devin has challenged Cam to compete with him in the hot-dog-eating contest. Would you please be on hand to get shots of that event?"

"I wouldn't miss it for the world."

The contest was a hit and a hoot. Everyone expected

the teenaged eating machine named Devin Murphy to win the day, but to his disgust and everyone else's amusement, when the final hot dog was consumed, Celeste Blessing was the last person standing.

Jack couldn't recall the last time he'd laughed so much. It had been one of the nicest days in memory. He'd been able to live in the moment and put his worry and grief and regrets aside. *Compartmentalizing again, but in a healthier way,* he thought.

The final item on the agenda was to be a statement from Cam to the people of Eternity Springs. What Cam didn't know—what nobody knew—was that Jack had an official bit of duty to perform himself. He had debated the best way to go about it, and finally decided this would be the most appropriate day, but the manner of the presentation would be private. He intended to take Cam aside after he made his remarks—which wouldn't last long, knowing Cam.

Mayor Hank Townsend asked the DJ to cut the music, then stepped up to the microphone. "On behalf of the town of Eternity Springs, I want to thank you all for sharing today's celebration with us. It's been fun and something I think we all needed as we officially welcome our hometown son back to Eternity Springs, to the place where he belongs."

The crowd cheered and clapped. Nic Callahan put two fingers in her mouth and whistled. Cam stepped up to the microphone. "I'm going to keep this short. On behalf of my son, Devin, and myself, I thank you all for this warm welcome. A lesson I've learned during the past few months is that it's important not to dwell on the past. A glance back now and again doesn't hurt anything, but a person needs to look forward. Life moves forward no matter what, and we miss a lot of living if we spend our time looking over our shoulder. So again, thanks for the welcome home. I look forward to life in Eternity Springs."

The crowd clapped, Cam stepped away from the microphone, and Cam Murphy Day was over. Almost.

"Hey, cousin," Jack said. "Can I talk to you for just a minute?"

"Sure." Cam gave Jack a second glance and asked, "Is everything okay?"

"Everything's fine. Just have a little family business to conduct." Jack drew Cam off to the side, stopping near the baseball field bleachers, a spot that offered a very nice view of Murphy Mountain. "It needs a little backstory, first, though."

"Then I'm going to sit down," Cam said. "My feet are tired."

The two men took a seat on the bleachers and Jack said, "This story goes back to the original friendship between your family and mine. When Lucien Davenport died, his eldest son inherited his title and with it, the entailed property. That included the contents of his library and his personal papers. My father descended from one of Lucien's younger sons. Do you remember the details about how you and I are related?"

"Your grandmother and my grandfather were siblings."

"Right. My grandmother was Shannon Murphy. She was a war bride and she never met her husband's family, which is a real shame because that could have changed everything. See, the British Davenports weren't much interested in any ties to Colorado, and with so much of the family wealth overseen by barristers, no one paid any attention until I got curious and shook the family tree."

"And I fell out," Cam said, flashing a grin.

"Swam out, more likely. The women are right about that shark's smile of yours."

"It's one of my best features."

"It's important that you know that I never did a thorough study of the ancestral library. It wasn't until Celeste contacted me looking for information after they discovered the Cellar Bride that I found the letters Daniel Murphy sent Lucien Davenport. Those letters helped establish the identity of the remains as being those of his lost fiancée."

"Yeah, yeah, yeah." Cam made a rolling motion with his hand. "You weren't kidding when you said this was a long story. Can you cut to the chase?"

"Patience, grasshopper." Jack gazed out at Murphy Mountain and continued his tale. "I need you to know that this information isn't something I have been holding out on you. I ran across these particular papers recently, and I wanted to be certain that I did the right thing with them. Honestly, this is why I wanted to get to know Sarah and Lori last spring—"

"You mean when you dated my fiancée?" Cam asked, baring his teeth in his signature smile.

Jack couldn't help but grin right back. "The woman's kiss does pack a punch."

"Would you please quit saying that?"

"But it's so entertaining." He expected he'd be throwing it out to Cam for years.

"Jackass. Get back to the point of your story, would you?"

"Right. Okay, here's the thing. I've been waiting for the right time to do this since last spring. Today is it. In fact, there's a part of me that thinks maybe the family guardian angel has been guiding events along because the timing couldn't be more perfect. So that's the backstory. Now for the action. I have something for you."

Reaching into his pocket, he withdrew an aged yellowed envelope. Words written in ink across the front in a masculine hand read: "To a righteous heir of Daniel Murphy."

"What's this?" Cam asked.

"A sealed envelope. Literally. See the wax seal? That's Montfort's seal."

"Who's Montfort?"

"Lucien Davenport. The Earl of Montfort."

"Why isn't he the Earl of Davenport?"

Jack recognized delaying tactics when he saw them. Obviously, Cam sensed his life was about to change and he wasn't certain that's what he wanted. "Just read the letter, Cam."

"You know what it says?"

"No," Jack said, exasperated. "Lucien didn't make a Xerox copy in 1892. It came with instructions to me as Lucien Davenport's heir, so I know some of it, but apparently, your letter reveals a big secret. You see that the seal hasn't been broken. I admit I'm very curious."

"Huh." Cam broke the seal on the envelope and removed three sheets of paper. He scanned the first page and half of the second, then looked at Jack. "The girls are going to be so jealous. They've been trying to solve this mystery for some time."

"What mystery?"

Wordlessly, Cam handed over the first two sheets. Jack read the neatly written words until Cam distracted him with a muttered epithet. "What's this b.s.?"

Ah. He'd read to the heart of the letter, obviously.

Cam lifted his gaze from the page and gave Jack a sharp look. "I don't get this. 'The Mountain is yours once again.' What does it mean?"

"It isn't clear?"

"No. It sounds like the Davenports are giving the Murphys the mountain. Murphy Mountain. That can't be right."

"No, it's not. What I'm doing as the Davenport heir is

ending the lease. The ownership of the mountain never changed."

Cam gawked at him. "I'm no Eternity Springs history expert, but even I know that Daniel Murphy drank away his fortune and sold Murphy Mountain when he was in dire straits."

"That's what everyone believed happened, but it's not what really happened. According to the information in the instructions letter to me that accompanied the letter to you, my ancestor owed your ancestor his life. Apparently, Daniel Murphy and Harry Cavanaugh pulled Lucien Davenport from a mine cave-in shortly before they made the Silver Miracle strike. So when Daniel needed financial help, Lucien was happy to oblige. He wanted to give Daniel Murphy money outright."

"Let me guess. Murphy was a proud Irish drunk and wouldn't take charity."

"Exactly. So, he believed he sold Lucien his mountain, but the earl had the paperwork written in such a way that it was a lease, not a deed."

"This whole thing blows my mind. I can't quite take it in and . . . Wait a minute." Cam's head came up. "What about Eagle's Way?"

"Technically, it's built in Waterford Valley, which always has been Davenport property."

Cam nodded, and then his eyes widened in alarm. "Holy hell. Does this mean I'll be responsible for taxes on a whole mountain?"

"Yes, but it's nothing for you to worry about. Lucien set up a trust and it's still funding expenses. It won't be a problem for you."

"But . . ." Cam rose to his feet. Shock gave way to pride. "No. No, sorry. You can't do this. That's charity and I'm no charity case."

"No, you're a head case. It's a legacy. Daniel Murphy

saved Lucien Davenport's life. Put a value on that and see who got the better deal."

"I'm a head case?" Affronted, Cam braced his hands on his hips. "You're the head case, cuz. Who here recently almost committed suicide by motorcycle?"

"I didn't—"

"Hey, you two," Sarah Reese interrupted. "What's with the serious looks?"

Jack glanced around to see Sarah approaching with Cat at her side. Cam sucked in a deep breath. His stare held Jack's, who said, "I'll make you a deal. I won't be stupid if you won't be stupid."

Cat began whistling the tune to "Impossible Dream," which made Sarah laugh as she slipped her arm through her fiancé's. Cam looked down into her eyes and the tension seemed to drain from his body. "You won't believe what Jack just gave me."

Cat gestured toward the pages Cam held in his free hand. "Those look old."

"They are old." Seeing the interest in her eyes, Jack said, "Cam, I have an idea. Since the *Eternity Times* is doing a special Cam Murphy Day edition, I think you should give Cat an exclusive interview. Let her break the story that the big mystery has been solved."

"What big mystery?" the women demanded simultaneously.

Cam nodded. "That's an excellent idea, Jack. I know that all of Sarah's friends will be interested in this. Why don't we all meet somewhere in an hour, and I'll spill the beans to everyone at once."

"At the *Times* office," Cat said. "Let's say around seven?"

"What's this about?" Sarah asked.

"Patience, my love," Cam told her. "Give Sage and Nic and Ali a call. Celeste, too."

"Give me a hint." Sarah batted her eyes at Cam.

"I don't want to spoil the surprise."

"That's okay. Go ahead and spoil it."

"No."

Sarah pouted and muttered, "Spoilsport."

"Now, if you want to revisit that decision about waiting until our wedding night . . ."

Jack interrupted. "I think Cat and I will mosey on over to the newspaper office while the two of you negotiate. See you at seven."

Once they were away from Sarah and Cam, Cat asked, "So what *is* this all about?"

From out of nowhere, a proposition similar to Cam's hovered on Jack's tongue. He bit it back. Barely. When his ex-wife reached out and slipped her arm through his, touching him voluntarily—an extraordinarily rare event—and turning warm green eyes his way, he had to bite back the suggestion again.

Literally.

EIGHT

❦

Excitement hummed in the air of the *Eternity Times* office at seven p.m., especially among the women in the group. Jack had confirmed to Cat that the letters he'd given Cam contained the answer to the mystery about how Daniel Murphy's "Lost Angel" had died and how her remains had come to be interred behind a false wall on Cavanaugh property. However, he refused to share it with Cat prior to the seven o'clock gathering, the dirty dog.

The Timberlakes and Raffertys arrived together, followed shortly by the Callahans and Cam Murphy and Sarah Reese. As they waited for Celeste to arrive, they discussed the day's events and took turns teasing Cam about having been the star of the day.

At five minutes after the hour, Celeste blew in issuing apologies for being late. "Had a minor emergency with a guest at Angel's Rest. She lost a necklace, and I helped her find it. That's why I'm running late. So, what did I miss?"

"Not a thing," Jack told her. "We waited for you."

"Thank you, dear."

Cat asked, "May I offer you something to drink, Celeste?"

"Thank you. I'd love a cup of black coffee if you have any brewed."

"We have a fresh pot."

Cat poured the coffee, then took a seat at the computer in order to directly enter her notes for the article she would write. The men made themselves comfortable leaning against the wall or the counter; Sage, Ali, and Celeste took the other two empty chairs in the room. Sarah and Nic each sat on the corner of empty desks. Once everyone was settled, Sarah said, "Okay, gentlemen, spill. What big mystery have you solved?"

Jack answered, "We know who murdered the Cellar Bride."

"I knew it!" Sarah slapped her hand against the desk. "Who?"

"Hold your horses, sweet cheeks," Cam said. "There is a story behind this, so we're going to tell it from the beginning. Jack, you're up."

Jack repeated the information he'd told Cam earlier regarding how the letter he'd given Cam that day had come into his possession. After that, Cam took up the storytelling by saying, "I'm going to read the letter to you. Okay?"

"Okay!" the women said, impatiently.

Cam opened the letter with a flourish. *The man's as much ham as shark,* Cat thought.

"To Daniel Murphy's heir. It is to my great regret that Daniel has already passed from the earthly plane as I compose this note. I would have preferred to sit down with Daniel and our friend Harry Cavanaugh to solve the problem in which I now find myself embroiled. As it is, I have made a decision based upon friendship and a similar debt owed to two different men. I beg you to understand, sir or madam, that this choice was not easily made. Enclosed, please find the letter I have recently received."

Cam shuffled the papers. On the second page, Cat

caught a glimpse of a feminine hand. Cam said, "This letter is signed Elizabeth Blaine Cavanaugh."

"Where does Elizabeth Cavanaugh fit in the family tree?" Nic asked, glancing toward Ali.

Ali thought a moment. "As I recall, Elizabeth was married to Harry Cavanaugh Senior. The one who helped found Eternity Springs. She'd be Cam's grandfather's grandmother and my grandfather's grandmother, too."

"Wait a minute," Cat said to Ali. "You are related to Jack and Cam, too?"

"My mother's maiden name was Cavanaugh."

"We can get the lineage down later," Sarah said, impatience in her tone. "Read the letter, Cam."

"Now, sweetheart, why don't—"

"If you tell me to be patient one more time, you'll live to regret it, Cam Murphy."

Again, he gave the pages a theatrical flourish, then continued, "Dear Lord Monfort."

"Who's that?" Nic asked.

"Lucien Davenport, Earl of Monfort," Cam replied.

"How do you know that detail?" Gabe added.

"Jack told me."

"Read the letter!" Cat and Sarah demanded simultaneously.

Cam continued, "I lie on my deathbed burdened by a secret I have kept for many years. As I await the arrival of my priest to hear my final confession to the Almighty, I recognize that I owe the truth to those good souls still among us who would wish to know the grievous sin I must confess. To my shame, the most important of these are already lost to this world. I have chosen not to share my admission with those he left behind because the term 'good soul' in no way refers to him."

Glancing up, Cam clarified. "The 'him' to whom she

refers, I believe, is Brendan Murphy, Daniel's son and my great-grandfather."

"I'm definitely gonna need family trees before I write this article," Cat murmured.

Cam continued, "Many years ago, after I married Harry Cavanaugh and our son, Harry Junior, was born, my family—my parents, my sisters, my younger brother— traveled to Colorado from St. Louis to see me. During that visit, my brother developed an unhealthy fascination for Miss Winifred Smith."

"Whoa," Sage said. "A brother. Did we ever know about a brother?"

"I don't recall one," Nic replied.

The women all looked at Ali, who shrugged. "I haven't investigated the Blaine genealogy. So, was the brother the killer?"

Cam picked up where he'd left off reading. "On the day that Miss Smith was to wed Daniel Murphy, my brother lost his mind. He abducted poor Miss Smith and kept her hidden in our root cellar. On the seventh day of her captivity, she managed to free herself of her bonds and she ambushed Alan when he arrived with her daily meal, hitting him over the head with a jar of pickled beets."

"Pickled beets?" Colt Rafferty muttered.

Cam's mouth twisted with a wry grin and he continued to read. "My brother went crazed. As Miss Smith fled for the stairs, he pulled his pistol and shot her dead."

Nic commented, "The theater group will need to rewrite their play for next summer's production."

"Pauline Roosevelt will be thrilled," Ali added. "As the unofficial town historian, she's never approved of the fictional account."

"There's more," Cam said. "Do you want to hear it?"

"I do," Celeste said, both her voice and her expression unusually subdued. "I hope Elizabeth Blaine offers an explanation of why she allowed dear Daniel to suffer the slings and arrows of suspicion for a crime committed by another."

Sarah's brow furrowed. "Dear Daniel?"

Celeste lifted her shoulders in a shrug, but she kept her gaze focused on Cam, who continued to read. "My brother was beside himself. He wasn't an evil man, truly he wasn't, but his unrequited love for Miss Smith was a poison within him. Once he realized what he had done, he came to me and confessed and begged me for my help in keeping his secret.

"I didn't want to see my brother hanged. I feared the damage to our family reputation, damage to my children. Eternity Springs was at times a cruel place, and in those days, Daniel Murphy was beloved. It is to my great regret that I acceded to my brother's request. Even worse, I pulled my husband into our conspiracy of secrecy and in doing so, caused him to betray his friend. With my Harry's help, we saw Miss Smith laid to rest in the place where she died, along with a symbol of the betrayal we committed."

Cam glanced up. "Wasn't there a stack of silver bars found with the Cellar Bride? And that's where Celeste gets the silver for her Angel's Rest medals?"

"Yes, she was entombed with thirty bars of silver," Ali said. "So, the mystery is solved. I figured the killer had to be connected to the Cavanaugh family in some way since she was found in the Cavanaugh House root cellar."

"What else does Elizabeth have to say, Cameron?" Celeste asked.

"Not much. I read the important stuff. She apologizes and asks for Lucien's forgiveness, then tells him to use the information as he sees fit. That's not all the news in this letter, though. Jack, you want to tell them the rest of it? I'm still having trouble wrapping my head around it."

Jack nodded and Cam handed him the letter penned in Jack's ancestor's hand. He read, "We will never know if learning the truth about his Angel's disappearance would have changed the path of Daniel's life. He remained a troubled soul until his death, and unfortunately, his son, Brendan, followed in his father's footsteps. My inquiries into the state of affairs in Eternity Springs has revealed that serious discord exists between the current Cavanaugh and Murphy heirs. It is for that reason that I have chosen to keep secret for now the news of the fate of Winifred Smith, Daniel's Lost Angel. I fear that were the truth to be revealed, history might repeat itself in that passions may overcome good sense and destroy lives. Thus, I have charged my own heir with the task of monitoring the situation in Eternity Springs and revealing the truth in its entirety at the appropriate time, to the appropriate person."

Cam interjected, "Note the 'truth in its entirety' part. It's important."

Jack nodded, met Cat's gaze, then finished reading the letter aloud. "I was with Daniel Murphy when he first set eyes upon the land that came to be known as Murphy Mountain. I watched his dream being born. He loved his mountain, he loved the town that he helped build. He loved the people who settled there.

"With the delivery of this letter into the hands of a righteous heir of Daniel Murphy, our family returns what we have held in safekeeping and preserved for your family in the name of friendship. The Mountain is yours once again."

It took the gathering a few minutes and further explanation by both Jack and Cam to grasp the news, and then the office erupted into excited questions and conversation. Observing the exchange, Cat noticed that Celeste grew quietly teary-eyed. Concerned, she approached her and asked, "Celeste, is something wrong?"

"Oh, no. Nothing is wrong, dear. Everything is finally right." A beautiful smile blossomed across her aged face as she added, "I'm so happy for Daniel."

Daniel, not Cam. Cat thought about the remark a little while later as people took their leave. Once only she and Jack remained in the office, she voiced her concern. "Celeste seemed a bit confused tonight, did you notice?"

"I noticed she was distracted," Jack replied. "She did a lot of work preparing for today. It was obviously important to her. Maybe she overdid."

"I hope that's all it is." Cat glanced down at her computer, mentally arranging her front page, wondering where she should start. She had a special section to put out. It was the coolest thing ever, but almost overwhelming.

"So, what do you want me to do?"

"You'll stay for a while?"

"Sure. I want to see this project through. This is my family heritage, and that makes it interesting to me. Besides, all this makes it seem like Cam is more closely related to me than he really is, and frankly, it's nice to have a family connection. I'm short on those."

Cat was inordinately pleased to have the company. To have *Jack's* company. She'd had fun with him today.

Her heart gave a little lurch at that thought. Quickly she pressed on. "We'll build the front page first, so I need appropriate shots for that. What do you have for me?"

For the next two hours they worked both together and independently. She asked his opinion and he gave it. Sometimes she took his suggestions and sometimes she ignored them. She had intended to mock up the front page and then quit for the night, but when the page was done, she was enjoying herself too much to stop. What she and Jack built together—six pages of news, town history, Murphy family facts, frivolity, and fun—made her proud.

Now, as she stared at the choice of photos of the face painting booth that he'd given her, her gaze was caught by a picture of little Meg Callahan painted up like a kitten, complete with a headband sporting kitten ears. Her smile was big and bright. Her eyes sparkled like sunshine reflecting off the waters of Hummingbird Lake. She wasn't looking at the camera, but toward something beyond the reach of the lens. "Who was she smiling at?"

"Her dad."

Cat heard a note of longing in his voice and it caused her heart to twist. She glanced up at him. *Not just longing,* she thought. *Yearning, too.* Acting on instinct, she reached for his hand. "Lauren would have made a darling kitten, don't you think?"

He subtly stiffened, then sent her a sharp look that turned searching once he realized that she wasn't on the attack. She saw his Adam's apple bob as he swallowed hard. "She'd have made a beautiful kitten."

Jack's thumb brushed Cat's knuckles. "Before today, I can't recall taking photographs of people except for surveillance purposes. Well, except for you. I took photographs of you."

"You took lots of photographs of me."

"Yeah." His lips lifted in a knowing smile and he shifted his gaze away from hers. Immediately, Cat knew what he was thinking about. "Tell me you didn't keep those photographs, Jack Davenport!"

He recited as if by rote. "I didn't keep those photographs."

She caught her breath. Heat flushed her skin. "You lying dog."

Jack broke into a full-fledged grin. "Now, Cat, those photos are some of my most prized possessions."

Chagrin battled with embarrassment and a ridiculous sense of, well, prideful pleasure. Jack had taken the photos in question on a private beach on a private Caribbean island he'd had access to due to his job during the second month of their marriage, when he'd finally managed to steal time away for a honeymoon.

Cat awakened to the sound of the surf rolling against the white sand and for a long moment, she lay tangled among the luxurious sheets with her eyes closed, soaking in the peace. When she finally summoned the energy to move, she stretched her arm toward the other side of the bed. Empty. No surprise. Each day during their weeklong honeymoon, Jack had awakened early and disappeared into the house's office before she stirred. Cat spent the mornings by herself, running on the beach, reading and writing in her journal, but he usually joined her for lunch and declared the office off-limits for the rest of the afternoon.

She dressed for her run and found coffee waiting for her in the kitchen—bless the man. She indulged in half a cup along with a small breakfast bar, then exited the house to enjoy the morning. A salty sea breeze blew gently off the water and she stood and stretched, listening to the call of the gulls as they soared and dived. She felt good, having slept like a rock last night, deliciously tired after a long, sweet interlude of lovemaking.

Now her body hummed with energy, so when she finished her stretches and took to the beach, she ran longer and farther than was her norm until she rounded the point and arrived at the turquoise waters of the island's isolated lagoon. The inviting lagoon. Cat was hot and sweaty. The lagoon looked cool and refreshing.

What the heck. The household help lived on the other side of the island, and when guests were in residence, they only worked from ten until two. No one was around to see her. Besides, what good was honeymoon-

ing on a private island if you didn't take advantage of the privacy?

In the broad daylight, feeling downright wicked, Cat stripped off her clothes and went skinny-dipping. As a city girl with minimal experience with isolation in Mother Nature, it was a new experience for her, and it took her a few minutes to relax. Silly, really, considering that the bikini she'd bought for her honeymoon was the next thing to naked. Yesterday, Jack had wanted to make love on the beach, but she'd been too shy. A girl didn't go from modest to wanton overnight.

But this was a good start.

Cat stretched with contentment as she floated on her back in the blue lagoon. Maybe if Jack were here now, she'd risk being risqué. If Jack were here now, rather than in the office working with her mother. It was a sad thing for a bride to have to compete with her mother on her honeymoon.

"Stop it," she scolded herself. She wouldn't go there. She'd promised herself she wouldn't let herself wander down that rocky path. Maybe she wished that she had her new husband's full attention, but she had gone into this marriage with her eyes wide open. It wouldn't be fair to Jack or their marriage for her to backtrack on the decision she'd made when she accepted his proposal. She had to share her husband with the U.S. of A. At least he fought the good fight from a building in Washington rather than on a battlefield. Cat rolled onto her stomach and swam the disturbing thoughts away.

Twenty minutes later, as she emerged from the water, the clicks of a camera shutter warned her she was no longer alone.

Years later, in a hundred-year-old building in a Colorado mountain town, the click of a camera shutter brought her back to the present. At some point while she'd been lost in the past, Jack had picked up his camera and started shooting her.

Click click click click click.

Cat licked her lips. "What are you doing?"

Slowly, he lowered the Nikon. "You looked so . . . wistful. What were you thinking about, Cat?"

She drew in a shuddering breath, then confessed. "You. Us."

He set down his camera and took her into his arms. "Me, too."

And then his lips touched hers, and with a soft sigh, she let him in.

Yearning washed through her like snowmelt in spring. His fingers tangled in her hair as one hand cupped her head and the free one skimmed up and down her spine. Cat quivered and lost herself in the moment, in the wood-smoke scent clinging to his shirt, in the taste of spicy mustard lingering on his tongue, in the oh-so-familiar drag of calloused fingers that had found their way beneath her shirt to stroke her bare skin.

This was Jack. Her Jack. The only man she'd ever loved. The lover who had left her empty and alone in the face of tragedy.

But he had been empty and alone, too. He'd just hidden it so completely that she'd never seen it.

How she had missed him. Missed this. Being touched by Jack, held by Jack. Kissed by this man whose kiss excited her like nobody else's.

Jack deepened the kiss, his tongue twining with hers. She lifted her hands and laced her fingers behind his neck. Melting against him, she let the current of sensation carry her away, seduced by the memory and the moment.

She lost all track of time. Arousal sizzled along her nerves as her breasts swelled and that hollow, achy feeling blossomed from her core. When he released her mouth and trailed heated kisses along her jaw to that sensitive spot on her neck just below her ear, she jolted. Shuddered.

Wondered what the heck she was doing.

He finally lifted his head and those mesmerizing blue eyes bored into hers. "Cat?"

She knew what he was asking. Knew how she wanted to respond. A sense of self-preservation held her back. "I think it would be lovely, but foolish."

"What's wrong with foolish?"

"Foolish has its time and place, but I'm not sure that time and place is now." She waited a beat, then asked, "Are you?"

Following a pregnant pause, he closed his eyes, then dropped his forehead to hers. "I guess not."

"I don't know what we are doing here."

"I know what I want to do," he murmured, a groan in his voice.

Reluctantly, she stepped away from him. "I enjoyed spending time with you today, Jack. It was fun. But this wasn't something I anticipated, and frankly, I need to think about this. If we take the next step, then I want to do it with my eyes wide open."

"You always did like watching." When she chided him with a look, he caught her hand and brought it to his mouth for a kiss. "As much as I hate to say it, I think that's probably a good plan for us both."

Cat tried to tell herself she was glad he hadn't pressed her. "Okay, then. Well. Um. I guess I'll get back to work."

"What can I do to help now?"

Leave. "I think we're set with the photos. You should probably go check on Fred, don't you think? Won't he be needing his dinner?"

He gave her a knowing look. "You trying to get rid of me, Blackburn?"

She forced a smile. "I need a little space, Davenport."

He packed up his camera bag and headed for the door. There he paused and glanced back at her. "Do you have dinner plans tomorrow night?"

Her heart stuttered. Was he asking her out on a date? "No, I don't have any dinner plans tomorrow night."

"I heard a rumor that Ali was going Moroccan tomorrow at the Yellow Kitchen. I expect her lamb tagine will be superb. Would you like to join me?"

Something light and hopeful blossomed in her chest. "Just to clarify, Mr. Davenport. Are you asking me on a dinner date?"

"Yes, I am."

"In that case, yes, I'd love to go to dinner with you. Thanks for the invitation."

"I'll pick you up tomorrow. Around seven?"

"That will be lovely. Good night, Jack."

"Good night, Cat. Sleep well."

Of course, she didn't sleep well. She tossed and turned for hours before she slept, and once she did sleep, she dreamed—of rolling naked on a Caribbean beach with her husband, the love of her life.

Jack thought the Saturday night date went very well, and when he walked her to the door of Nightingale Cottage, he kissed her thoroughly, then asked, "So, are you still thinking?"

She answered affirmatively.

As he climbed into his cold and lonely bed that night, he did suffer a few pangs of doubt. Was he making a big mistake? Was pursuing her the right thing to do? Yes, he loved her, but he'd always loved her and he'd been getting along relatively well without having her in his life the last few years. Perhaps he did take too many physical risks since nobody waited at home for him. Melinda had taken him to task for the dangerous choices he'd made in recent months. She'd be happy if he took to avoiding such situations because he had someone in his life who cared for him again. Except, considering that that someone would be Cat, maybe not.

It could be argued that getting involved again with Cat could be the riskiest move he could make. What if he offered her his heart again and she refused to take it? He'd rather take a steel blade to it than endure that sort of pain.

The next afternoon he invited her to go sailing with him on Hummingbird Lake, and again, at the end of the date, in response to his question and his kiss, she remained committed to "thinking." They spent part of each day together for the next week, sometimes on official dates, other times as reporter and photographer as she continued researching historical sites for her *Eternity Times* series.

The Cam Murphy Day special edition had proved to be a hit, selling out completely. Cat gave credit to the visual appeal that Jack's photographs added. He claimed the quality of the writing did the trick. They both recognized that everyone in town wanted the details of the Cellar Bride / Murphy Mountain news, and the special section could have been written in pencil on a Big Chief tablet and it would have sold out. Still, when he loudly gave her praise at the Mocha Moose sandwich shop while they ate lunch yesterday, she'd visibly preened.

A week after Cam's big day, Cat and Jack visited the original Silver Miracle Mine. The Eternity Springs development committee had the mine site listed for possible restoration and development as a tourist attraction, but for now it remained an isolated, all but forgotten scar upon an otherwise beautiful spot. And yet, Jack couldn't deny the allure of weathered timber and multicolored sludge, all that was left of the dreams of riches that had lured men into these mountains by the thousands in the second half of the nineteenth century. His own family history swirled through his thoughts as he shot photos of the place where Lucien Davenport had struck it rich, and Cat chattered about historical details she had gleaned as she researched her article. But when he spied a pair of red foxes scampering across a wildflower-dotted meadow below the mine, imaginings of the past faded away. Jack switched to his telephoto lens and began shooting.

He was excited. Though he kept it to himself, he had a "bag list" of animals he wanted to photograph in the wild before he died, and red foxes were one of them. As a result, he was careless with his equipment, setting the camera bag down in the middle of the trail. Cat was busy making notes about the mine and didn't notice that he had veered off the trail. She stepped right on top of the bag and Jack heard the sickening crunch of a lens breaking.

"Oh, no," she said with dismay when he removed a shattered wide-angle lens. "I'm so sorry, Jack."

"My fault. It was a poor place to leave my stuff."

"I'll replace it. Just let me know what—"

"I've been wanting to get a new one anyway. Tell you what. When you are through here, why don't we drive on over to Gunnison? We can stop by the camera shop, then have lunch in that Mexican restaurant Nic and Sarah rave about."

"That's an excellent idea."

During the drive, Jack sensed Cat's gaze upon him. Glancing over at her, he saw that she studied him with a considering look. "Thinking, Catherine?"

She rolled her eyes. "You have a one-track mind, Davenport. I'm thinking, but not about that. I'm wondering what's going on with you and your job. You don't appear to be working very much."

"I'm putting in the majority of my hours overnight since I don't have anything better to do."

"Now you're whining."

Actually, he was telling the truth. The project currently assigned to him had required a conference call at three a.m. Colorado time each of the past four nights. He'd taken to turning in early, then getting up for the call and staying up. Usually, he had put in a full day by the time he wandered into Eternity Springs to spend time with his ex-wife.

He had to make a trip tomorrow and he knew he should tell her about it. In the old days, she'd get quiet and sulky at similar news. In the old days, he'd wait until the last minute to tell her. Curious about her reaction now, he decided that now was as good a time as any to find out. Casually, he said, "I will be working the next few days. I have a trip planned."

She shot him a sharp look. "Tell me you're not going to Mexico."

Jack winced. It was the first time anyone had mentioned that idea to him since he ditched his crutches. "No, I'm not going to Mexico. I wasn't exactly thinking rationally then. I'm not planning a crusade against the cartels. Don't worry."

"I wasn't worried," she was quick to fire back. "Well, maybe a little worried. I figured it was the drugs talking, but you never know. You do know, don't you, that his death wasn't your fault? You didn't fail your friend."

"Sure, I failed him, but as much as I'd like to go to Mexico and kick some ass, it's not a rational plan."

"I'm sure you've spoken with your friend's widow. How is she doing?"

"She's hanging in there. She's strong." She'd called him the day before yesterday to thank him for the trust fund he'd established for her daughter.

"Good." Cat opened her mouth to say more, then shut it.

When she remained silent, he prodded, "What?"

"I know better than to ask. It's a work-related question. You never answer work-related questions."

"Try me."

"Okay, I will." She folded her arms. "On a scale of one to ten, what's the danger level?"

"Fifteen. I have a meeting on Capitol Hill."

She laughed, as he had hoped. Because he didn't want to put a damper on the mood with any more talk about Washington, he didn't mention the appointment he had with the detective assigned to her case or the meeting he'd called with his private investigators. No matter how easy technology made communication these days, nothing beat face-to-face ass-chewings. Almost a month had passed since the bombing. Somebody should have caught the bastard by now.

In Gunnison, he made the camera shopkeeper's day with a long list of purchases, then enjoyed the simple, sensual pleasure of sharing a delicious meal with a beautiful woman. He coaxed her into indulging in a sopapilla for dessert, and was so distracted by the way she licked honey from her fingers that he totally missed the question she asked. "I'm sorry. What did you say?"

"A one-track mind," she repeated, a gleam of amusement in her eyes. "I asked if you'd mind if we stopped by Keller Oaks. Sarah has asked that any time her friends are over here that we drop in and check on her mother."

"I got that memo, too, so I'd planned on it."

They entered the long-term care facility shortly after two and found Ellen Reese in the music room participating in a sing-along that was wrapping up as they arrived. She didn't recognize Jack, which wasn't a surprise since he'd only met her a few times. Though she'd never met Cat, she latched on to her like a long-lost friend, calling her "Honey." It wasn't long before Jack figured out that "Honey" was Ellen's method of compensation.

She thought she was supposed to know who Cat was, and this way her way of hiding it.

In her late sixties, Ellen Reese remained an attractive woman, trim and short of stature like her daughter, Sarah. She had a nice voice, a lovely smile, and a sadly vacant look in her pretty blue eyes. *Alzheimer's is an awful disease,* Jack thought as they made their way outside to the enclosed courtyard. They sat for a bit talking about the flowers and the hummingbirds at the feeders until a uniformed attendant approached with news that bingo was about to begin and that "Miss Ellen likes her bingo."

They said good-bye and started to leave when Cat hesitated. "Jack, would you mind if we took a little more time here? I'd like to speak with the director if she has a few minutes."

"That's fine with me." Then, because he knew her, he asked, "Did you see a problem?"

"No. Not at all. I'm very impressed with Keller Oaks. Something arrived in my email, though, about assisted living facilities, and since Sarah has shared her experience with her mom with me, the subject caught my eye. I thought that since we're here, it wouldn't hurt to ask a few questions."

Cat knocked just below a nameplate on the door that read LOUISE GALLATIN, EXECUTIVE DIRECTOR. She introduced herself as Catherine Davenport and him as her friend Jack, and said she wrote for the Eternity Springs newspaper. "I know that Sarah Reese is so pleased with her and Ellen's experience at Keller Oaks and she feels lucky to have found you."

"Ellen's transition here has been relatively easy," Louise said, smiling. "We do try hard to make it so, and I'm so glad that the Reese family is happy with our efforts."

"They definitely are. After speaking with Sarah, and

mindful of our aging population, I am considering doing an in-depth article about elder care options, including potential problems a family should be aware of as they begin their search for the right facility. Would you be willing to speak with me on the record? Not today, but sometime in the next few weeks?"

"I'd be happy to speak with you. This is a soapbox issue for me, to be honest. If you're willing to let me speak off the record, I have some particular warnings, too."

Cat leaned forward. "Really?"

Louise proceeded to relay her suspicions about mismanagement at an assisted living facility in the area. "They don't physically mistreat the residents or anything like that. This is more subtle, and they're very good at it. They ingratiate themselves with the residents and earn their trust. Then, they strike."

"What do they do?" Cat asked.

"They steal the residents' money." Louise squared her shoulders and declared, "They call it an investment club, but I know in my bones that it's nothing more than a Ponzi scheme."

Jack asked, "Why haven't you contacted the authorities? They can check them out."

"I actually did make a call to the state authorities who have jurisdiction," Louise replied. "They said that they'd look into it, but I have my doubts anything will come of it. They're overworked and I have no proof to give them. None. Just the fact that my instincts tell me it's a little too good to be true. Perhaps if you included something about it in your article, we could get some traction for an investigation."

Interest flared in Cat's eyes. Jack had seen that look before. Next would come a barrage of questions.

His prediction proved correct, and forty minutes passed before they finally took their leave of Keller Oaks. Cat remained quiet on the return trip to Eternity Springs while he debated the intelligence of cautioning her against diving into an investigation and putting herself at risk of discovery. Experience had taught him that sometimes, suggesting to Cat Blackburn that she take one path was sure to send her down another. That's why he began cautiously. "So, are you going to look into it?"

She gave him a blank look. "Look into what?"

"The investment scam."

"Oh." She gave her head a shake. "I don't know. I have to think about it. Until this whole thing with the firebomb is behind me, it's probably better I don't get too involved in any investigation."

Hallelujah. "So if not the investment scheme, what were you thinking about just now that had you looking so serious?"

Cat exhaled a loud sigh. "I was thinking about Ellen and Sarah and the mother-daughter relationship. Nic told me that Sarah fought hard to keep her mother at home as long as possible. They had their secrets and their differences, but at the heart of things, they were close."

Ah. Now he understood. "You were thinking about Melinda."

"I find it sad that my husband has always had a closer relationship with my mother than I have."

Her use of the term "husband" rather than "ex-husband" did not go unnoticed by Jack, but he focused on the substance of her comment rather than the detail. This wasn't the first time she'd made such a claim, and honestly, he couldn't argue with her. Melinda Blackburn was a peculiar duck. Brilliant, without a doubt. Driven, like no other person he'd ever met. In a crisis, the woman had the proverbial balls of steel. But in all the years he'd known her, he'd never seen her comfortable with the maternal side of her personality or, as a result, with her daughter. Still, he knew one thing about Melinda Blackburn that was undeniable. "Your mother loves you, Catherine."

She questioned that with an arch of her brow.

"You know she does."

"She didn't call me after my dining room exploded."

"She sent me."

"And that was an act of love?" When he chided her with a look, she pursed her lips into a pout. "Oh, all right. Yes, I know she loves me, but my mother and I will never be close the way Sarah and Ellen were. I know that sounds whiny, especially to someone like you who lost your mother way too young, and that makes my whining sound even worse. I thought I'd left this behind me a long time ago, and for the most part, I have. It's just that every so often, it gets to me. I wish I had as good a relationship with her as I do with my dad."

"I understand, and I don't think you're whiny."

"Thank you for that, Jack."

"You're welcome." He waited a beat, then asked, "So, will you take care of my dog while I'm away?"

She laughed. "Sure. I'll be happy to."

They passed the rest of the drive in relative silence. Jack's thoughts turned to tomorrow's trip. He didn't look forward to being grilled by the Intelligence committee chair. That never was much fun.

However, it would be a cakewalk compared to the meeting he had scheduled with Cat's mother.

Thoughts of Cat and her mother and their relationship continued to swirl through Jack's mind after he dropped his ex-wife off at Nightingale Cottage and decided to take a detour by the mineral springs before heading back to Eagle's Way.

Though he'd never admit it to another soul, he still felt deep tissue bruises from his motorcycle accident, and the hot springs worked the best magic on them that he'd found. He was pleased to see only a handful of visitors enjoying the pools, so he stopped his car, grabbed the swim trunks that he kept in his car for this very purpose, and headed over to have a soak.

The heat penetrated his skin like a song. A smelly song, but a song nonetheless. He reflected on the day spent with Cat. It had been a good day. He'd enjoyed himself and he thought Cat had enjoyed herself, too. Her eyes had certainly sparkled when she talked to the director at Keller Oaks. The enchiladas at lunch had left her groaning in delight. Her good mood had even lasted after he mentioned his trip.

The thought of his trip brought his mind back around to Melinda. It was too bad, he thought, that she and Cat couldn't put their mother-daughter relationship to soak in an Angel's Rest hot springs pool. It certainly could use the healing.

"Hello, Jack." He opened his eyes to see Celeste sitting on the rim of the pool, the hems of her jeans rolled up to just below her knees. Her bare feet dangled in the steaming mineral pool.

"Hi, Celeste." Nodding toward her feet, he asked, "Are your dogs barking?"

She laughed. "Oh, my. I haven't heard that old saw since I left the Carolinas, but yes, my feet are killing me. I climbed the trail above Heartache Falls today and I totally overdid it. How about you? Weren't you and Cat going sightseeing today?"

"We went up to the Silver Miracle Mine." He told her about their visit to Keller Oaks to see Ellen Reese, then mentioned he was leaving town for a few days. "I still don't think anyone could have tracked Cat Blackburn of Washington, D.C., to Catherine Davenport of Eternity Springs. I don't expect trouble, and Cam said he'd keep an eye on her while I'm gone, but I'd appreciate it if you'd keep your eyes open, too."

"Of course I will," Celeste said. "I do have a soft spot in my heart for your Cat. She is an advocate, isn't she? For the truth. For those less fortunate than her. For the good Lord's four-legged creatures. She puts herself on the side of the angels, doesn't she?"

He nodded and spoke a truth he'd recognized a long time ago. "She's like her mother, more than either one of them would ever admit." Scowling into the steam rising from the surface of the pool, he asked, "Do you have a daughter, Celeste?"

A shadow passed over her face. "No, unfortunately, I was never blessed with children. It is one of my life's biggest regrets."

Jack felt words he rarely ever spoke bubble up inside him, but he repressed the mention of Lauren. What was it about being around Celeste Blessing that gave him the impulse to blabber?

Instead, he focused on an issue he could do something about. "On our way home from Gunnison, Cat talked about Sarah and her mother. I think Cat regrets that she's not closer to her own mother. I'll be seeing her mom while I'm away, and I'm trying to think of the best way to encourage her to be open to it, too. What do you think a mother wants from her adult daughter, Celeste?"

"Why, that's easy. At the heart of everything, only one thing matters. We all want to love and to be loved and to be secure in that love."

"Melinda and Cat have the first two covered. It's the third that gives them trouble."

"Perhaps they need an angel to work on their case."

"Do you think you could help?"

She laughed. "I'm not Cat Blackburn's angel, Jack. That role is reserved for you. From what Gabe and Cam have shared, you've played that role in real life for other troubled souls, haven't you?"

"Me? An angel?" Jack thought of all the destruction

he'd instigated, all the people he'd killed. Every one of them had needed killing, but still. He was nobody's angel. "Maybe you should move away from the pools. I think the sulfur smell is getting to you."

She patted him on the head as if he were a child. "Don't sell yourself short. However, I say that with a caveat. Just because you rescue others, you shouldn't attempt to elevate yourself, either."

Jack didn't follow that. His puzzlement must have shown on his face, because she added, "The role of Savior is taken. You don't have to save the world, Jack Davenport."

"That's about as silly a thing as anyone has ever said to me. Maybe the reason I like these mineral springs so much is because the smell of sulfur reminds me of home— the old fire and brimstone."

Celeste's laughter pealed like church bells.

N I N E

᭢

Five days after her trip to Gunnison with Jack, Cat sat in a lounge chair on the bank of Angel Creek with Fred sprawled on the ground beside her. Putting the finishing touches on what had become a six-part story about the history of Eternity Springs for the *Times*, Cat was a happy woman. It was a gorgeous summer afternoon in the Colorado Rockies, and at that particular moment, Cat couldn't think of anyplace she'd rather be, or, for that matter, anything she'd rather be doing.

She was proud of the work and enjoyed the sense of satisfaction she felt upon finishing it. She realized she'd missed that. She'd learned something from it, too: Investigation into something besides criminal activity could ring her chimes as well.

She saved her file and opened her Web browser in order to email the story to Emily Hall, who had returned to Eternity Springs harried and stressed from dealing with her family emergency. Her brother's wife had packed up and left him and their three young children, and her brother was floundering. After hearing the story, Cat felt sorry for everyone involved.

She opened her email, sent off her work, then browsed her in-box. She had something from her old boss at the *Washington Post*. Curious, she read it first. He wanted her to call him as soon as possible.

"I wonder what this is about," she murmured aloud.

Fred's ears perked and he lifted his head. Soulful brown eyes seemed to scold her for interrupting his nap. She absently scratched behind his ears and considered ignoring the request. Did she want to allow that world to intrude on this one? If history were any indication, a phone call to Douglas Lowery was bound to disturb her peace.

"I shouldn't act rashly, should I?" she observed to Fred. "Look what happened last time I acted before thinking an idea through. I got saddled with you."

Was that reproach she spied in his eyes?

"Oh, stop it. You know I didn't mean it. I'm glad I offered to dog sit." Fred had proved to be good company, and with him around, she didn't miss Jack.

Liar.

Okay, maybe she did miss Jack. Maybe she caught herself listening for the phone or checking her email while glancing out the window at Nightingale Cottage to see if the car she heard on the Angel's Rest road might belong to him. The man's "few" days away had stretched to five with no sign of return imminent. It bothered her that she was bothered by it. Jack had wormed his way back into her brain in less than a month. What was wrong with her? Been here, done this. Jack had left. That's what he did. Why in the world was she wasting her time and energy missing him?

In order to avoid that question, she reached into the computer backpack lying at the foot of the lounge chair and dug around for her phone. She dialed her old boss's number from memory.

"Hello, Douglas. It's Cat Blackburn."

"Where the hell are you?" Douglas Lowery demanded.

"I'm in hiding." Sort of, she silently added, lifting a hand to wave at Celeste as she walked toward the footbridge spanning Angel Creek.

"Yeah, yeah, yeah," he grumbled. "That's no excuse. Especially not now."

"What's so special about now?"

"What, they don't have news wherever you're hiding?"

Cat sat up straight. Her heartbeat quickened. "What are you talking about?"

"Not what. Who. I'm talking about Bret Barnes."

Cat drew a blank at the name. "Who is Bret Barnes?"

"So you haven't heard? I can't believe that. You must be out in the boonies, but hey, that works for me. Bret Barnes is the scumbag who bombed your house. They finally caught him."

Relief flowed through Cat and she slumped back against the lounge chair. Funny, she hadn't realized she was still so tense about this.

"You will give me an exclusive, right?"

She ignored that and asked, "When did this happen?"

"This morning. So, where have you been hiding?"

She almost answered that one, then reconsidered. The last thing she wanted was for the media to descend on Eternity Springs and for it to be her fault. She'd heard plenty of complaints from the local citizenry about when Hollywood came to town in the guise of a television chef. "I'm out west. What do you know about Bret Barnes?"

"Hey, just who is doing the interview here?"

She couldn't help but grin. "Quid pro quo, Doug."

He sighed heavily. "Okay, but I want something you don't give to somebody else. Deal?"

"Deal."

"The guy is a nutjob fan of the singer you fingered in the dogfight ring."

"A fan?"

"When he missed with you and you disappeared, he went after someone else."

Oh, no. She'd been afraid of that. "Who? Was anybody hurt?"

"He targeted a woman named Pemberton. Jane Pemberton."

Cat's blood ran cold. She'd expected him to name one of the prosecutors or law enforcement personnel involved in the case, not her friend who headed the dog rescue group, Paw Pals.

"And no," he continued. "Nobody was hurt. He didn't get as far into the process as he did with you."

"Give me details."

"A private investigator turned up his name. Followed him around for a while. Turned up some evidence that proved Barnes had been casing the Pemberton residence."

A private investigator, or one Jack's guys?

"Guy's apparently a loon," Douglas continued. "When the cops executed a search warrant, they had more than enough evidence to arrest him. They picked him up, and get this . . . he sang his confession."

"You're kidding."

"Nope. Sang it to the melody of the tune the singer won his big contest with. According to my source in the department, Barnes blames you for the fact that the singer didn't get the lead role in next year's remake of South Pacific."

Cat couldn't help it. She started to giggle. She almost didn't hear the details when the newspaperman relayed Bret Barnes's age, hometown, and other salient facts, then demanded a statement—an exclusive statement—from Cat. "Something you don't write on your blog," he added. "Like, the circumstances of how you left town. One rumor going around town is that somebody snatched you and made a ransom demand to your father."

Oh, dear. "That's ridiculous. I left town with a friend of my family, and you can quote me on that."

She gave him some halfway decent quotes and enough details to satisfy her personal definition of "quid pro quo" without revealing anything that might compromise either her whereabouts or the facts surrounding her departure. When a click indicated another incoming call, she lowered the phone long enough to check the number. *Jack.*

"I have to go, Douglas. I have another call."

But as she moved her thumb to connect with her ex-husband, her ex-boss spat out words that made her freeze. "Wait! Don't hang up. I want to offer you your old job back."

Cat didn't hang up. She dropped the phone.

"She needs to hear this from you, Melinda," Jack said as he pulled his cell phone from his pocket.

"Ridiculous." Melinda Blackburn shuffled some papers on the desk of her home office. "The information is what is important. Not the delivery of it. You know that, Jack."

Jack bit back his exasperation. What he knew was that Cat needed to learn the news about Barnes immediately, and she should hear it from her mother.

Sure, he'd been the one to have all of Cat's friends and many of her acquaintances placed under surveillance, but once his hired guys came up with Barnes, Melinda had been the driving force behind taking him down. She'd been the one who called in markers to make sure that cops acted on the tips that surveillance developed. While Jack had been busy spinning stories for politicians, Melinda had closed in on Bret Barnes.

Sure, Jack had been the one to pay him a visit and . . . coax . . . information from him, but he would never have had the chance had Melinda not set the ball in motion. She went to great lengths to protect her daughter. Why couldn't she let Cat see how much she truly cared?

"The delivery of information will be important to Cat," he responded as the phone began to ring.

Melinda checked her watch. "I have a meeting."

"Be wild. Go late."

She drew back and looked at him. Jack didn't speak to Melinda that way, but times were changing. He was changing. Melinda and Cat needed to change their relationship, and this was a perfect opportunity to start. He didn't flinch as she gave him one of her disapproving stares, unwittingly reminding him of her daughter. "I don't have time now. I'll call her this evening."

Jack shifted his stance so that he stood between Melinda and the door. Planting his feet, he decided that this time, under these circumstances, if Melinda Blackburn chose to leave the room without speaking to her daughter, she would have to walk around him to do so. She wouldn't like giving way to him one bit. He jutted out his jaw, silently challenging her with a look.

At the other end of the call, Cat answered. "Hello?"

"Hello, Cat. We have news."

"I've heard."

Already? Well, hell. "Who told you?"

When she named her former boss, Jack scowled. He didn't like Douglas Lowery. He never had. Jack had kept an eye on Cat's professional life in the years since their divorce, and he'd thought it obvious that Lowery shuttled the good stories to other reporters. Jack suspected that when layoffs came down, Cat's name had made the list because she was so good at her job. She posed a threat to old Dougie. "How much did he tell you?"

"Not a lot, though I can fill in the blanks. The surveillance that identified Barnes . . . that was you, right?"

"Partially. Your mother directed things here for the

most part." He drew a breath, then made his move. "Here, let her tell you about it."

He handed the phone to Melinda, giving her no opportunity to refuse it. He expected the conversation that followed to be awkward and difficult to listen to, but it was a necessary start if they were going to make any headway in that "secure in love" part of the mother-daughter relationship problem that existed between these two women. Sometime in the past few days, that had become a goal of his.

"Hello, Cathy," Melinda said.

Inwardly, Jack winced. Though he could hear only one side of the conversation, he knew Cat didn't like to be called Cathy, and that wasn't the best way to initiate a meaningful conversation. *Forget meaningful, Davenport. That's overreaching. A talk that lasts more than thirty seconds will be a victory.*

"Yes," Melinda said crisply. "We put a man on everyone connected with the story."

Plus every one of Cat's friends, Jack thought. Melinda had added seven people to the list who Jack wouldn't have known to watch.

Listening to Melinda speak, he noted the detachment in her tone. Where was the warmth? Where was the caring, the concern? Had Melinda always been so . . . undemonstrative with Cat? Had it always been this way and he hadn't noticed? Had he been so busy trying to keep his own relationship with Melinda sailing smoothly that he didn't notice how she and Cat interacted?

Melinda opened a locked drawer in her desk and began sorting through the contents as she spoke. "I thought it likely he wouldn't stop at one attempt. Honestly, I expected a second attempt to come much sooner. It dragged out longer than I expected." Melinda listened a moment, then said, "No, of course not. This was privately funded."

Her gaze flickered to Jack. "No, he didn't. Your father and I are taking care of it."

He folded his arms and scowled at Melinda. She could insist all she wanted, but he had hired the security firm and he would damn well pay for it.

Melinda dismissed him by turning away. Next, she subtly stiffened as Cat responded to her mother's answer. When Melinda spoke again, she used what Jack thought of as her operational tone. In curt, clear, quickly spoken words, she summarized the salient facts about Bret Barnes and his apprehension, then, without giving her daughter another chance to speak, she neatly slid the desk drawer shut and finished, "I'm late to a meeting. Here's Jack."

No "good-bye"? No "Take care of yourself" or "I'll talk to you soon"? What the hell, Melinda?

She handed over the phone, and by the time Jack got it to his ear, she was headed out the door. His gaze lifted to the wall clock. Not thirty seconds, but a minute and a half. Progress? He wouldn't make book on it. "Cat? You there?"

"Yes."

She sounded distracted, and Jack began to second-guess his efforts. Had he done more harm than good? He'd always had a hard time reading her over the telephone, so he decided not to try. "How is Fred doing?"

"Fred is just fine."

"Good. I'll be by to get him first thing in the morning."

"You're coming home?"

He realized he liked it that she called Eternity Springs home. "I'm leaving here within the hour."

"Okay. Have a safe trip. I'll see you tomorrow."

She disconnected the call before he had a chance to respond. He sighed and dropped the phone into his trouser pocket, then turned to see his former father-in-law standing in the hallway, staring toward the front door with a bemused look on his face.

"George. I didn't know you were home."

George Blackburn fit the profile of a computer science university professor geek to a T, wearing his gray hair longish, his beard scruffy at times, and usually jeans and a button-up shirt at work. He carried a messenger bag, which his daughter teasingly called his man purse. From the very first time he'd met George, Jack had wondered how he and Melinda had gotten together, not to mention stayed together.

George tossed his bag carelessly onto the office's leather sofa. "I came home a few minutes ago. Couldn't concentrate with all the hubbub going on, so I gave my class a walk. I heard the tail end of Melinda's call. She was on the phone with Cat?"

"Yes."

"That's nice. I'm sure Cat was happy to hear from her mother. Was Melinda going back to work?"

"She has a meeting."

George Blackburn nodded. "From one crisis to the next, isn't it?"

"That's the job."

"Yes, it is, and this country is lucky to have people like you and my wife doing that job." George waved at Jack to follow him into the kitchen, where he crossed to the refrigerator and removed a gallon of milk. He held it up toward Jack in a silent offering. Jack declined with a shake of his head and George poured a glass. "Am I glad we have this nonsense behind us. Melly has been so worried about Cat. In all these years, I don't think I've ever seen her so fretful as she's been these last few weeks. Why, the woman has hardly slept."

"Really?" Jack couldn't imagine that. The Melinda Blackburn he knew was the definition of calm, cool, and collected, and he'd been around her during some seriously tense moments. "Fretful" wasn't a word he'd ever use in connection with Melinda. Determined, yes. Confident, yes. Reserved, definitely. She could be queen of the ice queens, but that's what made her so effective in her work.

Yet he knew she loved Cat. She'd been the proverbial mother grizzly, protective of her cub in the wake of the attack on Cat's house. She wasn't overt about it, but he'd known Melinda long enough to recognize the glint of steel in her eyes when she felt fiercely about a subject. She felt fierce about Cat. If George said she felt fretful, too, then okay. She felt fretful.

"I wish she would come right out and tell Cat she loves her."

"Cat knows her mother loves her." Now George's gaze shifted to the framed photograph of his daughter that sat on the wooden shelf hanging above the kitchen table. "Not everyone possesses a warm and fuzzy personality. I'm the first to admit that Melly can be more of a porcupine than cuddly kitten."

Jack managed not to snort at that understatement. "I've certainly found myself full of quills at various times in the past. It's amazing that I still have blood in my body."

"We've all felt the points of Melinda's barbs." George's gaze shifted to meet Jack's. "That said, she is a loving and caring woman. Shame on Cat if she refuses to see it."

Jack immediately leaped to his ex-wife's defense. "Just because a person knows something doesn't mean they don't like to hear it stated on occasion. There are times in a person's life when they need their mother."

"And their father. And their spouse."

Jack went silent. "We weren't there for Cat when she needed us most."

"No, we weren't," George agreed. "However, we can't change the past, and we've done all right this time out. In our own way, we were each there for her this time."

Jack smiled crookedly. "By the way, my investigator wants to know if you'll show him that hacking trick you pulled off."

"What hacking trick?" George asked, filled with innocence. As Jack smirked, George patted him on the back and spoke with quiet sincerity. "Thanks for taking care of my little girl, son."

"I was happy to do it."

"It's not over, you know."

A frown creased Jack's brow. "Everything points to Barnes being a lone wolf."

"That doesn't mean that Catherine doesn't need us to be there for her still. You, especially. She needs you, Jack. She always has. That's been obvious since the day you two met."

The question burst out of nowhere. "Then why was Melinda so against our relationship?"

"That one is easy, Jack. Right or wrong, Melinda never believed she had the skill set to be what Cat needed in a mother. Right or wrong, she always believed that you were too much like her to be right for her daughter."

"I wasn't Cat's mother," Jack fired back, annoyed.

"No, but were you right for her?"

"Yes. Yes, I was."

"Then why didn't you fight for her?"

Jack had no swift response to that, and George took pity on him. "So, Cat tells me you've adopted a dog?"

Jack conceded the change in topic by explaining how Fred came to be part of his life. As he spoke, George returned the jug of milk to the refrigerator. When the door closed, the crayon drawing that had decorated the front of the refrigerator for as long as Jack could remember slipped from beneath a magnet and floated to the floor. George bent and picked it up. "Isn't it funny how we see things every day without really seeing them?"

Stick figures. Mom, Dad, and Cat, Jack felt certain. "The picture has been there a long time."

"Since preschool. Different refrigerators. Same magnet." George blew out a heavy breath. "Different family in so many ways."

Jack wanted to ask him about that curious remark, but for once, George's expression appeared to be as closed as his wife's. Returning the drawing to its place of honor, George cleared his throat and said, "If I didn't say it clearly enough before, I'll say it now. Thank you, Jack, for stepping in to help Catherine. I don't know what her mother and I would do if we lost her."

"I was glad to help. I'm glad she let me help, and that you and Melinda wanted me to be part of the plan to begin with."

"I'll bet our Cat was spitting mad when the drug wore off."

"Let me just say that her claws are as sharp as her mother's quills." He checked his watch, then added, "I'd better be going. I told the pilot to expect me before the top of the hour."

"So, you're headed back to Colorado?"

"Yes. I'll get in late tonight."

As Jack shook George's hand, his former father-in-law said, "Give my little girl a kiss for me, would you?"

"I sure will."

Just before the door shut behind him, Jack heard George add, "Probably wouldn't hurt to give her one from you, too."

"I like the way you think, Professor. I like the way you think."

*　　*　　*

For the first time since Cat took up residence in Nightingale Cottage, sleep didn't come easily. She didn't find the rush and bubble of Angel Creek soothing or the scent of lavender drifting from beneath the window relaxing. The crisp night air didn't make her want to snuggle beneath the comforter and float into dreams. Not even Fred's now familiar muffled snore from the foot of her bed offered her comfort.

Her life was no longer in danger. She could go home. Go back to her old job. She could get her old life back.

Shoot, chances were good that she could get her old husband back if she put her mind to it.

So why wasn't she celebrating? Why hadn't she shared the job offer tidbit with Nic and Ali after word of the arrest broke on national news and they came by to dish? She'd kept it to herself, too, when Cam and Sarah stopped by with a bottle of champagne, and even when Emily called and interviewed her for the *Eternity Times*. It was crazy. It wasn't like her at all.

Why was she so confused?

She rolled over and pulled her pillow over her head and tried to clear her mind. Instead, she kept hearing Douglas Lowery's voice echoing through her brain. *I want to offer you your old job back.*

She threw off the pillow and sat up, reached for the television remote, and switched the channel until she found an old Hepburn and Tracy movie. She loved old movies. This would be the perfect distraction.

Her concentration on the story didn't last five minutes.

"Okay," she murmured aloud. "Obviously, you can't ignore it. So think it through. What's the problem here?"

Fred lifted his head and stared at her as if to say, *Excuse me, but would you please be quiet? Some of us are trying to sleep.*

"Tell me about it." She thumbed off the TV, punched

her pillow, and lay down once again. Then she sat back up, switched on her bedside lamp, and reached for the notepad and pencil lying on the nightstand. She divided the page into two columns, Pros and Cons, and prepared to make her list.

Her pencil hovered over Pros. And hovered. And hovered.

Finally, she wrote the word "Family." She missed seeing her dad, and yes, even her mother.

In the Cons column, without hesitation, she wrote "Family."

Next, she wrote "Friends." She missed Marsha and Janie and her other friends in Virginia. It would be nice to see them again.

In the Cons column, she wrote "Friends." When she returned to Virginia, she'd miss the new friends she'd made in Eternity Springs.

"That helped a lot." She tossed the notepad aside and her gaze landed on her cell phone. Acting solely on instinct, she picked it up and dialed the number she'd never forgotten.

After four rings, Jack answered. "Cat? What's wrong?"

"Nothing. Not really. My mind's buzzing and I can't sleep. Where are you?"

He hesitated a moment. "I'm close."

"Do you have a few minutes to talk?"

"Absolutely."

She told him the details about Douglas's call. "I don't know why in the world this makes me so crazy. I should feel great about the offer whether I take it or not. I was devastated when they let me go. I should feel vindicated, you know? Instead, I feel . . ." Her voice trailed off.

"You feel . . . ?" he prodded.

"Scared. I'm scared, Jack."

He waited a beat, then said, "Give me a minute, would you?"

She heard faint sounds in the background, then the squeak of hinges. Fred's head lifted and his ears perked. A moment later, she was startled to hear Jack's voice outside her bedroom window. "Unlock your back door, Cat."

"Here?" she said into the phone. "You're here?"

"I decided to check in to Cougar's Lair. Hurry up. It's cold out here."

She scrambled from her bed and unlocked the door. He strode inside wearing gym shorts and nothing else. Not even shoes. When he took her into his arms and held her, it didn't occur to her to resist.

"Now, what are you scared about?"

She couldn't remember. She couldn't think. He was so . . . bare. And cold. Dressed in only her thigh-length sleep shirt and panties, she was cold, too.

He could warm me up.

Temptation beckoned. Yearning called. It would be so easy to give in.

It would be so stupid under the current circumstances.

Eyes wide open. Remember?

She wasn't thinking clearly and now was not the time to act rashly, but it simply felt so good to be held. She *needed* to be held. Pulling out of his arms, she decided to take a risk. She climbed back into bed and scooted to the far side.

Almost imperceptibly, his eyes widened.

"This isn't an invitation for sex, but I'm cold and you're cold and I don't see why we can't act like adults about this."

"If we act like adults, I'll be making love to you in two minutes flat."

Oh, jeez.

She sighed. "Would you hold me, Jack? Just . . . hold me?"

Following a long pause, his mouth twisted in a rueful

smile. "You ask more of me than just about any human being on earth, Catherine."

Then he climbed into bed, tucked her against him, and said, "Talk to me, Kitten."

She did exactly that. She described how she'd felt about losing her job and how reinventing herself as a blogger had helped to heal the wound. She talked about missing her friends, her dad, and even her mom. She confessed to a longing for Thursday nights at the movie theater watching first-run films while munching on buttered popcorn.

"So what's the problem?" he asked when she fell silent.

"I like writing for the *Eternity Times*. I've made friends here who mean a lot to me. I love Eternity Springs."

He kissed her head. "It's a pretty special place."

"I don't know what to do."

"Do you have to decide tonight? Is Lowery going to call demanding an answer first thing in the morning?"

"No. Not that I know of, anyway."

"Then why don't you sleep on it?"

"I tried. I couldn't get to sleep."

"Try again. You'll sleep now. I'm here. I can feel you relaxing more every minute. That's not exactly easy on my ego, you know. You should be all excited, being in bed with me."

She smiled against his chest, breathed in the familiar clean scent of him, and lost herself in the comfort and pleasure of sleep in a bed shared with Jack Davenport.

TEN

Jack woke up aroused. He was in bed with Cat Blackburn. Go figure. She lay wrapped around him like a vine around a fence post. *Morning glory,* he thought.

He lay still, enjoying the moment. Holding her was like indulging in a tropical drink, what with the coconut scent of shampoo she used, the citrus body lotion she slathered on her skin at night, and the way touching her intoxicated him like high-dollar rum. He couldn't recall the last time he'd been so turned on. It would be so easy to indulge. She used to love it when he woke her up by making love to her.

But the salient words there were "used to." She specifically told him the invitation into her bed didn't include what he ached to do. He couldn't—he wouldn't—betray her trust.

Instead, maybe he'd lie down in the snow-fed waters of Angel Creek. Before he lost his resolve, he quietly slipped away from her embrace and out of her bed.

In his bed at the foot of hers, Fred opened his eyes, but he didn't bother to get up. Jack took a long look at Cat, thinking about the choice she faced and wondering just where whatever choice she made would leave him. He asked himself where he wanted it to leave him.

The answer was easy. As long as the words "leave him" had nothing to do with it, he didn't care what she

decided about her job. Because during the time he'd
been away—actually, right about the time he'd decked
Bret Barnes with a roundhouse punch—Jack had realized that he wanted to try again with Cat. She was the
only woman he had ever loved, and he loved her still
today.

He wanted her back. He wanted *them* back. After
spending time with her here in Eternity Springs, he believed they had a chance. The trick would be to make
her believe it, too.

He retreated to the cabin next door, pulled on a shirt
and shoes and went for a run. Upon his return, he showered, and dressed. When he came out of the bedroom,
he spied Fred on his dog bed in the front room and a
basket covered with a red gingham napkin sitting on the
kitchen table with a note in Cat's familiar handwriting.
"Banana nut muffins from Fresh. I'm heading to the
newspaper. Want to meet me at Ali's place for lunch at
12:30? It's Greek Week."

"Absolutely," he murmured. After scarfing down the
muffins, he took Fred up to Eagle's Way, where he
worked until eleven-thirty. Anticipation rode with him
down into town. He entered the Yellow Kitchen restaurant ten minutes early. Cat was already there, standing
by the hostess's desk chatting with Ali Timberlake. The
pleasure that flickered in her eyes when she spied him
made him walk forward with a little more confidence.
He said hello to Ali, then dared to lean down and kiss
Cat lightly on the lips. "How was your morning?"

"Interesting," she replied, following Ali to a table for
two that had a nice view of Murphy Mountain. "Emily
had to leave town again. Her poor brother is having an
awful time. I've promised her that I'll put the paper out
for the next two weeks."

After they took their seats and Ali handed them menus
and left, he asked, "Have you talked to Lowery?"

"He's called me three times. I haven't picked up. My work phone has been ringing nonstop with interview requests. I could have been on ABC, FOX, and CNN today if I'd wanted. It's just as crazy now as it was when the dogfighting story first broke."

They both ordered the lunch sampler special, and as they waited for it to arrive, Cat asked him about his morning. It appeared that she had no intention of referring to last night, so Jack took his cue from her. Some campaigns required a slow but steady pursuit. "I worked in the office, mopping up a few messes left behind after dealing with politicians. I'm free this afternoon. Do you have photographs you'd like me to take?"

"I do." She smiled warmly at the waiter who placed a half-dozen small plates of aromatic edibles in front of them. She inhaled deeply and moaned with pleasure. "That smells heavenly. I love the way Ali changes her menu to give her customers a variety, but I admit I could eat her lasagna every day."

When she selected a stuffed olive, savored it with sensual delight, then licked her fingers, Jack almost moaned himself.

"I'm doing an interview with Sage Rafferty about her art. I'd love to get some shots of her in front of one of her paintings hanging in Vistas. Emily has a shot from earlier this year in her files that I could use. But since you offered . . ."

After lunch, Cat suggested they take the long way around to the Vistas gallery. "I told Sage I'd be by sometime after lunch, so there's no rush. I ate too much. I need to walk off my meal."

Jack didn't buy that for a minute. He knew this woman. Cat had something on her mind and she was working up the nerve to talk about it.

They walked toward Aspen Street, then ambled north to Sixth. She veered into Davenport Park, and when they passed the bleachers behind the baseball diamond, she abruptly took a seat. "There is something I need to say."

He braced himself. "Okay. Say it."

"About last night . . ."

"In my experience, when a sentence begins that way, it's not good for me. Obviously, I made the wrong choice this morning. I should have followed my physical instincts rather than my mental ones."

She patted his knee. "Oh, stop it. You did exactly the right thing and you know it."

"Because of the eyes-wide-open thing."

"Yes. But that's not what I want to say."

That wasn't what Jack wanted to hear.

"Well, that's part of it," she corrected, which mollified him to some extent. "I made a decision about the *Post*. That is not what I want to do anymore. I'm going to tell Douglas no, and . . ."

For the first time, he heard real hesitation in her voice, and he braced himself for a challenge.

". . . I'm going to stay in Eternity Springs."

"Stay here? As in, live here? Move here?"

"Live here, yes. At least until winter comes. I'm not sure how much I'd like living here in the winter. But I do love it here now, and I love writing for the *Times,* and I can write my blog from anywhere. If I feel the urge to dive into an investigation, there's a Ponzi scheme waiting for me in Gunnison."

Jack cleared his throat. "This sounds like a cliché, but what about me?"

"Yes, what about you?" She offered him a warm but nervous smile. "I've enjoyed your company these past few weeks, Jack. I'm interested in taking that next step and seeing where it takes us."

"Define 'next step.'"

"Well, I guess it'd be testing the waters of a relationship. Slowly. With no strings attached."

"One that includes sex?" He wanted everybody clear on that detail.

"Well, yes."

"What if I'm planning to return to D.C. now that the danger to you is over?"

"Are you?"

"Would you care?"

"Yes, I'd care."

"But not enough to return to D.C. with me."

She stretched her legs out in front of her. Jack's gaze focused on her sexy heeled sandals and the coral-colored polish on her toes as she wiggled them—a nervous habit of hers. "That's not a matter of caring, but of commitment. I do care about you, Jack, I've always cared about you, even when we split. But it's too soon to have an answer to that question. I'm not ready to commit to you any more than you're ready to commit to me."

"Not to be argumentative, but you don't know how I feel. We haven't talked about the changes in our relationship."

"That's what I'm trying to do now."

Jack took a seat beside her. He didn't know why he was annoyed. It was stupid of him. After all, he was getting what he wanted, wasn't he? Cat back in his bed?

But—she "cared" about him. That's it? He loved her, he'd always loved her, and she "cared" about him?

Better than telling him to take a hike, he guessed, but really. "So, what do you expect from this 'next step'?"

She blew out a breath. "For one thing, I expect us to enjoy ourselves. I don't want high drama or expectations or strings. I don't want to go into another relationship thinking that I can change you. I'm older, and wiser, and I have those battle scars already."

"You didn't try to change me, Cat."

"Is that what you think? Really? I was twenty years old, Jack. Of course I tried to change you. That's what girls do."

"Well, that's stupid."

"Infinitely. Look, I think slow and easy should be our goal this time around. We shouldn't get hung up on 'what ifs' or 'if onlys.' I don't want us to fly high and then crash and burn again. I think we should give ourselves time to sift through the ash and figure out if there's anything left to build on."

Of course they had something left to build on. Otherwise they wouldn't be here now talking about it, would they? Jack knew better than to speak that aloud, however. If Cat needed to think that for now, then let her.

And yet, maybe she had a point. Yes, he wanted her back in his life. No doubt about that. But was he totally sure to what extent he wanted her back? Did he want to try for the whole thing again—marriage? And what about children?

His stomach rolled at the thought of traveling down that path again.

All right, then, she did have a point. Maybe they should take it slow and for the time being, anyway, let tomorrow worry about itself. They couldn't just step back into their old life. Nor would he want to do that. He wanted better, and he was a whole lot closer to it today than he'd been the day before. "Your plan makes sense, honey. Our goal is to enjoy ourselves. Enjoy each other. Life is too damn short to do otherwise." He didn't miss her slight shiver as he trailed a touch down her arm before lacing their fingers and bringing her hand to his mouth, where he placed a kiss against her soft skin. "You smell like oranges."

"It's the hand soap in Ali's lavatory."

"You know, we could be at Nightingale Cottage in five minutes."

"Can't. Sage is expecting me at Vistas." She stood and pulled him to his feet. "Now, if you were to ask me up to Eagle's Way later, I suspect I could be convinced to make my coq au vin for supper."

"I have an excellent Burgundy to serve with it." He dipped his head and nuzzled her neck. "My dear Ms. Blackburn. Would you do me the honor of cooking my dinner up at Eagle's Way this evening?"

She batted her lashes. "I'd be delighted."

"Excellent. I think that after we stop at Vistas, we should pick up Fred, make a stop at the Trading Post for groceries, then head up to my place."

"Sounds wonderful."

They held hands as they continued their walk toward Sage's art gallery. When a truck's horn beeped, Jack glanced up to see Cam's son, Devin, waving at them. As he and Cat waved back, he was struck by the wonderful simplicity of the moment. Walking down a small-town street on a pretty summer afternoon holding hands with a gorgeous woman—wasn't this how life should be? Weren't moments like this really what he and Cat's mother worked so hard to protect? The irony of that, of course, was that he seldom had the opportunity to enjoy them himself.

Well, he'd enjoy this moment, because in truth, it couldn't be much better. As they passed the Taste of Texas Creamery, he coaxed her inside for something sweet to top off a delicious moment. As they exited the shop moments later carrying ice cream cones—Rocky Road for him, butterscotch for her—he thought the day was damn near perfect. Only when they waved at Gabe Callahan, who had one of his twins seated on his shoulders with her little legs and arms wrapped around her daddy's neck as she giggled with delight, did he admit that something—someone—was missing. If he had just been able to buy Lauren an ice cream cone, the day

would have been sublime. Walking into Vistas and seeing a very pregnant Sage glowing with happiness put a
period on the thought.

"There you are," she said. "I was beginning to wonder if another breaking story about a bear might get my
Eternity Times article bumped to another week."

"You got bumped by a bear?" Cat asked.

Jack tore his gaze off her stomach. "I'd say she definitely got bumped by somebody. How much longer?"

"About two weeks, give or take a few days." Sage
rested her hand on her belly and beamed with such joy
that Jack reached for his camera. This was a look that
deserved to be captured for all time.

As Cat began the interview for the article intended
to focus on Sage Anderson the artist rather than Sage
Anderson Rafferty the mother-to-be, Jack focused on
his photography and barely listened to what the women
were saying, until Cat's horrified gasp brought him up
short. "They killed the children?"

"They massacred everyone there but me."

"Even the newborns?"

Sage's pained and weary smile answered that question. Jack was compelled to capture that expression,
too. Now as he framed his shots, he listened to the conversation. "For a long time, I wasn't able to talk about
it. I had demons chasing through my dreams."

Jack could relate to that.

"I used work to exorcise them."

Jack could relate to that, too.

"I've come a long, long way, and while I'm nervous
about motherhood, it's the normal sort of nervous."

Cat asked, "How did painting fairies tackle your demons?"

"Celeste has decided they're not fairies, but angels. I
spent my days immersed in happy, joyful images so that

I had the strength to battle the ugly ones that populated my nights."

Cat turned away from studying the fairy-filled forest hanging on the wall. "I've seen pictures of your dark paintings, but I've never seen one in person. You don't hang your midnight paintings at Vistas?"

"No. It's bad energy. A gallery in Fort Worth has an exclusive on those, and I haven't painted one in quite some time now." Her smile reappeared as she added, "It's a goal of mine never to paint in that style again. In fact, I'm all about puppies these days. After many hours of debate—okay, it was really argument—Colt and I decided on puppies as the theme for our nursery."

"I was always partial to ducks," Cat said.

Jack darted a look at Cat. Sure enough, her smile had turned brittle, though Sage didn't appear to notice.

Sage continued, "I could have gone with ducks. They're nice and traditional. Puppies were a compromise. We know we're having a boy, and Colt wanted a sports-themed nursery."

From Cat's expression, Jack guessed she was thinking about the fight they'd had not long before she lost the baby. She'd wanted to talk wallpaper when his mind had been full of hostages. He'd snapped at her, she'd taken it like a knife to the heart, and they hadn't spoken to each other the rest of the night.

Her gaze flickered toward him and he saw that he'd guessed right. Her next question steered away from babies and back toward Sage's art career. "Why did you decide to open an art gallery in Eternity Springs?"

Jack was momentarily distracted by the small white dog that trotted into the gallery from the back of the building. Before Sage responded to Cat's question, he asked, "Excuse me, but what is that poor dog wearing?"

Absently rubbing her back, Sage glanced around, then grinned. "I thought I'd better get Snowdrop's Halloween costume ready before the baby arrived. I was afraid I wouldn't have time afterward."

"Are those fairy wings?" Cat asked.

"Angel wings. Sarah said she plans to put Mortimer in a devil's costume, so I thought we needed balance. The Callahan girls will like it."

"That's the most ridiculous thing I've ever seen," Jack observed.

"I think Snowdrop looks darling," Cat countered.

"Thank you. I do, too. Now, back to your question about the gallery. Well, Vistas came about almost by . . . Oh, Snowdrop. Stop that." Sage bent to scoop up her dog, who had gone up on her hind legs to peer into the trash can placed inconspicuously behind a graceful antique writing desk, and abruptly she froze. Her eyes flew open wide and her hands flew to her belly. "Excuse me."

She dashed for her office, with its private restroom at the back of the gallery. Jack looked at Cat, who shrugged, picked up the dog, and began walking around the room studying the art on display as she scratched the white bichon frisé behind her ears. Jack watched with self-conscious pride as she stopped before a photograph of an eagle soaring above Waterford Valley. He'd taken the shot the previous spring, and upon seeing it, Sage had wanted it for her gallery. He'd learned firsthand how difficult it was to say no to Sage Anderson Rafferty.

The woman herself emerged from the back room wearing a different dress. Cat took one look at her and asked, "Your water broke, didn't it?"

Sage nodded, her cheeks rosy with embarrassment, her eyes bright with excitement. "I guess I'll be having a baby today or tomorrow."

Once his brain freeze thawed, Jack leaped to assist her. "What can I do to help? Here, let me get a chair." He looked around. "Where's a chair?"

"She doesn't need a chair," Cat said. "She needs her husband."

"I'll call him in a few minutes. There's no rush."

"Are you sure?" Jack asked.

"Yes. I . . . um . . . excuse me."

When Sage disappeared into the restroom once again, Cat turned to Jack. "Do you have Colt's number in your phone?"

"Yes."

"Then call him and ask him to come here."

"Here? Not the medical center? Should I go get my helicopter and fly her to . . . wherever?"

Cat rolled her eyes. "Sage is a physician. Her sister is a physician. I'm sure if they thought she'd need to fly somewhere to deliver her baby they would already have made arrangements."

Jack pulled out his phone and thumbed through the names until he got to Rafferty. As the line began to ring, he lifted the phone to his ear, but Cat smoothly swiped it from his grip. A moment later, she said, "Hi, Colt. Cat Blackburn here. I'm calling for Sage. Would you be able to meet us at the gallery in the next few minutes?"

After a pause while she listened, she said, "No, no emergency, and nothing is wrong. She needs your help with something whenever you can manage."

"Whenever you can manage?" Jack repeated after she hung up. "Shouldn't you have said 'Get your butt here ASAP'?"

"It's not an emergency, so it's not our place to spill the beans. Sage will want to see his reaction." At that point, Sage returned looking calm and cool and serene. Cat ignored Jack's question and said, "We called Colt and asked him to come, but we didn't tell him why."

"Thank you," Sage said.

"She didn't tell him to hurry," Jack added. He crossed the room and took hold of Sage's arm. "There's a chair over here. You can sit down. Should I call him back and tell him to hurry?"

"Oh, heavens, no. We have plenty of time. As much as I'd love my labor to be fast and furious, I sincerely doubt I'll be that lucky. And thank you for the chair, Jack, but I'm better off standing. Now, Cat, I think you asked me about why I chose to open Vistas?"

"Yes." Cat appeared to be as cool and calm as Sage, so Jack settled down. These were two intelligent women. Cat had experience in this arena. If they weren't concerned, he need not be concerned.

For the next fifteen nerve-racking minutes, he watched Sage Rafferty with an eagle eye. Mentally, he planned the fastest way to get to the clinic and gave himself a pat on the back for having provided the town with an emergency helicopter. He could fly it himself. Knowing that helped settle his nerves.

Still, he held his breath until Colt strode into the gallery, his body tense, his expression grave, until he spied his wife speaking calmly with Cat as she gestured to a tapestry on display. Visibly relaxing, Colt said, "Hello, you guys. Sage? What's up?"

Sage murmured something to Cat, then turned an easy smile toward her husband. "Well, you need not get all excited, but we're going to have a baby."

His gaze dropped to her belly and he gave an exaggerated drawl, "Really? I hadn't guessed."

Now a glitter of amusement entered Sage's eyes. "Tomorrow. Maybe even today."

His lazy grin disappeared in a flash. "Today?"

"My water broke. If I don't go into labor naturally within the next little while, we'll induce."

The color drained from Colt's face, and when he swayed on his feet, Jack grabbed the chair he'd been ready to get for Sage and shoved it under her husband.

Colt sank into it gratefully. "Today! I'm not ready. We're supposed to have two more weeks!"

"You better get ready, bud," Jack told him.

"Wait a minute. Why am I sitting down?" Colt shoved to his feet, stalked over to his wife, and took her arm. "You should be sitting down, Sage. Shouldn't you?"

Sage shook free of his grip and sighed. "No. Didn't you listen in any of our childbirth classes? Walking is the best thing for me at this time."

"You know I listened. I have three notebooks filled with notes. I just . . . oh, no. You have to stop it, Sage. They're back at the house. The house is ten minutes away. Ten plus ten equals twenty. I can't leave you for twenty minutes and I'm not taking you twenty minutes away from the clinic and I can't do this without my notes. Why didn't you tell me to bring my notes to town with me this morning?"

Sage reached up and held her husband's face with both hands. She gave him a little shake and said, "Colt. Stop. It's okay. We're probably looking at the middle of the night here. Maybe tomorrow morning. There's plenty of time for us to ride home, take care of the dogs, grab our go bags, and go to the clinic before anything too interesting starts happening."

The father-to-be scowled. "Answer me this. Are you having any contractions at all?"

"Well, yes. A few. But they're not hard and they're not regular."

"And we're not driving out to Hummingbird Lake," Colt declared.

"We'll go for you," Jack offered. "Just tell us what you need and we'll make it happen."

"You don't mind?" Sage asked.

"Not at all. We're glad to help any way we can."

Sage gave Cat a key to her house and Colt informed Jack of what the dogs needed carewise, then Cat gathered up Snowdrop and they departed the gallery. Neither of them spoke about the impending birth as they walked to Jack's SUV and drove out to Hummingbird Lake. They talked about Jack's trip and his visit to her parents' house. They spoke about the newspaper and what Cat had planned for her next article and for her blog. They even avoided speaking of the subject when they delivered Colt's backpack and Sage's packed tote bag to the clinic and discovered that Dr. Rose Anderson, Sage's sister and physician, had sent home the Rafferty family friends who'd begun to gather, predicting that Baby Rafferty wouldn't arrive anytime soon.

As they'd planned, Jack and Cat stopped at the grocery store before making the short trip up to Eagle's Way. They kept the conversation light while she fixed her coq au vin, and when they sipped after-dinner brandy while watching the moon rise from the balcony outside his bedroom.

Eventually, when the kisses they shared on the balcony grew heated, they moved to his bed, where they didn't speak at all, or at least, not with words.

It wasn't until afterward, when they lay sated and spent, and a big step forward along the "see where it goes" road, that he cradled her against his chest, gently stroked his fingers down her naked spine, and asked, "So, tell me, Catherine. When you went into labor with Lauren, did your water break?"

ELEVEN

❧

Cat blinked, wondering if she'd heard him correctly. Had he just asked her about Lauren? Now?

She attempted to sit up, but he held her tight and trapped against him. "No, honey," he said softly. "Don't. Talk to me. Let's talk. Tell me about what happened when we lost Lauren."

When we lost Lauren. We. Cat closed her eyes. "You've never asked me about that night before."

"No, I never have."

"Why ask now?"

"Because I'm finally brave enough to ask. Because I think you might be healed enough to answer."

Cat wanted to resist him. It would be so easy to throw up her defenses and storm out of his bed. So easy to attack him for making sure he got his rocks off before bringing up the topic they'd avoided since leaving Vistas.

But it wouldn't be right.

Jack had asked about Lauren's birth and now, finally, she would tell him.

Cat stood staring with dismay at the trash sack that reeked with the stench of discarded chicken bones from the soup she'd made late last week. It badly needed to go to the curb for today's trash pickup. She had forgotten to take it out on Monday and now it was Thursday and the garbage truck would be coming down the street at any time. Seven inches of new snow had fallen yesterday, and according to the TV weatherman the temperature had climbed all the way to seven degrees above zero. Oh, joy.

Nevertheless, the trash had to go, and she'd waited as long as she dared for Jack to come home and do the job. When he left four days ago, he'd said he'd be home by yesterday. Yesterday had come and gone.

At least he'd had the foresight to hire a neighbor boy to do the shoveling if he wasn't here to do it, and the young man had cleared a path from the front door to the mailbox first thing this morning. She pulled on her coat, earmuffs, and gloves, grabbed the trash sack, and opened the door. Bitter cold air enveloped her, stinging her nose and lungs. Cat liked winter as a rule, but not this year. This year she couldn't wait for summer and the long-desired, long-awaited birth of her and Jack's first child.

This summer, she'd have a baby to cuddle and a husband to hold at night. Jack had promised to cut back on his hours at work and to stop his out-of-country trips entirely once the baby was born. That concession had been a huge victory for her, so she tried not to feel annoyed that he'd been gone so much lately, all but disappearing off the earth while he was away. As a brutally cold gust of wind blew snow from the bare branches of the cherry tree in her front yard, sending a flurry of snowflakes to surround her, Cat kept her mind focused on summertime. Excitement thrummed inside her. She simply couldn't wait.

She dumped the black plastic bag at the curb just as the garbage truck turned the corner at the end of the street. Gratefully, she turned toward the shelter of her home and started back up the stone walk.

She never saw the icy spot. Her feet flew out from

under her and she went down, landing hard on her tail-
bone. Pain radiated up her spine. Fear clawed through
her and she screamed from the depths of her soul.

She heard the echo of it in her mind as she lay with
Jack in his bed in his Colorado mountain home. His
bed, his home. "Theirs" had ended long ago.

"Wait a minute." Jack sat up, his expression anguished. "You lost the baby because of a fall on the ice?
That's not what—"

"No, the fall wasn't the reason we lost her," she assured him. "Though it took me a very long time to accept that. The trash haulers called for an ambulance and
they kept me overnight as a precaution. Both of us were
fine when we left the hospital, and she moved just like
normal for the next day and a half. Then, I noticed . . ."
Cat's voice cracked on the words ". . . she didn't."

Jack lay back down and gathered her close. "That's
okay. You don't have to talk about it. I'm sorry I asked."

"No." She gripped his arm hard. "I'm glad you asked.
I need to tell you. I've always needed to tell you, even
when I couldn't. It's bothered me all these years that we
never talked about it.

"I didn't believe the doctor. I thought surely I dam-
aged her in the fall and I felt so guilty and careless. I
blamed myself and I blamed you. I shouldn't have blamed
you, Jack. I shouldn't have blamed myself. I was so full
of pain and loss and you weren't there and that made
you an easy target. I had no one to talk to. You weren't
there and Dad wasn't there. Even Mom wasn't around.
Maybe if she'd been there then, we could have found
some common ground that would have helped us ever
since. Dad told me that she'd had a miscarriage before
they had me."

"I'm so sorry I wasn't there, Cat. When I got home . . .
I felt helpless. Hell, I still feel helpless. Let's talk about
something else."

"No, let me get through it." She closed her eyes, took a deep breath, then said, "I've never told anyone about this before. You asked me once. I remember that. But I couldn't talk about it, and now I need to talk about it. Better late than never, don't you think?"

"Whatever feels right to you. This is your call."

She drew in a bracing breath and let it out with a sigh.

"No, my water didn't break. I knew she was gone even before I realized I hadn't felt her move for some time. I just . . . knew. I waited one day, hoping you would come home or at least call. When I finally worked up the nerve to call the doctor, she said for me to come in and bring someone with me."

"And I was gone. Your mother was with me."

"I tried to reach you both, but . . . it was one of those assignments where you're totally gone when you're gone."

"It was a mistake for me to take that trip. I've never forgiven myself."

She smiled sadly. "Dad was at a symposium in Prague. I don't know why I did what I did next, Jack. It was like I checked out and automaton Cat checked in. I went across town to a hospital where I didn't know anyone, where nobody knew me. The sonogram confirmed she was gone, and the doctor wanted to send me home to wait for labor to begin naturally. He said it'd probably happen within two weeks."

"You're kidding. That's the way they handle it? You have to wait, knowing . . . that's awful."

"I refused to leave. I couldn't go home. My belly was so still. I just . . . couldn't."

Jack's voice sounded raw. "I understand, honey. I do. You did what you had to do. I can't tell you how much I regret not being there for you. Maybe if we'd gone through that together . . ."

"We wouldn't have fallen apart?"

He lifted his shoulders, strain visible in his expression, his blue eyes soft and sad. "Who knows?"

For a long moment, neither of them spoke. Then Cat continued her story. "They induced labor, and blessedly, that went pretty quick. I blocked a lot of it out because it was simply the most horrible thing ever. The pain and the pushing and knowing that she wasn't alive and not knowing what to expect when she delivered. The terror of seeing her or of being too afraid to look at her. In the end, she was just like any other baby. Just small. She was so tiny, Jack. I held her for a little while. I wanted to know why, so they . . . tested her. They told me she had a heart defect."

"Nobody's fault," he murmured. "The fall was just a coincidence."

"That's what they said."

A minute ticked by before he spoke again. "How much did she weigh?"

"Fifteen and a half ounces."

"Did she have hair?"

Cat smiled faintly. "Little white fuzzy stuff. She had long fingers. Like yours. Mine are short."

"So she had my fingers, hmm?" He pressed a kiss against Cat's hair.

"Yes." Tears suddenly flooded her eyes and she blinked them back. "She was pretty, Jack. She . . ."

Cat held her breath, a revelation hanging on her tongue. Did she honestly want to share this most private detail? Before this moment, no, she never had. But now?

She'd never dreamed she would have this talk with Jack—or learn so much about him that she'd never suspected. These last few minutes, few weeks, had revealed that the man cared more about their loss than she'd ever suspected. Had he shown it back then, and she'd been so lost in her own misery that she'd been blind to it? Or had he totally hidden how he felt? She didn't know. She barely remembered when he finally came home.

She hadn't been fair to him. She swallowed hard, then confessed. "I have a picture of Lauren."

His body stiffened. "What?"

She blew out a breath. "The hospital had a protocol to deal with miscarriages. They had a counselor see me. She brought a little white burial dress made by volunteers. She took a photograph of Lauren and gave it to me."

"You never told me? Never showed me?" Jack pushed away from her and sat up, his gaze accusing, his tone anguished as he said, "For God's sake, Cat. I never got to see her or hold her, and you kept a picture of her away from me, too? That's just cruel."

"I . . . I couldn't . . ." As he rose and stalked naked across the room, disappearing into the master bathroom, her heart twisted. She had no defense. She'd never shared Lauren with Jack, and that was wrong. So wrong.

Cat sat up at the sound of the shower. For a long minute she sat frozen in place, her heart thumping. Breaking.

No. She wouldn't let this happen. They'd come too far. They'd lanced the wound—might as well get all the poison out.

She threw off the covers and marched into the bathroom. The shower stall was huge with spigots on all three of the tile walls, turned on full blast. Steam rose and collected on the fourth wall, made of glass, shielding Jack's form but not concealing him. He stood with his eyes shut, his jaw hard, face lifted to meet the pounding stream of water, his hands fisted at his sides.

Cat opened the shower door and stepped inside. "I'm sorry."

He jerked his head around. His stare was angry and wounded and she wanted to take him into her arms and comfort him. He warned her off with his glare, but she ignored him.

"I didn't know it mattered. All these years, Jack, you've hardly spoken Lauren's name."

"Damn you, Catherine. Of course she mattered. She was my baby, too. I wanted her, too."

"I was broken. I was angry that you weren't there when I needed you."

"You buried her without me!"

"I know. I know." Witnessing his pain made her sick to her stomach. "I'm so sorry, Jack."

"I tracked her down. Found the cemetery. I go every year to her grave site, just like you do. I wait for you to leave, and then I go to her."

Oh, Jack. She had a lump the size of a boulder in her throat. "I didn't know."

"I lost my family, Cat. Again! Once wasn't enough. I lost my family again!"

With that, he broke. The strong man broke. He bowed his head and his shoulders shook and a strangled, mournful sound escaped him. She went to him and wrapped him in her arms, crying. "I know, Jack. I know now. I didn't know then. I'm sorry. I'm sorry. I'm so sorry."

They mourned, together, for the first time ever, seeking comfort and offering comfort. Then, taking comfort. She could feel the tension pulsing through him, so she wasn't surprised when he backed her against the tile wall and took her. It was urgent and needy and filled with pain. His pain. Hers. Theirs.

It was fierce, fast, almost angry sex that moved from the shower to the plush rug covering the bedroom floor. It was the kind of sex she'd wanted to have with him during those months when their marriage was falling apart but instead, on the rare occasions when he turned to her, she'd done little more than lie there. Not this time. This time she gave. This time she took. This time she made war in the hope of finally finding peace.

But when it was over, they didn't cuddle and comfort. Jack retreated to opposite side of the rug, and feeling suddenly insecure, Cat grabbed a throw from the ottoman of a nearby chair and covered herself. He was still breathing hard. She watched him warily. Peace was obviously still beyond reach. Finally, Cat said, "Jack, I—"

He interrupted with a curse and rolled to his feet. Opening his closet, he grabbed the navy terry cloth robe hanging from a hook on the door and slipped it on as Cat climbed to her feet, gathered her clothes, and retreated to the bathroom to dress. She wanted to weep and she needed to think.

She was tempted to hide or run away, but wasn't behavior like that part of what had brought them to this point?

Maybe she took a little longer than necessary to dry her hair, and she probably expended more effort than necessary utilizing the makeup that she carried in her purse. Eventually, wearing the armor of her clothes and makeup and styled hair, she went looking for Jack.

She found him swimming laps in the pool. A bottle of bourbon and a crystal highball glass filled two fingers high sat on a teak table between two deck chairs. Cat strode over to the pool house and removed two bottles of water from the fridge. She set one beside the bourbon, took a seat in the deck chair, and waited, counting his laps.

At thirty-seven, he stopped. Cat wondered how many he'd swum before she arrived.

He climbed out of the pool and disappeared into the pool house. She heard the shower running and figured his skin must be waterlogged by now.

Five minutes later, he emerged from the pool house

wearing drawstring cotton pants, a sport shirt, and a solemn expression. He asked, "Did I hurt you?"

"Did I hurt *you*?" she responded.

His mouth twisted in a wry grin. He reached for the bourbon but picked up the bottle of water instead and took a seat in the deck chair next to hers. They sat without speaking for a long time. Finally, Jack broke the silence. "Will you show me her picture sometime?"

"Would you like to see it now? I have it in my purse."

He nodded, then lifted his gaze toward the sky.

Cat retrieved her purse from the house and, returning to the pool, saw that he'd switched on outdoor lighting. She'd had the original photograph reproduced, and she pulled a two-by-three-inch copy from where she kept it tucked away in her wallet. Silently, almost reverently, with fresh tears running down her face, she handed it to Jack.

He held it beneath a light, studied it, swallowed hard, and smiled wistfully. "You're right, Cat. She was beautiful."

She swiped the tears from her cheeks with her fingers as she took a seat beside him. "You can keep that if you'd like. I have copies."

"Thanks." After gazing at the photo for another long minute, he tucked it into his shirt pocket like the treasure it was. He switched off the outdoor lights and lifted his gaze to the sky. They sat in silence for a good five minutes before Jack spoke again. "We'll never forget her."

"No, we won't."

"We'll always miss her."

"Yes, we will." As a wave of that peace she'd been seeking washed over the raw grief the afternoon had exposed, Cat felt herself relax. Finally, Lauren's mommy and daddy had mourned her.

Jack's voice came from out of the shadows. "It wasn't her time to be born."

"No, I guess it wasn't."

Without lowering his stare from the starlit heavens, Jack extended his arm toward her, his hand open in silent request. Cat took his hand and held it and watched a twinkling star. "I like to think that she's up there watching over me. Over us. The littlest angel."

"Our angel. Our little angel, Lauren."

Somewhere in the heavens, a star twinkled just a little more brightly.

As Jack and Cat climbed into his truck to make the trip back down to town early the following morning, Cat checked her phone and frowned. "Sarah told me she'd text me with news about the Rafferty baby. Nothing yet. I hope there's nothing wrong."

Jack noted the way her teeth tugged worriedly at her lower lip. "Sage said it might be today before she delivered. Want to drive by the clinic on the way to Angel's Rest?"

"Yes. Good idea."

Her unspoken fear rode along with them on the trip down into town. Jack figured that considering her history, her mind probably always went to the "something's wrong" possibility first. As Jack turned onto Pinyon a few minutes later, approaching the clinic from the north, he spied a crowd of people outside, Cam and Gabe among them. He was already shifting his foot to apply the brake when Cat said, "I'd like to stop."

"Gabe is playing with his daughter and Cam's son is throwing a baseball around with Mac," Jack observed as he pulled into a parking place. "I don't think they'd be doing that if there was a problem."

"I'm sure you're right."

Jack placed his hand on the small of Cat's back and

escorted her toward the front of the clinic. At their approach, Mac, who stood a few feet off to the right from Cam and Gabe, held the baseball and waved a hello. Cam straightened away from the tree against which he'd been leaning, and when they approached the group, he asked, "Come to join the baby watch?"

"So, no news yet?" Jack asked, noting how Cat visibly relaxed at Cam's greeting.

"Not yet." He nodded toward the clinic. "The women are all inside."

"I'll go check it out," Cat said. "Excuse me."

Jack and Cam both watched her walk away, then Cam gave Jack a considering look. "You two are out awfully early, cuz. What's going on there?"

"Honestly, I'm not exactly sure." He nodded toward the building. "So, what's going on there?"

"Sarah came out with a report about twenty minutes ago. She said it shouldn't be long now. She's been here all night."

"Why? Are they expecting trouble?"

"No. No trouble." He shrugged his shoulders and added, "Colt and Sage are friends. We want to be here."

Gabe Callahan's boxer, Clarence, padded up to them and swished his crooked tail back and forth as his sniffed at Jack's jeans then looked up as if to say, "Well, where's my buddy?"

Jack scratched the dog beneath his drooping jowls. "Fred isn't with me today, boy."

"Dog. Dog. Dog." One of the Callahan girls toddled over toward Jack and Cam, her father following behind her. Cam swooped down and swept her up into his arms, blowing raspberries on her tummy. She squealed with laughter and wriggled until Cam set her down. Then she ran toward Gabe, hid behind his legs, and played hide-and-seek with Cam.

"Which one is this?" Jack asked Gabe over the giggles.

"Meg. Cari is in with her mother." Gabe frowned and wrinkled his nose. "Oh, for crying out loud, Margaret. I just changed your diaper. Excuse us, gentlemen."

Gabe scooped her up and headed for the clinic restroom. Mac sent Devin a high arching ball, then called after Gabe, "Get a status report while you're in there, would you?"

Gabe waved his consent and disappeared into the building. Cam said, "Those girls are just too darned cute. Smelly sometimes, but cute."

Jack noted the gleam in his cousin's eyes and casually asked, "So, do you think you and Sarah will give that another go?"

"What do you . . . Oh." Cam's eyes widened. "You mean have a baby?"

"Yes. Give Devin and Lori a little brother or sister."

Cam shoved his hands into the back pockets of his jeans and rolled back and forth on his heels. "Honestly, I don't know. Babies are a lot of work. I don't know if Sarah's ready to jump back into that pool. With her mother at Keller Oaks and Lori away at school, she's independent for the first time in her life. We haven't talked about it."

Cam's gaze settled on Devin, who missed the ball Mac sent him and jogged to retrieve it. "I didn't go through the baby stage with Devin, but I loved having a little kid around the house."

Mac signaled to the teenager that he was taking a break, tucked his ball glove beneath his arm, and stepped nearer to Cam and Jack. "How old was he when you adopted him?"

"Five." Cam spoke about the challenges of being a single father and observed aloud how hard single motherhood must have been for Sarah.

Twice Jack found Lauren's name on his tongue, but both times he bit it back. He'd never told Cam about the baby. He'd never told another soul. Why, he'd never even said her name to Melinda. Even with Cat, she'd always been "the baby." It hadn't been until the day he first visited the cemetery and read the name carved on her headstone that she had become "Lauren" in his mind.

They all looked up when Gabe exited the clinic sans daughter. He said, "No baby yet, but they're getting close. Mac, Ali asked me to tell you she needs to talk with you about something."

Mac disappeared inside, then Devin drifted off with friends who were headed toward Angel Creek with fishing poles over their shoulders. Gabe approached Jack and Cam, who observed, "You lost someone."

"Yep." Gabe looked pleased. "Lots of women in there to fuss over her. I'm glad the Raffertys are having a boy. Numbers need some balance." Gabe gave Jack a slyly innocent look and said, "Your Cat sure likes cuddling on my little girls."

And right then, in this town, at this moment, in front of these two men, the time was finally right. "We had a little girl. Her name was Lauren. She was stillborn."

In the beat of silent shock that followed the announcement, Cam's jaw gaped. "A baby? You had a baby? Jack, you never told me that."

"I don't talk about it. Well, at least, I haven't talked about her before now."

"When did this happen?"

Jack named the date and he saw it register on Gabe's face. Gabe had been mired in his own issues at that point. He put his hand on Jack's shoulder and squeezed it. "I'm sorry, man. Losing a child . . . it's bad. It just sucks. I know I'll have a hole in my heart until the day I die over losing Matt. I'm so sorry you and Cat went through that."

That's when Jack made another confession he had never expected to admit. "I was away on the job when Cat lost her. When I came home . . . I handled it poorly. I couldn't fix it. I couldn't give Cat what she needed."

The men stared at him in sympathetic silence until Gabe came to his rescue. "I get it, man. Believe me, I get it. But there really isn't a 'right' way to handle it, because the whole thing isn't 'right.' Don't hold yourself to some standard that doesn't exist, Jack. Sometimes shit happens, and when it does, you just have to batten down the hatches and hold on until the storm is over."

"Sometimes the ship breaks up before the seas calm," Cam, the sailor, observed. "Is that what happened to the two of you?"

"Part of it. The biggest part of it, I think."

"Because you lost the baby, or because of the way you reacted?" Gabe asked.

"Because we had trouble getting pregnant, because we lost her once we finally managed step number one, and because Cat and I mourned differently. And, to be perfectly honest, the baby wasn't real to me right from the first like she was with Cat. Love wasn't my first reaction when she said the stick turned blue."

"Fear," Gabe said.

"Oh, yeah," Cam replied. "When Sarah told me about Lori, I shook so hard my leg chains rattled."

"They put you in leg chains in juvie jail?" Jack asked, momentarily distracted.

"Nah. I was speaking figuratively."

"I didn't understand that I'd fallen in love with the baby until after she was gone," Jack explained. "Cat and I were both screwed up and we couldn't lean on each other. We grew so apart that there was no going back."

"What about now?" Gabe asked. "You've found your way back together in some respects."

"One very important respect," Cam added, giving a wolfish grin.

Jack considered the question. Where did they stand after last night? They'd stayed out beside the pool until almost midnight, then returned to the house and made slow, sweet love before falling asleep together. Conversation this morning had remained light and general. It was almost as if they needed to catch their breath after the emotional drain of the previous day.

And yet, something had healed between the two of them last night, forgiveness offered and accepted. It was important. He'd needed it, and he thought she'd needed it, too.

So, now what? Where did they go from here? She'd wanted to spend some time sifting through the ashes. To his mind, they'd pretty much taken care of that last night. He loved her. He wanted her.

Did he want to remarry her?

Whoa. That was a big, hairy question. Did they dare go down that road again? Yes, they'd finally mourned their child together, but what else had truly changed? He still had a job she hated. Hell, she'd hate his job now ten times more than the job he'd had when they were married. Even if the job didn't cause a problem, what about the baby issue? Would she want to try to have kids again? Would he? Fertility wouldn't be any easier now that they were five years older.

He exhaled a heavy breath. Maybe that stack of ashes was deeper than he thought.

The front door of the clinic opened and Sarah Reese stuck her head out. "He's here!"

The baby's arrival rescued Jack from the troubling questions, and what followed was a celebration the likes of which Jack had never experienced. Colt emerged

from the birthing room to briefly show off a healthy
eight-pound, seven-ounce bundle of boy with a head full
of red hair and lungs that didn't quit. Colton Alexander
Rafferty. Colt looked exhausted, excited, and elated,
and watching him, Jack experienced envy greater than
any he'd known before.

He glanced up to see Cat looking at him, her eyes
watery but warm. Standing beside him, Cam noticed,
too. He leaned over and murmured, "You know, cuz, I
discovered that a man can go home again. Maybe you
can, too."

TWELVE

The next ten days passed swiftly as the excitement in town began shifting away from the arrival of Eternity Springs's newest resident and toward the wedding of its favorite daughter to its redeemed rogue. Having been denied the big wedding she'd dreamed of as a girl, Sarah was going traditional all the way, including a long bachelorette weekend. She'd spent a considerable amount of time deciding what she wanted the theme of her party to be, and once it was done, she'd turned the planning over to Nic.

"The theme of the weekend is adventure," she told Cat when she stopped by the *Eternity Times* office to invite her along. "I've known Sarah most of my life, so I've come up with the perfect plan. We're leaving early Friday morning and returning on Sunday."

The sparkle of excitement in Nic's eyes made Cat wary. "We're not talking male hookers and blow, now, are we?" she teased, though a serious question lay beneath it. "Just what sort of adventure are we talking about?"

Nic laughed. "We're talking motorcycles, zip lines, and the Wild, Wild West."

"For motorcycles and zip lines, I'm with you. Could use a little more detail when it comes to the Wild West. I'm just over a firebombing incident, you know."

Nic dismissed her concern with a wave. "It's a mystery dinner place over toward Durango. Steampunk, southern-Colorado-Gold-Rush style, and you go in costume. It's role-playing."

"Ah, the *movie* called *Wild, Wild West.*"

"Actually, Sarah loved the television show reruns growing up. She had a thing for Robert Conrad because he wore tight pants."

"Sounds like fun." Cat hadn't been on a girls' weekend since college. "Count me in."

"Excellent. Especially since I already ordered your costume."

"Oh? Dare I ask what?"

"I couldn't help myself. I saw it in the catalogue and it just seemed too perfect. You're going to be Miss Kitty."

"A cat costume?"

"Miss Kitty as in *Gunsmoke.*"

"A saloon girl. Well, it's always been a secret desire of mine. I always thought Marshal Dillon was hot."

"You must watch old TV shows, too."

"I'm a sucker for *Gilligan's Island.*" She propped her elbow on her desk and rested her head in her palm. "So, who are you going as?"

"Now, I'm not going to spoil the surprise. They're all fun costumes, I promise."

"Fair enough." Cat's thoughts strayed to Jack, who, as Cam's best man, would be in charge of a bachelor party. She could easily picture him flying the guys to Monte Carlo to go gambling. "So, what are they doing for Cam's party?"

"A golf weekend at Pebble Beach. It's a lovely place—Gabe and I honeymooned there—and I do think it's cool that Jack has a house there, but we're going to have so much more fun."

Cat didn't know Jack had a house at Pebble Beach. "Are they going this weekend, too?"

"Yes."

"What are you doing with the babies?"

"My mother and aunt are coming in and they're going to stay through to the wedding. Sage is going to have to miss the party, of course. I feel bad for her, but not too bad. Colton Alexander is such a little doll. Her sister, Rose, was going to go, but she's scheduled to man the clinic for the weekend and couldn't find a sub. So it'll be Ali, Celeste, you, and me."

"Sarah's daughter won't be in for it?"

"Lori isn't arriving until Sunday evening. She's the maid of honor, but she didn't really mind missing this part of the wedding festivities. She and Sarah both agreed it would be weird for Sarah to have to worry about being a mom at her own bachelorette party."

"That's understandable. So, what do I need to bring?"

"I'm having the costumes delivered to the bed-and-breakfast where we're staying, so you won't need to worry about that. Pack light . . . but be sure to bring your sense of adventure!"

That's how Cat came to be riding a Honda Gold Wing motorcycle through the Rocky Mountains on a beautiful summer morning. The bikes were rentals, except for Celeste's—she drove her own—and Cat was surprised to learn that of all the girls, she apparently had the least experience riding a bike. "I'm almost embarrassed about it," she confessed during one of their breaks.

"It's because of Celeste," Ali explained. "She challenges you to attempt things you'd never dream of trying otherwise."

"She's our hero," Sarah added, throwing an arm around the older woman's shoulders.

Celeste laughed. "I've lived longer than you all. I've had time to try more things."

They stayed overnight in a bed-and-breakfast and sat

up late watching the DVDs of the TV show *Wild, Wild West* that Nic had brought.

The alarm sounded too early for Cat the next morning, and she had to drag herself from bed. Riding a motorcycle might be exhilarating, but it wasn't easy on the glutes. Nevertheless, by the time they arrived at the zip line site, she felt mellow and relaxed.

Then she spied a span of cable strung high above the forest floor and watched as a man strapped into what she considered minimal gear and hanging from a pulley mechanism stepped off a metal platform encircling a Ponderosa pine and soared through the forest. "I'm the bride-to-be," Sarah said. "Is it wrong of me to point out that the dude who just zipped past has a very fine ass?"

"Not at all, dear," Celeste said. "This is your bachelorette weekend, after all."

"Married doesn't equal dead," Nic agreed.

"It was definitely a fine ass," Ali added.

Staring upward as a woman stepped off the platform and zipped along the line, Celeste observed, "How cool is that?"

"Have you ever gone soaring before?"

"Not like this, no."

"It's a long way up there," Ali said, her tone a bit doubtful.

"You going chicken on us?" Sarah asked.

"No. Not at all. I've wanted to give this a try ever since I heard about it." She winced slightly as she added, "It's just awfully high."

Cat stared up at the treetop platform and wondered what she'd gotten herself into. "I went parasailing one time," Nic said. "That was fun."

"There's nothing like flying," Celeste agreed. "Hang gliding is fun, too."

"You amaze me, Celeste."

Celeste gave her a pointed look as she donned her

safety helmet. "Life is too valuable to waste on being dull."

"Leap like a lunatic," Sarah added. "That was her advice to me, and I have taken it to heart." Flashing her friends a grin, she added, "That's why I'm going first."

As a hoist lifted her up to the platform, she let out a whoop.

For the next few hours, they played like children. After learning the ropes, so to speak, on the first few runs, they began getting more adventurous, lying flat in the air, doing twists and flips and whatever other tricks they could come up with. The parallel racing lines proved to be the most popular, with Ali showing a seriously competitive streak, winning the head-to-head competition with Cat coming in second. Everyone agreed that the bride-to-be won the trick competition. "Sarah is so short that it gives her an unfair advantage," Nic complained.

By the time they were ready to leave, waiting beside their Gold Wings for Celeste, who had dawdled in the gift shop, Cat had squealed and screamed and laughed more than she had in years. "I'm going to have to bring Mac here," Ali said. "This was a blast."

"They promised thrills and delivered," Sarah agreed.

Nic nodded seriously, but the glint in her eye was wicked as she said, "Zip lining is almost as thrilling as having sex with Gabe Callahan." When Cat glanced at her in surprise, she added, "This is supposed to be a bachelorette party. We have to talk about sex."

Getting into the spirit, Ali said, "Excellent point, Nic. I'll add that zip line soaring is almost as thrilling as waterfall sex with Mac Timberlake."

Sarah gasped. "You had sex at Heartache Falls? But that water is freezing!"

"No, this was a waterfall at a resort in Hawaii. The water temperature was just right." Ali looked at Cat.

"Anything to add to the conversation? You were married to the mystery man of Eternity Springs, after all."

Cat made a show of staring at her fingernails. "As exciting as I found soaring through Aspen Alley a few minutes ago, it doesn't compare with Caribbean beach sex with Jack Davenport."

"Ooh," Nic said. "That's a good one."

Sarah grinned impishly. "I haven't had Caribbean beach sex with Jack Davenport, but I can vouch for the thrill of his kisses."

Cat scowled at her. "I do believe that I have some sympathy for Cam."

Sarah laughed, then exhaled a dreamy sigh. "Well, in another couple of weeks, I'll be having South Pacific yacht sex with Cam Murphy. Isn't that something?" She looked at Nic, her oldest and dearest friend, and shook her head in wonder. "Can you believe that? I'm marrying Cam Murphy!"

Nic gave her a quick, hard hug. "And we are all thrilled for both of you."

While Sarah blinked back happy tears, Ali said, "Here comes Celeste."

Nic noted the gift bag in her hand. "I swear, she never passes a gift shop without buying something."

"It's market research," Celeste replied. "I have to make sure that our shop at Angel's Rest is better than the competition's. They did have something unique here that I just couldn't pass up. Look."

She pulled a little figurine from her bag—an angel hanging from a zip line. Cat grinned as she mentally pictured the drawing room at Angel's Rest, otherwise known as the Angel Room. "It's perfect."

The others agreed, then they donned their helmets and roared off toward the next stage of the bachelorette adventure weekend—a trip to the Wild, Wild West.

*　*　*

Jack chewed the end of an unlit cigar and lined up his putt on the twelfth hole at Pebble Beach Golf Links on the Monterey Peninsula. The foursome of himself, Mac Timberlake, Gabe Callahan, and Cam Murphy had proved to be a competitive bunch. As it stood now, he and Mac each had three skins. Gabe had managed only one. Cam was ahead by one, but Jack would tie him if he made this putt. He stood over the ball. From behind him, he heard Cam channel his inner *Caddyshack* fan by saying, "M-m-m-miss it, Noonan."

Jack hit the ball cleanly and sank the putt. The others groaned. They walked off the green, then took advantage of the proximity of the halfway house to use the facilities. As Gabe stood in line to buy a round of beers, Cam said, "I think I'm going to call and check on the girls. I don't like this whole soaring idea. Sounds dangerous as hell to me."

"They'll be fine," Mac said. "I've done it with our sons. It's a lot of fun."

Cam wasn't pacified. "Why can't they have an ordinary bachelorette party? Go have a spa weekend or a shopping extravaganza? Oh, no. Our women want to go ride motorcycles and hang from trees."

"We are with extraordinary women," Gabe said as he walked up and passed out cans of beer.

"We may be with them, but we're not *with* them. That's the problem." Cam accepted the beer and stepped away, saying, "Looks like there's a bit of a backup on the tee box. I'll catch up."

Jack watched with amusement as his cousin pulled his cell phone from his pocket and placed a call, he was certain, to his bride-to-be. When the time came for them to tee off, Jack waved at Cam, catching his attention. He returned to the group saying, "They're all back on the ground, safe and sound, so you guys can quit worrying about them."

"I wasn't worried," Jack said. "Gabe, were you worried?"

"Not me. What about you, Mac?"

"Not at all."

"You are all a bunch of liars."

"No," Jack fired back. "We're golfers. You're up, Nancy."

Cam replied with a solid drive, and a smirk. "Who you calling Nancy, spy boy?"

The golf game and insults resumed, and everyone enjoyed himself. By the time they stood at the tee box of the picturesque eighteenth hole, Cam said, "What a great golf course. Thank you guys for being here."

"Wouldn't have missed it," Mac said. "Playing Pebble Beach has been on my bucket list for a long time. This was a great idea for a bachelor party."

"Not according to Devin." Cam studied his golf bag, debating his club choice. "I thought I was being a pretty cool dad inviting him along, but he declared our bachelor weekend lame."

Mac had honors and stepped up to the tee. "He's a teenager. To him, bachelor parties mean strippers and booze."

"True," Cam agreed. "At least the cigars are Cuban."

"We're living on the edge," Gabe observed after Mac split the fairway with his tee shot. "I will admit there have been a couple of bachelor parties I attended that I will never forget."

"There have been a couple I attended that I'll never remember," Jack added, stepping up to address the ball.

After Cam and Gabe hit their tee shots, Cam relayed a story about a bachelor party fishing charter he'd captained years ago. "Guys were out of control. I made them all wear vests the entire time, which was a good thing, because before the weekend was over, we had five instances of man overboard. One guy fell in twice."

The men exchanged bachelor party war stories as they finished up the round. Mac told one about barhopping along a seedy boulevard in Dallas. "The groom was a big-time Packers fan, so for his party, we took a road trip to the Dallas–Green Bay game. We're in some dive the night before the game, and the best man starts hitting on a woman who claimed to be a Dallas Cowboys cheerleader. She had big hair and bigger . . . pompoms . . . and before long she'd invited him to sneak onto the playing field at Texas Stadium."

"Touchdown," Cam said.

"Not hardly," Mac returned, grinning at the memory.

"She was a pro?" Jack asked. "The best man got rolled?"

"The best man made it back to the hotel with this wallet. He even got into the stadium. The problem was that the cheerleader turned out to be a maintenance man, and the best man had a heckuva time avoiding the interception, so to speak. The next day the poor guy kept looking over his shoulder the entire game. As far as I know, that's the last time he ever even thought about picking up a girl in a bar."

Mac's story left them laughing, and they finished up the round in high spirits.

Later, following an excellent steak dinner, the four men gathered on Jack's patio, smoked cigars, polished off a couple bottles of fine port, and watched a breathtaking crimson and gold sunset. The mood was mellow, and as the shadows of dusk deepened, Jack built a fire in an outdoor fireplace. Soon, cedar-scented wood smoke mingled with the salty fragrance of the sea on the night air.

Bouts of comfortable silence alternated with spates of convivial conversation. They talked sports and cars and dogs, and they sat in quiet reflection. Mac asked Cam if he missed the life of a sailor. "Sometimes, I do. More now, where I can smell the ocean and hear the surf, than I do at home."

"Did you and Sarah ever talk about living in Australia rather than Eternity Springs?" Jack asked.

"For maybe ten seconds. We have too many ties here, and frankly, I waited a long time to come home. I'm in no rush to leave."

"Hear, hear!" Gabe declared. "There would be no living with Nic if Sarah moved away."

At the sound of a cell phone's ringtone, Fred lifted his head from his place at Jack's feet. Absently, Jack scratched him behind his ears. Devin was taking care of Cam's and Mac's dogs, but Jack had chosen to bring his new pet along. One of the perks of being both pilot and host.

Cam dug his phone from his pocket and checked the number. Immediately, he stood. "It's Lori. Oh, man. I hope there's not a problem. Excuse me, guys."

Illuminated by the firelight, Jack and Gabe shared a concerned look as Cam stepped to the end of the patio and answered the call. Almost immediately, the tension in his stance dissolved, so the others relaxed. Ten minutes later, he rejoined the group wearing a wide smile. "Everything okay?" Jack asked, feeling certain that it was.

"Yeah. She called to tell me that she's been offered another internship next summer and now she has three to choose from. She's so excited." He paused a moment, then said, "She called me because she wanted to share the news. With me. Can you believe that? Said she couldn't wait until morning."

"That's really great, Cam." Understanding the significance of the moment, Jack topped off everyone's glasses, then lifted his in salute. After a tumultuous beginning over the Fourth of July weekend, Lori and Cam were trying to define their father-daughter relationship. Not an easy task considering that Lori was already an adult when the two first met.

Cam sipped his drink, stretched out his legs, and stared into the fire that crackled and hissed with the new wood Jack had fed it. Following a few minutes of reflective silence, Cam observed, "A moment like this is damn bittersweet. I'm so proud of the young woman she is, and at the same time, I know I had nothing to do with it. I missed so much. I regret it so much. I look at your girls, Gabe, and I just get this big old hole in my chest."

Me, too. Jack stubbed out his cigar and silently scolded himself. *Don't go there.* He'd had just enough to drink to be lured toward the maudlin. Tony's death was still too close to the surface, and the last thing he wanted to do at Cam's bachelor party was descend into depression.

It didn't help that Cam seemed determined to . . . emote. "I look at Meg and Cari, and I can't help but think of all those firsts I didn't experience. Lori's first step. Her first word. Her first day at school."

Jack picked up the poker and stabbed at the fire. It was either that or break out the scotch. Ordinarily, his cousin didn't open up this way. Jack chalked it up to fatigue and alcohol, and the import of the event taking place next Saturday.

Mac extended his hand toward the ground and snapped his fingers. No dummy, Fred rose and went to him to receive another one of the dog treats Mac had pilfered from the jar in the kitchen and had been doling out to Fred for the past hour. "The years when the kids are little just fly past," he said. "Ali and I always told ourselves that we were glad we started our family when we were young, but now that we're not so young anymore and neither are our kids, we're not so sure."

"You're not that much older than me, Mac," Gabe

said. "There are days with the girls when I seriously think I'm aging in dog years."

"You are looking a little long in the tooth these days, Callahan," Jack said, seizing on the crack like a lifeline.

"Bite me."

"Nah, I'm saving my appetite for my steak." Giving his friend a hard time was an automatic response, but his heart wasn't in it, and even as he spoke the words, a treacherous question formed right behind them. He surprised even himself by asking the question aloud. "Is being a dad to the twins harder because you lost your son?"

"Everything is harder because I lost Matt, but everything is also sweeter because of it. I try never to take a day or a smile or even a dirty diaper for granted."

"I call b.s. on the dirty diaper," Cam declared.

"Oh, all right. I think—" Gabe paused when his own cell phone rang. "I should ignore it," he muttered, fishing in his pants pocket. When he pulled out the cell and checked the caller, his indrawn breath was audible. His voice suddenly flat, he said, "It's Zach."

Zach Turner was the sheriff in Eternity Springs. He had no good reason to be calling Gabe, Jack thought. Only bad.

The possibilities ran through his mind—in light of the recent conversation, the first one being that something had happened to one of the Callahan twins. Jack mentally began preparing for the swiftest way to get home even as Gabe spoke into the phone. "What's wrong, Zach?"

Time hung suspended. All eyes were on Gabe, who listened for a moment, then loudly exclaimed, "They what!"

Noting the absence of fear in his friend's tone, Jack's tension eased. He knew Gabe Callahan well enough to know that fear made him deadly quiet. He wasn't quiet one bit as he snapped out the words, "All right. Yes. No. Hold on."

Gabe glanced at Jack. "Zach doesn't have your cell number."

Warily, Jack asked, "What does he want it for?"

"Not your work phone. Personal. He has a photo he's going to send you, to send all of us."

Jack repeated the number as Cam sat up straight. "Huh? What's this about?"

"Has to be the women," Mac said, rising to retrieve his phone from where he'd left it beside the dog biscuit jar.

"Are they okay?" Cam demanded.

Gabe held up his hand and continued the conversation. "You're damn right I want to talk to her. Have her call as soon as she's able. Have them all call."

Mac exited the house, cell phone in hand. "Yep, it's the women."

Gabe said, "Sure. Uh-huh. Yeah. Thanks, Zach. I owe you one."

The moment he disconnected the call, Cam demanded, "What the hell is going on?"

"Well, it appears that our women managed to get themselves into a little trouble. They're all okay, but I don't have a good explanation. I *think* what Zach said was that a picture is worth a thousand words. It was hard to hear what he was saying because he was laughing so hard."

Four cell phones made four sounds to indicate an incoming text message.

Jack watched the photo appear. He blinked. He tapped the screen to enlarge it. Mac said, "Well now."

Gabe asked, "Is that a corset my wife is wearing?"

"Look at the shoes on Sarah," Cam breathed.

Jack didn't look closely at the do-me pumps on Sarah Reese's feet. His gaze scanned right over the crown on

Celeste's head and the corset around Nic Callahan's waist. It snagged only briefly on the red leather miniskirt that appeared to have been painted onto Ali. What Jack focused on were the black fishnet stockings, stiletto heels, and red satin dress with a cutaway skirt displaying his ex-wife's wares to perfection. "That outfit Cat is wearing looks familiar," Gabe said. "I'm pretty sure I've seen it on a showgirl in Vegas."

Jack had to clear his throat to get words out. "But they're not in Vegas, are they? It appears that our ladies are in jail."

THIRTEEN

In a small town in southern Colorado, Cat gazed around the nineteenth-century jail cell and took a moment to marvel at the changes that had taken place in her life during the last month. "My mother is going to have a fit."

"About what?" Ali asked.

"This is the first time I've been arrested."

"Me, too." Ali tugged at her tight red leather skirt. "Your mother isn't a former federal judge, is she?"

Cat couldn't exactly come out and say that her mother worked for the CIA. "No."

"Count yourself lucky. Mac isn't in office anymore, but this won't set well with him. I don't even want to think about what the kids will say when they hear about it."

The satisfaction in Ali's smile had Cat doing a double-take. "You don't look too worried."

"Honestly, I'm not. You know, nobody was hurt tonight. Our cause was just, and by gosh, before the trouble started, I got propositioned by a man who had to be at least five years younger than me. All in all, I think Sarah's quest-for-adventure bachelorette party turned out to be a fine old time."

"We're in *jail*, Ali."

"But it's a quaint jail."

These Eternity Springs people are all a bunch of luna-tics. Her thoughts must have shown on her face, because Ali laughed. "It was a fun day. Admit it. Even tonight was fun."

" 'Fun' is not the word I would have chosen." But when the door to the outer room opened and Nic, Sarah, and Celeste swept in, their spirits high and the scrapes and cuts they'd received at the Wild, Wild West cleaned and bandaged, she couldn't deny that the day had been one of the most entertaining in recent memory.

Bar fight notwithstanding.

"We caught a break," Sarah said, smiling her thanks to the potbellied lawman who unlocked the cell door and motioned for the three women to join Cat and Ali. "Zach had a meeting here today and he's still in town. Sergeant Wallace called him once I told him where we're from. Zach is going to take care of everything for us."

Cat had met Zach Turner, Eternity Springs's sheriff, on Cam Murphy Day. He was a tall, good-looking man around her own age, she guessed. She understood he'd dated Sarah sometime in the past.

"Are you guys all okay?" Ali asked.

"We're fine and I'm feeling lucky. The doctor prom-ised me the scrapes would heal before the wedding, so the pictures won't be ruined."

"Excellent news," Celeste said, lifting the hems of both her emerald fake-ermine-trimmed queen's robe and her gold satin gown in order to perch regally at the foot of the cell's narrow cot. "I know how concerned you are about the photographs."

"She's obsessive about the photographs," Nic said with a snort. "I made them give her a tetanus shot. The fingernails on that chick were scary."

The women were comparing notes about the incident at the Wild, Wild West when Zach blew into the build-ing twenty minutes later on a wave of frustration and concern, stopping dead in his tracks at the sight of them. "I think I just swallowed my teeth."

"We'll take that as a compliment," Sarah said.

"Dressed—or should I say, not dressed—like that, it's no wonder you started a riot!"

"It wasn't a riot, and we didn't start it," Nic protested.

"That's not what Sergeant Wallace tells me. Why don't you share your side of the story?"

Sarah lifted her chin and folded her arms. "If it will stop you from being so snotty, I'm glad to share what happened. We arrived at the Wild, Wild West club about seven-thirty with the understanding that it was a venue for a steampunk-themed mystery dinner theater. Attending a mystery dinner is something I always wanted to do, and Cam said he had no interest in going since it involved costumes, so I figured my bachelorette party would be the perfect time for it."

"That's why we ordered the costumes we did," Nic added. "You were supposed to choose a character and her backstory when you made the reservation. I did that just last week. Last week!"

"So what happened?" Zach asked. "Did they change the script?"

"That's one way to put it. Sometime between last Thursday and last night, the Wild, Wild West went . . . wild. No dinner, but definitely theater. The theme was still steampunk, but more biker bar steampunk."

Zach's lips thinned. "You all must have been hit on the moment you walked inside."

"We were, but that wasn't the problem."

Celeste nodded. "We actually met some very nice people there before the trouble started."

Zach closed his eyes at that. "Celeste, I can't believe that you, of all people, got into a bar fight."

"Well, I didn't incite it."

"Why didn't you turn around and leave when you figured out the place was a bar?"

"We were on an adventure," Sarah defended.

Zach shook his head. "I feel for Cam Murphy. I truly do. You women are dangerous."

"We were," Cat agreed. "Once we saw what this woman was doing to a dog."

"A dog?" Zach asked.

"Cerberus."

"The three-headed dog? He's supposed to guard the gates of Hell, right?"

Nic said, "This poor dog was on the inside of Hell looking out. He was a pretty thing—a whippet. The bitch had a spiked collar on him."

Cat added, "With spikes on the *inside* of the collar, mind you."

"Oh."

"I didn't know who was going to blow a gasket first," Sarah said, "Nic or Cat. Turned out that Ali was the one who started the trouble."

"I went BMFH on her."

"BMFH?"

"Bitch Mom From Hell. She reminded me so much of one of my daughter's friends from high school that I just lost it. Her boyfriend took offense, and then the man Celeste had been talking to got involved, and it all just went downhill from there."

"Cat rescued the dog," Celeste added. "That's her specialty."

"I couldn't have done it if you hadn't kept everyone occupied," Cat replied. "You should have seen Sarah. She took a giant of a guy out with a well-placed kick to the knee."

Zach rubbed the back of his neck. "So the fight was over animal abuse?"

"Of course!" Nic said. "Do you think we'd just stand

around and let that go on? Just do nothing like the rest of those idiots? That poor dog was terrified and in pain. We had to help him."

"Right. Okay." Zach braced his hands on his hips and frowned at them, one after the other. "I do understand. I'm a dog lover myself."

Cat beamed at him. "Good, because we need your help with him. The deputy who arrested us wouldn't let us bring him along. He asked someone in the crowd to take him to the vet."

"I couldn't do it because I had my hands full with Sarah," Nic explained. "She had a little bit of a panic attack about scratches and wedding photographs. And then, of course, there was the whole arrest business."

"Arrest business," Zach muttered.

"Will you call the vet and ask how he's doing?" Cat finished.

"Sure. But look, ladies, this wasn't exactly the way to solve the problem. You should have called—"

Celeste waved a hand. "There wasn't time."

"Sage is going to be really sad she missed it," Nic added. "She's been bragging about her ninja moves. She could have put them to use."

Zach shook his head in wonder. "Scary. Just scary. You know your significant others will not be happy about this. Cam especially. After all, look at what the bar fight at the Bear Cave did to his world."

Sarah winced at the reminder of the incident that had sent a teenaged Cam Murphy off to juvie jail mere weeks after getting Sarah pregnant. "I know, but everything turned out okay in the end. And I have a first-class bachelorette party story."

"Which reminds me," Cat said. "I did get out of there with my purse. Would you get my phone and use the camera function to take a few photos of us for the *Times* before you spring us?"

"You want to put this in the newspaper?"

"Absolutely. The *Times* is a small-town human interest publication. Every human in town will be interested in this story."

"The dogs will be, too," Nic added, a twinkle in her eyes. "We'll be heroes of the canine crowd."

"You and Cat already are heroes of the four-legged crowd, but these events will secure your place in history." Celeste stepped in front of Nic and Sarah. "Zach, dear, it's been a long day and I'm afraid I am feeling my age. Can you help us secure rooms for the night? Unfortunately, there was a problem with our reservations at the B&B. The rooms were double booked. Also, my Honda and the girls' rental bikes are still at the Wild, Wild West, and we'll have to make arrangements for getting them tomorrow. The establishment is quite a ways from town."

"I'm happy to help you get a room, Celeste." A flicker of regret crossed Zach's face as he added, "But I'm sorry to say that those bikes won't be going anywhere."

"Oh, dear. They've been impounded as evidence?"

"No. They've all been vandalized."

"Wait," Ali said. "Our backpacks were on those bikes. Our clothes."

"You ladies made some people very mad tonight. Your stuff was completely destroyed."

Sarah folded her arms. "Now that ticks me off. Speaking of which, how come we are the only ones in jail? They didn't just arrest *us*, did they?"

"Sergeant Wallace is keeping you separated from the others. The newer jail is on the other side of town. It's bigger."

"Whatever. Just get us out of here. I'm calling dibs on the claw-foot tub at the B&B. I need a soak."

"Well, Sarah." Zach rubbed the back of his neck. "That soak is gonna have to wait. The sergeant is releasing Celeste to my care in deference to her age, but the rest of you aren't going anywhere until morning. You were arrested, remember? That's kind of how this all works."

"What?" Nic asked. "They're keeping us overnight? Here? In jail? But . . . you're the sheriff. Can't you fix it for us?"

"I did. You're going home in the morning, and we'll do the legal follow-up from there."

Cat sat on one of the bunks. She'd slept on worse. "That's fine. Thank you, Zach. Can you get us a jumpsuit or something to sleep in?"

"I'll see what I can do."

"And don't forget the photo."

"Your phone is locked away. I'll use mine." He directed them to approach the bars and line up. "Good. That's it. Now, grip the bars. Celeste, move a little to the right. Excellent. Now, everybody ready? Smile."

He took two quick shots, then Sarah said, "Maybe he should take one where we're not smiling. That might be fun."

Nic said, "Good idea. We can show that one to Sage. She's going to be so sad about missing tonight's adventure."

Zach took the smile-less photo and then thumbed through the images. A wicked smile began to flutter around his mouth, which made Cat wary. Ali noticed, too, and she asked, "What are you doing, Zach?"

"Just keeping my constituents informed."

Suspiciously, Nic asked, "What constituents?"

He looked up from his phone and flashed them a big grin. Cat knew then which constituents, and so did the others. He was sending the photo to the bachelor party. "Oh, Zach, no," Sarah pleaded. "Please don't! You can't."

"Sure I can. In fact, I've earned the right, because I

couldn't get out of my meeting in order to go with them. I've always wanted to play Pebble Beach."

"It's not our fault you had to work!"

"No, but it's your good luck I'm here to help. Legal strings are hard to cut through here in this county."

The sexy sheriff laughed like a little boy when he sent those photos off to Gabe, Mac Timberlake, Cam Murphy, and, unfortunately, Jack Davenport, too.

He was still chuckling when he escorted Celeste out of the cell and left them to fend for themselves. An hour later, stretched out on the thinly padded cot and dressed in an orange jumpsuit, Sarah spoke into the darkness. "Was this a great party or what?"

The following morning, as the Eternity Springs sheriff's van transported them to their hometown, she began to have second thoughts. She suggested to Cat that she might want to refrain from writing about their adventure, after all.

"Oh, come on," Cat declared. "What sort of reporter would I be if I ignored this story?"

"You would be a good friend reporter."

Nic laughed. "Lighten up, Sarah. It's a great story. Nobody was hurt, and the laws that were broken were minor. Ali's not worried, and her husband is a judge."

"Former judge," Ali corrected.

"But back to my point about the article, Cat. I don't want to be a bad influence on the young people of Eternity Springs."

Cat had already decided not to run the story if Sarah didn't want it printed. She had no desire to dampen her new friend's enjoyment of her wedding festivities. However, that didn't mean she wasn't willing to tease her a little bit first. "You should have thought of that before you ordered your first margarita."

Sarah wasn't one to give up easily. "It may have been a bar fight, but it wasn't a drunken bar fight. At least, *we* weren't drunk. That has to count for something. The story is not truly newsworthy. I'm certainly not the first bride-to-be to be carted home from her bachelorette party in a squad car."

"This isn't exactly a squad car," Ali pointed out. "It's a sheriff's van."

"A paddy wagon," Celeste contributed.

Nic sat up a little straighter and adjusted the corset. "You asked for adventure and you got it. I do wish they had let us keep those jumpsuits, however. I look good in orange."

"Not as good as you look in that outfit," Zach chimed in from the driver's seat of the sheriff's van, where next to him lounged the cause of the contretemps, the black-as-midnight whippet. After Zach confessed that the vet had told him that an overcrowded pound meant a dim future for the animal, the women had refused to leave him behind.

Nic beamed at the compliment. "Thanks, Zach."

Sarah groaned and buried her face in her hands. "The only saving grace is that Lori wasn't part of this *mis*-adventure. I'd feel terrible if I got my daughter arrested. I swear, I'm going to file police brutality charges against you, Zach. You had no right to send that picture to her and to the guys. Or, for that matter, to deny us our phone call."

Zach called over his shoulder. "You had your phone call. You spoke to Lori."

"Only after Cam refused to speak to me."

"It's not my fault that your significant others were having too much fun to talk to you."

"Too much fun? Lori told me they were sitting around a fire pit drinking port and smoking cigars when she called. They call that fun?"

"Not as much fun as getting arrested for brawling, I'm sure," Nic said, studying the bruise on her fist.

Sarah folded her arms. "What I find inexcusable is that our attorney wouldn't even talk to us." She fired a glare at Ali. "How could Mac possibly justify that?"

Ali shrugged. "It's what he always told our kids. 'If you ever get arrested, don't call me.'"

"Well, that just stinks."

"No, our kids needed to know we wouldn't automatically bail them out of trouble."

"Oh, come on, Sarah," Nic said. "You're not fooling anyone. You enjoyed every minute of it. Admit it."

Sarah maintained her scowl for another half minute before allowing the smile to spread across her face. "It was a blast. I admit I never dreamed the evening would end the way it did, but what other choice did we have, really?"

"None," Cat replied.

"Absolutely none," Nic agreed.

Celeste nodded. "There are some instances, some causes, for which a woman simply must make a stand."

Ali shifted in her seat, yanking on the hem of her skirt. "I have to agree with Nic. I understand that ladies-sized prisoner jumpsuits aren't plentiful in that little town, but I wish you'd scored some for our trip home, Sheriff Turner. We could have shipped them back."

Zach's gaze flicked up to the rearview mirror. "What? And deny myself the scenery? Being a small-town sheriff should have some perks, don't you think?"

"You know what you need, don't you, Zachary?" Celeste asked. "You need to find a nice girl and settle down."

"Hey, I tried. Right, Nic? Right, Sarah? Right, Ali? Even you turned me down, Celeste."

"Oh, you scoundrel," the older woman scoffed.

Zach was on a roll, so he continued, "So, Cat, what's the deal with you and Davenport? Are you two exclusive?"

Nic began to whistle "I Shot the Sheriff" as Sarah said, "Oh, yeah, I can see Jack putting up with that."

Ali laughed. "Seriously, Zach. Would you stop in the next town and let us buy some shorts and T-shirts? This skirt is so tight I think my circulation is being cut off. Don't you think parking your van in front of the local Baptist church so that we were the stars of a public perp walk was punishment enough?"

"Well, Mrs. Timberlake, you tell me. As the spouse of a former federal judge, do you think overnight incarceration in hooker clothes is a usual and ordinary sentence for kicking a man with a lethal weapon?"

"Hooker clothes!" Ali exclaimed. "And what lethal weapon, might I ask?"

"With all due respect, ma'am, those are killer heels. Even your husband agreed when I explained the details to him."

"You got a real charge out of giving our husbands grief, didn't you?" Nic observed.

"Busted!" the sheriff replied cheerily. "Ali, we're only twenty minutes from home. I'll let you borrow one of my department's orange jumpsuits if you'd like."

"You are so kind," she drily responded.

"We're going to stop by Sage's house first, though."

Celeste said, "Oh, good! We'll get to see that precious baby."

"How come?" Nic asked. "Is everything okay?"

"Yes, all is well at the Rafferty house. I spoke with her this morning and she asked me to bring you by. She wants to see you all dressed up."

"I missed her being with us last night," Nic said.

"Me, too," Sarah agreed. "But hey, it's her fault she had unprotected sex nine months before my wedding."

A short time later, Zach pulled the sheriff's department van into the Rafferty drive at Hummingbird Lake. As the women prepared to exit the van, Nic mused,

"Think Zach should put us in handcuffs? That would really be a photo op for your article in the paper, Cat."

"Not going there," Zach told them. "That would lead to too many intriguing fantasies about my best friends' wives, and I'm gonna have a hard enough time as it is."

Colt Rafferty opened the door with the baby in his arms. Upon seeing his visitors, he made a show of bugging his eyes out. "Okay, as of this moment, I shall entertain not one moment of jealousy for having missed playing Pebble Beach with the guys. Ladies, no wonder you ended up in jail last night. I'll bet you started a riot!"

"Not exactly," Cat replied. "It was more of a brawl."

Zach followed the women inside. "Personally, I think 'riot' fits the situation just fine."

Colt ran his tongue around the inside of his mouth. "Okay, then. Well, Sage is out back with Snowdrop. Hot Rod, here, just woke up from his nap."

"Perfect timing, then," Nic said.

Sarah asked, "Can I hold him?"

Colt frowned down at her high heels. "I dunno. Sure you won't trip and fall?"

"I'll take him," Celeste said, swooping the baby out of his daddy's arms. "Colt has a point."

"Oh, all right." Sarah glanced at the others and said, "Okay, ladies, let's strut our stuff for Sage."

They paraded through the house and out the back door, Sarah leading the way. Then she abruptly stopped, and Cat almost ran into her. When she spied the reason her friend had stopped, she muttered, "Wow."

The men flanked Sage, their stances wide, arms folded over broad chests. "My oh my, would you look at that," Ali said. "Isn't that an impressive collection of beefcake? Imagine how they'd look in leather, like that guy wearing the codpiece."

Behind Cat, Nic choked. In front of her, Sarah moaned.

Celeste advanced like the queen she was dressed as, offering a regal hello to the men as she took a seat beside the new mother, who was obviously trying not to giggle.

Gabe Callahan spoke first. "What in the world were you thinking?"

Nic's chin came up. "We attended a mystery dinner and rescued a poor, abused animal. Zach has him. He's our witness."

"The dog?"

She shrugged as Mac Timberlake said, "Alison, I'm ninety-five percent certain that your skirt is illegal in ninety-seven percent of the state."

Ali finger-waved at her husband.

Cam Murphy simply said, "Sarah, you may very well be the death of me."

The bride-to-be turned toward her fiancé and said, "Honey, you're home! How was the bachelor party?"

"Well, no one in our party got arrested."

Sarah beamed a smile. "How boring!"

Jack made an obvious effort to drag his gaze up from Cat's black fishnet hose and past her cleavage. His eyes were twin blue flames, but he kept his voice casual as he asked, "Are you ready to go, Catherine?"

She knew that look. Knew that tone. The man was furious, but he was also turned on. She vaguely wondered if anyone else noticed as her body responded to his unspoken question. Her reply sounded a little breathless to her own ears as she asked, "Where to?"

"Eagle's Way."

Lovely. Or, so she thought until he doused ice-cold water on her plans by adding, "Your parents have come to visit."

FOURTEEN

☙

The last time Jack remembered being this on edge, he'd been scaling a cliff in Afghanistan. This time, though, Cat Blackburn was perched on the tiny rock shelf right beside him.

"Here? They're really here?" she repeated as he put the SUV he'd driven from the private airstrip outside Gunnison into gear and prepared to leave the Rafferty property. "Why?"

"I don't know," he replied, his tone grim. "Melinda left me a voice mail. I heard a helicopter fly over about forty-five minutes ago."

"But her message said she and Dad were coming?"

"Yes."

Cat exhaled a heavy breath. "So, this isn't an 'I've come to tell you that your father has died' visit."

"No." Jack was sure of that much. Melinda would have warned him if that were the case. She wouldn't bring George on an "official" visit, either. Still, something was up.

Suddenly, Cat reached out and grabbed his thigh. "You have to take me by my cottage. I need to change."

"Absolutely."

"Where do they think we are?"

"I sent a text to both of their phones telling them

we've been out of town for wedding-related events for my cousin and that we'd be back around noon."

She checked the clock on the dashboard. It was quarter to the hour. "Ten to Angel's Rest. Fifteen from Angel's Rest to Eagle's Way. Five minutes to change. We won't be too late."

He'd told the Blackburns they'd be there around noon, not an exact time. He had business he intended to take care of with Cat at the cottage, and her parents could wait. Uninvited visitors didn't get to set the agenda.

At least, not until he took care of his own agenda with his ex-wife.

It didn't help his mood that she appeared to totally ignore him. It didn't help his concentration that she drummed her fingers on her thigh, bare but for those amazing hooker hose.

"What on earth do they want?" Cat wondered. "Do you think they came because of the arrest?"

"Yours, or your arsonist?"

"Mine . . . and he wasn't *my* arsonist."

"Whatever. I sincerely doubt your arrest had anything to do with their visit. It wasn't exactly a high-profile brawl."

She wrinkled her nose but didn't argue with him. They lapsed into silence until they approached the bridge over Angel Creek leading into town, at which point Jack cleared his throat and asked, "What character were you supposed to be?"

"Hmm?"

"At the mystery theater. Mac said something about characters and scripts and that's why you wore costumes."

Obviously distracted, she said, "Miss Kitty. Nic ordered the costumes."

Jack blinked and shot her a look. "The madam from *Gunsmoke*?"

"Mmm-hmm. Has Melinda ever visited Eagle's Way before?"

"No. What does Miss Kitty have to do with steampunk?"

That got her attention, and she frowned at him. "I don't know. She ordered it because of my name. And I don't think the show ever came out and said Miss Kitty was a madam. She owned the saloon. Not all saloon girls were whores."

Jack had never been a fan of westerns, so his knowledge of the genre was limited. He didn't want to argue with her.

He wanted to peel those stockings off her. "Tug up your skirt a little bit."

"What?"

"I want to see the garter belt. It has to be a garter belt."

"For heaven's sake, Davenport. My mother is waiting at your house!"

He pulled the car to a stop in front of Nightingale Cottage and said words he knew were guaranteed to turn her on. "Let her wait."

She went still. Jack reached over and slid his hand up her thigh. When his fingers found the tab of the garter, he sucked in a breath past his gritted teeth. "I knew it."

"Jack . . ."

"Get inside, Cat."

The moment the door shut behind them, he pressed her up against the wall. He'd been hungry for her since . . . well, forever . . . but it had gone to Level Orange when he got his first look at "Miss Kitty."

Despite the fact that he'd always considered their sex life to be adventurous, it had never included role-playing and costumes. Maybe they'd need to change that. When she pulled away from him, backed away from him, crooking her finger while she swished her skirt to flash that blessed black and red garter belt supporting those fishnet hose, he figured that any more adventure would likely kill him.

He scooped her up and deposited her on the bed, and when she began to laugh, the sound bubbled through him like fine champagne. At what point the sex turned to lovemaking, he couldn't say, but it did exactly that. He made love to her with his hands, his mouth, his entire being, and when he joined his body with hers, he gazed deeply into her eyes and wordlessly offered her his heart. Again.

Emotion swam in her soft green eyes, an emotion he had not seen there for so long. Hope rose within him, followed almost immediately by despair.

Her parents waited at Eagle's Way.

Why now? Why at this sensitive moment when they were trying to find their way back to each other?

Afterward, he refused to look at her bedside clock, and lay on his back with Cat tucked against his side, her head resting on his chest. When a muted beep signaled an arriving text message on his cell phone, he uncharacteristically ignored it.

Cat lifted her head and gave him a questioning look. He kissed her hair, then nudged her head back down onto his chest. "I talked to Mac while we were in California," he said. "Did you know that he and Ali separated not so long ago?"

She paused a long moment, then said, "I knew their marriage had weathered a rough patch."

"Mac says that for him and Ali, life and love are sweeter the second time around. He says that they've rebuilt their marriage stronger than ever."

A half a minute ticked by before she sat up, the sheet

clutched to her chest, and solemnly met his gaze. "I'm confused, Jack. What are you trying to say?"

In the end, it wasn't difficult at all. "I love you, Cat. I love you and I need you to know that and believe it. That day at the park you told me you cared for me. Well, you know what? Whether you're ready to admit it yet, I think it's more than that. I think you still love me, too."

"You've never lacked confidence."

"Sure I have. I just bluff better than most. Look, I don't know what awaits us up at Eagle's Way—"

"My mother," she muttered.

Jack grinned, grabbed her hand, and kissed it "—but whatever it is, I don't want to lose what we've found over these past few weeks."

"I don't either, Jack. But we have so much standing in the way. Our relationship didn't just hit a rough spot. It broke. My heart broke. It will take more than garter belts and hot sex to fix it."

"It isn't all about sex, Cat," he said, annoyed.

"I realize that. I don't mean to suggest otherwise. I'm just . . . unsure. I don't think going forward will be easy."

"When have you and I ever done what was easy?"

He repeated that thought an hour later when they arrived at Eagle's Way to see George Blackburn in the front yard, throwing a tennis ball for Fred.

Melinda Blackburn watched them from the shaded area of the front porch.

From a wheelchair.

"Mom," Cat said, gasping.

Jack reached over and took her hand, giving it a comforting squeeze. Even through her shock, she took note of the slight tremble in his grip, driving home the fact that in many ways, Melinda was as much his mother as her own.

Fred ran toward the SUV, barking a welcome. George tossed a look toward his wife, then crossed to greet Cat as she flew from the car. "Dad! What happened? What's wrong with Mom?"

She couldn't see a cast or brace or any outward sign of injury. Somehow, that frightened her all the more.

"Hello, Pumpkin," her father said. He gathered her into his arms and wrapped her in a hug.

"Daddy?"

"Don't be afraid, now. Let's go up and let your mother speak to you." Over her shoulder, he added, "Hello, Jack. Sorry to barge in on you this way."

Jack sounded dumbfounded as he replied, "You are welcome anytime, George."

Cat's pulse pounded. She approached her mother, searching her face for a clue to what might be wrong. Well into her fifties, Melinda Blackburn could pass for ten years younger. She kept her hair a flattering shade of blond with just enough gray visible to give her authority. She was shorter than Cat at five feet five inches tall, but between her usual two-inch heels and no-nonsense attitude, people ordinarily believed her to be taller. Her jewelry consisted of plain gold studs in her ears, a simple gold chain around her neck, and a modest wedding set worn on her left hand.

Despite an excellent application of makeup, Cat detected lines in her mother's face that she'd not noticed before. The sour frown was infinitely familiar, however. "Don't look like that, Cathy," she said in way of greeting. "I'm not dead yet."

Typical Mother. "Hello, Mother. This is certainly a surprise."

Melinda looked past her to Jack. "Jack, you'll find a file on your desk that needs immediate attention."

"Welcome to Colorado, Melinda." He placed his hand on the small of Cat's back, offering her unspoken support.

He did not immediately jump to do her mother's bidding, leaving Cat flabbergasted. When was the last time Jack had stood up to her mother that way?

George walked up behind them and suggested, "Why don't we all go inside. It'll be more comfortable and we can have a talk. I could use something to drink. Your dog wore me out."

Melinda nodded once, shot Jack an unspoken "back off" look of warning when he took a step toward her, then deftly turned the wheelchair around and rolled herself toward the front door. Upon reaching it, she waited like the queen she was for one of her minions to open the door. Jack, of course, stepped up.

As the familiar bitter thoughts swirled through her head, Cat stepped into the great room wondering just what the heck was the matter with her. For all she knew, her mother was about to confess some dire condition or the fact that she might be dying, and she couldn't get past the old anger and resentment she felt over Melinda's relationship with Jack? What kind of daughter was she?

"Take a seat, Cathy," Melinda said, indicating the plush couch upholstered in earth tones, one of the few pieces of furniture in the house that faced away from the glorious mountain view. "Jack, I will join you in your office in a few moments."

Jack, bless his heart, moved to stand behind Cat.

Melinda gave him a deadpan look. "Excuse us, Jack. This is family business."

He rested his hand on Cat's shoulder, and she had a sudden vision of him being as strong and unmovable as the mountains behind him. She sat up a little straighter.

Her father walked to the wet bar and filled one glass

with ice water and another with two fingers of bourbon. He handed the water to Melinda, who nodded her thanks, then met her daughter's gaze. "Very well. Cathy, I have a tumor."

A tumor. It took a moment for the shock to sink in. *A tumor. Oh, dear God, no.* Tears flooded Cat's eyes and she blinked them back. Jack tightened his grip on her shoulder as she shifted her gaze toward her dad. He didn't look devastated. The fact calmed her.

Melinda continued, "It is a completely benign, encapsulated tumor that is pressing on my spine. As a result, I am often dizzy and disoriented. I am at risk of falls, which is why I am restricted to a wheelchair. Surgery is scheduled for the seventeenth of next month."

Her mother spouted this all off like statistics. Typical. She probably had the entire ordeal, surgery, recovery, and convalescence planned out to the tiniest detail. She might have sought her husband's opinion, but not Cat's. Never Cat. "Why so long?"

"Waiting will not affect the outcome. The surgery itself is not without some risk. Your father and I prefer to wait for a particular surgeon."

"Dr. Hubbard is the best in the business," George interjected. "Besides, this little break gives me and your mother time to do a few things we've been wanting to do." He smiled and added with just a hint of curiosity in his tone, "Like visit our baby girl and our favorite ex-son-in-law."

"Those are the salient points you need to know. So, now you know them. Jack, if you are through ruffling your male plumage, I wish for you to join me now in your office."

Frustrated and angry and a little afraid, Cat snapped, "Mom, this is Jack's house. You can't order him around."

"Yes, this is Jack's house, but location doesn't excuse

him from seeing to matters that require his attention."
With that, Melinda wheeled herself off toward the office.

Jack hesitated, obviously torn. Cat sighed, knowing it
was a waste of time to fight the inevitable. She reached
up to pat him on his hand. Only then did he follow
Melinda into his home office. She heard her mother ask
him to shut the door. It clicked shut, and Cat collapsed
back against the couch cushions.

Same old thing. Even a tumor couldn't keep Melinda
from being Melinda. Then she turned a disapproving
frown toward her father. "Why?"

He had the grace to look sheepish. "Why what?"

"Why everything! Throw in a few whats. A when or
two would be nice." She folded her arms and said, "Spill
everything, Dad. Start with why you didn't tell me."

"You know your mother. She doesn't know how *not*
to play things close to her vest. She didn't share her
symptoms with me until it became obvious that something
was wrong. She fell. Twice at our house. Apparently once at work."

"Oh, wow. She must have hated that."

"In the beginning, they were concerned about it being
a poison of some sort. That's why we thought your situation
might have been connected to hers. It was the
fog of war, so to speak. We just weren't sure what was
going on."

"Wait a minute. Did Jack know about this?"

"No. She told him there was a threat against her, but
that's as much as he knew."

Mollified by that much, anyway, she said, "So, they're
certain it's benign?"

"Yes. And as far as the surgery goes, I will be honest.
The tumor is situated such that there is some risk of
paralysis. However, the surgeon we have chosen is truly
the best in his field, and he told us that while he couldn't

guarantee anything, he'd put the chances of that at less than ten percent."

"Mom would rather die."

"Yes, I believe she would."

Cat thought about the things her father had revealed, and tried to work out the one thing that still made no sense. "So, why the trip to Colorado?"

"We thought it best to tell you the news in person."

"Why not call me back to Washington? I'm not in danger anymore. There's no reason I couldn't have gone. All you had to do was ask."

For the first time, her father looked a little less than certain. "Well, your mother had something work-related to discuss with Jack."

The file she'd put on his desk, Cat thought. That probably meant he'd be leaving again today on some spy task. *It better not be too far away. The wedding is right around the corner.*

Or maybe there was another explanation. Maybe she wanted an excuse to see what was keeping Cat in Colorado and whether she and Jack were getting close again.

"Plus," her father continued, "we wanted to visit Eternity Springs. It sounded like such a lovely spot, and your mother and I decided we needed to get away for a little while. I have time before the semester starts and she's on leave. The more Celeste told us about Angel's Rest, the more it sounded like the perfect place for us."

Shocked and stunned, Cat took a moment to process what he'd just said. Holding up her hand, she said, "Wait a minute. Celeste? You've been talking to Celeste Blessing?"

"Yes. Such a lovely, friendly lady. I can't wait to meet her."

"You've been talking to Celeste Blessing," Cat repeated. She'd never said a word. One word.

"We have a cottage reserved there beginning tonight."

"You and Mom are staying at Angel's Rest!" *Beginning* tonight? "For how long?"

"Our reservation is open-ended. Celeste assures us that there are plenty of activities to keep us busy. She and your mother have gotten to be quite chummy."

Celeste chummy with Melinda.

The world had tilted on its axis. This just wasn't right. The child in Cat wanted to whine, *But they are* my *friends. She can't have them, too!*

Her father was no dummy, and he must have sensed what was going on in her mind. He came and sat beside her, draped an arm around her shoulder, and gave her a hug. "Look, I know it probably seems like your mother and I are butting in on your new life. Ordinarily, I wouldn't have dreamed of coming out here uninvited. But I have to tell you, Cat, something downright strange happened when your mother was talking to Celeste. Something about Angel's Rest touched a chord inside her. Celeste talked about a healing energy in the valley, and I swear, I almost think some of it came through the phone lines to your mother."

"I thought you said the tumor is benign."

"It is. It is. Truly, you need not worry about that. I'm talking about something, well, spiritual, almost. I've heard your mother laugh more in the last week than she has laughed in years."

"Mom? Laugh?"

"Yes."

"How long has she been in the wheelchair?"

"Ten days."

"That's very strange."

"Strange, perhaps, but wonderful, too. Your mother deserves some time to be carefree. For the last thirty years, she has worn the weight of the world on her shoulders."

"By her own choice." Cat worked to keep bitterness

out of her voice. "Please, let's not have this conversation again. I know she's patriotic and dedicated and all of those things. I respect that. But what I cannot and will not respect is the attitude that we're all supposed to jump when Melinda Blackburn barks an order. Look how she treated Jack! In his own house! After he stopped his life to help me out, she acts like he's her servant."

"Catherine, that's not fair. Their roles are defined. She's his—"

"Boss? Superior? Dictator? What?"

"Cat, please."

She folded her arms, her temper rising with every minute that ticked by with her lover and her mother ensconced in the office. Since her dad insisted that her mother's illness wasn't life-threatening—and her father never lied to Cat—then Melinda didn't get a bad behavior pass as far as Cat was concerned. Shoot, *she* was the one whose life was being threatened—the life she was trying to put back together with Jack.

"Mom blows in here like a tornado with no warning, and he has to scramble to do her bidding. It's ingrained. It's never going to change. If Jack and I get back together, I need to know that going in."

Her father drew back. "*Are* you and Jack getting back together?"

That stopped her tirade flat. "No. Maybe. I don't know. It's complicated."

"Life usually is. This world we live in definitely is, and that's what you need to remember when you think about your mother." Cat snorted, but he pressed on. "Somebody has to be the hero. It's because of people like your mother and their service to our country that we are able to enjoy our way of life. Melinda might not wear a uniform, but she is just as much a soldier as the man who carries a gun onto a battlefield. The physical risks might not be as great, but the mental ones can be devastating."

Cat's thoughts drifted to Jack. Her father wasn't telling her anything she didn't already know. Hadn't those stresses been why she'd tried to resist Jack's lure to begin with? Hadn't those stresses contributed to the breakup of their marriage?

Weren't those same stresses causing her to guard her heart against him now?

This morning, he'd come right out and said the words. *I love you. You still love me.*

Did she? She didn't want to. She'd barely survived the destruction of the marriage the first time. Going through that again would kill her.

"How did you do it, Dad? How did you manage Mom's job all these years?"

He eyed her curiously. "It hasn't always been easy, I admit. But your mother is a very, very special woman, Catherine, and I love her. That's all that ever mattered."

"But sometimes love isn't enough."

"Isn't it? Or maybe it's a case where the strings we place on love are holding it back from being what it is meant to be."

She frowned, hearing what he'd undoubtedly intended for her to hear. Her father always had been an excellent educator. Had she placed conditions on her love for Jack? Put tethers on the eagle? "That's possible. But I wonder if perhaps sometimes, some loves are meant to be grounded. Maybe that's what sets them free."

Free as in secure, certain without a doubt that love would be there to share, strengthen, and support in the hard times.

George Blackburn gave his daughter's cheek a kiss. "Could be, Sunshine. Could be. No one's life path is the same. You asked me about mine and your mother's. What I know is that we loved each other and wanted to make that love work. The sacrifices we made for each other strengthened us."

Cat stiffened slightly at that. "What sacrifices did Mom make for you?"

He studied her, surprise showing in his eyes. "You don't know?"

Baffled, she shook her head. "I'm sorry, but your marriage always seemed one-sided to me."

"Oh, Cat." He smiled wryly. "I know we haven't made a secret of what happened back then. You surely know all this."

"All what?"

"First, I suppose you've realized that your mother's pregnancy wasn't planned?"

"Yeah, figured that one out when I was in fifth grade and discovered that pregnancies lasted nine months, not seven."

He grinned sheepishly. "You were loved from the moment we knew about you, though, sweetheart. At the time, I was a grad student with a part-time job. Your mother already had a government job—with security and benefits. She was our breadwinner. It made sense that she continue to work after you were born, and my hours as a student allowed me to spend more time with you. Then I got the offer to come to Georgetown and your mother's boss recommended her to the Agency. The plan was for me to get established and then your mother would quit and become a stay-at-home mom."

"What?" If her dad had claimed her mom wanted to be a Rockette she'd have been less shocked.

"We wanted more children."

"What!"

This was total news to her. If anyone other than her dad had been telling her this, she wouldn't have believed it, but her father didn't lie to her. He never had.

"So what happened?"

"Her two-week vacation when you were eighteen months old. Don't take this badly, Catherine, but you

were a clingy child. You and I had bonded. You threw
tantrums when I left you with your mother. You truly
were a little monster."

"Well, that's lovely to know."

"It shattered her confidence. She was young and she
believed she was a terrible mother. Nothing she did for
you was right—or so she thought. And she tried. Oh,
how she tried. When her vacation was over and she returned to work, she was recruited into the . . . human
resources department . . . and her responsibilities, well,
broadened. We adjusted. Our goals and desires changed.
Your mother is a brilliant woman, Cat. I think she would
have made a wonderful stay-at-home mother of three,
given time. But that wasn't to be, partly because of the
choice she made early on, the sacrifice she made for me
and, frankly, for you, to be this family's primary breadwinner. It put us on a different life path."

Cat's mind spun. Her father had been correct. She had
known these basic facts—well, except for the part about
her being a brat—but she'd never put all the pieces together in a puzzle like this. Her father had painted a
different picture of her mother than she'd ever before
seen or considered.

No wonder she'd always been closer to her dad and
distant from Melinda. It started early on, and while it
wasn't anyone's fault . . . it simply evolved over time. "I
need to think about this," she murmured.

He patted her leg. "You do that. And while you're
thinking, be aware that everyone encounters crossroads
in their lives, but unless you're riding in the same car,
you don't usually arrive at the intersection at the same
time."

"All right, Professor. You lost me on that one."

"You'll figure it out. You know me, I like to make you
work for your answers. Now, tell me about this bache-

lorette party you attended. Celeste told your mother that you all got arrested and spent the night in jail?"

Jack shut the file folder and closed his eyes. A sickness of spirit washed through him. "I had no clue, Melinda."

"It's been the biggest disappointment of my career up until now."

"Do you believe this offer is legitimate?"

"Who knows?" She removed her reading glasses and set them on the desk. She rubbed her eyes. "I haven't managed to give the problem the focus it deserves."

Jack made certain to keep any sign of pity or concern wiped from his face. Melinda Blackburn would appreciate neither. "What do you want from me?"

"We must follow through. We need boots on the ground to analyze the situation and make immediate decisions."

He winced and glanced at the pile of mail on the corner of his desk. Somewhere in the stack was the invitation to Cam and Sarah's wedding. "My cousin is getting married. I'm his best man."

"I know, Jack. I'm sorry."

"There must be someone else who could go. What about Dixon?"

"He's already in the field."

"Dammit, Melinda." Jack shoved to his feet and paced his office. He rubbed his forehead with his thumb and fingers. How could he possibly go? How could he possibly not go? The lives of three good men . . . three of his fellow operatives . . . were at stake. If he abandoned them now he couldn't live with himself. He already had enough ghosts haunting his soul.

Cam would understand. He'd be disappointed, but he would understand. Sarah, maybe not so much. After all, she had the balance in the wedding photos to deal with. Someone could take his place. He and Zach Turner were of a similar size. So, Cam and Sarah he could deal with.

Cat wouldn't like this one bit. This was exactly the sort of thing she held against him. The job. Always, the job. And once again, her mother was involved. Could this get any better?

"Maybe I can get back. I have six days. If I leave immediately, grease some palms to speed up the process, maybe I can get back."

"The budget won't allow for greasing anything."

"Then it's a good thing that I have plenty of my own grease to spread around." The decision made, his mind immediately began to calculate what steps were required, what preparations he needed to make to pull this thing off in order to get back in time for the wedding. Mentally, he had left his office, left Eagle's Way, so when he noticed that Melinda had repeated his name— with an obvious bite in her voice—he realized she must have been trying to get his attention for some time. "We have another matter to discuss before you go. Sit down, please."

Frustration rolled through him. He didn't need a delay. He needed to get moving now. "Melinda, every minute counts at this point."

She leaned forward, her spine snapping straight, as her eyes flashed. "You think this is news to me, under the circumstances?"

The wheelchair. The surgery. *Well, hell.*

"Sorry." Jack took his seat and made a conscious effort to stop his toes from tapping. "What else do we have to discuss?"

Melinda Blackburn sucked in a bracing breath, folded her hands in her lap, and said, "My retirement."

Jack drew back. Retirement? Melinda? She wasn't at retirement age yet. Real fear skittered through him. "Is there more to this illness than you've shared?"

"I'm not dying, Jack. I have decided to retire and I am actually looking forward to it. I want to spend more time with George. I want to have a taste of life outside of Washington."

He studied the face he knew so well. All right, he concluded. She wasn't dying, and maybe she was trying to look forward to retirement, but she wasn't there yet. And he spied a vulnerability inside her that he'd never seen before.

It was a good thing he was already sitting down, because she would have knocked his feet out from under him when she added, "I've been authorized to offer you the job."

"Me?"

"It should come as no great surprise. I groomed you for the position for years."

"Not the past few years," he returned. Not since he'd left Cat. A cocktail of pride, excitement, panic, and dread swirled in his stomach. "I'm a field agent, not a planner."

"You've been a runaway."

"Excuse me? What do you mean by that?"

"You fled from my daughter. Fled from your marriage."

Jack's lips thinned. "I don't discuss my marriage with you, Melinda."

"Then don't ask me questions about it." He opened his mouth to protest, but she gave him the Evil Boss Eye, so he swallowed the protest back. "Your marriage and your job have been intertwined from the first. I'm not saying that running away was the wrong thing to do. You needed to separate your marriage and your job. Honestly, you never would have been right for my job if you didn't learn to do that. You did manage to refrain from discussing your marriage with me, Jack, but that doesn't mean you didn't broadcast details about your life in other ways while you were with Cathy. Your body language was unmistakable. It was a weakness."

Insulted, he snapped back. "Then why in the world would you offer me your job now? Because I'm divorced?"

"Because you're ready for it. I'll be honest. Yes, the divorce is part of it, because the divorce helped shape you into the man you are today. You've always had the intelligent, analytical mind necessary to be successful in this job. You've always had the passion needed for the work. But your field experience of recent years has matured you, and I am confident that you now possess the dedication needed to lead and succeed in this position."

"What about Cat?"

"Yes, what about Cathy?" When he didn't respond, she quietly said, "She's different from her father. George has been content to be the spouse of a director. That's not what Cathy needs or wants."

"So that's why you sent me to her? You thought we needed one more fling to get each other out of our systems?"

"Both of you made the decision to split when you were wounded and thinking unclearly. Now you're healthy, and you need to confirm that decision once and for all. It's time, Jack. You've both lived in limbo for the past five years. Take the job and it will be a clean cut for you both. Finally."

"I don't know, Melinda. I'm not sure . . ."

Her tone quiet and encouraging, she said, "This is what you've wanted, what you've worked for since the day you and I were introduced. Lives depend upon the work my department does. Many more lives are affected by our successes. It's important work. You'll be wonderful in the job, Jack. I think it's the job that you were born to do."

Softly, he murmured, "I wanted to be a fireman."

"I'm sorry. What did you say?"

"When do you need an answer?"

She lifted her chin. "Do you honestly need to think about it?"

A year ago, no, he wouldn't have needed to think. Six months ago, he'd have accepted on the spot. One month ago?

One month ago, he'd already carted Cat off to Colorado, so yeah, he'd have wanted to sleep on it. If she'd asked him this question a week ago, he'd have wanted to think long and hard about it. Today, his answer hung on the tip of his tongue, and the fact that he did react so instinctively made him literally bite his tongue and suck in a deep breath.

"I love your daughter."

"Does she love you?"

He hesitated. He believed she loved him, but since their reunion, she had never said those words. Not yet, anyway. She would. She loved him. He knew she did. "She will."

"And then what? You will destroy each other all over again?"

Anger flared within him. She didn't know that. That outcome wasn't written in stone.

But now wasn't the time to argue with her. "You know what? I need to focus on my trip. This discussion can wait until I return." He picked up the file folder from his desk, then hesitated. He felt bad about running out on Cam. Leaving Cat under these circumstances almost felt worse. "What is your schedule? You and George are welcome to stay here for as long as you'd like, of course, and this office has everything you should require."

"Thank you, but George and I have a reservation at Angel's Rest. I don't expect that I will need secure communications during the next few weeks, but if something does come up that requires my attention, I will appreciate access to your equipment."

The next few weeks? That confused Jack. She'd said

she was looking forward to her retirement, not that it had already taken place. "Who is my contact?"

"Mark Ellis is filling in at my desk until you get back. I am officially away on sick leave, but if you have need of me, of course I'll make myself available." She glanced at her wristwatch. "I expected you two hours ago. What extra time we had built into the schedule is gone."

Jack nodded brusquely, turned, and headed for the door. At the threshold, her voice made him hesitate. "Choose your path carefully, Jack Davenport."

"I always do, Melinda. I always do."

That's why he almost went straight upstairs to grab his go bag without detouring into the great room, but Jack was done running from Cat. She stood beside her father at the telescope set up in front of the windows. "Sorry to interrupt, but Cat? Could you join me upstairs for a couple of minutes?"

She took one look at his face and subtly stiffened. "I'll be right up."

Jack took the stairs two at a time, mentally dragging his feet. In his bedroom, he took his bag from his closet and set it on the bed just as she walked in. She eyed the bag, then pasted on a smile that looked surprisingly carefree. "Another meeting on Capitol Hill?"

He hesitated. "No. I'm headed west this time, not east."

"How far west?"

Jack did something then that he had never done—he talked to her about his trip. "I'm going to Manila. A couple of our own have gone missing and it's my job to help find them."

Her smile faded, but the scowl he expected failed to appear. Instead, she seemed surprised that he included her. "Sounds dangerous."

"My part shouldn't be. I'm determined to make it a

turnaround trip and get back here as fast as I possibly can."

Her eyes narrowed and he anticipated her next comment. "The wedding."

"I'll do my best to get back."

"Cam is your cousin, Jack. Your family."

She didn't say "Your only family" out loud, but he heard the words loud and clear anyway. "I know. Believe me, I know, but this trip truly is a matter of life and death. Cam will understand."

"Sarah will kill you." Then Cat drew back, shaking her head. "I'm not telling her. You better call Cam."

"I will."

He reached for the touch pad on the wall that operated the bedroom's recessed lighting—among other things— and rapidly punched in a series of numbers. A lock snicked and a bookshelf behind Cat swung away from the wall. She startled, but quickly recovered. "Of course there's a hidden wall safe."

Jack didn't even attempt to hide the guns, the bundle of cash, or the three passports he pulled from inside it. It struck him that Cat had never known about the safe hidden in the house they lived in after they married. He'd kept so much from her during that part of their lives.

No more. He was done hiding from her. He added the items to his bag, then approached her. "I'm sorry. This is the last thing I wanted for us. The timing just—"

She put two fingers against his lips, her green eyes filled with sadness, resignation, and acceptance. "No. Don't worry about me. I knew exactly what I was getting into when I said I wanted to test the waters. No strings attached, remember?"

Frustrated, Jack dragged her against him and kissed her hard and fast. "I love you, Cat. When I come back, we're gonna talk about diving into the deep end, talk about strings and knots and for better or worse. Now, leave a candle burning in the window for me, would you?"

Before she'd fought her way back from speechless, Jack Davenport had turned and left Eagle's Way.

FIFTEEN

❦

Three days before Sarah's wedding, Cat felt more like Alice down the rabbit hole than an adult woman, an award-winning investigative reporter who supported such causes as animal rescue and wounded veterans' charities. Here in Eternity Springs, reality had transformed into fantasyland. Alternative-reality world. What else would explain the fact that she was sitting at a table in the attic workroom at Angel's Rest with Celeste Blessing and Melinda Blackburn—the same Melinda Blackburn who was her mother and a spy for the CIA—and they were scrapbooking?

Scrapbooking. Her. Her mother. Together. Cat fully expected the world to come to an end sometime that morning.

She'd come because Sage, Nic, and Ali were supposed to be here to work on a scrapbook of the bachelorette party to give to Sarah. Then Sage's baby started running a fever, Gabe had a work issue come up so he couldn't babysit the twins, and Ali needed to be at the Yellow Kitchen to take delivery on some special ingredients she'd ordered for the wedding meal she was catering. By the time that all happened, Cat was stuck.

It was a surreal sort of stuck. In all her life, she and her mother had never sat and done crafts. Never. They'd never baked cookies together or worked on school projects together. They didn't sew or dye Easter eggs or make sock puppets. It was just weird to be sitting at a craft table with Melinda Blackburn.

It didn't help that this was her first foray into the scrapbooking phenomenon and she hadn't known what to expect. Before she'd sat down to work, she hadn't understood the attraction of the activity. Now, after half an hour of work, she would admit to finding the paper cutting machine to be a fun toy.

"Do you have any more of those cute little gold halos?" Celeste asked.

Cat fingered through her pile of paper. "I have silver."

"That will be fine."

Cat handed Celeste the little scrap of cardboard, and a moment later, she lifted a completed page to show it off. "Is this not the cutest thing ever?"

Celeste's masterpiece portrayed the zip line part of the party, and she'd combined photographs with paper cut-outs of mountains, trees, and animals. Strings ran from tree to tree to portray the cable, and an angel figure complete with wings representing each of the partygoers dangled from the wire. The Sarah figure wore a bridal veil, Celeste the halo, and Nic, Ali, and Cat wore horns.

Cat laughed just as a knock sounded at the open door of the workroom. Cat's father stood on the threshold, a shipping box in hand. "Your package arrived, Mel. I knew you'd want it."

Melinda Blackburn lit up. "Wonderful. Thanks for bringing it up, George. How was the fishing?"

"Those trout are wily little beggars."

"That bad, hmm?"

"I'm sure the problem is with the tackle I'm using. One of your friends, Cat, Mac Timberlake, said he'd show me how to tie his most successful fly this afternoon."

"That's nice of him," Melinda observed.

"Mac is a wonderful, generous man," Celeste observed.

George set the box down in front of Melinda, then kissed both his wife and his daughter on their cheeks and took his leave. As Melinda opened her package, Celeste continued, "Eternity Springs lucked out when Mac decided to follow Ali to Eternity Springs and reconcile. Their marriage experienced some rocky times and came close to ending. It would have been such a shame for them both and for their children had that happened. They are so happy now, but it took time and effort and commitment for them to heal their relationship."

"Ali told me about it," Cat said. "I noticed the angel's wings necklace she wears."

"The official Angel's Rest Healing Center and Spa blazon," Celeste said.

Melinda glanced up from her photos. "Your friend Nic wears one. They're simply lovely."

"Aren't they, though?" Celeste agreed. "They are a Sage Anderson design—our own Sage Rafferty—and they are fashioned from the silver that was left with the poor Cellar Bride."

"Are they for sale in the gift shop?"

"Oh, no. The blazons are not for sale. They are awarded only to those who have embraced love's healing's grace."

"Sarah told me she was so jealous of her friends when they got their medals. She said she never expected to earn one of her own . . . and then Cam came back to town."

Celeste's smile was beatific. "Sometimes miracles do happen, Cat."

Nothing veiled about that message, Cat thought. Looking for a distraction, she turned to her mother and was once again struck by the absurdity of seeing her mom with a glue gun in her hand rather than a Glock. "What's in the box, Melinda?"

"Some family photographs I had at the office. I want to include them in my scrapbook."

Family photos from the office? On the rare occasions she'd visited her mother's office, Cat had never seen photographs on her credenza or walls or desk.

Celeste said, "Oh, do share, Melinda. I simply adore family photos."

Cat watched with surprise as her mother drew a tattered photo album from the box. It was the sort of inexpensive album once offered for sale in drugstores with sticky-back pages and clear plastic sheets to cover the pictures. Melinda wore a bittersweet smile as she flipped back the cover to reveal her wedding photo.

Celeste said, "Aren't you two a handsome pair!"

"We were so young," Melinda replied.

Cat had seen the photograph before—her father kept it on his desk both at home and at his office on campus—but she hadn't really looked at it in a very long time. Now, it struck her just how much she looked like her mother.

Melinda flipped the page and all of a sudden, Cat was looking at her own wedding photo. She barely noticed when Celeste excused herself, saying she had to cover the front desk while her employee took her break and she'd return in twenty minutes. Cat's heart twisted as she stared at the photograph. Girlfriends who'd married before her had warned Cat that she wouldn't remember the moment, that the details of the ceremony and her wedding day would be one big blur in her mind. That's not how it'd been for Cat. The important moments of that day were etched into her memory, and she could recall them today as though they'd happened yesterday.

They had eloped to Las Vegas, but instead of doing the deed at a tacky wedding chapel or even one of the fancy chapels in a hotel, they had found a Methodist church in a residential area of town and a real, ordained minister to conduct their ceremony. She'd bought a wedding gown off the sample rack at a bridal shop and he'd purchased a tux at the mall—no rental for Jack Davenport even back then. She wondered if Jack still had that tux.

The minister's wife had played the organ and the office secretary and youth minister had served as witnesses. At the time, a part of her, admittedly a very small part, had missed having family or friends with her to mark the event.

But it had been right for her and Jack. He didn't have family, or really any friends outside of work, and under the circumstances, having work friends at his wedding wouldn't have been appropriate. She recalled the first notes of the bridal march and stepping to the back of the aisle. Then Jack had turned, and the fierce look of love and admiration on his face had her gliding up the aisle.

"You're so beautiful," he said to her as he met her at the altar. "You make me weak at the knees. If I faint, you have to catch me."

"Are you kidding? In these heels, no way I'd keep my balance."

They stood at the altar of a Methodist church, the minister asked them to bow their heads in prayer, and moments later, she was facing Jack, holding his hands and gazing up into his serious blue eyes. They had chosen traditional vows, and when he repeated the minister's words, his voice rang with such sincerity, truth, and promise that she was struck by the fact that this was what the term "vow" truly meant.

When she repeated those same words back to him, she meant them with every fiber of her being. Cat's heart swelled with love and joy as the minister announced they were husband and wife. When, a few moments later, he took a snapshot of the newly married couple in front of the altar with the small camera Cat carried in her purse, she truly believed their love was strong enough to defeat whatever trials came their way.

Now, seated at a table in the attic workroom of a Victorian house in a little Colorado mountain town with years of heartache behind her, Cat stared at the photograph and stated, "You didn't want me to marry him."

Following a long pause, Melinda said, "No, I didn't."

"You never came out and said it, but it was obvious. That's why we eloped. Neither one of us wanted to deal with your disapproval."

She paused, waiting for her mother to speak in her own defense, but when Melinda remained stubbornly silent, Cat said, "I always wondered what you held against us. Care to finally clue me in? Wasn't I good enough for your golden boy?"

"Oh, don't be silly."

Cat folded her arms as questions that had brewed within her for years demanded answers. "I'm not being silly. It's a legitimate question. Why didn't you want Jack to marry me?"

"I didn't think the two of you were right for each other. Jack was committed to his career and you made no secret that you despised that career. I thought you both would be happier with other people."

"Were you glad when we split up?"

"No. You suffered, Cathy. You and Jack both suffered, and I hated that. Once it was done, however, I hoped you both would get on with your lives. You did a good job of it. I've been proud of how you recovered from the miscarriage—"

"Lauren was stillborn."

"I'm sorry. Of course. I'm proud that once you recovered from losing your child, you took control and found purpose and focus in your work and charitable activities. I admit I've been disappointed that you haven't found someone else to love. I want you to be happy, Cathy. Believe it or not, that's what I've always wanted for you."

Inexplicably, Cat found her eyes filling with tears. This wouldn't do. Dipping her head to concentrate on getting the black dog's tail positioned just right on her Wild, Wild West theme page, she willed them away. Once she'd managed to find control again, she asked another question that plagued her. "Why send Jack when I was in trouble? Surely there was someone else you could have trusted to help protect me."

This time the answer was a little longer in coming. "It was my judgment that the two of you had unfinished business that prevented both of you from taking the next step. I thought this situation provided the perfect opportunity for you to deal with those issues."

"Kill two crises with one kidnapping."

Melinda laughed, and Cat started at the unusual sound. "That's a fair way of looking at it, I guess."

"The way he's talked, Jack hasn't been working for you for some time. Not directly, anyway?"

Melinda gave Cat a considering look. Ordinarily, she'd never respond to such a question, and Cat honestly didn't expect her to do so now, but again her mother surprised her. "He transferred out of my department and into a section where his talents are utilized in more physically challenging situations."

Cat's stomach took a little roll. "Dangerous situations."

"Well, yes."

"Have you heard from him? Is he in danger now?"

"I am not being kept apprised of the situation, but I did request to be notified should he run into trouble. This trip isn't as dangerous as it is arduous. Jack keeps himself in good shape, but frankly, the job he's been doing is better suited to a younger man. He needs to leave that job." Melinda set down her glue gun and looked Cat straight in the eyes. "That's why I offered him mine."

Confused, Cat lowered her hands to her lap. "*Your* job?"

"I have put in for my retirement."

Retirement? She's actually retiring? Maybe she really is dying.

"Jack's transfer and promotion have been approved."

His promotion to her mother's job. Jack was taking her mother's job? It finally got through to her, and Cat's heart twisted as a dream she hadn't admitted to nursing died. "When did he apply for it?"

"He didn't apply. I recommended him."

Of course you did. Cat closed her eyes. Of course Melinda recommended Jack for her all-consuming job. He was the perfect person for it, right? She'd known that for more than fifteen years.

Cat couldn't keep the bitterness from her voice as she said, "So you thought *I* was the unfinished business he needed to deal with before taking your job?"

Melinda obviously chose her words carefully. "Jack needed to stop running from you, one way or the other."

"He's not running from me," Cat snapped, her temper flaring. "He's been sleeping with me!"

A glint of emotion flashed across her mother's face so quickly that Cat wasn't sure she actually saw what she thought she'd seen. It almost looked like . . . satisfaction.

Surely she was mistaken.

"When did he accept it?"

"He hasn't yet. Apparently, he needed time to think about it."

Cat's chin came up. "What if he says no? That could happen, you know. What if he turns it down?"

Melinda flipped the photo album page back to Cat's wedding photograph. "I don't know. Yes, he could refuse the job, though that wouldn't be in his own best interests at all. I imagine in that case, he'll stay in the job he's in now, doing what he does now, for as long as possible. Of course, he could quit the service entirely. He doesn't work because he needs to financially, of course. Jack does the job because he wants to. He needs to emotionally. He's spent his whole adult life honing his skills to do it to perfection." Doubt permeated her tone as she added, "Perhaps he could find another occupation that he would find just as fulfilling."

Cat stifled the sudden urge to stick out her tongue at her mother, let out a sigh instead, and reached for her scissors. She would finish up this page, then find something else . . . anything else . . . to do. Maybe she'd give Fred a bath. He'd had a playdate with Cam's devil dog yesterday and he'd smelled funky ever since. She didn't know what those two had gotten into, and she didn't think she wanted to know.

"I'll be honest, Cathy. I didn't support your marriage to Jack because I didn't want you to have the kind of life your father has had. I wasn't blind to the worry and the fear and the stress—it was hard for me and your father and obviously for you, too. But while your father has the personality to be an agent's spouse, you didn't when you started seeing Jack, and in my opinion, you still don't."

"So it's all my fault." As always.

"I'm not saying that at all. Fault has nothing to do with it. You are who you are, Cathy. You are a wonderful, kind, caring human being and I'm so proud of the woman you've become. The reality is that life as Jack's wife isn't right for you—not as long as he does the work he does. If you must place blame, Jack's shoulders are a good fit. After all, he could have changed jobs when you two married, or before you divorced. He could have quit to be here for his cousin's wedding rather than go to Manila. He didn't. You need to ask yourself why that is. Believe me, I've asked the question."

Melinda laced her fingers and leaned forward. "Believe this or not, Cat, but there is nothing I want more than to see you happy. I love you. And I love Jack, too. I want him to be happy, too. I just have my doubts that the two of you can make each other happy in the long run. However, you are both adults and you have to make your own decisions. It's not my place to interfere in your private lives."

"But you always did. You were my husband's boss, his mentor. That interfered."

"Well, that won't be the case now, will it? I'll be retired. Oh, look at this." Melinda pulled another picture from the box and turned it toward Cat. "This was your first bicycle. Do you remember it?"

With that, the topic of Jack and his job was left behind as Cat suffered through another fifteen minutes of family photographs before Celeste returned and she managed to make her escape. As she made her way downstairs and out of the house, her thoughts bounced around like a pinball. Her mom had kept a family photo album at her office. She'd offered Jack her job. Melinda was retiring. What about Dad? Did he intend to keep teaching? Mom had offered Jack her job. Maybe her parents would do something even stranger than taking an extended visit to Eternity Springs, like move to Florida.

Mom had offered Jack her job.

And what had he said to Cat almost immediately afterward? *I love you, Cat. When I come back, we're gonna talk about diving into the deep end, talk about strings and knots and for better or worse.*

Strings and knots, for better or worse.

She wanted to cry.

Instead, she stopped by the supply building, secured buckets and an old towel, and headed for Nightingale Cottage. There, she filled both buckets with warm water and carried them outside to the fenced yard behind her cabin where Fred lay lounging in the sun. At her approach, he bound to his feet, his tail wagging hard, his tongue extended and ready to lick.

Cat expected to get soaked, but Fred turned out to be one of those rare dogs who love getting a bath. Cat didn't consciously think as she sudsed him up, rinsed him off, and patted him dry, but once the task was complete and he happily scampered toward Angel Creek to shake and chase his tail, she realized that somewhere along the way, she'd come to a conclusion.

She loved Jack Davenport. She'd never stopped loving Jack Davenport. And Jack Davenport loved her.

"He's going to turn the job down," she said to Fred, knowing in her bones that she was right.

At the same time, she knew in her bones that her mother was right, too. Jack had been born to do the job he'd been offered, maybe not on the day his mother gave birth to him, but surely on the day when she lost her life in the fire that spared him, leaving him to the guidance of the guardian who had brought him to Melinda Blackburn's attention. He saved lives. He made lives better. He truly was a hero.

Either way, she would make him miserable.

If he took the job, misery was inevitable. Oh, she could try to change. She *would* try to change—just as she'd tried to change when she married him the first time. She'd tried so hard to accept his job, to support his work, to be the wife a hero deserved, but it hadn't worked. They'd loved each other then, too. They'd made each other miserable, even before Lauren died.

And if he quit his job? Then what? How long would it be before he missed the life? How long before he resented her? A month? A year? It was bound to happen at some point. Jack Davenport was born for the job. And would she take that away from him? Could she take it away from him and still live with herself?

Cat looked back at the window of Nightingale Cottage where, out of sentimentality and silliness, she'd placed the electric candle that she'd purchased from the Christmas section of the Angel's Rest gift shop. *Now, leave a candle burning in the window for me, would you?*

She thought of the hours they'd shared at Nightingale Cottage. She thought of the time they'd spent together at Eagle's Way. She thought of their life together in Washington. Loving him was easy. Living with him was . . . another story.

Jack Davenport was the Eagle. Eagles weren't meant for strings and knots and tethers to the ground or white picket fences.

"I have to set him free."

SIXTEEN

Cam Murphy woke on his wedding day to the ringing of the telephone. He bolted upright in bed and stared at the land line as if it were a moray eel. "She's calling to call it off."

Brring. Brring. Brring.

"Dad, answer the phone!" his son, Devin, yelled from his room across the hall.

"I can't. What if it's Sarah calling to call off the wedding?"

"Dad, you are so lame."

He was lame. Sarah loved him. She wasn't calling off the wedding. However, she could be calling to tell him that she'd decided they needed yellow satin bows on the ends of the pews instead of white. Thank God he was marrying for life, because this wedding nonsense was driving him crazy. But after all she'd had to go through all these years by herself, he owed it to her to do what he could to make her day perfect.

Just as he reached for the phone, it stopped ringing.

Cam thought his heart might have stopped beating. What if Sarah had called to call off the wedding?

"Dad. Pick up. It's Jack."

"Thank God." He grabbed the receiver from the cradle. "You better be home!"

Static crackled and told him the answer before his

cousin spoke. "I'm still in the air. Should be able to make it in time, but I'll probably need to come straight to the church. I'm arranging for someone to meet my jet with a tux, but I need to know which vest Sarah finally decided on."

"Last I heard it was silver, but it could be animal print by now."

"Going that well, is it?"

"Let's just say I'll be really glad when it's over. She wants you and Devin in the silver."

"Okay. Look, Cam, I thought I should give you a heads-up, since Sarah is so particular about her photos. I'm looking a little ragged. It won't hurt my feelings if she wants me to—"

"You okay, cuz?" Cam interrupted.

"Yes. Let's just say I'll add a little color to the photos that I don't think your bride is counting on."

Cam didn't hesitate. "Look, Sarah talks a big game, but what she really wants . . . what we both want . . . is you there with us when we say out wedding vows in—" he glanced at the clock "—six hours."

Oh, wow. Six hours.

"I'm doing my best." Static crackled. "How is Cat?"

Cam scratched his bare chest and considered his response before finally saying, "She's worried about you. Have you called her?"

"She didn't answer her phone."

"Yeah, well, she left it in reach of the Boston Terror-ist," he said, referring to his dog, who had an eating disorder—Mortimer ate everything. "It's history."

As if he knew he was the topic of conversation, Mor-timer lifted his head from where he slept at the foot of Cam's bed.

"Oh. Okay."

Jack sounded relieved and Cam would have felt guilty, only it was his wedding day. When he hung up the phone a couple of minutes later, he spied his son standing on the threshold, his arms crossed, a disapproving frown on his face. "You lied to your best man?"

"Co–best man," Cam automatically replied. "Damn straight I'm going to lie. He can't do anything from cruise altitude, so what's the point in telling him. I don't want anything interfering with Sarah's dream day."

Devin scratched his stubbled jaw thoughtfully. "Makes sense. So, old man, you gonna lie around in the fart sack all day, or you gonna haul your butt out of bed and make me some breakfast?"

"Excuse me?"

Devin laughed. "Actually, I thought I'd take Beelzebub for a walk and stop by the Mocha Moose and pick up some cinnamon rolls."

"Don't let your mother find out that you're shopping at the competition," Cam replied.

Both men stopped and shared a grin. "Thanks for giving me a mom again, Dad."

"My pleasure, son. My pleasure."

Sarah Reese awoke on her wedding day to church bells.

The Catholic church one block over from her house didn't ordinarily ring their bells on a Saturday morning, but Father Tim was a frequent customer at Fresh. He'd told her with a twinkle in his eye that he would ring the bells in mourning today since her bakery would be closed for the next month while she and Cam were away on their honeymoon in the South Pacific—either that, or in joyous celebration of her happy day. Lying in bed, Sarah stretched languorously and laughed out loud.

Moments later, her daughter showed up at her door. "I thought I heard you stirring. I was beginning to think you'd sleep through your own wedding."

"I needed my beauty sleep," she replied. "I'm older

than the average bride, after all, and I don't want puffy eyes in the wedding photos."

Lori rolled her eyes. "You and your wedding photos."

Sarah sat up and grabbed her robe off the foot of the bed, then asked, "How is your grandmother doing this morning?"

"Good. I like the nurse, Mom. She's soft-spoken and so gentle with Nana. It's obvious she loves what she does."

"It takes a special attitude to care for the elderly," Sarah agreed.

"This morning during breakfast she told me that someone Cat Blackburn knows did an investigative news report about an investment club that was taking advantage of seniors in the Gunnison area. She said the people running it packed up in the middle of the night and left town."

"Yes. Cat found out about it when she visited Mom, and she got someone from Denver to look into it. I don't understand how people can be so cruel."

"*I* don't understand how Cat can give up on Jack," Lori said. "He's rich. He's mysterious. He's to-die-for sexy."

Sarah's exuberant mood dimmed just a bit. "One thing I've learned along this road I've traveled with your father is that it's impossible to understand anyone's relationship from the outside looking in."

"My father," Lori repeated, pleasure blooming on her face.

"Your father." Sarah reached out and gave her daughter a quick, fierce hug. "Speaking of which, did you get the paperwork all done?"

"I did. I was just getting ready to wrap it when I heard you. Want to see?"

"I do." Then she laughed. "That was good practice. I do, I do, I do."

Lori rolled her eyes once more in that special way that daughters can do with their mothers, then left her mother's bedroom to return moments later. With a flourish, she handed a piece of paper to Sarah, who looked at it and sighed. "This is going to send Cam over the moon. You couldn't have given either of us a more perfect wedding gift—Lori Elizabeth Murphy."

Cat awoke on Cam and Sarah's wedding day to a sloppy wet kiss. "Fred, I really wish you could learn to let yourself out."

Then she recalled what today was and realized that this was the last time Fred's potty habits would matter to her, and she fought back tears. She'd miss Fred. Then again, it would be hard for Jack to give the dog the attention he needed once he started the new job. Maybe she could offer to take him if . . .

"No. He won't neglect you. He'll probably hire a home day care service for you." And she wouldn't need the constant reminder Fred would provide of her time in Eternity Springs.

She had all her arrangements made. Melinda had told her yesterday that Jack had safely accomplished his mission and was headed home, so she'd been able to set her plans in motion. She'd been tempted to leave him a note and sneak out of town before he returned, but that would be cowardly of her and unfair to him. One thing she could say about her mother: Melinda had been right about unfinished business. Cat intended to finish her business with Jack Davenport today—once and for all.

But as the day progressed and the two o'clock time for the wedding approached with no appearance by Jack, she began to wonder if she'd have the chance. "Is he here yet?" Sarah asked in the bride's dressing room as Nic laced up the corset back of her gorgeous shantung silk strapless gown.

"Cam has been here since noon," Sage said, leaning forward to better see her reflection in the mirror as she touched up her lipstick.

"Not Cam. Jack."

Ali shook her head. "No, honey, he's not here yet. Don't worry about the photos. Zach is dressed in the tux and ready to step in."

"I don't care about the stupid pictures. I care about Cam. It's important for him to have Jack here."

Cat gave Sarah's arm a comforting touch. "It's important to Jack to be here. Don't give up on him, Sarah. He won't let his cousin down."

Sarah folded her arms and gave Cat a scathing look. "Hello! I wish you'd listen to what you just said. I'm not giving up on him. Why are you?"

Cat winced. She had told her new friends that it wasn't going to work out with her and Jack, and they hadn't taken the news well. Glancing around the crowded dressing room, she spied only one sympathetic face— Celeste Blessing's. When the organ music swelled in the church, she took the opportunity to escape. "I'd better go find a seat before they're all taken."

"Come sit beside me, dear," Celeste said. "I'm liable to need help. At Sage's wedding I started bawling and dropped my handkerchief. I could hardly see it to pick it up for the tears."

The church was packed. At ten minutes to two, Cat heard the distinct *whop whop whop* of a helicopter. She exhaled a small sigh and Celeste reached over and patted her leg. At five minutes to two, Gabe Callahan escorted Sarah's mother to her seat. As soon as Ellen was settled, the organist quit playing, a side door opened, and Jack stepped into the church, followed by Devin and Cam Murphy.

Cat gasped audibly. Celeste leaned over and whispered loudly, "That had to hurt."

The left eye sported a shiner, he wore a bandage across his cheekbone, and his left arm was in a sling. She saw his gaze sweep the congregation, then lock onto her, and he smiled.

Cat trembled, barely noticing as Nic, then Lori, made their way down the aisle. She wanted to look away from Jack, but she couldn't force herself to do so. It wasn't until the organist sounded those familiar notes of the bridal march and the congregation stood that she jerked her attention back to the matter at hand.

The look of devotion shining in Cam's eyes as he watched Sarah walk toward him brought tears to Cat's eyes. But since she'd been tearing up over everything today, that was no real surprise.

The ceremony was lovely, the bride and groom beaming with happiness. Cat's gaze kept straying to Jack as she imagined different scenarios for how he got his injuries. None of them eased her worries.

The reception was being held outdoors at Angel's Rest, which would prove handy for Cat. She'd rented a car the previous day and packed up most of her things before leaving for the church. Her plans were to wait until Jack's best-man duties were done and ask him to walk her back to Nightingale Cottage, where she could inform him of her decision, change her clothes, and make her escape. Now all she had to do was to get Jack to fall in with her plans.

However, by the time the minister announced that Cam and Sarah were husband and wife, Cat realized that she needed to make some alterations to her plan. She couldn't bear it. No matter how much she liked her new friends, despite her sincere wishes for their happiness, if she had to witness much more of this bliss, she was afraid that she'd break down and bawl like a baby.

After escorting the matron of honor up the aisle, Jack waited for Cat in the back of the church. "Hey, there," he said, bending down to kiss her lightly on the lips. "You look gorgeous."

"You look bruised. Are you all right? What happened to your arm?"

"I'm fine. Just a little banged up." He avoided the question about his arm as he stared intently into her eyes. "You okay?"

"Yes. I'm fine, too." She worked to find a smile. "I'm so glad you made it back in time."

"I was determined to get here." Again, he gave her a searching look. "What's wrong?"

"I get a little emotional at weddings."

Just then, Devin interrupted them. "Jack, my mom wants you back at the altar for pictures."

"I'll be right there," he replied, not looking away from Cat. "You'll wait and go with me to the reception?"

"No, I'm helping. I need to go on. I'll see you there."

She rushed off, her heart pounding as she fought back tears. She'd known today would be difficult, but she hadn't anticipated it being so gut-wrenching.

Rather than taking the straight route up Fifth Street toward the footbridge over Angel Creek along with the rest of the crowd headed to the reception, she ducked down an alley to steal a few minutes to herself. There, digging in metal garbage can behind the barber shop, she spied Cam's dog, the Boston terrier named Mortimer who was the biggest escape artist in town.

"Oh, Mortimer," she said with a sigh. He lifted his head from the can and turned to look at her, most of a hamburger bun protruding from his mouth. Somewhere along the way, he had ditched his collar. She could smell the spilled trash from where she stood.

Cat hesitated. Devin Murphy was in charge of Mortimer's care until Cam and Sarah returned from their honeymoon. She could just move on and pretend she hadn't seen him. "'Yeah, in what world,' says the dog rescue volunteer."

Despite Cam's efforts to improve the dog's looks and lot in life, he remained one of the ugliest dogs Cat had ever seen, and at this moment definitely the most odoriferous. She tried everything she could think of to get him to follow her, without success. She looked around for something—anything—to adapt to a leash and finally admitted she had no choice.

She picked up the stinky mess of a dog and carried him off toward Nic Callahan's veterinary office, the closest place where she knew she would find somewhere to secure ol' Morty. Halfway there, she realized she'd stumbled upon the perfect excuse to skip the reception. She couldn't go stinking to high heaven. She'd have to go straight to Nightingale Cottage and take a shower. The jeans and sweater she'd left out of her suitcase were great travel clothes, but totally inappropriate to wear to a wedding reception.

Maybe she'd write Jack a note, after all, and quietly take her leave.

If the barks Mortimer sent after her as she walked away from the Callahans' sounded more like a chicken's *bawk* than a bark, well, surely she was imagining things.

Jack couldn't find Cat.

When he didn't see her upon first arriving at the reception, he wasn't too concerned. She'd said she had to help, so he expected she might be with Ali's catering assistants in the kitchen or checking the playlist with the band. But when he didn't see her with Sage or Ali or Celeste, he began to grow concerned. Something about her smile had been off at the church.

He had a sneaking suspicion about what the cause might have been.

What were the odds that Melinda had told Cat about

the job offer? What were the odds that she'd gone into full snit because of it? When she'd met his gaze at the church, he'd figured fifty-fifty. Now that she'd gone MIA from Cam and Sarah's reception, he figured it at closer to seventy-thirty.

Moving to intercept Sage, who was descending the steps of Cavanaugh House with her new baby in her arms, he asked, "Have you seen my wife?"

"Cat?"

He managed to stop the frustrated snort. "Yes, Cat."

Sage wiped a milky bubble off the round-faced infant's cheek. "I saw her at the church, but now that you mention it, no. I haven't seen her here at the reception."

"Did something happen with her while I was gone?"

Sage's wide eyes went just a little too innocent. "I know she did some scrapbooking with her mother and Celeste."

Jack knew if he grilled her, he could get the truth out of her, but she still had that soft new-mother glow about her and he simply didn't have the heart. "The little guy is growing like a weed, isn't he? He's a pretty baby, Sage."

"I know. He looks just like his dad."

Jack didn't hold back a snort at that. Next he tracked down Nic and asked if she knew Cat's whereabouts.

"Honestly, I don't know where she is. She seemed a little emotional before the wedding, but a lot of women are like that."

The shadow of concern that flashed across her expression didn't escape his notice. She pasted on a bright smile in an obvious attempt at distraction and asked, "Have you rehearsed your toast?"

"What's going on, Nic?" He gave her a hard, demanding look that silently reminded her to whom she owed her loyalty.

She gazed toward the spot where Cam and Sarah stood accepting congratulations. "Look, I'm not sure exactly what's going on in her head. She didn't go into a lot of detail. She just said that you had an important new job and it's obvious she isn't happy about it. I'm sure you'll be able to work it all out once you talk to her."

Jack muttered a curse beneath his breath, though he couldn't say that he was surprised. Melinda never played fair where Cat was concerned. She wouldn't have lied to Cat, but she wasn't past using a clever turn of phrase to make the truth appear to be something it wasn't.

That explained the stiffness he'd detected in her attitude. He smothered a sigh. He was weary to the bone and he didn't look forward to the discussion Melinda had forced on him. He'd wanted to enjoy his cousin's wedding and have a soak in the hot springs, then go to bed with his woman. Now, because of Melinda's flapping jaw and Cat's conspicuous absence, it appeared as if he'd have to have a "talk" first.

Great. Just great.

"Thanks for the heads-up." Jack leaned over and kissed Nic's cheek. "I'm sure she'll show up eventually. Maybe Celeste has her tied up with something."

"I'm sure you're right."

Later, when Sarah asked where Cat was he said, "Got all teary-eyed at your ceremony. She must have stopped to fix her face."

He gave Ali the same excuse, then acted as if he didn't see the doubt in her eyes. Throughout the reception, as he did his best-man duties—dancing with the bride, toasting the newlyweds, making sure that whatever the bride or groom needed or wanted happened—he searched the crowd for Cat. By the time the limo arrived to transport Cam and Sarah to Gunnison airport to catch their flight to Denver where they'd spend their wedding night, it was clear that she had no intention of attending the party. Jack was torn between anger and concern. If she'd skipped the reception in a snit because of him, then she'd been a poor friend to Sarah, and shame on her. If she missed because she was ill or something . . . well, that worried him. It wasn't like Cat to ditch a friend. Jack gritted his teeth and silently wished the Murphys would speed up the good-byes.

Finally, the pair came out onto the front porch at Cavanaugh House. Well-wishers lined either side of the path, throwing not rice or birdseed but white Angel's Rest feathers toward the departing couple. Standing beside the limo, Jack assisted Sarah into the backseat. "Welcome back to the family, cuz," he told her. "Have a wonderful honeymoon."

Sarah's eyes pooled with tears. "Thank you, Jack. Thank you for being my friend and Cam's friend and for trying so hard to get back here on time."

"Sorry about messing up your pictures."

She laughed. "You made them perfect. They'll have character. Who wants boring old wedding photos anyway."

She leaned up and kissed him. "I'm going to give you once piece of advice. I have some experience with second chances. Sometimes that second chance is hello again, but sometimes it's good-bye. Sometimes it takes a second chance at good-bye to open the door for a new hello."

Jack drew back. "I think you've been hanging around Celeste too long."

Cam looked on, wearing a put-upon expression. "Are you ever going to stop kissing my woman, Davenport?"

"Probably not. She's the first kissing cousin I've ever had." He grasped Cam's hand for a handshake, then the two men clapped each other on the shoulder in their version of a man-hug.

"Thanks, man," Cam said. "Good luck with Cat."

Jack shot his cousin a hard look, but before he could demand further explanation, Devin and Lori arrived with a picnic basket from Celeste and hugs and kisses and good-byes to deliver.

Jack thought about good-byes as he watched the limo pull out of the drive. What did Sarah know, and what had she been trying to tell him?

The time had come to find out. He'd check Nightingale Cottage first, and if she wasn't there, he'd head to Eagle's Way. The four-minute walk from Cavanaugh House down to the cottages took him a frustrating five because people kept stopping him to ask him how he'd gotten hurt. He made a point to always move forward even as he replied with his canned—and truthful—response, "Lost my footing and took a tumble off a hill."

Finally, he exited the rose garden and the cottages came into view. The sight that met his eyes brought him up short. A small SUV he didn't recognize sat parked in the gravel-lined parking spot beside Nightingale Cottage. Its rear door stood open, revealing a suitcase and familiar laptop case in the cargo area.

Cat sat in the Adirondack chair facing Angel Creek. She wore jeans, sneakers, and a sweater. Fred lay with his head in her lap. He heard Sarah's voice echo in his mind. *Sometimes that second chance is hello again, but sometimes, it's good-bye. Sometimes it takes a second chance at good-bye to open the door for a new hello.*

Well, the hell with that. Anger flared and built with every step he took. Once he was close enough to speak without shouting, he said, "Did you have to do this today? You couldn't have waited for me to get some sleep first?"

Her chest rose as she took a deep breath, then she rose from her chair and faced him. "I'm leaving, Jack."

"Yeah, well, that one's not too hard to figure. You have your suitcase and laptop packed up and ready to go. That's a good clue."

"Shall we go inside where we have some privacy for this conversation?"

"Sure, why not." Fred trotted over to greet Jack, and he spent a moment scratching the dog's ears and rubbing his tummy before following her inside.

"Something to drink?"

"Scotch."

"Actually, all I have to offer is water."

"Water is fine."

She walked straight to the refrigerator and pulled out two bottles. Glancing at his arm in the sling, she twisted off the cap and handed it to him, saying, "Is this okay? I've already washed the dishes."

He wanted to throw the bottle against the wall. Instead, he said, "I hear your mother told you she offered me her job."

"Yes."

"So your reaction is to pack up your bags and run away?"

"I didn't run away. I stayed to have this conversation."

He paused with the bottle halfway to his mouth and, spoiling for a fight, spoke with a hint of a sneer. "Or did you just want to pout through your friends' wedding until I showed up and begged you to stay? It's a damn shame you took out your feelings toward me on Sarah and Cam. I'm surprised at you, Cat. You're usually not this petty."

"Actually, no." She told him about Mortimer and the ruined dress, then added, "Everything appropriate I had to wear is packed, and by the time I showered, well, frankly, I didn't have the heart to attend the reception."

"You didn't have the heart?" He folded his arms. This

was a petty grudge, that's what this was. "It wasn't about your clothes. It wasn't about you or me or us. It was their wedding. My cousin's wedding. The only family I have, remember? You threw that in my face before I left, and I moved heaven and earth to get back here. For them. For you. And you couldn't even go? What the hell, Cat?"

She didn't respond to that, but instead said, "If you hadn't stopped by here, then I'd have gone up to Eagle's Way to find you. I want to tell you good-bye this time. We didn't do that last time. I think that's why, as my mother put it, you and I were unfinished business."

"Your mother? Since when did you ever care about her opinion? You're right. We weren't finished. We may have divorced, but we never were finished."

"Well, I believe we are now."

Shocked, he allowed his arms to fall to his side. Seriously, he wanted to shake her and tell her to pull the stick from her butt and drop the drama. "Why are you saying this? Because I left? Because I didn't tell your mother no? Damn it, I told you I couldn't. It was a matter of life and death."

Abruptly, exhaustion took hold of him. He sighed heavily and raked his fingers through his hair. "You know what? I can't do this now. I'm tired and my arm hurts like a son of a bitch."

He pulled the flat pack of ibuprofen from his jacket pocket, ripped it open with his teeth, and tossed the two pills back. He finished with a long sip of water. "And besides all that, you can relax. There's no need for this. I've already decided that I'm not going to take the job."

Jack didn't expect her to jump for joy, but he did anticipate some reaction, a sign of relief or pleasure, something that indicated that she was happy about his choice. Instead, she looked stricken, and the tears that pooled in her eyes weren't tears of happiness.

"You have to take the job, Jack. You were born for it."

"Stop it." He made a chopping gesture with his hand. "Just stop it. You sound like your mother now, and frankly, that's not attractive."

Now she reacted, drawing back with a gasp. He set his bottle down on the counter, then rubbed the back of his neck. "Cat, I'm sorry. Can't you see? I'm whipped. I ache all over. My eyes feel like they're made of sand. Can't we please just let this discussion wait until tomorrow?"

He saw the refusal in her expression and like a little kid, he closed his eyes. The words he heard her speak surprised him.

"You know what? You're right. It can wait." His eyes flew open in surprise. Her smile was bittersweet. "It's no more right to do this when you're exhausted than it would have been to leave you a note. I guess the ceremony made me a little melancholy and Mortimer ruined my new dress and barfed on my shoes. It hasn't been a good day for me, either. Want to go take a soak in the hot springs?"

Tension flowed out of Jack's muscles and for the first time in hours, in days, he relaxed.

"Isn't your swimsuit packed?"

"Yes, but I'll unpack it. I wish I'd dug out a dress and gone to the reception. By the time I dealt with the dog and cleaned up, I thought I didn't have time."

"A soak sounds great, but honestly, a nap sounds better."

Cat gestured toward the bedroom. "My cottage is your cottage. Why don't you lie down and I'll see if I can scare up some swim trunks for you. I'm guessing you're not wearing them under your tuxedo."

Relief rolled over Jack, and he stepped toward Cat and wrapped his good arm around her, holding her the way he'd dreamed of doing since the moment he'd left Colorado a week ago. "I missed you," he murmured against her hair.

"Lie down, Davenport. Later, I want to hear what happened to your arm."

He stripped out of his tux and all but fell into the bed. After he slept, they'd hash out the rest. Within moments, he was asleep.

He awoke to full darkness and the sensual pleasure of a woman—*the* woman—cuddled up against him. He turned his head into her hair and nuzzled her, kissing her temple, nipping at her neck, licking that sensitive spot he knew so well just below her ear. Soon she stretched against him, arching, purring. Then she was above him placing sweet, gentle kisses across his sore face and bruised brow, taking care to avoid his injured arm while devoting her attentions to the notion of kiss it and make it better. After she drifted her way down his torso and made sure that all of him felt better, Jack drifted back to sleep content and sated, lying to himself that he hadn't noticed the warm sting of her tears against his skin.

The next time he opened his eyes, moonlight beamed through the window and illuminated a rectangle of the quilt pulled up to his shoulders—the double wedding ring pattern. How he knew that fact or why it occurred to him then, he couldn't begin to guess. He also realized right away that the space next to him was empty, but at the same time he sensed that she remained nearby. "Cat?"

"I'm here." Her voice came from the shadows in the corner of the room where the wooden rocking chair sat.

"What time is it?"

"About four. How do you feel?"

He'd slept a long time. He started to sit up, but his muscles protested, so he remained right where he was.

"Sore. The hot springs sound really good to me right now."

"I left swim trunks hanging in the bathroom for you."

"Great. Thanks."

"Jack, could I ask a favor of you?"

"Of course."

"I'd like you to listen and not interrupt. I have something I need to get off my chest."

He didn't like the sound of that. "Cat—"

"I love you, Jack Davenport," she said, effectively shutting him up. She had not said those words to him in years. Then she ripped his heart right out of his chest by adding, "I love you, but I cannot be married to you."

She talked about heroes and heartache, about babies and bygones, about dreams and desires and birthrights. He heard her mother's assertions, but also Cat's own reasoning, and while arguments and contradictions lingered on his tongue like a fine Bordeaux, he didn't offer them up. Her voice resonated with certainty. And besides, if he tried to speak, he feared his voice would crack.

She was leaving. Eternity Springs. Him. Them. She was moving on.

When finally she fell silent and he sensed she'd said all she had to say, he fought back despair. *Don't leave me. Please don't leave. I'm so tired of being alone. I've always been alone, except when I'm with you.*

Rather than begging, he spoke from his heart. "I love you, too, Cat. I want to be married to you. You are more important to me than any cause, any job. I want a life with you, a home with you, and God willing, another child with you. Don't give up on us. Don't give up on me."

"Oh, Jack, I'm not giving up on you. I *believe* in you. Finally, after all these years, I get it. It's not about you and me and our life together or about our trouble getting pregnant. It's not about losing Lauren. It's not even about your job. This is what you do. Who you are. I've done a little rescue where animals are concerned, but you rescue people. You save people. This is bigger than us."

You save me! "Why am I hearing a tinny piano playing 'As Time Goes By.'" He laughed bitterly. "What am I supposed to say, Catherine? We'll always have Eternity Springs?"

Why didn't she believe him? Because the past was bigger than either of them wanted to admit? Because she'd convinced herself—with Melinda's help—that he could never change? That she wasn't as important as the job?

Or maybe she didn't have the heart to try again? If that were the case, how could he change her mind?

The rocking chair creaked as she rose and approached the bed. "This is about who you are, Jack, and why you and I can never be. You're the Eagle. I can't change that. I don't want to change it. You are who you are, and I am so proud of you."

She leaned down and kissed his lips, quickly, softly, sweetly. "Good-bye, Jack. Spread your wings and soar."

He didn't return to Eagle's Way that day, but instead spent the next two days holed up in Cougar's Lair, soaking his sore bones and weary soul in the hot springs twice a day, ordering in meals for himself and Fred, and thinking about Cat. Why hadn't he fought harder for her to stay? Was it ego that had stopped him? He'd felt rejected, so he needed to lick his wounds? Or, deep inside, did he think she might be right?

At dawn on the third day since Cat left him, after a night spent mostly tossing and turning, he arrived at his favorite hot springs pool to find it occupied. "Good morning, Celeste."

"Good morning, Jack. Come on in. The water is wonderful."

"I'm going to miss these pools when I leave here."

"Speaking of that, I was going to wander down to the cottages to speak with you later. I'm afraid that if you wish to remain at Angel's Rest, you will need to switch to another cabin. Cougar's Lair is reserved by a couple from Kansas starting tomorrow. It's an anniversary trip for them. They take the same cabin every year."

"Oh. All right. I should probably check on things up at Eagle's Way, anyway. Maybe the change of scenery will do me good. I'm at a crossroads, Celeste. I'm having to make the biggest decision of my life, and I'm not sure which way to turn."

"Yes, I gathered as much. Knowing you and Cat and Melinda, knowing Melinda's situation, it wasn't difficult to draw a conclusion. Care for a little advice?"

"From you? Any time. The guys—Gabe and Colt and Cam and Mac—have told me that if you ever have something to say to me, I should listen."

"Smart gentlemen," she said with a laugh. "Here's my advice to you, Jack. Forget your past."

He waited a beat and when she didn't say more, repeated, "Forget my past?"

"Yes. Don't concern yourself with the boy who couldn't rescue his family from a fire or the man who wasn't home to help his beloved through a tragedy. Ask yourself who Jack Davenport is today. Decide who you really are now, not who you have been in the past. Make that decision carefully and consciously and deliberately. Make it with the knowledge of yourself that only you possess, and then you won't be concerned with trudging in one direction or another from a crossroads, you'll have the heavens to soar. Make that decision, Jack, and then you'll have the power to discover who you will become."

She lost him a little with that last bit, but the rest of it . . . she'd definitely caught his attention.

Forget the past.

Decide who he is now, today.

Discover who he will become.

He barely noticed when Celeste left the hot springs, so intent was he on the advice she had shared. Forget. Decide. Discover.

Three hours later, he hailed a sailboat out on Hummingbird Lake and gestured for the man at the wheel to bring the boat ashore. When it pulled alongside the pier, Jack caught the lines, secured the boat, then spoke to the passenger. "Melinda, I need to talk to you."

SEVENTEEN

෫

Hagerstown, Maryland
February

It was a balmy winter day, much warmer than on her
last visit to Rose Hill Cemetery a year ago. As she sat on
a bench across from her daughter's grave, Cat added a
little prayer of thanks for the nice weather to the usual
prayers she said during this visit. In the five months since
she'd moved to Texas, they'd only had snow once. She
didn't miss it one bit.

She was glad to have relatively warm hands and feet
this year. She was thankful that her heart was warmer,
too. Oh, it still ached for little Lauren. It always would.
But her summer in Eternity Springs, and the time spent—
and, yes, the love shared—with Lauren's father had
helped her heart to heal.

She didn't hurt quite so much. Didn't grieve quite so
deeply. She'd begun to move forward with her life. It
hadn't been easy, but it had been necessary.

Today, as she placed the bouquet of yellow roses
below the grave marker, pressed a kiss to her fingertips,
and touched the raised letters of the name recorded there,
the sense of loss didn't overpower the love. "Happy
birthday, baby. I love you."

She wasn't the least bit surprised when she heard Jack say, "Happy birthday, Lauren. I love you, too."

Cat had expected him to be here and she'd braced herself for it. In all honesty, she had hoped to see him. She'd missed him desperately and she'd wondered how he was doing in the new job. She'd forbidden her Floridian-resident parents and her Eternity Springs friends to mention his name, and they'd respected her wishes. But she'd thought of him, worried about him, and hoped he was doing all right, so she figured a brief conversation with him once a year on the anniversary of their daughter's birth wouldn't set back her effort to move on.

"Hello, Jack." Smiling, she turned around. "I thought I might see you here."

He looked gorgeous, of course. A quick study of his face revealed that that incident in Manila had left no permanent scars. Dressed in a black knee-length cashmere coat over a dark suit, he looked rested and well—though a little on guard.

"I told you I visited," he said, walking toward her.

"I remembered."

He stopped beside her and for a moment their gazes met and held. She thought he might touch her, maybe kiss her cheek, but the moment passed. Disappointment washed over her, though she tried to deny it.

She wanted to touch him so badly.

He carried a bouquet of white roses. For a few minutes, they stood side by side in companionable silence beside their daughter's grave. Lauren would have been six today. A first-grader. Maybe missing her two front teeth.

Jack said, "I think she would have had curly hair. Curly red hair."

"Do you? I always picture her with your dark hair—and your blue eyes."

A few more minutes of silence passed, then Jack knelt

on one knee and set his white roses beside Cat's yellow ones. He, too, trailed his fingers across Lauren's name, and when he stood, he sank his hands into his coat pockets. Clearing his throat, he said, "I'm sorry we've paid these visits separately all these years. It helps to have you here beside me."

"I agree."

After another few minutes, she said, "I need to be going, Jack. It's been—"

"I'll walk you to your car." His blue eyes challenged her to deny him.

Wary, she wondered what he had in mind. Would he push her to have some big serious talk? That wasn't what she wanted or needed. Not today of all days.

However, she couldn't exactly stop him from walking beside her. All she had to do was get to her car. She'd get right in and go—before she did something stupid. *Like throw myself into his arms.*

He waited until they'd left the children's section of the cemetery to say, "I understand you're living in Texas."

"Who told you?"

"Don't worry. Our friends and parents explained that you didn't want them telling me about you. But I know how to check on people, Cat. It's not difficult."

True. Especially for a spy. "It's a little town at the north end of the Hill Country called Cedar Dell. It's not far from Gabe Callahan's hometown. I work for the newspaper there."

"Yes. I read your column about the abandoned pet problem." When she looked at him in surprise, he added, "I subscribe."

She didn't know how to respond to that, so she didn't say anything. It was easier to keep her mouth shut because the questions that hung on her tongue—how is the job and are you dating anyone—were better left unsaid.

A short distance from the car, he asked, "Would you

come with me to get a cup of coffee, Cat? There is something I'd like to tell you about."

A wariness in his eyes triggered a suspicion. *A woman. He's found another woman. Maybe he's getting remarried. Maybe they're having a baby!*

I'd rather jump naked into the Potomac than listen to him tell me that.

Or was he going to make an attempt to lure her back to his house for an . . . interlude? A long weekend before she returned to Texas? The thought was tempting . . . and devastating. As much as she loved him, she could not, she would not, go down that road again. Though she found it excruciatingly hard to do, she said, "I'm sorry, Jack. I have a plane to catch."

He touched her arm. "I'll drive you to the airport. We could talk on the way."

"No, thank you." He was trying, and it tore her up. She glanced back toward the cemetery and added, "The drive is part of my ritual for today. I need the silence. Besides, I honestly don't think it's a good idea. Closure, and all that."

He gave her a long, steady look. "Are you sure?"

It was all she could do not to throw herself into his arms and beg him to take her back. "I am sure. Goodbye, Jack. Take care. I'll see you next year."

She thumbed the remote to unlock the door, and he picked up his pace to open it for her. Cat slipped behind the wheel, fitted the key into the ignition, and started the car. She smiled up at Jack, her heart aching, and said, "Lauren would be proud that you're her daddy."

His smile came slow and sweet. "Travel safely, Kitten. I'll see you around."

"He'll see me around?" she murmured as she pulled out of the cemetery. What did he mean by that?

The comment nagged at her during her trip back to Texas, but once she returned to her little rental house and dived back into her work with the Cedar Dell *Clarion*, she was able to put the remark and the man out of her mind.

Mostly.

Therefore, she was taken totally by surprise when she walked into her kitchen on the first day of March and found an intruder in her kitchen. "Fred?"

He bounded toward her. *Arf, arf. Slobber slobber. Lick lick.*

Her attention on the dog, she never noticed the man dressed all in black until he swooped in, grabbed both her hands in his firm, unyielding grip, and began wrapping her wrists in . . . something hot pink? "Is that a bandage?"

"The self-sticky kind," Jack said, his hand moving rapidly as he secured her wrists together. "I wanted yellow, but you always did look good in pink."

He continued to wrap her with the bandage roll until he used it all up. "What are you doing!"

"What does it look like I'm doing? I'm abducting you. Now . . . your choice." He held up a hypodermic needle, and said, "I'd rather not go this route, but I will if you force me to do it."

"Jack Davenport, you wouldn't dare."

"Probably not, but you never know." Moving quickly, he grabbed another bandage roll from the counter—why hadn't she noticed that when she walked in?—and went to work binding her ankles. "I am determined, Cat."

Made as immobile by shock as by his actions—Bandages? Really?—Cat asked, "Determined about what?"

"To take you home where you belong, of course. Now, I have duct tape, too, and I will use that. You won't scream or anything, will you?"

Her head was spinning, partly because he had just lifted her and dangled her over his shoulder. *Oh for cry-*

ing out loud. She squirmed, she squealed, he slapped her butt. "Stop it. Fred, let's go."

"Put me down, Davenport."

"In just a moment." He carried her outside, and with nowhere else to look, Cat focused on his ass. Had she seen a prettier view since leaving Colorado?

Then they were at the curb and she found herself being shifted forward. He heaved her like a sack of potatoes into . . . a black limousine? Jack climbed in after her, saying, "C'mon, Fred. Here, boy."

When the dog bounded inside, she heard a stranger's voice ask, "Next, sir?"

"The airstrip."

"Very good, sir."

The door shut. Cat scrambled to a seated position. Jack sat stretched out on the seat like a Regency rogue, a satisfied smile on his face and a wicked gleam in those gorgeous blue eyes. "Are you crazy, Davenport?" she demanded. "Have you lost your mind?"

"No, Kitten. I've figured out who I am."

Fred climbed up on the seat beside her and began licking her face. Cat laughed—she couldn't help herself—and turned her face away. "Would you get these stupid bandages off me, please? I feel like I'm in a bad remake of *The Mummy Goes Girly.*"

"I don't know." He reached out and scratched Fred behind the ears. "It might be better if I wait until we're in the air."

Cat hadn't been miserable since moving to Texas, but she hadn't felt like singing and dancing and floating on air while she was at it, either. Right now, even though she might pretend otherwise, the fact that Jack had come after her had given her heart wings. "Get rid of these bandages and tell me why you're here."

His gaze scorched a trail over her from head to toe. "I

don't know, sweetheart. You and I never did the bond-age thing before. Maybe we should give it a go."

"Jack!" Her gaze darted toward the front of the limo, but the privacy screen kept everything black.

"Don't worry. That can wait for later. At least until we're in the air."

"In the air?"

"You know I don't take a car on my kidnappings. I have more class than that."

He reached into the bar and pulled out a soda, lifting it toward her in silent offering. She declined with a shake of her head. "Okay, Davenport, what are you up to? I know my abandoned pet article didn't bring out the crazies this time, so what are you trying to prove?"

He sipped from the can, his gaze never leaving hers. Cat had the sudden sensation that she was prey being sized up for a meal.

"I should be angry." She wasn't angry, though. How could she be angry when she was so glad to see him and he sat there watching her with that smug, knowing smirk? He'd gotten her good and they both knew it.

Besides, she was thrilled to see him. "Where are you taking me?"

"You wouldn't have coffee with me in Maryland, so that kind of forced the issue. I have something I need to say and I need you to listen."

"You could have tried a phone call."

"No. It's too important."

Cat tried to convince herself that she was annoyed, but that was a lie. She wasn't annoyed. She was excited. Anxious. Hopeful.

Had she been unconsciously waiting for him to come to her ever since she left him?

The drive to the private airstrip took less than ten minutes, and the limo pulled up beside the same Cita-tion jet that had taken her from D.C. to Eternity Springs more than half a year before. Once again, Jack served as copilot, and after the plane was airborne and reached cruising altitude, he joined her in the cabin. "I truly should be furious with you," she told him.

"Probably so, but I'm not taking any chances. I figure that no matter how badly you want to get away from me, you won't jump out of a plane all on your own."

"Are there parachutes on board?"

"I'm not telling. I have something to show you. Join me at the table in the back?"

While she took a seat, he reached into an overhead compartment and withdrew a thick file folder and a rolled set of plans. "I want to show you what I've been doing since I quit my job in August."

Everything inside Cat froze. "You quit your job?"

"A week after you left Eternity Springs."

That confused her. "But . . ."

"You're wondering why it took me seven months to tell you?"

"Yes."

"I asked them not to. I wanted to do this in my own time, my own way. I was going to tell you when I saw you last month, but . . ."

"I wouldn't go for coffee."

"Yes, but that turned out okay. This is better."

She folded her arms. "I can't believe my dad didn't say anything."

"Your mom is the person I feared might spill the beans. She wanted me to chase after you immediately. She said that you should know I gave up what mattered to me most for you and that it was a grand romantic gesture." When Cat's eyes widened at that, he shrugged. "I told her she was wrong. I know you better than your mother knows you. You didn't want a grand romantic gesture from me. It wasn't that easy. Besides, I'd told

you I wouldn't take the job and you still left. I knew I
needed to prove myself. To both of us."

"I didn't want to change you. I wanted you to be you.
I just couldn't live with the 'you' that you were."

"You couldn't live with the 'me' that I *used* to be. I'm
a different man now. That's what I had to come to understand."

"You're not making sense."

He took her hand and kissed it, his blue eyes shining
with sincerity and peace. "I was at a crossroads when
you left me and Eternity Springs. I took a few days and
did a lot of soul-searching. Oh, I knew the moment you
left that I would come after you. I wanted you and I
wasn't going to let you go for good. But I wanted to do
this the right way. I was sure of you, but I wanted to be sure
of myself. To do that, I had to jettison some baggage—
thus, the soul-searching. In doing so, I figured out that it
was never the job itself that I found so rewarding and
fulfilling, but the outcome of the job."

"So, you've quit?" she asked, worry rolling through
her. "You don't help people now? You don't rescue
them?" *He'll shrivel up and die.*

"I like to think I do more rescuing than ever before.
Look." He unrolled the paper, and she saw it was a set
of plans. Buildings. Roads. A big project. "This is the
first undertaking of the new foundation. It's a summer
camp, the Rocking L Ranch, and it's for kids who have
suffered a significant loss, to give them a little time in the
healing atmosphere of Eternity Springs. It's been built
on Murphy Mountain—I had to track down Cam on his
honeymoon to get him to sign the paperwork."

"You did what? Jeez, Davenport. It's a wonder Sarah
didn't feed you to a great white!"

"She is still cranky with me for that, but she'll come
around. Gabe Callahan did the design with Mac Timber-

lake in charge of the legal work and Colt Rafferty over-seeing all the safety aspects."

"And you paid for it?"

"Lauren's Gifts paid for it. That's the new foundation."

"Lauren's Gifts?" she repeated.

He cleared his throat. "I decided that our daughter needed a legacy. She'll always be in our hearts, but why not share her with the world?"

"Oh, Jack." Her eyes went wet with tears. "You did all this? For her?"

"For her. For you. For us."

"Tell me everything."

He cleared a thickness from his throat before explaining that Lauren's Gifts had been organized as a children's charity that awarded grants based on a broad mission statement. "We're completely separate from the Davenport Foundation and the Bade Foundation. For those charities, I write checks like I've always done. But I'm hands-on when it comes to Lauren's Gifts."

"Let me get this straight. You quit being a spy to run a children's charity?"

"I was too old to become a fireman." He flashed a grin that quickly faded to serious. "Your mother gave me the opportunity to do what I couldn't do as a child— save people from the proverbial fire. What I have learned is that there are lots of ways to rescue, Cat. You know it. You've lived it. Look at your volunteer work, your professional work. I don't know why it took me so long to see it. I can do this for the rest of my life—no guns, no danger—no intrigue. Face paints and pig races are a lot more fun. I've found perspective, and I've found it be-cause you showed me the way.

"There's a problem, though. It's a big job, Cat. I can't do it all myself, and frankly, I don't have the background in nonprofits. I'm hoping you'll come aboard as my executive director."

"So, you're offering me a job."

"I'm offering you a lifetime. Do this with me. Take the risk. I promise you this isn't just a grand romantic gesture to get you back. This is for keeps. For life. For better or for worse."

For better or for worse. As much as she wanted to throw herself into his arms right now, she couldn't help recalling the "for worse" part of their previous relationship. Her hesitation must have shown, or else he could read her mind, because he added, "I know I wasn't the best husband. I was younger and full of myself. When our infertility became an issue . . ."

Cat went on guard. This was the touchiest of all touchy subjects.

". . . I know I let you down. I was a jerk about the fertility treatments. I don't have a good excuse other than the fact that I was young and selfish. I'm definitely older and I hope wiser. If you give me—give us—another chance, I give you my word that I'll be on board if you want to try to have another baby. If you don't want to go there, I'm good with that, too. If adoption holds any appeal, well, I have a special place in my heart for orphans. All I want . . . all I need . . . is you. I love you, Cat Blackburn."

Emotion clogged Cat's throat. He was offering her everything she'd always wanted, everything she'd always dreamed of having. "I love you, too, Jack Davenport, and the idea of Lauren's Gifts and the Rocking L just blows me away. It's perfect for you, and as a career volunteer worker, I have to admit I'm dismayed that I didn't think of it. I do see three potential problems, however."

He visibly tensed. "What are they?"

"First, where is the home office of the Lauren's Gifts Foundation?"

"It's currently in Eternity Springs, but I'm willing to discuss relocation if that's a sticking point. What else?"

Cat pursed her lips but she knew her eyes must be twinkling. "This executive director thing. Is it a full-time position?"

"Do you want it to be?"

"Well . . ." She studied her fingernails. "Emily Hall sent me an email just yesterday saying she's decided to move to be near her brother and she's putting the *Times* up for sale."

"Oh, yeah? I didn't know that. It's a weekly newspaper. I don't see why you couldn't manage both. I'm sure your photographer would be happy to pitch in to help whenever necessary. And the last potential problem?"

Cat found it difficult to hold back her smile as she sat back in her seat, folded her arms, and lifted her chin. "Well, in all that heartfelt talk, I don't believe I ever heard a particular question posed that, frankly, should have preceded the others."

The last furrow in his brow eased. "Oh. That." He checked his watch. "Can you give me about forty-five minutes?"

"Why do you need forty-five minutes?"

"Well . . ." He gave an exaggerated wince. "I'm afraid that once again, I listened to your mother."

Cat groaned and hung her head.

"It's a good thing. Really."

"What is it?"

"I don't want to spoil the surprise."

She narrowed her eyes. "Spoil it."

He sighed. "Oh, all right. It's my grand romantic gesture. I decided that you did deserve one this time around. I also realized I needed to give you one."

Her heart simply melted. "Oh. Okay. Forty-five minutes, hmm?"

"Give or take."

"Well, then." She circled her lips with her tongue suggestively. "Whatever will we do to pass the time?"

His slow smile was downright wicked. "I have another roll of sticky bandage. We could play doctor."

"That's an idea. Or . . . since you're a pilot and this is your plane . . . I've always had this fantasy about being a flight attendant." She rose up onto her knees and straddled him. "What do you say, Captain? Coffee, tea, or me?"

Cat stood on a snowy slope high on Murphy Mountain and said, "Paragliding? Really? I thought this was to be a grand romantic gesture. Tell me something, Davenport, do you have something against keeping both feet on the ground?"

"I'm the Eagle, remember?" Jack double-checked the strap on her helmet, then the fastenings on their tandem rig. "Trust me."

"You're the Eagle. If you make me a widow before I'm a bride, I'll kill you."

He laughed and gave her a quick hug. "Do I need to repeat the instructions?"

"No."

"You ready?"

"You've done this how many times?"

"Hundreds, maybe thousands of times."

"Okay. I'm ready."

On his signal, she started to run, and in just a few steps they caught the air and began to fly. Expertly, he guided them away from the mountain, and soon they soared over the valley where the first wildflowers of spring had begun to bloom, and dozens and dozens of flowerpots filled with yellow roses spelled out the question she'd been waiting for.

Marry me.

In her ear, the Eagle murmured, "I love you, Nightingale. Come share my sky."

ACKNOWLEDGMENTS

My thanks to the entire team at Ballantine for the fabulous support. Libby McGuire; Gina Wachtel; Scott Shannon; Linda Marrow; Lynn Andreozzi and the art department; Janet Wygal and the production department; my editor, Kate Collins; and Junessa Viloria. A special thank you to Robert Steele who created the breathtaking art used for the covers of the Eternity Springs books. To Mary Dickerson, Christina Dodd, Lisa Kleypas, Nic Burnham, and Susan Sizemore, you've helped Eternity Springs come to life and I am forever in your debt.

Read on for a preview of
Emily March's next novel
in her Eternity Springs series:

REFLECTION POINT

O N E

"There's a new girl in town."

Sheriff Zach Turner first heard the news from Cam Murphy when he arrived at the man's outdoor-sports shop, Refresh, on his day off. The fly rod he'd noticed on his previous visit was proving to be quite a temptation. A sports equipment junkie, Zach had been both delighted and dismayed when Murphy's shop opened in March. Having such a great selection of gear within spitting distance of the sheriff's office was playing hell with his wallet.

Zach lifted the rod from the rack, tested its feel, and replied, "A troublemaker?"

"A looker."

Ah. "And you are compelled to share this information why? Still threatened that Sarah will come to her senses and decide that she can't live without my superior kisses, after all, Mr. Murphy?"

"I'm too sexually satisfied to respond to that dig, Sheriff."

"Ouch." Zach set the rod on the counter, then wandered over to the bicycles where a red Enduro Evo caught his eye. He'd been wanting to move up from his Stumpjumper, but he couldn't justify the cost. Not now anyway. Maybe this summer . . .

"Actually, I'm giving you a heads-up," Cam continued. "The quilt group met at my house last night and your love life—specifically, your lack of a love life—was one of the main topics of conversation."

"You're kidding."

"Nope. The women have matchmaking on their minds."

Zach groaned aloud. "Does it never occur to them that they don't know everything they think they know about my love life?"

Cam folded his arms and arched an inquisitive brow. "You have a fish on the line we don't know about, Turner?"

Zach's thoughts went to the ski instructor he'd been seeing over at Wolf Creek. Inga Christiansen was a lovely, tall, talented woman who was as athletic in bed as she was out of it. He'd enjoyed the time they'd spent together, but they'd both gone into the relationship knowing it was seasonal. "Actually, I recently cut one loose."

"Someone I know?"

Zach gave a slow smile. "Inga."

"Inga?"

"She's going home to Sweden and I just didn't want to move with her."

"Ah, a Scandinavian! I used to love it when we had snow bunny Scandinavians sign up for dive trips," he said, referring to the dive boat tour business he'd owned when he lived in Australia. "Nice scenery."

Zach mentally envisioned Inga the last time he'd seen her naked. "Very."

"Although, I will repeat that the new Southern comfort we have to enjoy is pretty scenic."

"Southern comfort?"

"Ms. Savannah Sophia Moore from Georgia. Wait until you hear her accent. I told Sarah that the way she says 'sugah' sorta licks up and down a man's spine."

"And your bride didn't take a knife to you?"

"No. She was too busy trying to figure out a way to set the two of you up."

Zach snorted and decided it was time to change the subject. "So have you heard anything about how the rainbows are biting on the Taylor River?"

The conversation turned to fishing, and Zach forgot about the newcomer to town as he went about his errands. His next stop was the local vet's office to pick up his whippet, Ace, who he'd left with Nic Callahan first thing that morning. The tall, blond mother of twin daughters had an appealing girl-next-door beauty and friendly demeanor, and she gave him a welcoming smile as he opened her office door and strode inside. "Hey, Zach."

"How's my dog?"

"Ace is a doll, and I'm happy to say that he's doing just great. Even better, he seems to have gotten his spirit back. You've done a great job with him, Zach. Aren't you glad we talked you into keeping him?"

Ace had been in pitiful shape when Nic and her friends rescued him from a bad situation the previous summer. Scarred, starved, and scared, he had needed extra doses of TLC to be nurtured back to health. Surgery had helped his hip injury, the likely result of being hit by a car, but the speed-demon escape-artist days enjoyed by most whippets were behind him. "He's a good dog. Good company."

Nic snapped her fingers. "Speaking of which, have you heard the news? Eternity Springs has a new permanent resident. Savannah Sophia Moore. Isn't that a lovely name? She's from Georgia and is a dog person. She adopted a pocket beagle recently and she brought her to me for a checkup."

"Purse pets," Zach said with a disdainful snort.

"Don't be snotty," Nic said with a frown. "The world

needs small dogs, too. Savannah is a soapmaker. She's rented Harry Hobson's old place on Sixth Street and she'll use the shop in back as her workshop. She's a little quiet and standoffish at first, but once I got her talking, she opened up. She said she mostly sells her stuff at street festivals and craft fairs, but she intends to open a retail shop in town during tourist season."

"That's exciting," Zach replied in a tone that clearly suggested the opposite.

"It *is* exciting."

"You are such a girl, Nic. Cam opening a sporting goods shop was exciting. A soap shop? I don't think so."

Nic's expression turned knowing. "Want to make a bet you're singing a different tune after you meet her?"

Zach decided to put a stop to this matchmaking business right now. Choosing his words carefully—Zach didn't like to lie to his friends—he said, "The woman I've been seeing in South Fork wouldn't be amused to learn that I found a soap shop exciting."

"You're seeing someone?" she asked, shock in her tone. She folded her arms and scowled. "I didn't know that. Why don't we know about this?"

"We? Do you mean your coven?"

She sniffed with disdain. "Now, that's just mean, Zach."

He reached out and thumped her on the nose. "I adore you, Mrs. Callahan, but I don't need you and your friends sticking your noses into my love life."

"We care about you, Zach. We don't like seeing you alone."

"Then, rest easy. I'm not alone." *I have a dog. And a new fly rod.* "You and the girls can turn your attentions to somebody else. Now, let's talk dog food. The Trading Post has begun stocking a new specialty brand." He named it, then asked, "Is it worth the extra money, do you think?"

Zach left Nic's office ten minutes later with Ace on a leash and a spring in his step, telling himself he wasn't the least bit curious about a soapmaker from Georgia. He had more important things than women on his mind—namely, a free afternoon breaking in his new fly rod at his favorite fishing hole on Rainbow Creek up above Lover's Leap. When he strolled into the Mocha Moose a few minutes later with the intention of getting a boxed lunch to go, he almost pivoted on his heel and marched out. Sarah Murphy, Sage Rafferty, and Celeste Blessing sat at one of the tables eating lunch. During that split second of indecision, Sarah spied him and then it was too late.

"Zach!" she said, waving him over to the table. "We were just talking about you. Have you heard the news?"

He swallowed a groan and ordered a sandwich.

"I suppose this breaks a law or regulation or rule," Savannah Moore said, speaking to herself as much as to the dog she held in her lap. She sat atop a bench at Lover's Leap, gazing out at the mountain vista stretching before her, where spring was in full bloom. "Not that I care."

Sarah Murphy had suggested this spot when Savannah mentioned she wanted to visit a high, peaceful, isolated place where she could meditate. Of course, Savannah hadn't confessed the true reason behind her request. What she did here today was private. Besides, until she knew her new neighbors better, she didn't dare let on that she was anything less than a straight-arrow kind of woman. If they only knew.

The dog, Innocent or Inny for short, lifted her head, her ears perking up. Savannah glanced around, making sure they were still alone, but a lone hawk sailing a wind drift high above was the only other visible sign of life. Yet, even more than usual, she felt her grandmother's spirit all around her.

"It's a beautiful place, Grams." She blinked back tears. "The mountains are higher, but the sky is just as blue as it is at home, the smell of the air is just as crisp and clean. I hope you would agree with this decision. After everything that happened, I couldn't bear the thought of stepping back onto your mountain. I just couldn't bear the thought of leaving you behind. I need you with me, Grams."

Savannah had planned today's events for a very long time, working out all of the particulars before she ever left Georgia. Well, except for the site itself. That had to wait until she found the right spot. "It's called Lover's Leap. It's not the highest elevation around, but the canyon floor below us is a long way down. This is a perfect place for an angel to fly, Grams."

And now, it was time to get started.

Savannah tied Inny's lead to the picnic table, opened the large wicker picnic basket lined with a red bandanna and removed a Mason jar of clear liquid, two glasses, two Haviland china plates, a dinner knife, a yellow gingham napkin, a homemade pimento cheese sandwich—Gram's recipe—an apple, a lavender-scented candle, and her smart phone. Then she opened her totebag and removed the battered cookie tin that Grams had used as a button box for as long as Savannah could remember.

Setting the tin in the middle of the picnic table, she used the knife to cut both the sandwich and apple in half, then divided the food onto the two plates. She began to eat her lunch, sharing bites with Inny as she carried on a one-sided conversation with her grandmother. "I think I've settled on my initial line of fragrances for the retail shop. I've decided to limit what's sold through the store to five. I thought of you when I went into the fresh handmade soap store in the upscale mall in Dallas. Their products are fabulous, but the scents assault a customer when she walks in. I want my store to be inviting, tempting, but not cloying. Not over-powering."

She munched her apple and pictured the building she'd rented. "I had intended to call my store Fresh, but believe it or not, Eternity Springs already has a business called Fresh—Sarah Murphy's bakery. What do you think of Heavenly Scents? Or maybe Heavenscents? Heavenscents, featuring Savannah Soap Company hand-made products. Maybe I could do some cross promotion with Angel's Rest."

She could almost hear her grandmother's voice whis-pering on the wind. *Why, Savannah Sophia, I think that would be right fine.*

She was accustomed to hearing her grandmother speak to her and she conversed with her all the time. She didn't ordinarily share a meal with her, but this was a special event. "Will I quit hearing you, Grams, once we do this?"

That depends.

"On what? Just how crazy I am?" Savannah sighed and polished off her half of the sandwich.

Hearing voices in her head wasn't unusual for her. She'd conversed with an imaginary friend—Mandy—when she was a child. When she first arrived at Em-manuel, she'd resurrected Mandy, fully aware that doing so was a defense mechanism. Mandy's voice had morphed into Grams's in the weeks after Grams had passed away.

If pressed, Savannah wouldn't swear that Grams's spirit wasn't with her, in fact.

She eyed the other plate and said, "Grams, you still eat like a bird. Shall I finish this off?"

Another time, Savannah would have been embarrassed by her playacting, but not now. She'd been headed up the mountain to have lunch with her grandmother the day her world fell apart. During those awful weeks that followed, she'd promised herself that someday she would pick up her life where she'd left off. This was the best she could do.

With lunch over, she moved to the next item on the agenda, opened the Mason jar and sniffed. Her eyes watered. "Whoa."

She splashed a small amount of moonshine into each glass. Lifting one glass in a silent toast to the old days, she said, "Making family proud, one Mason jar at a time."

The liquor burned like fire going down. Savannah shuddered. "Grams, I cannot believe you drank this every day and lived to see eighty-five."

All natural ingredients, my dear.

Savannah laughed, then made sure Inny's leash was still secured to the picnic table so that she wouldn't wander too close to the edge while Savannah was busy. Picking up the button box, she carried it and the second glass of moonshine toward the edge of the overlook and the large flat rock that stretched out over the valley like a plank on a pirate ship. She stood there for a long time, her thoughts spinning back through the years, and she mourned. When the time felt right, she held her glass high. "Here's to you, Grams."

She quoted the Irish blessing that her grandmother had cross-stitched in green thread against a cream background and hung in her parlor: MAY THE ROAD RISE TO MEET YOU, MAY THE WIND BE ALWAYS AT YOUR BACK, MAY THE SUN SHINE WARM UPON YOUR FACE, MAY THE RAINS FALL SOFT UPON YOUR FIELDS, AND, UNTIL WE MEET AGAIN, MAY GOD HOLD YOU IN THE HOLLOW OF HIS HAND.

She tossed back the drink, swallowed, shuddered,

then drew back her arm and sent the empty glass flying. She watched it until it dropped out of sight, listened for the crash of glass against rock but heard only the wind.

And the sound of her smothered sob.

Not good. Savannah didn't cry. She'd sworn off tears ten years ago and she'd only backslid once. Okay, twice.

Get this done, Savannah. It's time.

"Yes." She blew out a heavy breath. Closing her eyes, she recited a prayer and swallowed the lump of emotion that had lodged in her throat. Tears welled, overflowing to trail down her cheeks as she removed the lid from the tin and stepped closer to the guard rail.

She wasn't a fan of heights. Gazing out over the valley was fine, but when she leaned forward and looked straight down, her knees went a little weak. The 'shine hadn't helped.

She tested the rail. It seemed sturdy enough. Good. She needed to be able to fling Grams out beyond the rock shelf so that the ashes sailed, soared, and flew on the breeze before falling back to earth. However, she didn't want to join her.

Maybe this was a bad idea. Maybe she should forget the plan entirely, put the lid back on the tin, take Grams home, and put her on the mantle. Didn't her grade school friend Annie Hartsford keep her cat's ashes in a shoebox beneath her bed? Hadn't Eloise Rankin left her husband's ashes on a shelf in the garage for almost a year before her children convinced her to put him in the vault? She could—

Savannah Sophia.

"Okay. You're right. It's time." Inside the button tin was the cream-colored muslin bag tied with a blue ribbon containing her grandmother's remains. Grams had sewn these bags herself, filled them with soaps or salts for sale at retail shops in town. Savannah knew her grandmother would approve of her use of the bag and button tin rather than the funeral urn the mortuary had wanted to sell her. Amaryllis Moore hadn't liked waste.

Savannah removed the bag from the button box and set the tin on the ground. She untied the ribbon, watched it flutter in the soft breeze, and in that moment, a wave of grief struck her so hard that she literally swayed, then broke. Tears fell and she released the sobs she'd held back for so long. She cried for her grandmother, for herself, for the cruel acts committed against her family. She wept for the losses she'd endured.

It was a fierce storm, but also a fast one. Cleansed of the dark emotion, a calm, warm sense of peace spread through her and strengthened her. She lifted the open bag up in front of her like an offering at an altar and said, "Rest in peace, Grams. You were my teacher, my nurturer, my family. You were my rock. I will miss you until the day I die."

Leaning over the railing, she shook the bag, waving it back and forth like a flag, and the fine particles of ash spilled from the bag and floated on the breeze. Savannah watched the ashes float and dance and dissolve against the blue springtime sky with a bittersweet smile upon her face. "Goodbye, Grams."

Once the bag felt empty, she checked inside it and frowned to see a significant amount of ash clinging to the inner seam.

She turned it inside out and, holding it by one corner, she leaned over the railing once again and shook the bag hard. Once. Twice. On the third shake, she lost her grip and the bag floated to the surface of the rock just beyond her reach.

Savannah scowled at the bag. She couldn't leave it lying there. It wasn't completely empty. Besides, she wanted it for a keepsake.

Did she want it enough to climb out onto the rock?

Great. Just great. At some point, the breeze would certainly blow it off the rock surface and it would fall to the ground. Where it would lay and rot.

"Wonderful," she repeated. She glanced around for a stick or something else she could use to retrieve the bag even as a gust of wind scooted it closer to the edge of the rock. Savannah watched it and knew she should let it go. It was only a bag. The ashes were ashes, the dust was dust.

She wanted it.

Savannah gripped the railing and swung one leg and then the other over it. Without loosening her hold on the iron rail, she started to sink to her knees, planning to stretch for the bag while keeping herself safely anchored to the ground.

Two things happened simultaneously. When the breeze scooped up the bag and sent it scooting toward the edge of the rock, Savannah reacted instinctively, lunging toward it.

And something clamped around her wrist.

Savannah let out a startled scream and time seemed to slow to a crawl. Her gaze remained locked on the bag as it skittered over the edge of the boulder even when the vice around her arm yanked her backward.

She banged into the railing and pain shot from her hip. Then, she felt herself lifted and thrown backward in a fireman's carry. Her breath whooshed out as her diaphragm hit a broad, hard shoulder. For a moment Savannah was too stunned to struggle, too shocked to be afraid, but then a flashback to events when she was fifteen burst into her mind.

She'd been picking wildflowers in a high meadow above her grandmother's homestead when a big, burly, smelly mountain man emerged from the trees. The ratty jumpsuit he wore identified him as a prisoner, most likely someone who had walked off a road crew. He grabbed her and carried her off toward the trees, his talk nasty and promising rape.

Then, she'd used her intellect and her knowledge of the mountain to escape him before any real harm could be done her. Now, she didn't know the mountain, but she still had her brain, and she'd learned a whole new set of survival skills during the past eight years. She could fight dirty when necessary.

The question remained whether or not this would be an instance of "necessary." Only a handful of seconds had passed since he'd grabbed her up and begun toting her away from Lover's Leap.

Away from the bag that still held some of her grandmother's ashes and teetered precariously on the edge of the rock.

Just when she gathered herself to struggle, she felt her captor lean forward. Her body began to slip. Her butt landed hard on top of the picnic bench and she looked up into a pair of aviator sunglasses.

He stood well over six feet tall in a spread-legged, aggressive stance, wearing faded jeans and an unbuttoned blue-plaid flannel shirt over a tight white T-shirt. Reaching up, he lifted the sunglasses off a straight blade of a nose to reveal piercing blue eyes. But it wasn't his moviestar good looks with those mesmerizing eyes, chiseled cheekbones, and sexy, five-o'clock shadow that made her mouth go dry.

The gun holstered at his waist managed that.